TRYSMOON

Book Four: Sacrifice

By
Brian K. Fuller

TRYSMOON
BOOK FOUR: SACRIFICE

Edited by Jessica Robbins JessiLynRobbins@gmail.com

briankfullerbooks.com
facebook.com/briankfullerbooks

ISBN-13: 978-1502806543
ISBN-10: 1502806541

For Jeff and Jenny:
Your enthusiasm kept me going.

CHAPTER 70 – CHARADE

For three days Mikkik's armies marched up the narrow road to Echo Hold, and for three days the armies of men slaughtered them almost without casualty. Only the powerful longbows of the Uyumaak archers took some toll on the soldiers across the ravine, while their human counterparts devastated their enemies in return. Every new wave of creatures to ascend the mountain cast their dead comrades into the deep canyon, and the fresh Uyumaak often found themselves pierced by a well–aimed shot, tumbling over the side and down to join the dead.

The easy victories, low casualties, and balmy summer weather sent a surge of confidence through the ranks of besieged soldiers. Indeed, only the growing shortage of arrows to shoot at the reckless invaders concerned them.

On the fourth day Warlord Jarius of Aughmere extended the bridge across the ravine and sallied forth briefly to beat back a fresh wave of creatures and recover what few undamaged arrows they could find among the carnage. He returned, smile wide and face proud. "I believe I could push this whole army back down the mountain in a day!" he bragged.

Those with no sense of history took pleasure in what

seemed more like sport than warfare, while the smiles of those with more lore never reached their eyes as unsettling stories of the past preoccupied their minds with dark speculation. Mikkik had more than Uyumaak at his command, and he had more intelligence than to just throw away Uyumaak in droves day after day. The tales of the First and Second Mikkikian Wars held but few mentions of victory, and what victories there were cost plenty in blood and sacrifice.

Lord and Lady Khairn, safe within the keep, had little to occupy them during the long days of battle. Athan encouraged Chertanne to practice with the sword every day, though the nervous King could rarely stop fidgeting and pacing long enough to work up a serious will to accomplish anything. Dread cast his features into wrinkled contortions, and his muttered phrases of self-deprecation—uttered in long dialogues with himself—set the Chalaine to worrying. Athan's discipline allowed him to present a calm demeanor, but the Chalaine could pick out the little habits that revealed the Churchman's concern. She wondered if his thumb had a fingernail left at all.

What hope the Chalaine held to sprang from her protruding, uncomfortable belly. She felt like an engorged pumpkin propped up on two twigs, but the baby's pronounced and sometimes painful movements always brightened her heart, whatever the cost to her back. She wanted to believe herself a beautiful pregnant woman, but the giant lump of her belly destroyed whatever grace she could lay claim to. She mostly laughed at her awkwardness, realizing it signaled the end of one journey and hopefully the start of a better.

She rarely spent time with anyone other than Chertanne and Athan, and their thoughts rarely wandered from the potential doom that awaited at Mikkik's hand. Only her shy, though capable, handmaiden—handpicked by Athan to replace Mena—offered the occasional ray of excitement and cheer, although even that was subdued. Her mother and Gen, she knew, waited somewhere outside of Echo Hold, and she dearly wished for their company and fretted that outside the protective walls more sinister danger might befall them.

Soon, she thought. *Soon this will all be over, one way or another.*

A tightening across her belly ended all purposeful thought and clenched her jaw. The contractions had come with increasing frequency and pain all morning. She exhaled sharply as the tension increased. Chertanne, however, did not break from his pacing or even look up despite her increasingly obvious distress. Their wide room on the second floor of the keep provided an ample track for her husband to traverse in the throes of his anxiety.

Sometimes he would slide the sword from his scabbard and thrust it weakly about, and the Chalaine had to bite her lip to keep herself from critiquing his every move. She understood why Samian spent so much time teaching her to draw a sword and move about with it. Every time Chertanne unsheathed the sword, he seemed like a blacksmith's new apprentice staring at some strange implement pulled from an unfamiliar bag.

Her husband needed confidence, and the Chalaine could think of no way to lend it to him, especially considering her own doubts. Even with Gen at her side, she doubted she would face birthing the Child and confronting Mikkik with any degree of calm. At least she trusted Gen's ability and loyalty. As it was, she suspected that at the first sign of Mikkik's presence she would only catch sight of Chertanne sprinting in terror off into the distance just moments before the evil god annihilated them all.

Another tightening came and she gritted her teeth. *Is it really going to hurt* this *badly?* This time a grunt escaped her lips and Chertanne did turn, face screwing up into a question before he sheathed his sword on the second try.

She breathed deeply and quickly until the contraction passed.

"Are you all right?" Chertanne asked, not stepping closer but staring at her as if she had the plague. The Chalaine felt a sudden wetness.

"Get Athan!" she yelled. Chertanne scurried out of the room as if death dogged his heels.

"What is Mikkik up to?" Torbrand wondered aloud as he, Gen, and Falael lay on a precipice overlooking Echo Hold. They had split from Mirelle's army nearly a week before and scrambled into the mountains to watch Mikkik's host as they assaulted the mighty fortress. They hiked a goat track to the cliff that dropped nearly two hundred feet to the road below. In their packs they carried the cloaks of the elves with them and waited for the time when they would be able to drop from the cliff and strike.

"And why does Jarius keep shooting at them?" Torbrand continued. "Let them waste *their* arrows and starve, for Eldaloth's sake! I imagine they would start jumping over the edge out of sheer boredom. I know I've thought about it several times just sitting here."

Gen shook his head. He joined Torbrand in his puzzlement over Mikkik's strategy, or lack thereof. History told that Mikkik never marched with his armies, preferring to scheme and plot in the shadows and let his underlings do the work and take the risks. Whomever he sent to command the armies below certainly cared nothing for the piles of Uyumaak stacking up on the canyon floor nor possessed any sort of military creativity.

But the more he thought about it, the more it nagged Gen. In the first two Mikkikian Wars, the dark god had sent creatures of flight—giant birds of prey, swarms of needling and poisonous insects, and soaring, dog-sized lizards with wide mouths and sharp teeth. None had come this time. No Magicians sent lightning or hail or wind to harry the enemy archers or to strike at the carefree soldiers manning powerful ballistae and devastating trebuchets that tore avenues of slaughter down the ranks of Uyumaak advancing up the mountainside.

The three spectators conjectured that perhaps the short time since Trysmoon's return had prevented Mikkik from creating or breeding a significant force of creatures. But if that were the case, then why waste what army he had pounding away at a nearly impregnable castle? And if he had used Magicians against them during the journey to Elde Luri Mora to skew the weather, why not do so now? A good lightning storm over Echo Hold would likely kill more soldiers in a few minutes than the Uyumaak had in nearly four days.

Still, however perplexing the battle below, each day that passed brought them closer to Eldaloth's advent and what prophecy outlined as the final drama. With any luck, the Chalaine would give birth within the safe confines of Echo Hold and never see Mikkik's face. With a larger helping of luck, Chertanne's participation in events wouldn't doom them all to a lifetime of futile war against a mad god.

This is the final chapter, Gen thought. *I will see the Chalaine and Mirelle again and be content. H*e found that he felt more for a rekindling of that joy than for any other good that could come from Eldaloth's return.

After watching Jarius lead another attack across the retractable bridge, Gen returned to their meager camp. The rocky, steep inclines of the Far Reach Mountains challenged their climbing skills in their journey to reach their lofty overlook. Their cramped camp on a slightly sloping space between two granite outcroppings provided little more than a place to stow their gear and sleep, with a minimal chance of their rolling off the mountainside. Gen took up his waterskin and reclined, sensing another of the Chalaine's frequent contractions. They had started earlier that day and steadily increased in frequency and duration. Now they came almost unrelentingly.

Time is short. Eldaloth comes.

After a few more minutes, the pain coming from the Chalaine escalated, and he stood, feeling the need to *do* something and finding nothing more than a short prayer to offer. Gen waited in the shadow of an upthrust rock, trying to get out of the afternoon sun. The low booming of distant drums caught his attention just as Torbrand scrambled down the rocky track to meet him.

"I think the time may have come at last, thank Eldaloth!" Torbrand announced, wild excitement in his eyes. "We'd better gear up. How is the Chalaine?"

"I think the baby is coming."

"I think Mikkik is," Torbrand grinned. "At last, some fun! Eldaloth better leave a few heads to chop. He will, won't he?"

Gen shook his head, though he had expected his former master to be excited for all the wrong reasons. As quickly as they could, they donned their armor, Gen wearing the black and silver banded mail of the elves, while Torbrand donned his black and gold breastplate and greaves. Carrying all the weight of the armor up the mountain had nearly broken them both.

"Do not forget the cloak," Gen admonished his enthusiastic companion who had already started back up the hill.

"Oh, yes. Are you sure this cloak does what you say it will?"

"Yes. If it doesn't, you really won't have a chance to get angry at me."

The booming continued to mount, reverberating through the canyon and off the walls of Echo Hold. Gen and Torbrand reached the top, laying on their bellies and following Falael's eyes down the canyon road. Gen had to push the Chalaine's spectacular pain out of his mind to focus on the procession below. At first, only more Uyumaak ascended the road, but as the pounding drums grew louder, the gasps and oaths from Echo Hold's soldiers mixed in with the cacophony.

"What do they see?" Torbrand asked of no one in particular.

A few moments later, what the men of the castle saw rounded the corner. Uyumaak warriors, some pounding massive, skin-covered drums, surrounded a hideous figure sitting on an oversized throne of burned wood bolted to a simple platform. Severed human heads, spiked into the wood through the temples, formed a border around the sides of the platform, the dark wood wet with blood.

Two Gagons hauled the contraption up the mountain road. The Gagons stood a full fifteen feet tall and were covered in a thick, scaly hide the color of dried mud. They walked hunched over, but their stout necks could telescope five feet long, letting the flat snake-like head whip around unpredictably. Deep brows protected beady eyes embedded on the sides of a head that consisted mostly of thick bone and teeth.

The hideous rider slumping forward on the throne extinguished all the cheer and excitement that had built up during the preceding days' easy victories. In form, the creature was like the Millim Eri Gen had seen before, only twisted almost beyond recognition. Oozing pustules covered a skin that seemed to have been burned to black and then stretched over the hulking frame, angry red cracks crisscrossing everywhere to form islands of leathery flesh. Ebony earrings, three to an ear, swayed with the motion of the two Gagons. Only a loincloth adorned the naked frame, while a cloud of buzzing flies enveloped the dark passenger, feeding on the blood and pus and casting a shadow about the throne.

The bald head swiveled to take in everything around it, empty eye sockets filled with maggots and coalescing flies formed eerie eyes which scanned the fortress and canyon. A stench and feeling of dread clung about the creature, and even the nearby Uyumaak it passed shrank from it. Archers, trebuchets, and ballistae all let loose at once, but the veritable wall of projectiles simply evaporated into the summer air. The Gagons continued forward until they stood at the platform landing, Jarius calling a halt to the vain bombardment. Gen turned toward Torbrand and Falael, eyes widening. Both lay unconscious on the ground. A tingling sensation flooded Gen's body, and in a moment he lost a familiar connection.

He could no longer sense the power of Trys.

Startled, he rolled over. Two figures floated just behind him, and in an instant all strength left him. Joranne, young and beautiful, smiled at him. The other figure, tall, dressed in white and looking commanding, regarded him coldly, but not without satisfaction. Recognition pierced Gen's mind. Here stood Eldaloth's murderer, the progenitor of horror and death, and his creator. Unlike the creature below, Mikkik radiated beauty, though his person held no glory or brilliancy.

"What do you think of my creation down there, Gen?" Joranne asked teasingly. "At first I thought the heads spiked on the platform a bit much, but now that I see their effect, there can be no doubt that my first inclination was correct. The flies and pus are a nice touch, don't you agree? Everything horrible the simple race of men imagined Mikkik would be. I thought I would have him sit on a throne of bodies, but. . ."

"Enough, Joranne," Mikkik's commanded, voice deep and inviting. "Read him."

Gen pushed against Joranne's intrusion into his well-traveled mind, but her power battered away every defense he could throw against it as it had before. Once done, she

11

turned to Mikkik and he absorbed the information without expression.

"As you are aware," Mikkik continued. "I have stripped you of your power. You are nothing now. As a gift to you for your service in my behalf, I leave you your life, such as it is. You have played your part well."

"And have a part yet to play," Joranne added.

Confusion and helplessness rose within him. Had Mikkik really intended for him to do all that he had done? Had he duped the Millim Eri? The Chalaine's pain spiked for several long moments, and Gen could focus on nothing more. At last it faded, and Mikkik flinched, pulling back slightly and snarling.

"He is born," the dark god intoned gravely.

"Do you think you can unmake him?" Joranne asked.

"I must, but I cannot approach the creature. Its cries sear me like summer fire. The blood is much stronger than it should be, and I cannot come near it." His troubled face relaxed after a moment, though doubt left a residue in his eyes. "It is nearly time. Let the parley begin."

Joranne floated to Gen. "You'll appreciate the theatricality. Watch."

With a wave of her hand, she flipped him over and scooted his body forward until his head hung over the precipice. The two warring armies remained at a stalemate in the afternoon heat, an uncomfortable silence born of awe and terror radiating from the fighters of Echo Hold. Joranne concentrated and incanted softly. Her monstrosity hauled itself from the throne and stood at the precipice of the canyon, regarding the castle with a lazy disdain.

"God is born!"

The cry rose from a single voice three times and then swelled as voice upon voice bore it up until it reverberated through the canyon. Soldiers' faces beamed anew with hope, and handshakes and hugs of congratulations replaced the cowering of moments before.

Wake up, you fools! Gen thought. With all his might he struggled against the spell that trapped him to the ground. Joranne chuckling at his attempts.

"Not yet, Gen. Soon."

The monstrosity raised its arms, and dark clouds gathered about the base of the elevated castle, electricity crackling. "Hear me!" it bellowed, voice like black, boiling pitch poured into the air, so loud that every motion halted on both sides of the canyon. "Your revelry is in vain, worthless dogs of weak blood! Your race is a blight. Open your gates, and perhaps I will let the women escape the Uyumaak cook pots!"

"We will not open to you," Warlord Jarius shouted confidently from the walls above the gate. "Our god will find you, and you will end!"

Gen could just make out Athan standing exultantly at the Warlord's side. Lightning erupted from the clouds, and at least twenty burned men plummeted from the battlements.

"I will slay you!" the monstrosity said. "I will slay your god as I have before!"

"You will not!" Athan countered defiantly. "For here rules the Ha'Ulrich, one who holds the power of Eldaloth and your undoing! He comes to meet you and send you to your destruction. God is born, and *you* will soon be an unpleasant memory."

The creature waited a few moments before a laugh pulled out of the Abyss tore from its throat. Joranne crouched by Gen. "Your performance is almost ready to begin." The creature laughed for what seemed like hours, pulling down smiles and unpinning knees.

"Do you think," it finally said, "*do you think* I came here in ignorance? I know well what I face." The impostor Mikkik reached backward, and Gen felt himself yanked from the overhang and pulled downward toward the clawed, outstretched hand. It caught him by the back of the cloak, lifting him high. Gen, paralyzed, slumped like a freshly killed corpse. The soldiers gasped and murmured.

"Yes," the counterfeit hissed, "yes. You know my servant. Do I not know that your Ha'Ulrich is a coward? That his magic and his mind are weak? Do I not know that he trembles even now to face me? He is no King. Any one of the men on the walls has more mettle than he! Bring him forth! Extend the bridge! Prophecy says he must face me, so let's see if he can steady his shaky legs enough to walk out to see my face! Let's see how your faith fares when I turn him to ash!

"As for this one," it continued, indicating Gen, "he has done his work well and shall have a throne for his service."

A powerful force flung Gen backward. He landed hard on the engulfing chair on the platform, an unseen hand pinning him up strait. Tears flooded his eyes. Mikkik had won. They could not match him, and the Chalaine would die. No one could see the truth, and even if he were freed, no one would believe him anymore.

Only the healing power of Padra Nolan and the virtue of the Training Stones allowed the Chalaine to shuffle forward next to her husband so soon after the birth of her perfect Child. She wanted to hide away from the world and pull her son to her breast, to stroke his smooth, peaceful face and sing to him. A soft glow surrounded his tiny body, a glow that invited reverence and awe. But almost no sooner than the midwife had placed the tiny infant in her arms did she hear the first grating demands of her enemy. Only the Padra's steady magic kept Chertanne from diving under the bed.

Minutes later they stood on the street as the retinue of Padras and soldiers surrounded them. Athan and Warlord

Jarius joined the group last, Jarius and his Aughmerian soldiers in the lead and Athan coming to stand by Chertanne. Dason joined them. While not permitted to be her personal guard, Athan had allowed Dason to serve in Echo Hold after he took an oath of fealty to Chertanne. He squeezed the Chalaine's shoulder from behind, and the Chalaine thanked him for it.

"I'll take it from here, Nolan. Thank you," Athan said. "Jarius, do not move until I tell you. Padras! This is the time. Raise your wards. Guard the Chalaine and Chertanne at all costs. We must get the Ha'Ulrich near enough Mikkik for him to strike the final blow. Chalaine, take Chertanne's hand."

The Chalaine shifted the sleeping Eldaloth to her left arm and took Chertanne's clammy hand in her right hand. He placed his remaining hand on his sword hilt, clenching it to steady his trembling. Athan incanted and Chertanne straightened.

Unexpectedly, Athan turned toward her. "You should know, Chalaine, that Mikkik has Gen. You will see him when the gate rises. I am sorry. It seems Mikkik did use him, as I feared."

The Chalaine's mouth fell open and her heart sank. *Faith,* she told herself. *It will be over soon. Justice will come.* She focused on her Child, a deep, unexplainable love for and attachment to the infant filling her heart with purpose and hope.

"Have them extend the bridge, Jarius," Athan ordered.

"Extend the bridge!" the Warlord yelled, the baby's eyes fluttering at the harsh sound. Grating and rumbling filled the air, scaring away scavenger birds and silencing the men on the wall. A thud and sudden silence signaled the end of the platform's traverse, and the Chalaine looked up, finding that the soldiers of Echo Hold had formed a line around them, kneeling in prayer.

"Open the gate!" Jarius ordered. It rose too quickly for

the Chalaine, and she could feel her husband's shaking despite Athan's steeling magic. Chertanne nearly fell down upon first seeing his enemy, and the Chalaine gasped. This was not the Mikkik who Aldemar had shown her in vision. *What has happened?* A curse, surely, had stricken Mikkik for his crimes, and the Chalaine wondered at how such a horror had befallen a being once so mighty and glorious. As they marched resolutely forward, she could just make out Gen sitting on a dark throne behind Mikkik.

"Deafen him, Nolan," Athan whispered. Nolan nodded, and Chertanne looked around in surprise at his sudden loss of hearing.

"Is this *him?*" Mikkik mocked, and the Chalaine understood Athan's precaution. The Chalaine wanted to turn and run. "And with his lapdogs all around. Come! I will meet you halfway!"

"Hold fast to him, Chalaine!" Athan said urgently. "Your healing touch will keep him alive until he is close enough. Faith, child! Faith!"

Mikkik walked casually forward, unaccompanied by any of his army. Clouds of flies swirled around the bridge, and the Chalaine swallowed hard, pulling her son close. The baby slept calmly cradled in her arm, but as they neared Mikkik, she practically had to drag Chertanne forward.

Mikkik said, "Let's peel away your vanguard so I can get a look at you!"

Warlord Jarius, his twenty soldiers, and their equipment turned to glass, forward momentum toppling them to the bridge road, chunks shattering away from the impact and into the clouded canyon below. The procession stopped.

"Now, let's away with meddling Churchmen and their pathetic wards."

"It's gone!" Nolan exclaimed. "They're all gone! We are nothing!"

Mikkik stood twenty feet away. Chertanne's hand nearly crushed the Chalaine's. Athan remained rooted and pale.

"Nolan," he said, voice barely controlled. "Get the Padras inside the walls. You are of no use here." Powerless, the Council of Padras turned and sprinted back inside the gate while Mikkik laughed.

"That's better. Come, Ha'Ulrich. Come and know your enemy!"

The Chalaine could barely control her shaking, and Athan sweated with the exertion of his steadying magic. The Padra gently pushed Chertanne forward, glass crunching underfoot. Mikkik's stench overwhelmed them as they approached, and as they neared, a swarm of flies poured from his eye sockets and swirled around them for a few moments before buzzing back inside his head.

"Now I see," Mikkik rumbled. "It is time for you to die, Ha'Ulrich. You, your woman, and your Child. It is time for me to sit upon the throne of Elde Luri Mora and rule this world!"

"Now, Chertanne!" Athan yelled, but Chertanne did nothing, staring everywhere but at Mikkik, who laughed uproariously.

"Goodbye, Churchman!" Mikkik flicked his hand, and Athan skidded backward through the broken glass until he lay at the gates bleeding and unmoving.

"Goodbye, Protector."

The Chalaine shrieked as Dason suffered the same fate, armor clanging as he skidded along the stone. Chertanne now knelt, crying on the stones as Mikkik moved toward him, mocking him.

"And now for you, Ha'Ulrich!"

"Chertanne," the Chalaine yelled, "do this. You can. You can!"

Suddenly, Chertanne's eyes went vacant and his face slack. He stood quickly and drew his sword stiffly like a puppet.

"Do you think swords are any good here?" Mikkik thundered.

17

Chertanne stepped forward and thrust his sword into the thigh of the creature. Mikkik bellowed, an orange light glowing from the cracks in his burned skin.

"Impossible!" Mikkik screamed. Wracked and clenched, he writhed in agony and then exploded in a shower of ash, fire, and flesh. The blast flung Chertanne and the Chalaine backward, and she lost hold of her Child.

She lay dazed and senseless, for how long she could not guess. Vaguely, she heard cheers as if from a great distance. A light gathered around her, but she could only think of her Child. Frantically she felt around herself, light and smoke obscuring her vision.

"Milady!"

It was Dason. He grabbed her arm and pulled her upright.

"No!" she yelled. "Eldaloth! My Child!"

"Wait! Something is happening!" Dason said, grabbing her head gently and tilting it upward. "It's wondrous!"

The Chalaine ignored him as the light gathered, searching the ground for the baby. Finally, she found the blanket and the tiny clothes, but the Child was missing. In despair she cast around, finding Dason staring just ahead of them. A being, shining and splendorous, hovered over Chertanne, descending and landing just in front of him. So bright was the glory of him, that the Chalaine could hardly keep her eyes on him.

"Rise, my servant," he said, voice reassuring and kind. "I am Eldaloth. You are victorious. You have saved the world. I have returned, and you will have a great reward. You shall have the peace of the faithful."

Something struck the Chalaine as familiar about the voice, and she pressed forward. *It's over!* She thought, hope surging through her veins. *We did it! Athan was right!*

"My servant, the Chalaine," Eldaloth said. She stumbled forward eagerly, tears coming to her eyes. At last she would see her God. At last she would be free of the burden she had carried for so many years. At last she could *rest*. She lifted her veil and examined the countenance of the one she had sacrificed so much to bring back to the world. But when she finally saw his luminous features clearly, her world fell out from under her. His face she knew. The voice she could now identify. Aldemar's vision had shown her this god, and he was not Eldaloth. Reeling, she let her veil drop, peering past Mikkik to find Gen. The two Gagons near the throne and the rest of the Uyumaak were fleeing back down the mountain, leaving her Protector motionless, eyes bulging, on the throne.

Come to me, Gen, she willed in her distress. His face was distorted with struggle, but something pinned him to his seat.

"Hear me, all the ends of Ki'Hal," Mikkik called, luxurious voice filling the air with its assured tones. "For these I have reserved a throne in the paradise of Erelinda. By their deeds they have shown themselves worthy of a much greater glory than this simple realm. To them I impart a gift I wish to give all, transcendence and peace. The legend of the Ha'Ulrich and the Chalaine shall live forever on the lips of the men and women here this day! Their names will be holy. They will never be forgotten. Continue your oblations. Stand, Chertanne! Stand, Chalaine! Today is your victory!"

Chertanne took her hand and turned toward Echo Hold to receive the adulation of the survivors. "I did it," he told her, confidence and contentment blooming on his face for the first time in months as the praise and adoration washed over him. "At the end, it's as if something took over and I did it!" The Chalaine didn't answer, swallowing hard, frozen in panic. "Chalaine?" Chertanne questioned, perplexed by her demeanor, but the Chalaine just squeezed his hand and answered nothing.

The jubilation died down, and Mikkik spoke. "Chertanne, will you enter into the rest I offer you?"

Chertanne closed his eyes. "Yes, my master and my god."

Mikkik stretched forth his hands, a light gathering around her husband before he dissolved into thin air, to the amazement and delight of the onlooking soldiers. The Chalaine stepped backward, fearful and uncertain. Dason, standing proudly behind her, whispered, "Take me with you."

"Chalaine, will you enter into your rest?" Mikkik invited, voice affectionate and kind.

"What have you done with my Child!" she managed to squeak barely loud enough for herself to hear. She could just detect the barest twitch of Mikkik's brow and a brief hesitancy, but she knew all too well that she had failed, and now, she was finished.

CHAPTER 71 - BUTCHERS GAP

A moment after the Chalaine glanced at him from behind Mikkik's illuminated form, Gen felt himself freed from the invisible bond that nailed him to the abominable throne. With his power stripped from him and with Mikkik between him and the Chalaine, few options presented themselves. He cast his gaze upward to the promontory, but saw no sign of Torbrand or Falael.

Are they dead? Captured?

The Chalaine, Chertanne, Mikkik, and Dason all had turned toward the battlements as the people cheered their "victory."

Then he saw it—the sword of Aldradan Mikmir. His sword. The sword Chertanne had killed the impostor with. The explosion had melted away the blade about halfway down, and the ragged tip still glowed white. While he couldn't be certain the sword still possessed any of the virtue that had displayed itself so powerfully in destroying the warped creature, he had no other means with which to strike.

As the cheering died down, he realized his dilemma. Everyone on the wall thought him a monster and a traitor. If anyone saw him move, they would alert Mikkik, and he wouldn't get close enough to touch his enemy. He couldn't believe that Mikkik would let Chertanne live, and as the dark god proffered the Ha'Ulrich transcendence and rest, Gen knew he had to act. The spectacular light gathering around the Ha'Ulrich provided the distraction he needed.

Launching himself from the throne, he hit the ground at a dead sprint, slowing only slightly to scoop up the blade, hilt warm in his hands. Gen ran just behind the luminous figure of Mikkik, though he knew he had little cover. Mikkik offered the Chalaine her transcendence, the Chalaine said something in return, and then shouts of horror from the walls filled the air. Gen grinned. It was too late. Just as Mikkik started to turn, he lifted the blade high and rammed it into the small of Mikkik back. It sank in and stuck.

Mikkik howled in agony, his aura fading as he shot backward into the air, as if pulled by a string, and disappeared over the mountain, leaving a stunned and horrified audience. "The Ilch!" someone screamed. Gen knew he had little time before the Padras would work their magic upon him.

"Gen!" the Chalaine cried. "What has happened?"

"Die, filth!" Dason yelled, stepping forward to strike. Gen stunned him with lightning fast punch to the throat and grabbed the Chalaine's arm, pulling her to him and launching off the side of the extended bridge. Howls of disbelief and agony washed over them and faded as they fell through the air, ground rushing toward them. Gen held her tight, and she clung to him just as hard, eyes closed and wind whistling in her ears. When their feet settled lightly on the canyon floor, she opened her eyes.

Gen regarded her kindly, extending his hand beneath her veil and rubbing her face. "I am so sorry, Chalaine," he said, face sad.

"What happened, Gen?"

"He tricked everyone, Chalaine. He has won today."

"My Child! What has he done to my Child?" she cried, hands trembling.

"He unmade it, Chalaine. The baby's gone. I am sorry. I could not get to you sooner to warn you."

She collapsed on the ground and wept. "How? It's impossible!" Gen pulled her to him for several moments and let her cry before picking her up and moving. They had to hide. If the Padras chose to pursue them, he had nothing with which to counter their magic. Uyumaak corpses lay everywhere in grotesque shapes, and he hiked away from them until their sight and stench no longer assaulted their senses. A nearby boulder-fall among a copse of fir trees provided seclusion, and he set the Chalaine down in the shade. She refused to relinquish her grip on his neck, and he pulled her onto his lap and held her as she collected herself.

"I have failed, Gen," she finally said. "I am a wretch."

"No, Chalaine. You did everything the prophecy said you would. The rest of us have failed you, and I not the least."

"What happened to you?" she asked. "Why did that creature have you?"

Gen explained the story to her, and she listened, numb. "And so, Chalaine, the world thinks I am a villain now, and perhaps I am. If the Padras come, you will need to leave me behind. Your mother and Lord Kildan's army should be here soon, if all went as planned. I'd hoped they would be here now. The Shadan and an elf named Falael were also supposed to join me, but it is possible they, too, think I have betrayed them."

"I won't leave you, Gen," she promised softly. "I know the truth. What happiness have I ever known without you? If the world is to suffer from my failure, please take me where I cannot hear their accusing voices. Take me where I can forget the beautiful face of my son!" Gen mourned with her as she sobbed, finding no words to offer her.

"Chalaine!" someone yelled.

"Dason?" the Chalaine asked, wiping her eyes and disengaging herself from Gen. "I've got to explain to him!"

"Gen!"

Gen pulled his sword. "It's Torbrand, too. Let me talk to them."

"No, let me," the Chalaine offered. "Dason will listen to me."

"Together, then."

They stepped out from their cover, finding Dason, Torbrand, and Falael walking toward the place of their concealment, Dason—face decorated with new bruises—pointing the way.

"I have done her no harm," Gen said. "Please hear me out! You have been deceived! What happened was not. . ."

"Shut up. We know," Torbrand said.

"How?" Gen asked.

"Joranne. After Mikkik had descended in his 'glory,' she woke us up and explained the whole ruse, telling us we had to save Chertanne and the Chalaine at all costs. One out of two isn't bad. After Gen stabbed Mikkik, she kicked us over the edge and fled. Chertanne was transcended, and you had jumped with the Chalaine. Soldiers started flooding out onto the bridge. We grabbed Dason. Had to beat him a fair bit to get him to listen."

Dason strode forward and pulled the Chalaine protectively aside. "Is it true, Milady?" he said, voice gravelly.

"It is true, Dason. Your Queen has failed, and Mikkik will destroy us all."

"None of this can be laid to your charge!" Dason asserted.

"I must sit. My legs will no longer carry me," she said, and Dason helped her down to lean against a tree.

"Any sign of Mirelle and that army of hers?" Torbrand asked.

"No," Gen answered.

"Odd," Torbrand said. "Well, I suppose with Chertanne dead that I am now the Shadan of Aughmere again. I turn command of this little party over to you, Gen."

Gen turned to the elf. "Falael, you and I will scout down the canyon and see if they are near."

"Don't leave me, Gen, please," the Chalaine begged. Dason eyed him narrowly.

Gen turned to explain when Torbrand grabbed his arm. "I'm just as good in the wild as you. Stay with her. My son-in-law is with Mirelle, remember?" Gen nodded, and Torbrand and Falael ran out into the canyon. Gen returned to where the Chalaine sat, head in one hand with Dason stroking the other.

"If you have the strength, your Grace," Dason said, "a little healing would not go amiss."

"Leave her be, for pity's sake, Dason," Gen chided him. "The black eye will heal, and you'll have your looks back. Help me find a couple of straight branches for a litter." Dason scowled at him but complied.

They stayed near the grieving Queen, and Gen ached for her. His time with her had taught him that she feared one thing above all—to prove a failure and doom the world. While any rational creature would never assign her any blame in the day's events, he knew her diffident heart pounded her with guilt. He understood what it was to feel as she did, and it had taken a great deal to pull himself out that hole.

She needs her mother, and she needs a purpose, he thought.

While Dason cleared a branch, Gen crossed to her and removed his cloak. "Chalaine, listen to me. This cloak is special. We will make your litter with it, but do not lose it. It is elven and imbued with magic. By its power we were able to survive the fall from Echo Hold. It can be very useful in the right places."

"Then you keep it," she said. "You should take your

stones back, too."

The numb apathy in her voice shocked him. "No. Mikkik is not going to come for me, Chalaine. He wants you."

"Why? I am unimportant. Chertanne is the one who had Eldaloth's blood."

Gen furrowed his brow. "What?"

"Padra Athan explained it to us. It was a part of the Apocraphon they kept hidden. Chertanne's blood was what held the power to destroy Mikkik."

Gen sat as he absorbed the information, trying to puzzle something out that tickled in the back of his mind, but the Chalaine's renewed weeping pulled him back to her.

Leaning close, he whispered so only she could hear. "Chalaine, please. Nothing that has happened today is your fault! It's more mine than anyone's! Even if you had done something wrong, I would not love you less. If you had never borne the title of Chalaine or been as beautiful as every sunny spring day piled on top of each other, I still would have fallen in love with you in that canyon. I know it was a mistake you fault me for, but I could hardly help it. Please remember that while all of Ki'Hal only knows you as the Chalaine, there are those of us who know you as much more."

She hugged him fiercely. Dason returned quickly, frowning.

"What did you say to her?" he asked grumpily.

Gen disentangled himself from her arms and stood. "Just the truth, Dason, just the truth. Be at ease."

"Ho!" Torbrand shouted some distance off. "Gen! We have a problem!"

"You cannot do this! There are too many!" the Chalaine

yelled a short while later, voice hoarse and frantic with desperation. Rather than the friendly forces of Rhugoth marching to their aid, a column of Mikkik's host two thousand strong surged up the canyon. Torband mentioned a narrow gap where they might bottle the army for some time, and Gen had decided immediately—he and Torbrand would buy escape time while Falael and Dason bore the Chalaine away.

Gen smiled at her as he and Shadan Khairn adjusted and tightened their armor. Gen's eyes were hard and resolute, while Torbrand's lit up with childlike anticipation. The heat of the late summer afternoon beaded sweat upon their brows.

"Don't worry, Chalaine," the Shadan said happily. "We can hold the gap for a good long while. I give us one chance in four of surviving the entire onslaught, unless they have magic, in which case I calculate one in ten."

"Listen to me, Gen," the Chalaine pleaded from her litter. Her veil obscured the tears sliding down her face, but the pain in her voice could not be hidden. "Two cannot stand against two thousand! Please don't do this. Please, Gen. Obey me just this once."

Preparations done, Gen crossed to her and took her hand, eyes clear with purpose.

"Chalaine, we must hold them until your mother's army arrives. Torband and I are the only ones who have a chance to stall them." He lowered his voice to a whisper. "Chertanne is dead now, Chalaine. Happiness and love is at last yours to have." He drew her eyes to Dason scowling nearby. "I will see it done. Never forget that you are the best of women, and that I am never wrong. Farewell." He grinned affectionately at her and stood. In her grief, the Chalaine lay back, limbs flaccid as if the bones had been pulled from her body.

"Dason," Gen said, "may I have a word?" Dason nodded, and Gen stepped apart with him. "Dason, the plan was to meet with Mirelle's army and climb out of the canyon on a path to the south that I told you about. From there, we were to head south until we passed the Kord Forest and then strike west for Tolnor and Rhugoth. It is quite possible that Harband's army was defeated by what approaches us now. If so, you must make the journey alone."

"I understand."

"Also, the Chalaine will need you in the coming days. You know how she tortures herself. She has an affection for you that will be important."

Dason nodded. "I have always loved her, Gen. You know that. You do not think to survive this day, do you?"

"No, and you shouldn't be too optimistic about your chances, either. Please don't tell the Chalaine that, if you would."

"Of course. I will praise your memory for this last sacrifice."

Gen returned to the Chalaine's litter and knelt beside her, taking her hand. "You must survive. If you chance to see your mother before I do, tell her that I love her and that I am sorry. Will you do that for me?"

"Yes."

"Thank you. I leave you with my love. Make haste."

"And I leave you with mine," she returned. "Come back to me, Gen. Please don't throw your life away."

Gen smiled at her and turned to the others. "Get going, Falael, Dason. Go as fast as you can, in case the Hunters get by us."

Torbrand ascended to the gap while Gen watched Dason and the elf lift the litter and go. A sadness overcame him momentarily, but he had done everything he could to secure a pleasant future for the Chalaine in their poor circumstances. As her litter disappeared into the trees at the first switchback, he joined the newly reinstated Shadan between the two massive red stones that formed the sides of the gap.

"How long do you think we have?" Gen asked, rechecking his armor.

"By the dust, the main body will arrive shortly. We may see Hunters any moment now. They will be the most important to kill in the short term. If it comes to it, we let the slower ones pass."

Gen nodded in agreement.

"So tell me, Gen," the Shadan asked. "Are you really the Ilch?"

"Yes."

Torbrand shook his head and smiled. "I thought the story a concoction to discredit you for a long time. Does that mean you can use Trysmagic?"

"Not anymore. Mikkik stripped the ability from me."

"Pity. That would have improved our odds. Should we stand and intimidate them or hide and ambush them?"

"Hide. If we are out in the open, the archers may be able to pick at us from a distance."

"I concur." The Shadan breathed out heavily, excitement playing upon his features. "I confess, this is perhaps the most alive I have felt in years."

"And while you are confessing," Gen said as he pulled himself out of sight behind the rock opposite from Khairn, "explain to me how you can be brutal and cruel to everyone on Ki'Hal yet treat Mena as if she were a goddess of some sweet religion unknown to the rest of us?"

"Ah, Gen, you should know better. Love is capricious! I first saw Mena when she was five years old placing my wine before me at dinner. I cannot explain how her dark looks and innocent, fierce eyes threw a net over my heart, nor do I wish to understand it. I think understanding would ruin it. She was the dearest of my soul from that instant, and I have labored to elevate her against her culture. My affection for her came from no will of mine and was contrary to my nature. It was meant to be just as the sun was meant to

29

shine or the wind to blow. That's the best explanation I have."

Gen grinned and turned his gaze to canyon. The sound of marching feet and the pattering Uyumaak swelled as they army narrowed the distance. "So you think we have one chance in four?"

"Of course not. This will see us both dead. The only question is how long we can hold out, which is a question I am quite excited to find the answer to. As for my bogus odds, the Chalaine seemed so overwrought that I thought I might soften the blow of your demise a bit so she would be quiet and leave. I really can't abide such blubbering."

"And here I thought you had at last learned to be considerate."

"No. Isn't it strange that if you give people even the smallest sliver of hope they will grasp it and build their lives and dreams around it, regardless of how ridiculous and unreasonable it is? Owing to our illustrious reputations, the Chalaine and her companions probably think we really do have one chance in four." He paused, the din of the Uyumaak horde complicating their conversation. "Any regrets, Gen?"

"Plenty, and none I wish to talk about."

"I have just one: I never got to fight you. I so hoped that you would do the noble thing and challenge me during the birthday celebration in Rhugoth."

"You shouldn't have been so persuasive in your letter, then."

"Was it good? I've always felt I was a rather pedestrian writer."

A skittering on the loose gravel on the other side of the rocks ended their banter and brought them to the ready.

"Fight well," Torbrand shouted, and as one they charged the gap.

The first two Hunters met the men's blades at a full gallop up the hill, falling beheaded without a chance of defense. Gen and Torbrand yelled at the top of their lungs as they waded into the midst of the vanguard. So fierce was their initial assault that the army stopped, the Hunter advance hastily retreating backward. Gen and the Shadan returned up the incline and hid behind the rocks.

"That will give them something to think about." Torbrand grinned. "How many did you kill?"

"Seven."

"Ha! I downed eight. One thousand nine hundred eighty-five to go. Did you see a Chukka or a Shaman?"

"No."

"Me neither," Torbrand yelled over the thumping and pattering that erupted from their enemies. "Well, they are cooking up something. If they use magic, we are done for."

"Yes," Gen agreed, "but they won't try it yet. They have no idea what is waiting for them on the other side of this hill, and they'll save their strength. Let's pick at them while they discuss their options." They sheathed their swords and pulled bows.

"Youth first," Torbrand offered, signaling Gen forward. Gen nocked an arrow and turned the corner, catching his first good glimpse of what they faced. The army stretched down the canyon ahead of them, disappearing behind a bend in the towering walls. Formations of Bashers, Warriors, and Archers waited anxiously as a Chukka consulted with the Hunters at the head. To Gen's dismay, two towering Gagons hunched in the middle of the army hefting massive crossbows. Throgs loping along the flank released their yellow eyes into the air.

The target was obvious. Gen loosed the arrow at the Chukka, who turned just in time to take it in the face. Gen pulled another arrow and fired it at a nearby Throg before slipping behind cover. Torbrand went next, firing twice. As he retreated behind the boulder, a flight of arrows swarmed through the gap, clacking as they bounced around the stones. The archers kept up a steady stream of missiles to discourage any further forays into the narrow space.

"They've got Gagons!" the Shadan exclaimed excitedly. "I hope we get to fight one."

Yellow eyes floated over the columnar stones of Butchers gap, staring at them and behind them before floating away.

"Now they know we're alone," Gen commented calmly. He dropped his bow and drew his sword.

The Shadan followed suit. "Gen, in all your reading, did it ever mention if Uyumaak can feel stupid? Or perhaps display admiration for a clever foe?"

"No. The momentary genius of our little ruse is lost on them all, unless they have any Chukkas left."

Heavier, slower footsteps approaching signaled the arrival of a company of Warriors.

The Shadan laughed. "Sounds like they sent about twenty to clear us out. You ready, Gen? This will be interesting. If we get through this, they will be angry. Don't let them push you back if you can help it. Only two or three can fit through the gap at once."

As before, Gen and Torbrand broke cover and killed the first four with such speed that the rest flinched backward. The meaty Warriors held massive clubs and thick, hide-covered round shields, and once over the initial shock, they clumped together and charged. Gen knew he had to be careful not to be lured forward away from the gap, allowing his enemies to surround him, but he also couldn't allow too much daylight between the Warriors and himself, lest the Archers find a clear shot. The Warriors, in their haste and anger, didn't let him ponder the particulars of strategy.

A wicked sidearm club swing whistled over his head and hit the red sandy rock of Butchers gap, sending chunks of the weak stone showering around him. Gen thrust upward, gutting his opponent and chopping down another at the knees as he dodged the falling corpse. The next threw its club—Gen whirling away—and then charged, hoping to catch his human foe off balance. Against a slower opponent, the Uyumaak's gambit may have succeeded, but Gen's reflexes were too quick, and he simply stepped aside and slashed a deep cut across the creature's back.

The Shadan met a club with his sword, grunting as he absorbed the force, disengaged and chopped deeply into a Warrior's side. As it fell he stepped back and let the next Uyumaak over-swing and miss, cleaving its skull before it could recover. As the initial wave turned back, Gen and the Shadan pressed the attack forward, their footing tricky as they negotiated steps between the corpses. Not one of the Uyumaak Warriors had encountered such skill at arms, and the alacrity of the two men's assault rendered any attempt or thought of retreat impossible. Twenty Uyumaak warriors lay dead at the two men's feet, and they retreated behind the boulders as more arrows sped toward them, chipping away more stone and lodging in the creatures that were dead or dying in the gap.

After a few moments the arrows stopped, and the Uyumaak again communicated amongst themselves. The Shadan and Gen grabbed their bows and fired two shots each before the archers pinned them again.

The Shadan turned to Gen, face and armor covered in gore. "If you hit your targets, we are down to one thousand nine hundred fifty-seven . . . I think. Any guess as to what they will do next?"

Gen tightened a shoulder strap. "If they have a brain among them, they'll just send the army forward in a steady stream. They must realize we aren't inexhaustible. It's almost like they are afraid to fully commit to pressing forward."

"It's quite possible," the Shadan shouted over the noise, "that they think this is part of some ploy despite our apparent lack of support. Two people defying an army this size is too ridiculous to be true to them." The slapping and thumping stopped. "Let's see what they decided."

They both peeked around the edge of the rocks. The army had split to allow an enormous Gagon to lumber forward surrounded by a ring of squat Bashers carrying battle-axes. Gen swallowed hard as he pulled back. He judged they had at least a minute to consider their options. The Gagon's massive black crossbow hung in muscular, four-digit hands swaying at its side.

"What do you think, Gen?" Torbrand asked, eyes alight with anticipation.

"Crouch, wait for its head to clear the rocks, and shoot its eyes. If we can blind it, we can try to deal with the Bashers while it stumbles about. With any luck, we can kill the thing and get it to fall in the gap."

The approach of the Gagon drowned out any further attempt at strategy. Its footsteps boomed amid the clang and clatter of its squat entourage, and as it neared the gap, it stopped, head telescoping forward to survey its prey.

Gen and Torbrand fired their arrows toward the eyes, Gen's finding its mark while Torbrand's deflected off the bony skull. The creature stumbled backward, dropping its crossbow and crushing one of the Bashers with a wide, three-toed foot. A drumbeat from behind was the signal, and the Bashers charged the gap while the Gagon collected itself.

"Cut the bowstring on the crossbow!" Gen shouted as he rammed his sword into the eye slits of a Basher helmet. As if sensing their intent, the Bashers clumped in front of the weapon, protecting it and the suffering Gagon.

Gen doubted that if he were to live another twenty years he would find himself in a fight that rivaled the one he now sought to survive. While slow, the Bashers struck with deep power. Parrying their heavy axes would be as useless as it would be fatal, so the Shadan and Gen danced around the gap, using speed and movement to confuse their foes. Within seconds, however, the Gagon had recovered, grasping its weapon and firing it at the Shadan. The heavy thwack of the bolt's release momentarily stalled the fighting, the massive projectile crashing with terrific force into the red sandstone to the Shadan's right.

The bolt hit shoulder-high and at a slant, grit and rocks exploding from the impact point. In the confusion that followed, the Bashers were able to push the two defenders backward out of the gap. Blood ran down the Shadan's face where some of the fragments had cut him, though Gen couldn't watch him long enough to assess the damage. A low swing bit through the armor on his thigh, pain shooting up his leg. He retaliated by chopping into the narrow space between the Basher's helmet and shoulder armor.

The Gagon tossed its weapon down and swung a heavy fist at Gen, who rolled to avoid it. The ground shook at the blow, and Gen stood quickly, jumping away from another ax-blow aimed at his knee and feeling another Basher flanking him. Desperately, Gen swung his sword at a Basher in front of him, hitting its helmet hard enough to stun it and knock it aside. Then he took a chance.

In a desperate gambit, he sprinted between the muscled legs of the Gagon and into the relative clear between the gap and the rest of the army. The Gagon's head twisted about, trying to use its one eye to find its escaping quarry. The Shadan, finding himself alone, retreated farther backward. Gen watched the army closely and saw what he had hoped for—the archers taking a careful bead on him.

Just as they were about to fire, he turned and ran back between the calves of the Gagon, whistling arrows intended for him peppering the legs of the monster, the heavier arrows of the Uyumaak sinking deeply into its hide.

The Gagon's tongueless mouth went wide with agony and it fell to a knee, slamming its forearms and fists into the sides of the gaps to steady itself. Thumping its chest loudly, it stood, turned, and ran unsteadily and angrily back toward its own army, head cocked askew as it focused on the front line of Archers with its remaining eye. The Archers cast about frantically, wondering what to do, until the beast tore into their ranks, killing some and scattering the others.

Gen and the Shadan quickly dispatched the remaining Bashers and took cover behind the stone as the enraged Gagon madly slaughtered its frightened comrades. Gen checked the Shadan's injuries. Chunks of rock had deeply lacerated the right side of his face and head, blood flowing freely. The injuries did nothing to diminish his enthusiasm.

"Mikkik's breath, what a fight!" he exclaimed. "If I had two hundred horsemen right now I would drive all these Uyumaak into the Abyss. That was a clever maneuver, Gen. You are a smart one."

Together they peeked around the rocks, finding the Gagon covered in feathered arrows, still stomping and crushing everything around it. As they enjoyed the slaughter, they spied the rear ranks splitting to allow something to come forward.

"What do you think they'll come up with next, Gen?" the Shadan asked, resting against the rock.

"It is hard to say. It appeared as if their commander was riding to the front, so maybe he will have the sense just to pour his army into the gap. Surely they know that we are the only ones here."

An earthshaking thud signaled the fall of the Gagon, and they spied on their enemies once more. Their commander approached, riding just behind the head of an enormous, undulating black snake. The hood of his dark cloak was down, revealing a weathered and scarred elven face. He was bald, and even from a distance, Gen could feel the dark intelligence in his eyes. His only adornment was a row a silver earrings edging his left ear. He held no reins, no weapon, and no standard, and after a few minutes of communicating in Elvish to a group of Chukkas gathering around him, he turned and slithered back from whence he had come.

Shortly, the deep booming of drums echoed down the

long line of Uyumaak between the canyon walls, and at a final deep drumbeat, the army moved forward as one, feet set for the gap.

Torbrand smirked. "Whoever that dark elf was, he apparently is the genius of the army. I would have liked a chance at the snake."

"I think I've had enough of snakes."

"This is it, Gen. Let's hope the Abyss is not as bad as they say."

Gen swallowed hard and exhaled, turning to scan the trail behind him, unable to see the Chalaine's party.

Run, Falael. Run, Dason. Get her away from here.

The wave of scaled bodies, claws, clubs, axes, and teeth washed into the gap as Gen and Torbrand stood against it and commenced the work of death. All semblance of planning or thought disappeared, trained instinct commandeering the task of survival. In seconds they had felled a sufficient number of opponents to choke the gap with their bodies, but this did not slow their advance for long as a wall of creatures pushed Gen and Torbrand out of their advantageous position as they scrambled backward to prevent the Uyumaak from flanking them.

Torbrand fought fiercely, the Uyumaak paying dearly for coming within the reach of his blade. In the brief glimpses Gen could snatch of his master, he finally understood why Torbrand would always be his better at the sword. Gen fought out of necessity, the Shadan for pure pleasure. Torbrand yelled, he taunted, he laughed, and—despite being hopelessly outnumbered—intimidated his foes. Gen used his speed to his best advantage, stringing his enemies out so they could not bring their collective strength to bear upon him.

But there were simply too many. How long they had fought, Gen could not guess. Bruises and cuts decorated them both, but the pain merely whispered to their minds, easily ignored, while they immersed themselves in the chaotic swirl of violence around them. Gen heard Torbrand grunt as a Basher cut him down at the knees. A swarm of Uyumaak warriors surrounded the Shadan as he continued fighting from the ground. The Warriors' clubs pounded him over and over until a wicked strike caved in his skull. Torbrand Khairn was dead.

Gen swallowed hard and tried to keep his wits about him as a group of Warriors surrounded him and started to close. He was limping badly, and he could barely use his left arm after intercepting a club blow with it. Blood covered him from head to toe. One of the Warriors thumped, and they rushed him.

This is how I end.

Dimly he was aware of the rest of the army now pushing forward through the gap and toward the trail. The thought of them catching up to the Chalaine infused him with enough energy to stage one last rally.

The Chalaine, hearing the booming of the drums, stirred for the first time since Gen had bidden her farewell. She tried peering through the foliage to the battlefield below, but the trees grew too thickly. Twisting, she attempted to see what lay ahead of them.

"Have a care, Chalaine," Falael warned, accented voice tender, as she jostled the litter. "We would not want to drop you. What do you look for?"

"Find somewhere you can see the battle and stop. I must know what is happening."

"Chalaine," Dason said, "I think it would be better if we moved on as quickly as we can. They are buying us time to escape."

"Stop when you can see, Falael," the Chalaine ordered, ignoring Dason's argument. Reaching inside her dress pocket, she could feel the warm animon and knew that Gen yet lived. Within a few seconds, the battle below was joined once again, and after a steep climb, they encountered a small promontory that provided a clear view of the valley floor.

While the figures below were difficult to distinguish from one another, Torbrand and Gen created snakelike paths of enemies alive and killed as they worked an irregular retreat away from the gap. Clumps of Uyumaak would form around each briefly, only to have to have Gen or Torbrand burst through, a frustrated mass of enemies trailing in their wake and stumbling over their slain companions.

Dason and Falael watched the battle transfixed, chatting gravely to one another and pointing their long fingers at the field below. Gen and the Shadan heroically decimated the vanguard of Mikkik's army, but elements already passed them by and started toward the mountainside path.

"We should go, Milady," Dason gently suggested. "The main group now marches toward this trail. The Hunters could catch us very quickly."

The elf nodded his agreement. But the Chalaine could not tear herself away, a portentous dread, not of fancy or speculation, compelled her to spectate as fate unfolded on the stage before her. Before she could offer a rebuttal to Dason's suggestion, Shadan Khairn fell underneath an overwhelming onslaught.

"And so passes Shadan Khairn," Dason intoned softly. The Chalaine barely heard him. Within her heart terror swelled, for there, unmistakable, fought Gen, alone, wounded, and scrambling for his life amid butchered Uyumaak felled by his hand. A group surrounded him and charged, and just as the wave hit, a thunderous peal of drums reverberated through the canyon. As one, Gen's attackers and the army which slowly poured onto the battlefield below reversed course and commenced retreating back through the gap.

"Lord Kildan has caught them from the rear, I believe," Falael surmised.

With difficulty and pain, the Chalaine rose from her litter and scanned the carnage below for any sign of Gen. Her heart leapt as she felt the animon, still warm within the folds of her pocket. At last she spotted him, using his sword as leverage to push himself up. His left arm hung useless at his side, and he stood unsteadily for several moments before staggering tentatively forward, the sword a crutch supporting a leg that he could barely drag upon the ground.

Easily healed! the Chalaine thought joyously. *Just one touch is all I need.*

She turned to Falael. "I need to get down there as quickly as possible." But Falael's eyes remained riveted on the battlefield. The Chalaine turned back, hand coming to her mouth. One of the retreating warriors detoured away from the main body and walked toward Gen, who had managed only a scant few feet in his progress toward the trail. Gen's back was turned, but he heard the creature approach and tried to turn to meet it, falling to his knees.

It took but a moment. The Uyumaak raised its heavy crossbow and fired it into Gen's chest at a range of ten paces. The bolt punctured his breastplate and threw Gen backward to the ground with stunning force. The Chalaine flinched and stumbled as if the bolt had struck her instead, landing hard on her litter.

The animon in her pocket shattered.

For the young Queen, time stopped flowing. All thought halted. All emotion evaporated. Her breath pulled back into her chest and died. She existed, stunned and frozen, in the moment just before the Uyumaak loosed the fatal bolt, unwilling to step forward into an unfathomable reality. In this space the Chalaine hovered for many moments, but grief could not be denied, clutching its victim's hand and dragging her forward into an unwanted life. She lay still, for

40

how long she cared not.

"What is your will, Lady?" Falael asked, face concerned.

"Go down."

"No!" Dason countered. "We wait until we are sure of the outcome. Should Lord Kildan fail. . ."

The Chalaine pulled herself from the litter in frustration. Weak and tired she stumbled down the path, Falael and Dason pleading with her to stop and lay back on the litter. She ignored them, tired of resistance. She wanted nothing to do with anything or anyone. She tripped and fell so many times her knees bled. Dason tried to help her, but she shoved him away.

Dimly she heard Falael comment that the horses of Mirelle's army had emerged onto the plain, but the Chalaine barely registered anything around her. She existed alone in a barren country of anguish until she reached the bottom and picked her way across the field to where Mirelle sat amid the wrack cradling Gen's body in her arms, weeping in unchecked agony. Cadaen crouched beside her, pained. Only when the Chalaine joined her mother on the ground could she admit the presence of another into the arms of her grief.

CHAPTER 72 – IMPOSTOR

When the Chalaine had read of the epic battles of the past, they always started with two armies gathered against each other on opposite sides of the field, horses stamping and footmen nervous as the leaders parleyed in the center of the field. Parley failing, the leaders returned, and after raising a shout, two waves surged across the intervening space to mash against each other in chaotic thunder.

After General Harband and Lord Kildan fought their way through one of Mikkik's lesser legions at Butchers gap, they heard the drums of war arrayed against them again, but not the percussive thunder of the Uyumaak. The combined armies of Tolnor and Aughmere now pursued them on their southward track. Lord Kildan and General Harband had pushed Mirelle's forces on through the night, but the soldiers behind them matched them for speed and endurance.

Spies of the Church of the One had no doubt warned Athan and the Padras that a sizable force marched on the floor of the canyon, and that Mirelle rode in command. The Chalaine could only imagine what they thought of her mother, Gen's unflinching supporter, who had, to their view, attempted to slay Eldaloth on the day of his reemergence into Ki'Hal. How would she and her mother ever convince them of the truth? What arguments could they possibly proffer to persuade the Churchmen that the bright shining being that now favored them with such beneficence was indeed the force of evil that they had so long feared would wrap his crushing embrace about Ki'Hal and destroy it?

Even worse, the Chalaine marveled at how she hardly cared about what became of the world. She had failed, and neither of the dreams that had plagued her for so long had come true. The man she had married to save the world had died without a whimper. The man whose love she sacrificed to save the world had died in a valiant struggle to save her when it was worthless to do so. The world would fall, and any comfort she could have taken in Gen's affection would have faded as the deceitful Mikkik destroyed them all.

But oh, how she had wanted her faithful friend and Protector!

The young summer days brought sunshine and little shadow to the vast stretch of flat prairie that slid by her in a tear-soaked blur. The Chalaine's body hurt from the birth, her head spun with weakness, and her heart felt so numb with grief that she of doubted it beat at all. Her Child was gone. Gen was gone. Her hope was gone.

Her mother rode to her side, her mask of control set aside so that sorrow could roost upon her features and project clearly to anyone that her heart had broken. The Chalaine doubted she had ever seen Cadaen so pained as he rode dutifully behind, powerless against the enemy that tormented his charge. The Chalaine had caught glimpses of her mother's love for Gen in the past, but now that oft-hidden text read plainly in her eyes, forced to light by the loss of one most dear.

The Chalaine tried to choke down her own distress, but something within her bid her to simply stop, dismount, and let the wave of soldiery knock her to the ground. The thundering hooves would pound away what miserable shred of life she could still lay claim to. At the very least, she wished they would return her to the side of Gen's quiet body so she could fade away with him into the dust. But haste had denied him even the small courtesy of a proper burial. The only honor they could bestow besides the sad volume of honest tears was to arrange his body so that he was embracing his sword as he was wont to do, only now in the grasp of eternal sleep.

Lord Kildan and General Harband called for a halt, her mother working at her own hair and face in an attempt to fashion a mask of dignity. The Chalaine cast her gaze over her shoulder, finding that the pursuing horde of men had also stopped about a mile away. Their metal glinted in the sunshine, the number of soldiers easily doubling the small force commanded by her mother's leaders.

"It appears they wish to parley," Dason informed her, riding close. "Do you see the emissary?"

Between her veil and her tears, nothing in the distance could be seen easily, but after a few minutes, a number of horsemen approaching at an easy pace resolved to her vision. Lord Kildan and a contingent of soldiers separated from their ranks and rode out to meet them. Murmurs and whispers broke out among the soldiers who, for the most part, had obediently followed them despite not knowing the full drama of what had occurred at Echo Hold.

With Gen dead, the Chalaine was the only witness of Mikkik's duplicity. Aldemar had shown her the face of her enemy, and that vision alone held the truth that the being masquerading as Eldaloth was a fraud. Her mother believed her implicitly, as had all those connected with her. But hopelessness welled up within her when she realized that no one else would. Who would embrace the horror of truth while the rest of the world reveled in victory?

Lord Kildan returned from his parley on the plain, and the inner circle of Mirelle's leadership gathered at the center of their forces. The Chalaine wanted no part of it, but her mother—somehow functioning despite her grief—helped her daughter down from the horse and brought her into the circle where Duke Kildan, General Harband, Ethris, Maewen, and Gerand waited.

"Who commands the host?" Mirelle asked, unable to mask the unsteady quiver in her voice.

"It is Padra Athan," Lord Kildan answered. "He's got enough scars to rival Gen, now." It took Mirelle looking away and wiping her eyes for Kildan to realize his blunder. "I apologize, Milady. I express my condolences."

"What does he want?" Ethris asked, eying Mirelle with concern.

"At first," said Lord Kildan, "they just wanted Mirelle, and anyone connected with her, to be held for interrogation and prosecution for aiding Gen. Besides trying to kill Eldaloth—or who they think is Eldaloth—they believe that Gen murdered the Chalaine by tossing her off the bridge. I informed them of the truth, which brought them great relief but new demands."

"What terms?" Mirelle asked, crawling on top of her emotions.

"They want you and the Chalaine to return with them to Echo Hold immediately, claiming they are under orders from Eldaloth himself. They wish for Ethris, General Harband, and me to disperse the troops immediately and submit ourselves to their custody. If we do not obey these terms, they will purse us and take what they want by force of arms and magic."

"Did you inform them of Mikkik's fraud?" Ethris asked.

"I tried," Lord Kildan answered, "but they mocked me for even suggesting it, demanding proof and witnesses. Are we sure that the being that appeared was Mikkik and not Eldaloth?"

Lord Kildan's eyes communicated his desperate desire to avoid bloodshed.

"It is Mikkik," the Chalaine confirmed. "With Gen . . . gone . . . I am the only witness. I could open my mind to Athan so he could see the vision Aldemar gave me, so he could know Mikkik's face and voice as I do."

"If you get within eyesight of Athan, he'll take you," Harband warned.

"I agree," Lord Kildan said.

"I can get the memory from her and share it with Athan," Ethris suggested. "He may not believe me, but it is worth the attempt. Lord Kildan, do you think that Athan would agree to a council if we promised to offer evidence of our claims?"

Lord Kildan thought for a moment. "I cannot say with certainty, but I can attempt it. We must try. They claim to outnumber us three to one, and from what I could spy from my vantage point, I believe them. If we are forced to fight, we will lose."

Mirelle stood tall. "Let me be clear about one thing, and this is for all of you. I will not turn my daughter over to Padra Athan. I would ask that if the need arises, that the forces loyal to me buy time for the Chalaine to escape southward and then west to Rhugoth. She must live."

"No, Mother!" the Chalaine exclaimed amid the nods of assent. "My life is not worth the blood of these men! Let me go, if Athan requires it. I would rather join Gen in death than see the blood of good men spilled to save my worthless life! I have failed, and nothing can change that! My time is over!"

"Mikkik wants you," Ethris said tenderly, taking her by the shoulders, his gaze boring through the veil. "If you weren't important or a threat to him, then Padra Athan would let you go. I'm sure that in his mind, he simply wishes to return you so that Mikkik can usher you out of this world. But the truth is that you are the only member of the prophecy of his destruction that still exists, and you are the only hope we have!"

The Chalaine wrenched herself from his soft grip. "I will not. . ."

"You will!" Mirelle interrupted, face severe. "One of the best men I ever knew just sacrificed his life so you could live. You will not dishonor his memory by throwing that life away." Her mother closed her eyes and steadied herself. "I do not mean to burden you or be cross during this time of mourning. You know I feel this wound as deeply and as painfully as you, but do not compound it by suggesting I give away what I have treasured above all."

The Chalaine nodded in acquiescence, and the council relaxed.

"It is settled, then," Ethris said to solidify the decision. "Chalaine, I must intrude upon your thoughts. I need your memory of Aldemar's vision and what passed between you and Mikkik on the bridge of Echo Hold. Will you allow me?"

"Yes."

"Thank you, dear," he said tenderly. "Do not let pain overwhelm you. We cannot see all ends. When I am done, Mirelle and Lord Kildan will accompany me to talk sense into Athan. There may be a way out yet. Lord Kildan, please approach Athan again and let him know we have evidence of our claims."

The Chalaine bowed her head as Ethris placed his hand upon it, but despite his comforting words, no serious hope took root in a soil she feared too hardened by tragedy to let any seed creep in.

Mirelle kissed the Chalaine's cheek before she mounted her horse, joining Ethris, Kildan, Cadaen, and a retinue of soldiers ready to ride toward the center of the yawning space between the amassed armies. Athan had agreed to hear their arguments, though Mirelle doubted the conniving Churchman would take them seriously.

Mostly, Mirelle was grateful for Ethris, a Mage powerful enough for Athan to respect and a loyal friend who had generously taken up the slack in her leadership that the fog of her grief had left. She hardly had the will to command anything or anyone, having Gen's pale face and marred body cradled in her arms the only memory that mattered to her. Only the need to protect her daughter had roused her to activity, and she clung to that steadying purpose to will her mind to turn again toward strategy and negotiation.

They moved at a steady pace toward a pavilion that Athan had ordered erected in the field between the two factions. Mirelle tried to understand the matter from the perspective of everyone at Echo Hold, save those few who knew the truth. The day before had proceeded just as prophecy had dictated—until Gen had stabbed the impostor Eldaloth in the back and wounded him, turning the bliss of victory into terrifying uncertainty. That Mikkik had commanded Athan to retrieve the Chalaine and her supporters meant that the dark god had survived Gen's attack on the bridge and was in command.

What terrified Mirelle the most was Athan's pride. He would take his inability to control Gen as a personal failure that had led to the wounding of his god. This task from Eldaloth would provide him a way to save face in a small way. If Ethris's demonstration of her daughter's memory was not sufficient to convince the Padra of the true identity of the being he thought a god, there would be no way to avoid bloodshed.

The noon sun shone warmly upon them as they approached the pavilion, a cadre of eunuch Eldephaere ringing the outside and stiffening to attention as they dismounted. Padra Athan stood outside in his robes of office, eying Ethris and Mirelle as they approached. Padra Nolan stood at his side. Athan's face and hands bore recently healed scars, but the power of his piercing eyes remained alight, filled will divine purpose. Without a word he stepped aside and signaled for them to enter.

The dim tent sweltered in the afternoon heat, the ground covered with functional rugs and rough camp chairs that circled the interior space. A third Padra waited inside, already seated with a quill and paper on his lap. They exchanged no greetings as they sat, Athan staring at them all with barely checked contempt.

"Let me be clear that I allowed this parley as a courtesy," he began. "I fully intend to recover the Chalaine. I was gratified to hear that Gen was slain and will have my men search among the corpses so that we can drag his body through the streets of Echo Hold and then burn it. If I have my way, Mirelle, you will suffer the same fate. I hope you can see where your naive trust of Gen has led us. You *knew* he was the Ilch and chose to give him honor and position despite it all! Now Eldaloth bleeds with a wound that cannot be staunched. His wound has no power to take his life, but no power to be healed, either. Only the Chalaine can help him. She must come with us!"

"Gen saved the Chalaine's life, Athan! He died at Butchers gap, destroying Mikkik's creatures to keep them from catching and killing her," Mirelle countered.

"The Chalaine was set for Erelinda before the Ilch interfered! She would now be partaking of the joy that Eldaloth gave to Chertanne. . ."

"That is not Eldaloth, Athan," Ethris said forcefully.

"Ah, yes," Athan said, "the delightful story Lord Kildan warned me about. What proof could you possibly have? What circumstance could confirm it? The world now rejoices! Mikkik's creatures are in retreat as we crush them and drive them east! Eldaloth sits upon the throne in Echo Hold rewarding the faithful and healing the sick, and you come with wild tales. Who concocted this story? Gen?"

"It is the Chalaine that confirms it," Ethris said, "though

a thoughtful consideration of the events at Echo Hold might tender its own evidences. Don't you think, Athan, that the battle went just a little too easily? In the first two Mikkikian Wars, tens and even hundreds of thousands were killed. So Mikkik returns and just throws his soldiers at Echo Hold with no plan or military purpose? I doubt even a hundred of our defenders were killed. Then Mikkik crafts some creature for you to believe is him, and you all play along."

"Ridiculous!" Athan thundered. "If you have real evidence, then let us see it. If all you have is words, then return to your soldiers and tell them it's time to die."

Mirelle's doubts about Athan's willingness to negotiate became all too real as Ethris rose and approached the zealous man. Athan would not leave without her daughter. He had already carved his intended path, and only a confession from Mikkik himself would deter him down a different road.

Ethris stopped in front Athan. "My evidence consists of two memories I have copied from the Chalaine's mind. The first is a vision given to her from Aldemar in which he showed her Mikkik when he slew Eldaloth. The second is the Chalaine's encounter with Mikkik on the bridge of Echo Hold just before Gen pulled her into the ravine. It is very clear to the Chalaine and anyone who sees this memory that the one who killed Eldaloth hundreds of years ago stood on the Bridge of Echo Hold and unmade Chertanne and the Holy Child using Trysmagic. You may enter my mind and view these memories. I know it is in your power."

Athan, clearly unconvinced, stood and invited Ethris to sit in his chair so he could place his hands upon Ethris's head and do the reading.

"Do not try to wander where I do not wish it," Ethris warned. "You would regret it."

The spectators fell quiet as the two men concentrated,

Athan whispering the words of his spell. For several minutes both sat motionless as the memories gleaned from the Chalaine's mind played before Athan, whose controlled facial expression revealed nothing of what he might have thought or felt. At last it was over, and Athan backed away, eyes refocusing outward as Ethris returned to sit with Mirelle. For a moment, Athan actually seemed to consider seriously what he had seen, Mirelle's hope rising. But his words crushed it in an instant.

"You call that evidence?" he said with derision. "These are images from the mind of a frightened young woman whose faith Gen had poisoned her from the moment he met her. And let's not forget that the memory given her was from a race of creatures whose purposes and intentions are as unknown to us as Gen's were. If you have nothing better than that to offer, then I suggest that you turn yourselves over peacefully now. I will allow Lord Kildan to return to your lines and order the soldiers to surrender their weapons. They will be free to return to their homeland once we have reached Echo Hold with the Chalaine."

"See reason!" Ethris pleaded, standing. "You have been hopelessly deceived!"

"Guards, seize them," Athan ordered, nervously eying Ethris.

"Wait!" Mirelle yelled as the Eldephaere entered the tent, weapons drawn. Cadaen shoved his way forward to stand by Mirelle.

She stood toe to toe with Athan. "If the Chalaine goes with you, can you promise that she will come to no harm?"

Ethris said, "No, Mirelle!" She silenced him with a look.

"Of course!" Athan exclaimed. "It is you who is taking her into danger! I only wish to do as Eldaloth wills! She will be far and away more protected in Echo Hold than riding through the wilderness where the remnants of Mikkik's forces roam leaderless."

"Then let me speak with my daughter," Mirelle said,

doing her best to act defeated. It came easily because she felt it. "I would inquire of her will and see what she wishes."

"Then be quick about it," Athan said. "I expect a report within the half hour."

Mirelle's mind raced as they left the tent and mounted the horses, polishing every detail of the plan that was born as soon as she saw Athan's determined, implacable face.

"You can't be seriously considering this," Ethris said quietly, face questioning. "But I see that you aren't. What do you propose?"

Mirelle waited until they were farther from the tents before she explained, signaling for Ethris to lean in close so Cadaen couldn't hear. "If Mikkik uses impostors, then so can we. I will take the Chalaine's place with a little help from your magic. After we have pretended to counsel together, we will send Kildan back with the deal. He will say that the Chalaine has agreed to return with Athan, but only if he lets everyone else go free. If I'm right, he will agree. Getting the Chalaine is everything to him, and punishing the rest of us of far less import. I will take Dason and ride to their camp to complete the illusion. If we're lucky, he'll be so excited to get underway that he won't submit me to any close examination."

"What about. . ." and Ethris cast a glance back to Cadaen.

"You or I will have to drop him and keep him under for as long as it takes," she said. "He will ruin everything if he comes chasing after me."

"Athan was serious about dragging you through the streets, Mirelle. Are you sure you want to do this?"

Mirelle nodded. "If that is what it takes to keep my daughter away from Mikkik, I'll suffer it. But I think Athan knows that if he hurts me, the Chalaine would never forgive him or get anywhere near his control. I'll remind Athan of that if it comes to it."

Ethris nodded as they arrived at their lines to a sea of expectant faces. Taking care of Cadaen would be easy compared to convincing her daughter, but Mirelle had to try. If need be, she would have Ethris put her into a slumber along with Cadaen. Her council gathered about them, but Mirelle asked for privacy, pulling her daughter away toward the rear of the camp where they could speak alone.

"We've little time, daughter. I am going to ask something very difficult of you, and I need you to be strong for me."

"You've decided to let me go with him after all," the Chalaine said, resigned and even relieved.

Mirelle took her daughter's face in her hands. "No, my love. I need you to let me go with him." As she explained the plan to her daughter, the expected resistance came.

"I cannot lose you and Gen both! Not now!" the Chalaine exclaimed.

"That is the point!" Mirelle countered. "If you go, Athan will have no qualms about torturing and killing me and maybe others besides. If we refuse, his army will destroy us. If I go as an impostor, you can flee. By the time he figures out our little trick, you will be out of his reach. He cannot kill me. He knows that doing so would turn you against him forever, so he will keep me safe. In more ways than one, I will be much safer than you."

The Chalaine began to weep, and Mirelle embraced her tenderly, knowing that her arguments had broken down the Chalaine's defenses. She signaled for the council to come to them and quickly explained her plan.

Cadaen, incensed, objected. "I will not put you within reach of that man or. . ."

Ethris incanted and Cadaen fell to the ground, unconscious.

Mirelle regarded him softly, tears coming to her eyes. "I am sorry, old friend. You cannot follow me this time.

Please see that he is treated with dignity and honor."

"It will be done," Lord Kildan assured her.

"Dason," Mirelle said, "are you prepared to come to Athan's camp with me? I cannot say what he will do with you."

"I am loathe to leave the Chalaine in this peril," he said.

"Please, Dason," the Chalaine said. "Do this for me. If he allows you to stay with her, please do. It is the greatest gift you could give me. I would be in your debt forever."

He bowed. "Then I will."

"Let's hurry," Ethris prompted. "There is little time. Kildan, ride to Athan's camp and let him know our terms. There is a small hedge just a little way off. Mirelle and the Chalaine will trade identities and clothes there."

They worked quickly in the heat of the summer afternoon. They had to conjure a replacement veil for the Chalaine, though Mirelle knew that the powerful beauty that had once exuded from the Chalaine had already dimmed, the darkness around her red-streaked eyes dulling her once-powerful radiance.

When they were finished, she signaled Ethris over.

"You are of the same height and build," Ethris observed, "but the problem is in voice and bearing. The voice I can change. The Chalaine's bearing is yours to imitate, Mirelle. You are used to ruling and commanding and getting your way. Right now, you need the humility, fear, and exhaustion of your daughter. I mean no offense, Chalaine."

"I feel those things, too," Mirelle said. "I plan on saying little." To her daughter, she said, "Since you spent a great deal of time with Athan, I will need you to inform me of any significant events that he may bring up casually, though there is no time for detail."

While Ethris incanted, the Chalaine rattled off a number of meetings she had attended and conversations she had had with the Padra, but Mirelle doubted they would help much. When Ethris finished, the voice of her daughter issued from her lips, surprising her.

"It will be strange," Ethris warned her, "and it will only last for about a day. If you can keep up the ruse that long, we should be far enough out of Athan's reach."

"I'll do my best."

Duke Kildan returned, galloping directly to where they waited. "He has agreed," he reported. "He demands she come at once. There is a lot of activity in their lines, and I am worried he means to attack anyway."

"Let's get this over with," Mirelle said, embracing her daughter one last time. "Remember your worth, Chalaine. Remember who died for you. I hope we may meet again soon, but if not, remember me for my love, whatever my mistakes have been."

Prying the reluctant Chalaine away, Mirelle signaled Dason over to her and steeled herself. If she failed to convince Athan of her identity, she had little doubt Athan would see her run through on the spot. Ethris hugged her and the rest of the party bowed.

"Remember," Ethris said, "you are your daughter. Diffident, quiet, and not prone to sharp remarks. Speak as little as possible and you'll get through."

Mirelle nodded, and, with Dason in tow, mounted the horse and rode away from the line of soldiers who, unaware of the ruse, whispered among themselves about the Chalaine's departure. Course decided, she allowed one last look backward at her daughter and let the grief she had held at bay finally have its just due.

Ahead, Athan waited next to a prison wagon, and as Lord Kildan had observed, the lines bustled with movement and preparations that indicated that more was at stake than just an unforced departure. Men donned armor and checked weapons, and Athan's bearing bore the hallmarks of impatience. He bowed as they approached.

"Most Holy Chalaine," he intoned reverently. "I thank

you for the wise decision to return to Eldaloth's embrace. I am afraid we must depart rather hastily. Some of Mikkik's creatures still have the will to fight on without him. I had intended less confined accommodations for you, but I am afraid you must bear a little discomfort for your own protection, as during the caravan to your wedding."

"It doesn't matter," Mirelle said, the Chalaine's voice still feeling strange in her throat. "We're doomed no matter what we do."

Athan furrowed his brow in concern. "You are mistaken, Chalaine. When you see Eldaloth, you will understand your error and feel of his kindness and mercy. Then you will find hope again."

Mirelle mounted the prison wagon, and Dason tried to follow, only to have the Eldephaere guards rebuff him.

"Dason, you are dismissed," Athan said. "Return to your people."

"I will not leave her!" he exclaimed, and Mirelle was impressed by the sincerity of his voice. Lord Kildan's son was quite an actor, after all.

"Go, Dason," Mirelle said, keeping the despair at the forefront of her voice. "You can do me no more service, now. Go help my mother. Keep her safe, and you will be rewarded."

He bowed stiffly. "Your will." He mounted the horse and took the other by the reins, leading them away.

Padra Nolan approached as the Eldephaere bolted her in. "If we are to avoid the vanguard of Mikkik's host, we must leave now. We will barely make it to Echo Hold as it is."

"Is there time for the tent?" Athan asked.

"Leave it," Nolan replied.

Mikkik's host? Mirelle thought. *From where?*

The small contingent they had destroyed on the canyon floor was the only body of Mikkik's army not attacking Echo Hold that the scouts had run across.   Athan had

56

made it seem like Mikkik's forces were scattered and leaderless, but if the army of six thousand that had chased them south could be put to flight by whatever was coming, then something had gone wrong. Her daughter might have been safer going to Echo Hold after all. Mirelle peered out the bars as the wagon rumbled north, wanting to scream a warning to those she left behind. But she was just as powerless to help them as she had felt holding Gen's lifeless body to her breast. Desolate, she slumped against the sides of the carriage as the only thing left in the world she wanted to fight for disappeared beyond the horizon.

Chapter 73 - Driven and Bled

"We've got half a day, Lord Kildan, and then we'll be in their power," Maewen reported after dismounting her lathered horse. "It seems they've no interest in Athan's party heading toward Echo Hold. They come for us alone, and we must press on."

The late afternoon sun hung over the plain where they had thought to encamp for the night, the heat sucking sweat from their skin while the warm light painted their faces the color of flame. After Athan's party had departed, Lord Kildan had ordered a more leisurely pace south to rest the horses, but Maewen smelled something on the breeze blown in from the east and returned with the poor news—an army of Mikkik's creatures of unknown number moved across the plain, coming directly for them.

"We can't rest," Maewen said. "We ride south as fast as we can to the Blackwood, even if it kills the horses. The forest is dense and dark and will give us some advantage. If we're caught out here on the plain, and if that army is the size I think it is, we will be slaughtered. If we ride through the night, we'll make the Blackwood by dawn and have several hours to rest before they fall upon us."

Lord Kildan swallowed hard at the news. His son

Gerand stood next to him, every inch the soldier his father was.

"Father, let me take a group of a hundred of our heaviest cavalry and ride along the eastern flank some distance from the main party so we can sound the alarm if some group of the host catches us early."

"Do it," Kildan agreed.

"I'll send Falael with you," Maewen added. "He can see and sense things you cannot."

Lord Kildan nodded. "Dason, Kimdan, and Tolbrook will stay with the Chalaine at all times and ride on the extreme western flank. If we are attacked, we will slow the advance to buy time for the Chalaine to escape."

"I will ride with her as well," Ethris offered, concern in his eyes.

The Chalaine could hardly speak. Something was happening to her, both in body and spirit. It felt like the undoing of everything that she was. In the hour after her mother left, her skin began to darken and dry as if held over some invisible, scorching flame that desiccated her flesh but didn't burn. It worsened with every hour of the sweltering afternoon until chips of graying skin flecked away and fell like ash to the ground. She wore her riding gloves to hide it, but it hadn't escaped Ethris's notice.

But worse was a mounting despair flooding down a channel already worn away by her grief over Gen's death and her mother's departure. The events of the last two years had sent her soaring to the greatest heights of emotion and dashed her just as far down. But she realized now that even in dark times some anchor of hope had kept her grounded, some purpose had pushed her forward against the driving wind of resistance that always seemed to blow in her face. The anchor was gone, and a deadness just as heavy now replaced it. The sunshine around her mocked the storm that swirled in her mind. It reminded her of the demon's poison that had pulled Gen so far into despair that it had nearly killed him. Who would come into her mind and pull her out?

"We ride!" Lord Kildan shouted, jolting the Chalaine out of her mind and into the dangerous world outside. Lord Kildan's men took up the refrain and mounted their horses, though even the general clamor couldn't mask the groans of weary men unready to be forced back into movement. Gerand, Volney at his side, split off and rode east with the cavalry until they were barely visible in the distance.

"Let me help you mount," Dason said sweetly, offering his hand. She took it and then snatched it away self-consciously, feigning rearranging her improvised headdress and veil before taking the saddle and pulling herself up. Dason sidled up to her horse, making a show of adjusting the stirrup straps. His dark hair had grown wilder in the days of marching and battle, and his once-crisp uniform was rumpled and dirty. A strange glow of expectancy still filled his eyes, despite their harrowing circumstances.

"Milady, I know you have wandered through many sorrows. You have lost your husband and Gen, whom I know you esteemed as a great man of arms. I stand ready, as your ever constant friend, to succor you in these woes." He lowered his voice. "And with the . . . obstacles . . . now removed, I might hope that the warm regard we have always shared might bloom into something more blessed than just friendship."

The agony and deadness within her spared her from feeling the full horror of Dason's unlooked for and unwelcome invitation. Her mind refused to even accept it as real, the social machinery meant to respond to such a forward declaration jammed and stuck fast in a mire. Esteemed Gen as a great man of arms? How could Dason be so ignorant of her feelings? She blinked to clear her head and then spurred the horse onward to join nearly two thousand men racing forward in a desperate attempt to reach the forest before an army of dark creatures overtook them.

The interminable night favored them with a clear sky, the full light of the three moons beaming down to ease their way through a light mist that clung to the grass like a gauzy veil. Horses and men fell during the night, exhausted and drained. The others rode on without them. Lord Kildan and General Harband refused to let up. The indomitable Maewen rode back and forth between the main body and Gerand's defensive column on their eastern flank. The Chalaine never heard the reports she brought back, but by the army's unrelenting pace, the news spurred them forward rather than invited rest.

Several times during the solemn hours of the night, threading through the wisps of mist, the Chalaine nearly fell out of her saddle from a leeching exhaustion. Everyone needed sleep, but few carried a heavier burden than hers. More men and horses succumbed to the forced march, the wrenching cry of screaming horses and deserted men driving everyone's sanity to the breaking point. Even the Chalaine's leaden heart jumped to her throat when the first, barely perceptible thumping of the Uyumaak assaulted her ears, only to be followed by the frantic yells of Gerand's men. A battle ensued, dimly heard by those in the main column, the noises of weapons and the tone of Gerand's barked commands hinting at the ebb and flow of the fight.

The altercation was brief, and the tenor of the night air returned to the slow rumble of horses riding ever south. Maewen came back from the fight, and Ethris rode forward to listen to the report she gave to Kildan and Harband, returning the Chalaine a short while later.

"Gerand's men skirmished with the Hunters scouting ahead," Ethris told her. "Time is short. We are nearly to the wood and have three hours at best to prepare for the main body. How is your skin?"

The Chalaine regarded him dully. "Does it matter?"

Ethris frowned, but three horses approaching drew their attention away. Volney slumped in the saddle, riding between two of his fellow soldiers. A dark arrow protruded from his shoulder, and the other two bore deep gashes on their legs. The Chalaine cringed, knowing what they would ask.

"We need healing," Volney said, wincing. "Damn Archer hit me out of the dark."

They stopped the horses as the column proceeded forward around them. Hesitantly, the Chalaine removed a hand from her riding glove, surprised at the amount of flaked, ash-like skin that fell from it. Her skin appeared fully burned and black now, and Volney, even in his discomfort, drew in a startled breath.

"Mikkik's beard!" one of the soldiers exclaimed, earning him a stern look from Ethris. The Chalaine reached forward, hand seeming like a dark claw, and grasped Volney's arm, more skin falling away at the friction. She closed her eyes and tried, as she had a hundred times before, to sense the wound and heal it, but the power had fled. No amount of concentration or effort produced even the slightest healing effect. Tears came unbidden to her eyes. Even her gift had been stripped from her. She was truly worthless now.

"I can't," she said, pulling away.

"I have some skill, there," Ethris said. "Dason, Kimdan, keep her moving."

The Chalaine barely recognized the passing of night, wondering what sort of dark transformation was upon her. Was this punishment? Was this retribution for failing to protect the Holy baby? For loving Gen instead of the monster she had been married to? Wasn't her regret and the world's undoing enough punishment? Wasn't watching Gen hammered to the earth by a wicked bolt enough torment?

"We're there!" Dason trumpeted loudly, again bringing

her from her dark reverie. The eastern horizon bore the barest hints of dawn, washing away the easternmost array of stars. Before them loomed the Black Forest they had driven for. While perhaps a trick of the darkness, *black* was an apt description. Rather than large, thick trees, the Black Forest consisted of many thin pine trees crammed together in tight spaces. The needles and branches grew only near the top, the thin trunks shooting impressively high into the air. Fallen, dead trees lay at angles, interrupting the uniformity of the dense, vertical poles. The bark of the trees was dark, like her skin, and its layers peeled away from the trunks in feathery strands.

As they neared, it became clear that riding horses through the tight spaces of the Black Wood would be impossible. Their original route would have led them farther east around the wood and then back west toward Rhugoth. Heading directly west would trap them against an impassible ravine and put them in an indefensible position. Almost as soon as they arrived, Dason and Kimdan helped her from her horse and led her into murky sylvan darkness and away from prying eyes.

Lord Kildan and General Harband formed their troops into ranks, Gerand and his men returning from the east to join the rest of the party. The orders were given for alternating shifts of sleep and work, and Gerand and a handful of his men were sent back into the plain to see if they could recover any of the recently fallen soldiers before the Uyumaak butchered them and stuffed them into cook pots. The Chalaine sat heavily against a tree trunk, a knot burrowing into her shoulder. She was too tired to care. Dason told Kimdan to get some rest. A trio of soldiers lay Cadaen's slumbering body behind a thick tangle of a fallen trees not far from where she reclined, and the Chalaine wondered how long they could do without his sword. Even if awakened, she thought he might just try cutting through the entire Uyumaak column to get back to Mirelle.

The woods burst into activity as men hauled brush to the forest edge to create a dense wall that would slow the Uyumaak advance. For the few who had been wounded in their flight, a small camp was set up near where Cadaen was laid. Nearly half of the soldiers simply lay down in the forest and immediately fell into an exhausted sleep so profound a casual observer might have thought them dead. The Chalaine joined them shortly after, the scent of the Gen's Ial stone rising with the heat of her body.

Ethris woke her some time later, Maewen with him, and gave her hunk of bread and apple slices. "We have a bit of good fortune. It appears the Uyumaak are as weary and hungry as we are. We've only seen a handful of Hunters. The rest appear to have stopped to light their cook pots."

"Give the food to someone who will fight," the Chalaine said glumly. "I need little to get me through sitting on the ground."

"You will eat, child," Ethris said firmly, penetrating eyes boring through the veil. "Either take it or I will use my magic to force you."

The Chalaine took the proffered meal and nibbled at it. If they wanted to waste the food, she supposed she couldn't stop them. Ethris relaxed as she ate, Maewen looking around and listening.

"I wanted Maewen to see what is happening to your skin," Ethris said. "I will try to help it, but I have never seen anything like it before and wondered if she might have come across it in her travels."

Placing the food in her lap, the Chalaine removed her riding glove, and Dason sucked breath through his teeth at the ghastly sight. The Chalaine was surprised herself to see just how blackened and flaking it had become. It truly appeared as if she had fallen asleep with her hand in the fire. When she clenched her fingers, chips would drift away to the ground. Maewen, face barely masking her horror at the sight, stooped down and took her hand, rolling up the sleeve a little.

"So it covers your body?"

"Yes," the Chalaine confirmed. "It is uncomfortable. It started coming on after my mother left me."

"I have never seen any poison or sickness that acts as this does," Maewen said, releasing the Chalaine's hand and standing again. "In the Mikkikian Wars, there were many afflictions, and I do not know them all, but no, Ethris, I can be of no assistance here."

"It's a curse for my failure," the Chalaine mumbled.

"What failure, Chalaine?" Ethris censured. "You have nothing to be ashamed of. You did everything that was required of you and more. What happened at Echo Hold was none of your doing. Your mother told you this. If Gen had the chance, I'm sure that he would have said the same thing. You are not cursed!"

"I failed to love my husband! I failed to protect the babe! My baby!" she cried at the memory of his perfect form and the short time she had to embrace and suckle him.

"No one loved your husband, and Chertanne and Athan failed to protect the baby," Ethris reasoned forcefully, trying to break through her guilt. "You were not supposed to have the magic to fight Mikkik; Chertanne was. Mikkik tricked everyone, and that is not your doing."

"But if I hadn't loved another man, maybe I would have tried harder with Chertanne," she said, noticing Dason look away as if embarrassed. In horror, she realized he thought that *he* was the other man.

"Chalaine," Ethris said, taking both of her hands. "Give it time. You will see that none of what has happened can be laid to your charge. You are as guiltless as Maewen or me or your mother. Now hush, child. Let me see if something can be done for your condition."

Ethris began chanting and the Chalaine closed her eyes. For a brief moment, she felt relief from the dry, raspy itch of her skin, but once Ethris's chanting stopped, it returned. She remembered Gen's sickness in Elde Luri Mora that would only abate when she touched him. He had been Mikkik's creature that couldn't abide the holy city. *Perhaps I am so unworthy that I am unfit for even a place as this,* she thought, misery compounding.

Ethris shook his head and stood. "It is beyond my knowledge," he lamented. "I am sorry, Chalaine. Maewen, when the fighting starts, I would like you to stay with her. If it looks as if the battle is turning against us, take her into the woods and try to get her to Mikmir and the protections of the castle. If I can follow, I will."

They left, Dason remaining nearby. "I am sure it will fade soon," he consoled. "You have always been a creature of such beauty that it will return to you naturally, I am sure of it. Your radiance will shine again, and everything will be as it was at first."

The Chalaine declined to answer, and Kimdan arrived a short while later to let Dason rest. Kimdan made himself useful by constructing a crude shelter for her to afford her some privacy and some protection from any inclement weather. The day had come as hot and bright as the one before it.

"The Uyumaak will wait to come until it cools and begins to darken," Kimdan said. "If you can rest, you should. We may need to flee in the night."

She nodded and leaned her head against the tree. She didn't want to flee. She just wanted to lay down, and if she never rose again, then all the better.

"Hunters!"

The urgent scream brought the Chalaine out of a dead sleep, and she dashed her head against the side of Kimdan's lean-to, shaking the entire structure. In the weak light of dusk, she could almost imagine that the form standing in the black uniform of a Dark Guard was Gen. But it was Kimdan, youthful bravado tempered by training and now war. He squinted toward the edge of the forest and out into the plain, eyes searching for the camouflaged beasts gathered in the tall grass. The Uyumaak thumping echoed among the tree trunks, filling her with dread and chasing the grogginess from her mind.

The Chalaine, whose crude accommodations faced backward into the woods, craned around to get a better look, her tight, dry skin cracking and peeling with the effort. From her position behind the front line, the trunks obscured nearly everything save the barest of slits of light that provided narrow windows to the battlefield beyond. Her veil and the constricted view prevented her from seeing anything save the fleeing passage of men darting to their positions. Crunching footsteps nearby brought her heart to her throat, but it was only Dason arriving from wherever he had taken his rest.

"We've come to it now," Dason said gravely to Kimdan. "At least they let us rest. How do you fare, your Highness?"

Awful. Horrible. "Fine."

"I see Kimdan made you a little castle! I had thought to do the same myself. We should fortify it if we get the chance."

"Get down!" came another yell from the front, and the woods exploded with the whistling of dark arrows ripping through the trees to hammer hard into the trunks or skitter into the underbrush. Kimdan pushed her farther behind the tree as he and Dason crouched.

"It is a typical tactic," Kimdan explained. "They rain down arrows to keep our archers from doing any damage while they send in the Bashers to knock down our fortifications. It should let up in a minute."

The Chalaine huddled on the ground, covering her ears

to mute the awful racket punctuated by the painful wails of those felled by the mighty bows of the Uyumaak Archers. Few arrows fell as far back in the woods as she was, but the loud pop of a sleek dark arrow nearby snapped her eyes open, the polished shaft quivering in the trunk of a tree.

As Kimdan predicted, the hail of arrows stopped, providing for a brief respite until the relative silence ended with the horrifying crash of the Bashers smashing into their hastily constructed fortifications. Orders and shouts and screams mixed with the sharp sound of branches being snapped and split and chopped. Kimdan and Dason waited, swords at the ready, itching to help those who fought in the dwindling light before them. The voices of General Harband and Lord Kildan rang out clearly above the din, first calling for reinforcements toward the middle, and then frantically warning everyone to watch the flank.

"If they spread us out, we're done for," Kimdan said soberly.

A soldier sprinting back toward their position startled them. "They're breaking through!" he yelled, eyes filled with terror as he bolted toward the interior of the forest. Kimdan tripped him, sending the panicked Rhugothian soldier and his weapon flying. Angrily, Kimdan hauled him up by his breastplate and slammed him into a tree.

"Get back to the line, you. . ."

Two Bashers charged into camp from their left flank, both carrying massive war hammers and wearing thick hide armor and metal helmets. Kimdan released the soldier, who continued his flight into the twilight of the branches beyond. Wordlessly the Bashers struck, and while their short stature brought them only chest-high with their human enemies, their thick limbs struck with fierce power. The first drove its hammer in a side stroke toward Dason's hip. Dason jumped backward and away, the strike breaking a thin tree trunk to his right in two. Dason returned with a downward strike to its helmet, the impact hard, but the blade did little damage as it skipped off the metal.

Kimdan took a risk as the other charged him and he leapt at it before it could throw its arm over to strike. The sword's arcing trajectory aimed for a small space between the helmet and shoulder and missed, impacting with the dense armor of the shoulder and doing nothing. Desperately Kimdan tried to pull back, but the Basher wound up its unfinished hammer stroke and brought it down on Kimdan's extended leg, cracking it with a sound so awful that the Chalaine shrieked. Dason could do nothing to help his comrade as the other Basher pushed him backward. Dason tried quick stabs, seeking to insert his blade in some gap that would damage the creature.

Kimdan, eyes pained, tried to roll out of the way of another strike, but the Basher pounded him again, shattering his sword arm. The plight of Regent Ogbith's son finally penetrated the Chalaine's fear and self-pity, giving her the mettle she needed to act. She spied the sword discarded by the fleeing soldier and dove for it, Samian's hours of nightly instruction making the hilt and the blade familiar to her hand though she had never wielded a sword in the waking world.

The Basher hammered down on Kimdan again, crushing the left side of his chest, ribs snapping. The Chalaine stood, and with a skill not quite her own, aimed a sword stroke at the same spot Kimdan had tried for before. Unaware of her, the Basher made no move as the sword edge drove into its neck, blood spurting onto her dress as she retreated a step in preparation for its retaliation.

It reeled and turned, horrible line of gray eyes fixing on her from the depths of its helmet. The Chalaine brought her sword up instinctively. Dason still hadn't finished his opponent, and three more Bashers that had broken through the front line now marched toward their position. The wounded Basher charged unsteadily, its hammer swinging wide. The Chalaine struck quickly, chopping into the neck from the opposite side and severing the head. The Basher fell hard at her feet. At that moment, an arrow took Dason's opponent down, and with a yell Gerand, Volney, Maewen, and two Tolnorian soldiers broke into the fray and dispatched the remaining Bashers quickly. Blood covered everyone.

"Volney and I will stay with the Chalaine, now," Gerand said, eyes hard. "You four return to patrolling the flank."

"I'll stay, too," Maewen said. "We may need to flee into the wood if the tide doesn't turn soon."

The Chalaine ran to Kimdan. Gerand, noticing his sword mate, joined her. Kimdan barely breathed, eyes vacant and blood running from his mouth and nose. With every ounce of will and desire she had, she tried to heal him, but as with Volney, nothing would come. Her gift had truly gone. In despair she watched as Kimdan exhaled for the last time, face slackening. Shaking, she stood and went into the lean-to he had built for her. The sudden energy that had come upon her was gone, and she curled up on the ground and wept for the blood spilled for one as useless as she.

The sun dropped fully as her Protectors formed a solid perimeter around her, the darkness becoming ever more impenetrable. A change in the thumping brought them all on alert, but gradually the sounds of fighting ceased, replaced with the moans and cries of the injured and dying.

"I'm going to scout to make sure they haven't secreted any force inside the wood that could come upon us," Maewen said.

"How can you see anything?" Dason asked.

"Eleven eyes aren't defeated by the dark, and the Uyumaak aren't as blind as you are, either. Stay close to the Chalaine. And start no fire! If I cannot return, find Falael and do as he says."

"We need to bury Kimdan," Volney said sadly. "He deserves a better resting place than this cursed wood."

"We need sharp swords and eyes right now," Gerand returned. "Let's pull him back a space and arrange his body with what dignity we can. Dason, stay with the Chalaine."

"As you wish, *little* brother," Dason said with a firm tone of dominance. Once Gerand had left, he turned to the Chalaine. "I think someone is getting a little carried away with showing off for my father. I think he's always resented that I am the elder son. Curse this miserable darkness. At least the Uyumaak can have cook fires."

The Chalaine, tears falling silently now, said nothing. The movement around the forest was slow. Men flung curses into the night at scrapes and trips that could hardly be avoided. But stumbling about was better than light that would provide targets for the Uyumaak Archers. The moons again shone brightly on the plain, though stray clouds would drift overhead and shroud patches of the ocean of grass. The Chalaine drifted in and out of consciousness, for how long, she didn't know, but when she woke, everything was unnaturally still.

"What is it?" she asked weakly.

"The drums have stopped, Milady," Gerand said. "The Uyumaak have gone completely silent. I can't imagine what this portends. Be at the ready. We may have to move."

"Fall back! Run!" came the cry from the front line. As dissolute as she was, fear struck her heart as she realized that Ethris had raised the call. The Chalaine bolted upright as a curtain of fire rose on the plain, the light sending shadows wavering through the forest. At first she thought the flames some trickery of the Uyumaak or their Chukkas, but Maewen arrived seconds later to correct her assumption.

"Ethris buys us time," she said, frantically. "Keep the sun to your left in the morning!" she yelled to everyone. "We meet at the ridge."

They pushed southward toward the unknown chambers of the forest, Dason gripping her arm painfully as he vainly tried to guide her around obstacles he himself couldn't see well enough to avoid. Once the boles had swallowed the light of Ethris's fire, going forward became a matter of blind feeling about in the darkness. All around, the voices and footfalls of panicked men created the strange sensation of everyone being together in a dark room where the only comfort was knowing someone else shared the same affliction of blindness. Branches and undergrowth continually clawed at their feet and clothing like restless corpses trying to pull them down into an inky grave.

They had hardly gone two hundred feet into the sylvan abyss when a new sound creeping up from behind them stopped every foot and turned every head. Something moved along the forest floor, scrabbling and scraping among the dried needles and branches, coming for them like a wave in a steady, crescendoing roar.

"Lanterns!" someone yelled, the cry echoing through the forest.

None of her Protectors possessed one, but after a few moments, several pockets of light bloomed around them in the gloom. The uneven retreat had scattered the soldiers haphazardly around them, and the Chalaine shuddered to think of what had already become of those too wounded to flee.

Relentlessly, the sound grew, men drawing their weapons to face the unknown threat. This was no Uyumaak horde, the persistent thumping of their language unheard among the approaching cacophony, but when their enemy did arrive among the forward ranks, oaths and screams punctuated the night. The Chalaine, despite her weariness of soul and body could not stifle the scream ripped from her by the revelation of the horror that came for them.

Along the forest floor, a horde of black, lustrous beetles the size of a man's fist scrambled in an anxious advance toward them, the lamplight casting a fiery reflection along their obsidian backs, giving them the appearance of a flowing river of fire. A single snaking tubule hung between wicked pincers, adding to the uncomfortable appearance of their pointy, jointed legs and ridged backs.

Such was the speed of the insect host that none thought to flee. Swords, boots, hammers, and shields all pounded down with fury on the mass of carapaces, the crunch of popping insects and the explosion of pus and slime bursting all around them. To the Chalaine's amazement, the creatures avoided her, circling around her instinctively as if she were a warding pillar they could not abide. But her Protectors and every other soldier caught in the unyielding wave eventually succumbed to the beetles, the creatures' pincers lancing through boot leather, puncturing legs. The insects' tubules wiggled into the pincer cuts, sucking blood.

The Chalaine huddled against a tree trunk, powerless as the beetles took their fill of the soldiers' blood, and then just as quickly as they had come, turned and scrabbled away back to the north. Blood dribbled from the beetle wounds, the wounded staunching the blood with their hands.

The pale soldiers around her slowly recovered enough to stand, and as tough and indomitable as the Dark Guard was trained to be, the Chalaine could see in Gerand's and Volney's eyes the flicker of fear that would plague lesser men in less dangerous circumstances. No more did screams and yells punctuate the forest, only the pitiful sounds of whimpering and crying from an army of men pushed beyond the reach of hope.

"We've got to move," Gerand said, the first to rise, looking sickly and wan. "Let's keep the lanterns lit until the Uyumaak give us a reason not to."

Maewen found them moments later, a haggard Ethris at her side. A stunned, upset Cadaen followed, eyes hollow, Falael bringing up the rear. Several bites gashed Maewen's legs, though her hard eyes betrayed no weakness. Ethris was untouched, though Cadaen fared as poorly as everyone else. They examined the Chalaine, looking for injuries.

"They didn't bother with me," she said to get their prying eyes off of her. "I can walk."

Maewen inspected the cuts on her legs. "They bit me, but died immediately on doing so. The same for Falael. They didn't like the taste of elven blood."

"They liked mine just fine," Gerand fumed. "What was that?"

"One of Mikkik's abominations," Ethris said sourly. "I could feel its mind challenging me just before it attacked. Awful, horrible thing. What it wants with our blood, I cannot guess. We are in dire circumstances, now."

Gradually, the call to move echoed through the forest, and those with the strength to do so hauled themselves up and forward under the power of fear and will. Cadaen joined her group of Protectors, and the Chalaine wondered what bargain Ethris had struck with the man after awakening him. Whatever it was, she knew he would bolt at the first opportunity to find Mirelle or die in the attempt.

They marched through the night, and the Chalaine could only guess what the toll in men would be between those that simply got lost amid the trackless forest and those who collapsed from exhaustion. From the glances between Ethris and Maewen, she could tell they noticed the same thing as she—the soldiers looked more exhausted and sweaty than they should have. Even their breathing seemed forced.

Near morning, they encountered a pleasant glade blooming with wildflowers and bisected by a gurgling stream. There they ordered a halt, Lord Kildan and General Harband crossing to where Ethris, Maewen, and Falael talked in Elvish. Both leaders appeared as wan and unsteady as the men.

"The men, well, all of us are of a fever and weakening," Lord Kildan said. "We go no farther."

Maewen shook her head. "We should at least get to the treeline on the other side so the Archers can't butcher us on a whim. I know the men are weak, but it must be done. It's not far. . ."

Lord Kildan collapsed to the ground insensate, twitching with fever. All over the glade, men dropped prone as if compelled to a sudden slumber they could not refuse. In minutes, the entire clearing appeared like a battlefield where the battle had long ended and only the corpses were left behind. Only the fitful fever sleep revealed that something else was at work.

The Chalaine, Ethris, Falael, and Maewen still stood amid the stricken army to witness the sun cresting the tall pines, revealing a glorious morning. The beauty of the glade and the teeming life of insects flitting among the blossoms mocked the terror of the passing night and the moaning men scattered everywhere.

"Ethris," Maewen said, voice empty, "do you have anything to aid this?"

"I will try," he replied, "though I am close to spent. Is there any elven lore that might help? Falael?"

Falael shook his head. "Not that. . ."

Maewen aburptly stood erect, eyes distant, her hand going to her chest. Her lips parted slightly as if she wanted to exclaim, but she snapped her mouth shut. While the Chalaine couldn't be sure, it seemed some thought or hope had struck the half-elf.

"I . . . I remember now," she finally said, "a woodsman I once knew who used to frequent these woods. He used to dwell in a place not far from here. He may have wisdom to aid us. Let me see if I can seek him out."

Ethris furrowed his brows. "Would he know more than you?"

She nodded. "In some things, yes. He is the only hope I can see for us now."

CHAPTER 74 - THE MASTER OF THREE

Sore Kam helped his sister Sarina arrange Gen's lifeless body on a white granite boulder in the heart of the Black Forest where the old trees grew tall and round. Night had fallen, and the fireflies attended them as they waited for their father and Aldemar to come counsel together, the last of the Millim Eri.

"Let us remove the armor and clothes," Sarina said, "and wash the body. He deserves that service, at least, for what part he played."

Together, brother and sister went about their work, discarding the ruined armor and torn clothing, fetching water from a pool formed by a clear, flowing brook.

With a tender touch they washed the blood away from the cuts and the gaping hole of the crossbow bolt. When finished, Sarina arranged his hair and limbs to afford him dignity, while Sore willed the leafy vines of the forest to shroud his nakedness, leaving his still face uncovered. Fireflies flew about his head, their yellow glow on his pallid skin lending his cheek a false color of life. A cool summer breeze teased the mighty pines about them, the moons clear in the sky above them.

Two ravens crossed the sky and then fluttered to a clear space at the foot of the boulder. As avian feet touched the earth the birds transformed into Aldemar and their father, Norus Kam. Like all of their race, their father was built powerfully. While he enjoyed the eternal youth of those of powerful blood, the white hair and the faded blue irises of his eyes aged him. He had the wise and troubled countenance of one who had seen the passage of centuries and the death of three gods.

He and Aldemar stared at the body for a moment before Norus spoke. "I see that you bear the fruit of your meddling, my children. I have watched this drama unfold with great interest and with great sorrow. Even I began to hope that my advice to you to remove yourselves from the affairs of men would be proved wrong. But woe has always followed whatever attempts we have made to right Mikkik's wrongs. It had been better if our strength could have veiled Trys forever than to have Ki'Hal suffer this shameful fate. But we are weak now, and all our devices have failed. It is time for us to enter our rest."

"Not so, father," Sore disagreed. "It is true that Mikkik has turned our carefully crafted prophecy and its prepared actors against us and will now accomplish his design. Yes, it is a pity that the race of men is so weak and we are so few. But you must see that there was in this man something more, as in the time we elevated Aldradan Mikmir and helped him save many peoples."

"Gen proved that the race of men can be noble and strong," Sarina joined in, Norus listening expressionlessly. "Mikkik owned his body, but for one created without a soul, he was indeed powerful. Oddly, our guiding hand had little to do with what he accomplished in the end. His love for the woman we chose and for her mother guided all his actions. If only the Ha'Ulrich could have loved the world or the woman as much, then this might have ended well."

Norus nodded. "It is as I have always said. To make a man a king is to make a man a ruin."

"It would not have ruined this one," Sarina said, indicating Gen. "He possessed the power of knowledge and the firm purpose of love. He despised fame. He craved no authority."

Norus grasped his daughter's shoulder. "Perhaps, Sarina, but he is dead now. And from what I saw of his heart, it was a small tent that only admitted a few. For Gen to have succeeded in his purpose, he would need to have enough room to love the whole world. He would have failed, too, I am afraid."

"But he could love, and purely," Sarina argued. "If one has the ability to love just one other selflessly, then to love more just requires a little stretching. He could have done it. The Chalaine did it."

"Her love was not for the whole world," Aldemar contradicted, surprising them all. "I saw into her mind and her heart. She was willing to sacrifice all for the love of a few, Gen among them."

Norus raised his hand. "It is enough, Sarina. We could not have anticipated this. Mikkik is too clever. However far along the path we think we are, he has walked farther and left snares for us to fall into. There is nothing more to do! He will glean what power he can from their diluted blood until he can silence the beating heart of Elde Luri Mora forever, and Ki'Hal will wither and dry like the autumn leaf fallen from its home."

"The Chalaine's blood still has the power to kill him," Sore said. "Eldaloth's blood runs in her veins. A weapon could be crafted!"

"We do not craft the implements of war with blood magic, as he did!" Norus said, voice rising. "Eldaloth forbade it, and only Aldemar among us knows its secrets from his former master. Creating the Chalaine and the Ha'Ulrich using Eldaloth's blood was blasphemy enough. I only permitted it to appease you."

"I know, father, that you see no hope," Sarina said, voice soft and placating. "But if we are to pass into our rest, then let us at least use what power is in our blood to make such a man as never has been known upon the face of Ki'Hal! If the world is meant for its end, there can be no harm in this one last desperate attempt to thwart our ancient enemy."

"Just what exactly do you propose?" Norus asked, face concerned.

"Here in this bower we have masters of Myn, Duam, and Trys. In our blood flows the pure sensibility to the power of those moons. Never before has a human been a Master of Three. Aldemar can use his knowledge to put within him our blood, and the blood of immortality. Let us fashion this one last hope for men. If all is doomed to fail, as you say, Norus, then whatever harm you think he could do is irrelevant."

"And so then is the attempt!" he retorted. "Can you do this, Aldemar?"

"I can, Norus," Aldemar answered. "It is the same magic I used to help them create the players of the prophecy during the time of my mourning."

Norus shook his head. "We saw what happened when we gave the power of Trys to the humans during the Mikkikian wars. I regret that choice to this day."

"But it saved them," Sore added. "Yes, it caused division and destruction, but in the end they survived."

"They survived because our people exhausted themselves shrouding Trys's light to weaken Mikkik's power," Norus contradicted. "Were there enough of us now, I would do it again."

"But there aren't, father," Sarina said. "Besides, with no soul, Gen can never have progeny. The magic will stay with him and him alone for eternity or until he decides it is time to end his existence. If there is the slightest chance, we must try! There is no need for us to spill our blood uselessly on the ground when it might offer some hope, however slight. If you withhold, father, then Sore and I will contribute our essence to this task, but a Master of Three, where Trys is the third, has a greater chance than only a Master of Two! Please father, humor your children this one last time. Let this man carry some part of us, whether it be to this world's ending or to its salvation. Let him be the legacy of our race."

Norus paced around the body, face calm and eyes upon the countenance of the youth on whom Sore and Sarina had placed such heavy expectations. Patiently his children waited. Aldemar stood beside them with a look of solidarity. Four hours they waited as Norus paced, the night waning and the stars dimming as dawn approached. At length he stopped at the head of the boulder.

"Uncover him, Sore," Norus commanded. With a word, the enveloping leaves retreated. "If he is to be a king and a new creature, then his body must be clean and strong."

Norus stretched forth this hand, and Sarina stepped forward. "Do not undo the branding on the center of his chest. It is his connection to the Chalaine."

Norus nodded and concentrated, and the multitude of scars and wounds that crisscrossed Gen's body faded, his skin renewing and undoing the marring of Torbrand's cruel instruction.

"The virtue of our blood will provide all else he requires," Norus said. "It will be a majesty that the humans will not see, but they will feel it about him. What knowledge of Trys you left with him will remain, but we must imbue him with the arts of Myn and Duam. Sarina, Sore, bestow the knowledge upon Aldemar, and he can pass it to Gen when life again courses through his veins.

Aldemar placed his hands on his companions' heads, the deep knowledge of Sore and Sarina passing into his mind. The ever lightening sky brought a chorus of birdsong, another brilliant summer morning waiting to be born.

"Let us be about it and march to our ending," Norus said as Aldemar finished. "I am weary of the world and its trouble, and I long for peace."

Norus concentrated and, with the power of Trys, created within the boulder a depression around Gen's still body to hold the blood they now prepared to spill. As one, they placed their arms inside the new bowl, and Norus used Trys to undo the skin and the walls of the veins in their wrists. Golden blood spilled freely as Aldemar looked on, face doleful. Sarina and Sore smiled at each other in a last farewell.

As Norus weakened, he turned to Aldemar. "You will be the last of our kind, old friend. Do not be afraid to come to us. You heart and your conscience are clean. It is because of you that there was any chance at all."

Aldemar nodded and watched as his companions gradually slumped over the side the boulder, closed their eyes, and then fell to the ground. The tears that he had long cried for the horror of Eldaloth's death returned, brought forth by a new pang for the loss of his friends and the end of his race.

Breathing deeply, he arranged Sore, Sarina, and Norus respectfully among the trees, wishing each a farewell, and then he returned to the boulder where Gen's body waited. The warm, golden blood did not quite cover him, and Aldemar used his hand to ladle it over the corpse until his skin was stained with its hue.

Drawing upon the knowledge of his former master, Aldemar thrust his hand into the pool of blood, its combined power staggering to his perception. He spoke the dark words, the blood seeping into Gen's skin, destroying the old blood and filling Gen's veins and body. Pulling in the remaining virtue, he gave Gen life, his heart reigniting and his chest rising and falling just as dawn broke fully into the sky. The blood now spent and gone, Gen stirred within

the hollow of the boulder

Before his eyes could flutter open, Aldemar used the power of Mynmagic to put Gen into a sleep, allowing him the opportunity to infuse the young man's mind with the learning that Sore and Sarina had shared with him. Once done, Aldemar looked upon the creature he had created, remembering his encounter with the Chalaine. There was good in the race of men, and he hoped that Gen reborn would retain the love and devotion he once had and not succumb to the pride and vanity that so often plagued his race.

"I give you one last gift," Aldemar said. "If you are to be our legacy, then it is wisdom that the legacy is passed on to be as immortal as you."

Aldemar gave his gift, a gift Norus did not intend.

He blessed Gen with a soul.

Lifeless, Aldemar fell to the forest floor with his companions, never to rise again.

Gen sat upright, the memory of the savage crossbow bolt loosed upon him shocking him awake. He had known that he was too far gone to even attempt to avoid the attack and awaited the terminal blow that would finally end his tempestuous life. The impact had come, his body thrown back with the stunning force of the missile. Surely it had killed him.

But instead of the sandy cliffs of Butchers gap, the dark bark of pine trees surrounded him, and by the position of the sun to his east, he saw that morning had come instead of dusk. Weak light provided scant illumination, but he found he could see quite well. The unnatural scoop in the boulder where he lay and his nakedness brought him up short, his mind struggling to fabricate an explanation for his whereabouts.

But when he regarded his body and came into his mind, his amazement stunned him. Only his branding to the Chalaine remained, the rest of his grotesque scars having disappeared altogether, his skin a healthy, burnished hue that seemed just a shade darker than he remembered. He could sense the Chalaine in the distance only a scant few hours from where he was. She had survived!

Alive with renewed purpose, he clambered out of the boulder to find his second shock—four dead Millim Eri, including those who had concealed Mikkik's lessons on Trysmagic from him. The two others he did not recognize. He would have to sort the mystery out later. He had to reach the Chalaine, for he didn't doubt that Mikkik would pursue her relentlessly until he unmade her just as he had done to her pathetic husband on the bridge of Echo Hold.

As Gen cast about for something to wear, he felt the familiar awareness of Trysmagic. The Millim Eri had returned it to him! Reaching within, he sought to use its power to fashion raiment for himself. As he turned inward, he found more. Two other forces awaited his command, and he found the knowledge of the phrases and gestures needed to use them at the tip of his tongue.

Reeling under the weight of his new knowledge, it became clear. The Millim Eri had changed and empowered him, but to what end? Tentatively, he used the magic of Duam to change his face and disguise himself, growing a close-cropped beard and lengthening his hair so it hung about his shoulders. Pleased with the results, he drew upon Trys to fashion the simple leather garb of a woodsman about himself, including a wide-brimmed hat to further conceal his face.

Casting one last look at the strange bower and his stranger benefactors, he turned westward toward where he felt the Chalaine waited, feeling through the Im'Tith her exhaustion and the dry, itching discomfort of her skin. If she had fled into the wood, then they were indeed desperate. Calling on Duam again, he fortified his body and ran with the fleet foot of Maewen's father, the thicker trees giving way to thin ones that clumped more tightly together the farther he ran from the bower. The joys of Duammagic infused him with the agility and speed of a deer, dodging and jumping through the tangle with such alacrity that he couldn't help but smile within himself.

He had run for an hour when he caught sight of a solitary figure making her way through the forest in his direction. Upon seeing him, she stopped and leaned against a tree to rest. Maewen. Gen rejoiced and ran to her. As he approached, she squinted at him, unsure for a moment of who he was. At last the glimmer of recognition bloomed on her face and she smiled one of her rare smiles.

"It is you," she said in Elvish. "But, it is not you."

"I am not sure what I am, either," he answered in kind. "But I am the Gen you knew. I still bear the brand of the Chalaine and know she is not far from here. Is she in danger?"

"Grave. I'll tell you while we run. Let's see if you are as good as you once were!"

They pressed forward against the clawing tangle of branches and underbrush with as much celerity as they could manage, Maewen's tale souring his mood the more she told. Mikkik had played them all masterfully, and whatever the dark god had in mind was clearly within his reach. He wanted the Chalaine, sending Athan for her, which evidenced there was some purpose left that Mikkik had not yet fulfilled.

"So I do not believe it will be wise for you to return as Gen," she said, stopping as they approached. "Your appearance is so different now that if you keep your distance and talk little, you can pass for someone else. You need a new name, something humble and nondescript."

"Call me Amos. I will be a woodsman you met on your

excursions searching for Elde Luri Mora. Explain that I am an expert in the healing arts, and if I can help the fallen men, I will. We must keep my existence secret. If Mikkik learns that I am alive, I will be a liability to the Chalaine, not to mention that most of the men may not trust me as Gen, no matter what Mirelle tried to tell them or how different I look."

"I agree," Maewen said, "but it cannot last. Gen, you must see that you have been given great gifts for a greater purpose than just protecting the Chalaine. Think on it. But we must hurry. I fear the Uyumaak will again come for us with nightfall, and it already approaches midday."

Gen nodded and used Trysmagic to conjure up a phony bag of herbal remedies to mask his use of Duammagic's healing power. They ran forward again, emerging into the clearing to find that most of the fallen men had gone, Gen sensing the Chalaine on the other side of the glade within the confines of the forest. Some few corpses remained, and he and Maewen inspected them, finding gaping wounds and blood around them as if something had burrowed out of their insides.

"This does not bode well," Maewen intoned gravely. "They were all unconscious when I left. Let's see if the soldiers can move. We must leave before the beetles or the Uyumaak arrive again. Remember, keep your hat low and talk little."

They crossed the clear brook at the center of the glade, passing some men filling water skins, all bearing bloody bandages on their extremities, all wan and shaky. Crossing into the wood on the other side, they found General Harband and Lord Kildan leaning against the tree trunks, a tired Ethris nearby. They all gave Gen the once-over as he approached, but no flicker of recognition sparked in their troubled eyes, their attention turning to Maewen.

"Did the stupor pass?" she asked, noting the bandages on Lord Kildan and General Harband.

"Oh, it passed," General Harband answered grumpily, "after we all birthed a beetle or two out of those bites they gave us last night. Mikkik's beard! I'm not a fainting man, but the little baby beasties damn near crippled the entire army before scurrying away into the woods toward the rest of them! I will not be used as a breeding cow for beetles! I won't!"

"At least the Uyumaak didn't come for us," Lord Kildan said. "I had feared that the beetles were meant to weaken us."

"The Uyumaak may fear the creatures," Maewen said. "They ceased their speech when the beetles neared. They only do that for stealth, to hide."

"Whatever it is, the beetles' emergence claimed the lives of some of the weaker men," Ethris explained. "Most survived, but the wounds are painful and infected. I healed what I could, but there are many more that could use your herb craft, Maewen, though there are likely too many for you to help."

"I will try," she said. "This is Amos, a man I met in my travels. He knows herb craft, as well, and he has some small skill with Duammagic to aid us."

Ethris raised his eyebrows. "That is welcome news, indeed."

"We'll get to work immediately," Maewen said. "We need to get this army moving. I'll start near the center of the camp." To Gen she said, "Go to the north and start anywhere."

Surreptitiously, Gen angled his way near the Chalaine, seeing Volney, Dason, and Gerand surrounding her as she slept beneath a small lean-to. He had to resist the urge to run and embrace his old friends, though they obviously needed assistance, and instead he went to the first man he found upon the ground, a Rhugothian soldier who appeared half out of his wits.

As General Harband had described, the beetle bites had

indeed turned to beetle nurseries, and as the young had burst forth, they left ragged craters in their victims that were grotesque and painful. Gen sprinkled the innocuous herbs on the soldier's wound, and, while rebandaging it, used the gift of Duammagic to heal it enough to take away the sting of the pain.

After treating the first few men, he realized the enormity of the task; there were simply too many men scattered throughout the woods, and he would run out of strength long before even half of them were well. He could also use Trys to knit the flesh back together, but that wouldn't last him long, either. He tried to perform triage to treat the most severe cases, but time seemed to run on the fleetest of feet, the afternoon sun was angling down at a hurried pace.

And then he felt it, the slight tickling in his mind. The touch upon his thoughts was dark. He stood and turned toward the glade, wondering what it portended. It felt similar to what he had experienced with Ghama Dhron, but he did not feel it as strongly. A powerful mind approached, something not human that was bent on destruction. He reached out to it with Mynmagic, gesturing the proper patterns instinctively. When the contact came he staggered, nearly stumbling into a tangle of branches.

Who dares to see my mind? the ancient evil clicked in odd tones. *You think to challenge the might and will of Hekka Dhron? Come, and let my children feast upon your blood and use your flesh as their womb! From those that stand against me, I gather might!*

Gen gasped and broke contact. Hekka Dhron. Wrath of Blood.

Chapter 75 - Hekka Dhron

Gen worked his way back to the edge of the clearing. Ethris stood by Lord Kildan, face transfixed. The old Mage had sensed the presence of the foul mind as well. Rather than expose himself to questions, Gen backed away and let Ethris deliver the bad news to a haggard Lord Kildan, who swore in response.

"Get up!" Gerand's father yelled, voice echoing through the trees. "Get the men up! Anyone who can move, retreat southward into the woods! Anyone too ill to be moved must be left behind."

Gen retreated, watching to ensure that the Chalaine was up and moving, Maewen there urging the Dark Guard to better efforts. Gen signaled the half-elf over as the retreat began in earnest, more men than Gen would have liked simply giving up, lying in the pine needles and waiting for their doom. Ethris, already spent from healing the men, left with Lord Kildan, joining the Chalaine's entourage.

"I'll stay behind. I may be able to slow it," Gen said. "I'll come when I can. The Chalaine will guide me."

"Don't throw your life away again," Maewen lectured him sternly, then lowered her voice. "I know you would save all these men, but your life and your abilities are worth more than all of them. Come quickly."

Gen understood her point, but it was not in his nature to feel above anyone. He would save whom he could. Gathering his wits, he strode out of the forest into the beautiful glade. The late afternoon sun cast long shadows and warm tones across the wildflowers and green grass. With every passing moment, the mind of Hekka Dhron pressed upon his consciousness, ever inviting him to open up to let it in. Ghama Dhron he could command because he was Mikkik's creature, but he understood instinctively that Hekka Dhron would not respond to any wish of his.

A swarm the beetles poured out of the tree boles on the opposite side of the glade, though they caused little more than a slight agitation of the tall grass and wildflowers across the length of the field as they skittered toward him by the thousands. The hard carapaces and the clicking sound of their mandibles and legs filled the air with a harsh noise that chilled Gen's spine. He breathed, remembering Shadan Khairn's training, seeking the stillness of mind and emotion he needed to confront an enemy that would overrun him in seconds.

As the first of the obsidian beetles emerged into view, Gen sifted through his mind for some way to deal with them. The Dhrons had come late to the war, Mikkik's last innovation of destruction before he weakened and disappeared, and none of the memories of the masters in the Training Stones and none of the instruction of the Millim Eri could aid Gen. The purpose of the Dhrons became immediately clear as he watched them roll in like a tide. To take down a single large creature would be easy for a Trysmagician. Trying to deal with a horde would be nearly impossible. Some few could be disintegrated or disabled, but not enough to keep the whole from its dark path of destruction.

He needed time to think, but that luxury was denied him. With an incantation he brought down fire around him, blasting a charred circle in the meadow with him in the center. The beetles burned and died, but where any fell, others simply swarmed forward to take their place. They made no attempt to avoid the flames, pushing forward heedless of their lives as if driven by some implacable force. For every one he burned, twenty passed by, and Gen panicked, realizing the futility of his efforts.

Helpless and his Duammagic draining, he turned and fled the wave, hoping to outpace the insects. His mind raced with his legs, and as he reached the forest edge, a thought struck him. While he couldn't destroy tens of thousands of beetles, only one mind controlled them. Was the mind imbued within them all, or did it reside outside the swarm? He turned inward, feeling the pressure of the evil mind still trying to break down and enter. But this time, he found something else—directionality. The push came from somewhere, and he could feel it.

Pushing away his fear, he turned back toward the wave, running to where he felt the vile intelligence moving amid the cover of its fellow creatures. Again calling upon the virtue of fire, he scoured the path before him, boots pulverizing the crisp remains of the beetles as he charged past. His power over Duam was fading fast, and with it the ability to keep the creatures from attacking him. The presence was moving with the rest of the swarm, and in dismay he realized that finding the right one would be akin to singling out an ant in its hill. He had to find a way to reveal the one among the many.

A sting on his calf let him know that his efforts at self-protection were failing, the pincers of one of the creatures puncturing his boot leather and his skin. He kept running as the beetle's tubule sank into the meat of his lower leg. The pain he could ignore, and the beetle fell away almost immediately. Nearing exhaustion, he knew he had one desperate chance left. He would have to do war with its mind. Preparing a mental attack meant to daze and confuse, he opened a connection to Hekka Dhron and unleashed it. The effect was immediate but short-lived. The linear march of the beetles suddenly broke, the insects running to and fro in a mad dash of disorientation.

Fool! Hekka Dhron roared into his mind, the impact staggering in its weight of ill will and singular purpose. The enslaving force was again reasserted, and the beetles regrouped, moving into the wood as one. The wounded and weary men who had been left behind began to scream as they fell victim to the vanguard.

Desperate, Gen struck again, but this time Hekka Dhron was ready and pushed back with the weight of an anvil and the force of a hammer. Gen reeled and nearly fell to the ground. Two beetles latched onto his legs and cut in as Gen tried to keep his focus and move toward the being attacking his mind. Again, the snaky tubules penetrated his flesh, but as he looked down to swat them off, they fell away dead.

The blood of the Millim Eri that ran through his veins was poison to them. He stowed that fact in his mind, trying to keep calm to let his mind work.

Resuming his sprint, he tried a new tack, sending the sharp, stinging emotion of fear into the intellect of the mind that sought to overwhelm him. He knew he could chance no half measures with something so determined and strong. He pulled on every last ounce of Mynmagic he could muster to inject terror into the thoughts of the enemy. As one, every beetle turned from its forward course and flowed toward a central point some fifty yards away. Like scared children trying to shove their way through a single door, they piled on one another, a black mound swelling, rising from the floor of the glade.

They are forming a shield around the one, Gen reasoned. The power of Trys was all that remained within him. He would form a large rock high above the pile and crush the beetles and, with any luck, the corporeal vessel of Hekka Dhron. Concentrating, the rock, large and flat, formed some twenty feet in the air, but just as it began to fall, the entire mass suddenly shifted and rose, powering at him. The rock fell uselessly behind it, smearing a handful of stragglers into the earth.

But what faced him now was not just a shambling mound of beetles. Thousands of the creatures clung to the carapace of a single, massive parent, pincers wedged within it. The tubules of the many injected their sack of blood into the chosen host, inflating it. As it moved, it swelled ever larger, the hides of its children forming a shiny armor. With the instinctive will to attack the enemy that had triggered its fear, it barreled at Gen with a ghastly hiss.

Magic gone, Gen fled, but only for a moment. At once he knew what his last chance would be, and he turned to the creature, letting loose a mighty yell and charging it without a weapon. The sudden assault brought it up short, and with another hiss it stopped, a tubule the size of Gen's forearm snaking out between the mandibles. Gen raised his arm, and the hooks of the tubule enveloped his wrist and began their work, his golden blood pulsing down its length. He immediately weakened and fell, pain lancing up his arm and into his chest. Vision dimming, he watched as the first bulge of blood pulsed down the tubule and into the creature.

It staggered, the suction on his arm ceasing. The beetles along Hekka Dhron's outer shell fell away limp, cracking and popping as they dropped to the ground in heaps. The massive beetle released the hooks of its tubule, stumbling drunkenly about as if trying to find somewhere to flee. With a final hiss, its legs collapsed and it crashed to the ground, the remaining beetles scattering in every direction. The powerful mind had gone. Hekka Dhron was no more.

Gen rolled over, weakened and weary. It was done. He felt far too dizzy and weak to even consider marching into the woods. From his supine position he watched the sky dim toward twilight, remembering Ghama Dhron's first words to him: *I am one of four fell servants of Mikkik*. What were the other two horrors at Mikkik's command? Ghama Dhron was still out there, too, and its poison was likely worse than the bite of the blood-harvesting beetles he had just tangled with.

After what seemed like an hour, Gen rolled and sat up, dizziness swirling his mind. Full dark had nearly come when he noticed Maewen approaching cautiously out of the woods. He raised his hand to signal his position and she jogged to him.

"Are you well?" she asked.

He briefly related the tale of his encounter and then asked, "Do you have any sunlock leaves?"

"I'm afraid not," she said.

"No matter. In a couple of hours I'll be well enough to heal myself."

"Have you seen any sign of the Uyumaak?"

"No," he said. "But I've been flat on my back for some time."

"Stay here and rest," she ordered. "I'm going to scout forward. With the beetles gone, they may yet pursue us."

Gen put his back on the ground and closed his eyes, soaking in the rays of the radiant moons above him, their soft light slowly filling the wells of power within him. Maewen returned an hour later, face twisted in a scowl, and helped him stand.

"They are coming," she said. "The Hunters will get here within the hour. Can you walk?"

He nodded and took Maewen's proffered hand to help himself up. As he walked carefully through the wood, following Maewen's lead, his strength slowly returned, and he healed what he could of the beetle bites on his legs, hoping the blood would ensure that no grotesque insects were breeding within his skin.

The main party had continued on into the night hours, and by the time he and Maewen caught up, the night was deep. A single lantern burned to provide some light for moving about, but the tree boles cast wild shadows everywhere.

"How long until we reach the ridge?" Gen asked Maewen as she prepared to leave to report to Lord Kildan and Ethris.

"I gauge it at two days with a steady march," she replied. "You and I could make it in less than a day, but with the wounded in the party and the difficult path, two days may be an optimistic guess. I hate to say it, but as much as I love the woods, it will be nice to get somewhere where we can have a clearer vision of what's around us. Once we get to the ridge, we'll need to take a short jog to the east to catch a sheep track that leads to the other side. It will be treacherous going for those with unsteady legs."

Gen nodded, and Maewen turned away. He needed sleep. He could sense the Chalaine nearby but stayed out of sight, curling up on the forest floor with little care for any kind of protection.

For the next two days, they rushed to stay ahead of the Uyumaak army. Gen kept mostly to the rear away from everyone, and only Maewen knew that he was to thank for their remaining just out of reach of their pursuers. While the company of soldiers rested, Gen would perform his healing on whom he could, and when they marched he would turn back and deal as much death to the Uyumaak as possible to keep their pace cautious.

But the more they marched, the more Gen worried for the Chalaine. From his discreet vantage points, she appeared almost as an old woman, thin, weak, and hunched over like a small tree in a stiff wind. Through the brand he could sense her physical exhaustion and the discomfort of her raspy, peeling skin. During his ministrations to the soldiers, he would hear the men comment about how she was cursed for displeasing Eldaloth. Even worse, many began to wonder if they were on the wrong side of the battle, if Eldaloth had truly won and if they should have returned with Athan to Echo Hold after all.

"The Uyumaak will catch us in the morning, Gen," Maewen told him as the exhausted and demoralized camp settled in for the night. "We've about two hours before we reach the ridge line, but the Uyumaak may catch us before then. I would push us through the night, but we'd lose half the army if we did."

Gen leaned against a tree, watching the sky darken with a summer storm. "I'll do what I can tonight to fortify the men. For all my forays and ambushes, I still can't get a solid idea of how many Uyumaak are out there. I think they at least double our number."

"We need your leadership, Gen," Maewen said.

"I'll be exposed if I do. Most of the people in this camp think I'm the Ilch. Well, I am—or was—but they won't listen to me."

"With the Chalaine's endorsement. . ."

"They think I put the Chalaine and the First Mother under my power," he replied. "I must stay concealed. I can work through you. If we are to have a fight with the Uyumaak, then we must do it on our terms. We can't just let them fall on our rear while we run. Have the men take shifts. We need to build choke points with the forest detritus to inhibit the movement of the Uyumaak, particularly the Bashers. If we can get them entangled and stymied, we can hit them hard with bows while their own Archers will be practically useless. Let's scout the points together. But this is the most important thing: when the morning comes, the Chalaine and the Dark Guard need to proceed toward Rhugoth. Whether we win or lose, she must get free."

Maewen nodded, and they walked the length of the camp, Gen marking the points for the men to work piling brush and trees and placing crude traps. After reviewing the placement of men, Maewen returned to the camp to speak with the generals while Gen walked among the soldiers, using the power of Trys to sharpen swords to rival the blade of Aldradan Mikmir that he had wielded. He reinforced armor, created bow tips that could punch through armor with the same ease with which would pass through flesh, and healed what wounded he could. A light rain fell for about two hours during the night, eliciting curses from the men who were still awake.

As he rose from healing a man with an infected cut, he heard a familiar voice. "Excuse me, Amos?"

Gerand Kildan.

"Yes?" Gen answered, thankful for the concealing dark and his wide-brimmed hat.

"The men have told me you've demonstrated a great deal of skill at healing."

"I do what I can," Gen said, trying to keep his sentences short for fear the prince of Tolnor would recognize his voice.

"Then I wonder if you might aid me," he said. "An Uyumaak arrow grazed my shoulder a few days back. It was nothing, but it's turned swollen and painful now."

"Come near one of the lanterns and let's get a look," Gen said. "You're Lord Kildan's son and a Dark Guard, correct?"

"Yes."

"You fight well," Gen said as they neared the lantern at the center of the camp where Maewen was the hub of the preparations against the Uyumaak. "Let's take a look. Uyumaak arrowheads are unsavory things."

Gerand removed his shirt, revealing a wicked, infected gash. Gen went through the motions of his worthless herbs, binding the wound and using Duammagic to heal the cut to where it would no longer fester or hamper Gerand's movement.

"There. What I gave you will numb it and heal it quickly. Get what rest you can."

Gerand grabbed his shirt and began to pull it on as Gen turned to leave. "Wait a moment, if you will. I would speak with you about another matter."

Gen turned, keeping his head low. "And what is that, sir?"

Gerand glanced over his shoulder and lowered his voice. "It is the Chalaine."

"I can see that she is suffering."

"Yes, in mind and body, I fear."

"I have heard the men speak of her skin," Gen said, "but what of her mind?"

Gerand sighed. "It is the loss of her baby, the absence of her mother, and the death of her Protector, Gen."

"Most believe him the Ilch," Gen said.

"I do not and neither does she," Gerand stated, bringing Gen a sense of relief. "She cared for him a great deal, I think. I wondered if there is some remedy for her mind or her body that you can conjure. Ethris and Maewen have both tried their arts and failed. It is as if, well, I hesitate to say it."

"As if she is cursed."

"Yes, though I cannot believe it," Gerand continued. "I cannot see what fault was hers. To me it seems a dark hopelessness and lack of purpose gnaw at her. It has robbed her of her gifts and her beauty. I cannot think of what might help but hoped you might have some cure."

"You are a true friend to the Chalaine," Gen said, proud of his once-faithful comrade in arms. "If the arts of Ethris and Maewen have failed to heal her body, then I doubt I can be of much use. But you are wise to see that it is the heart and mind that may be the seed of her sickness. While she may not be able to heal as she once did, she can bind wounds and speak words of comfort. Remind her of her trips to the Damned Quarter, and what she did for the children there. Remind her she is free to love whom she will now. She lacks a sense of her own strength, but it is there. Remind her."

"You seem to know her better than I would think a wayfaring woodsman should," Gerand said, Gen fearing the searching gaze now directed at him.

"I don't spend all my time in the wild," Gen answered obliquely. "Remember what I said, and be ready to leave this camp with her when danger arrives. It is clear the enemy still wants her."

Gerand nodded, and Gen retreated into the night to rest and regain his strength. He slept for two hours once the rain stopped, rising in the dead of the night. A second shift of workers labored to fortify the positions he had marked earlier, the snapping and popping of deadfall dragged from place to place swallowed by the abyss of the forest. Gen found Maewen and let her know he was leaving to scout behind them.

The infusion of Millim Eri blood had improved his eyesight in the dark, and, with the help of damp ground, he passed stealthily toward an Uyumaak army he knew could not be far behind. Choosing every step carefully, he crept into a thicket some two hundred yards from their camp. He paused and waited, listening. Amid the sounds of trilling night birds and the occasional drip of water, something moved. Gen held perfectly still. A breeze brought in the sour smell of an Uyumaak cookpot, and he realized the their pursuers were closer than anyone thought.

A mighty Uyumaak bow creaked as an unseen Archer pulled it back. Gen dropped hard to the forest floor, the missile caroming awkwardly through the branches of the thicket. It had come from somewhere in front of him, but a second arrow from the side sank into the ground near his leg, and he rolled away and crouched, springing forward.

The familiar thumping from the Archers broke loose, and a volley of arrows slashed through the night from three sides. The heavy shafts drilled into wood and branches, one tip slicing his cheek before embedding itself in a tree just ahead of him. He had walked into their trap.

Apparently they grew tired of me picking them off.

With a burst of Duammagic, he kicked up a wind of pine needles and twigs, sending the spray up behind him in a swirl to conceal his location until he found a log thick enough to hide him lying athwart his course. He dove behind it and let his debris storm fade. The thumping started again and then died, the natural sounds of the forest returning, excepting the birds frightened away by the conflict. Gen lay perfectly still, attuning his senses to the night. Several minutes passed before he heard footsteps again, many of them, heading in his direction.

He kept his breathing shallow and his body as still as a corpse as an Uyumaak Hunter nearly stepped on him. With Mynmagic, he turned its mind against its companions, and it bolted away into the darkness. In moments, the sound of a battle in the darkness sent the Uyumaak running in the direction of his thrall until it fell. The thumping resumed as did the march, but instead of just the handful of Archers and Hunters, an entire wave of Uyumaak of every variety poured out of the darkness, marching directly toward the encampment. Gen used Trysmagic to disintegrate a portion of the log and the ground next to him, rolling inside the empty space and then creating a bark shell to conceal himself.

The heavy feet of Bashers and Warriors crunched all around him as the wave of Uyumaak passed by him in the night on their way to slaughter the army that would not be ready for them. Gen kept his awareness sharp and tried to gauge the numbers passing by him. Of the Tolnorian and Rhugothian army that once numbered two thousand strongly, only around twelve hundred remained. He guessed that twice that many Uyumaak marched on their crude fortifications. They had stretched their numbers in a long line, hoping, he guessed, to get around their fortified positions and prevent them from fleeing farther south to the ridge line.

Once they passed, Gen broke through the light bark around him and stood, wary of any stragglers. Once convinced of his safety, he formed a bow and arrow using the power of Trys, firing the arrow up through the canopy. With a quick incantation, he ignited the arrow mid-flight, sending a burning signal into the sky he hoped Maewen would see. Once the arrow burned and winked out, the familiar barking yells of Lord Kildan and General Harband erupted into the night, only the tone of their voices discernible from Gen's position.

Run, Chalaine, he thought as he crept forward. Once the battle started, he would harry the enemy from the rear, but doing so alone would be risky.

He didn't wait long. The human arrows he had improved with his magic shot through the night, punching through Uyumaak and tree trunks with equal ease, dropping multiple Uyumaak on the way through. The Uyumaak archers returned in kind, screams and yells indicating some few arrows found their marks, but the forest and fortifications lessened their effectiveness. Surreptitiously, Gen turned an Archer's mind against its fellows and watched as it killed five of its brothers before the Warriors turned and hacked it apart. All along the line Gen slunk, using Mynmagic to make traitors among the Uyumaak, conserving his strength with the other magics against greater need.

The battle raged for half an hour before thumping far behind him sent a chill up his spine. Turning, he jogged back at a cautious pace until he confirmed his worst fear. Another wave of Uyumaak approached from the rear. Cursing, he sprinted back toward the fray, and as he approached, he heard the words he had feared since the attack began—"Uyumaak are in the camp! Watch the flanks!"

Gritting his teeth, Gen ran right toward the middle of the fortifications they had created. Dawn had finally started to break, and in the dim, gray light, a pile of Uyumaak lay strewn about. A scant few Bashers hacked away at a wall of intervening deadfall behind which only a handful of defenders remained. The rest of the camp had split into two to intercept the waves of Uyumaak pressing them from either side.

The numbers appeared even but wouldn't be for long. Using Duammagic, Gen leapt over the Bashers and defenders, forming two swords in midair before landing in the midst of chaos. He cast about for Maewen, not finding her, and pressed farther south, the fighting swirling around him. The weapons and armor he had enhanced lent his allies the advantage, although the Uyumaak's numbers kept the fighting close.

At last he spotted the half-elf toward the rear near Falael, both elves using their bows to good advantage. "Maewen!" he yelled. "They've got another wave coming! We've got to run for it now. I'll hold these for as long as I can and then follow you toward the ridge!"

She nodded and raised a loud whistle, a prearranged signal for retreat. The men fought their way backward as Gen worked his way around to the right flank. His swords whistled as he sprinted through the forest, hacking down Uyumaak in droves to free the men engaged with them. With haste, he worked his way from one end to the other and then back again until the thumping beyond the fortifications signaled that the second wave had pushed forward. Saddened by the wounded he left behind, Gen turned and ran, bringing up the rear of the fleeing column.

The retreat was fast and unorganized, but they emerged from the wood onto a ridgeline much sooner than Gen expected. Before them stretched a deep gash in the earth filled with dense spruce trees that cast up a crisp smell in the dawn. The wetness of the night before veiled much of the depression in a deep fog, but from their vantage point on the ridge, the other side beckoned. Turning east, they ran along a sheep trail on the ridge. The place where the ridge curved along the outer edge of the depression and then turned back west waited a tantalizing mile away. There, the running would get treacherous.

Gen ensured that all the men who could run were ahead of him and then followed. The ruckus of the pursuing Uyumaak crashing through the forest to their left sounded dangerously close. As he brought up the rear, he extended his swords to his sides, their unnaturally sharp blades effortlessly passing through the tree trunks to his left and right, sending trees crashing about on the trail to complicate his enemies' movements.

Slowly, the trail made its precipitous turn, the sheep track they followed led along a narrow shelf that jogged southward. The path was strewn with loose rocks and provided a walking space so narrow that it required hugging the cliff face to avoid a deadly fall. As Gen expected, the company's movements backed up as the pace slowed to a miserly crawl so the men could safely negotiate the dangerous passage. Some had already fallen off the ledge. A quick look to the rocky floor of the ravine revealed three soldiers dead on the rough shale field below. Gen turned back toward the trail, the Uyumaak finally flooding onto the ridge line behind them. Hunters scrambled after the stalled line while the Archers pulled their bows, taking aim at the fliers.

Gen glanced over his shoulder to make sure he wasn't observed and used Trysmagic to create a bow and arrows for himself. With all the speed ingrained in him by his training with Samian, he launched an assault on the Archers opposite him to keep the arrows off the soldiers who were already pressed to keep balance. He had only taken down a handful of Archers before the Hunters rounded a boulder just behind the fleeing soldiers, dividing his attention. His piercing arrows ripped through two and three at a time, their bodies falling and tripping up the ones following.

With smooth, fluid movements, he kept the arrows singing through the air in a chorus of death, creating more in his hand as he needed them. His deadly assault turned the Archers attention on him, and he found himself forced to use Duammagic to nudge the uncannily accurate arrows away with bursts of wind. But despite his best efforts, he knew the sheer number arrows would overpower him and exhaust his magic. His resistance had allowed the last of the soldiers to push some fifty yards head, and he turned and ran down the dangerous trail after them. His training allowed him to negotiate the obstacles without the vertigo and balky movements of his companions. But the Uyumaak kept coming, the Hunters and Warriors pressing onward as the human army passed out of easy bow-shot range.

Again Gen bought time, the single file nature of the trail allowing him to hold it easily with nothing but his sword until at last the soldiers finally passed onto the southern ridge and safer footing. Muscles tiring and soaked in blood, Gen turned and sprinted ahead, the Uyumaak following cautiously. If they managed the southern ridge, they would hound the desperate army until every last man was dead. Gen turned, seeing the entire ridge trail lined with every type of Uyumaak, slowly making their way toward them.

Gen exhaled and dug deep, calling forth every last shred of Trysmagic he could muster. With nothing but a thought, he disintegrated a crack of rock across the entire bend of the sheep track. He stumbled, lightheaded, at the immense effort. Out of sheer will, he drew in the power of Duam and incanted the words to shake the rock he had just weakened. Exhausted, he collapsed in unison with the rocky shelf, the sound a thunderous roar through the ravine that shot frightened birds into the sky. The Uyumaak fell to be smashed and crushed in the avalanche of rock, a cloud of dust rising from the impact. Three Uyumaak that had pursued him the most closely escaped the calamity, but Gen's vision swam and his limbs didn't want to work.

A Warrior raced toward him, sword high for the killing stroke, when an arrow took him in the throat. His two companions fell in like manner, leaving everything in peace. Gen smiled as Maewen approached and bent over him, face concerned. Once convinced he was unhurt, she turned her gaze across the ridge.

"There are still a number of Uyumaak on the other side," she said, "though only a small portion of the original force, I think. Even if they do decide to take the long way round and pursue us, we should be able to deal with them. Well done. How long are you going to be useless?"

"I don't know," Gen answered truthfully. "I pushed it too far."

"It was a mighty work."

"You can push ahead with the rest. I'll catch up."

She answered by sitting down by him and pulling out her knife to work on her fletching. "I'll stay. It would be a shame for you to win such a victory for us and then be devoured by a wolf or a bear. Besides, there are a few arguments I wish to make while you are less able to reason."

CHAPTER 76 – REDEMPTION

"I will watch tonight, Gen," Maewen insisted. "You provided the victory today, and that is enough. You cannot go on without rest." Gen, eyes heavy, nodded a reply. Embracing his sword, he reclined against the gentle slope of a bulge of white granite rising out of the ground, his cloak behind his head serving as pillow. It had taken nearly four hours for him to regain his ability to walk in a straight line and another two for them to catch up to the main body of soldiers. The army had pressed on through the early afternoon but stopped early for a chance to rest.

Maewen and Gen camped well ahead of the rest of the party, both to scout forward and to keep Gen away from those who might recognize him. Behind them on the trail, the soldiers lit fires and started a victory celebration, breaking into song for the first time in weeks. After days of terror, their enemies were finally dead or miles behind and powerless to reach them. Maewen disliked the ruckus and told Gen as much. Gen smiled at her and said nothing.

Sitting cross-legged, Maewen watched over her stubborn friend until his chest rose and fell in a regular, slow pattern, and then she rose and turned back toward the trail that ran along the edge of the Blue Canyon. Rather than walk the trail, she skirted along the edge, threading her way between fragrant boughs of spruce and pine. Moonlight slanted through the boles along the edge of the forest, providing just enough illumination for her to see with clarity in the darkness. She drank from a gurgling spring that filled a small pool near the trail, the stars and dark trees reflecting on its surface until she dipped her hand in and scattered them. The water, borne underground from the mountains to the east, refreshed her and calmed her mind—and she needed all the peace she could muster.

As she approached the camp, singing, dancing, and shouting drowned out the sounds of wind, water, and birds and set her on edge. Humans lived short lives and possessed even shorter memories, and whatever Gen's indifference to the noise, Maewen knew that if the revelers had her recollections, they would still be cowering, cold and silent, in the hopes they could escape notice of things they could not fathom or imagine. The victory they won today meant nothing other than immediate survival. Mikkik had far worse creations than Uyumaak and blood beetles at his disposal, and when he found out that his army was defeated, he would send those horrors to find them. He probably had already.

Maewen stayed well outside the light of the fires and the celebrating, giving sign to the sentries of her approach. The Chalaine's camp always lay in the center of the caravan. The fine, colorful tents and camp arrangements had been left behind long ago, complicating the task of finding where the frail Queen slept, but as soon as she saw Dason standing guard over an improvised lean-to, she knew where the young woman lay. Maewen sat on a bed of pine needles just out of Dason's notice and started her long watch as a favor to Gen.

She could just make out the Chalaine huddled in a ball and leaning against the tree trunk that formed part of her shelter. Since losing her mother, the Chalaine had fallen into even greater despondency than before, talking little, eating little, and caring nothing for soldiers, strategy, or the impressive scenery around them. While Gen's death and the tortured appearance of her skin had started her withdrawal, the departure of her mother into the hands of Athan's men in a ruse to save her had transformed the young woman into a hunching, bitter recluse. Lord Kildan and Ethris no longer sought her for councils or approvals of their decisions, and her role as Queen no longer meant anything to anyone, save Gen.

Dason and Ethris did their best to revive her spirits, but every day the Chalaine grew more feeble and more apathetic, and Maewen worried. Dason's discomfort in her presence was obvious. The council had wished Lord Kildan's oldest son to marry her to unite Tolnor and Rhugoth under one rule, but it was clear—and to his credit—that her former Protector would not force the act on her. Maewen wondered if he did this out of respect for the Chalaine's pain or because her pitiful state dulled whatever feelings he might have had for her when she walked beautiful and vibrant.

Maewen sighed. While she cared for the girl and respected her for the pain she endured, Maewen agreed with most of the talk she heard swirling around her. The Chalaine's part in the shaping of Ki'Hal had failed and was over. The infant that was to be God had been unmade by Mikkik, and the mighty warrior that was to save him had been killed by the same power. Forcing the Chalaine to lead or to think she had further part to play only tormented her more, and it was obvious she hadn't the thought or wish to do anything but slink away from the world. But each time Maewen broached the topic with Gen—as she had earlier that day—he would disagree vehemently, claiming that if Mikkik still had interest in her, then she should not be cast aside and ignored. Whatever his words, Maewen suspected Gen watched over the Chalaine not from any desire to see her healed to seek some new destiny but because he cared for her.

Maewen had witnessed centuries of human passion, hate, love, hope, and despair, and Gen's unwavering and disinterested love for the Chalaine broke through her ancient, often cynical perception of the world and touched her heart. Alrdadan Mikmir was the only other human she had known who possessed such a simple, honest will, and Gen was like him, and better in many ways. If anyone had the power to lift the fog and confusion that hung over humanity, Gen did, and from the moment of his rebirth, Maewen had resolved to push him out of the background and into plain view of the world. But he resisted all of her attempts, and Maewen would not betray him. If he cared only for the welfare of the Chalaine, then Maewen would see her cared for. She hoped that one day he would notice the plight of his people and no longer remain silent and unseen.

Unexpectedly the Chalaine rose, and, after telling Dason something Maewen could not hear, she and Dason left and walked along the trail through the camp. Maewen rose and followed at a discreet distance. Wherever the Chalaine passed, the songs and talk died out and the dances stopped as the celebrants stared at what seemed a wraith's shadow passing by. So heavy was the power of the Chalaine's despair that it took a great deal to prompt a return to the festive mood from the suffocating pall that lingered behind her. Maewen heard "Cursed!" roll off more than one soldier's tongue.

The Chalaine led Dason, despite his objections, ahead of the camp and into the still, blue night. Maewen wondered at the Chalaine's purpose, trusting Dason to prevent her from doing anything rash. Maewen couldn't fault the Chalaine for wanting to get away from others, for jubilation only tortures the lonely and despairing.

After passing the last sentries, the two of them

continued on slowly for a few more minutes and stopped to sit on a long granite rock that was rooted in the ground. Their resting place commanded an expansive view of the canyon, dazzling and mysterious in the moonlight. A low fog hung over the river that roared through the gorge below, the mist threading through low-lying trees. Maewen worked to get closer to the pair, using all her skill to be silent. Getting her bearings, she calculated that Gen slept not seventy-five yards farther down the trail and was thankful the Chalaine hadn't pressed on.

The widowed Queen sat motionless for nearly an hour, the noise from the camp behind them waning almost completely as the night deepened and grew colder. Dason fidgeted restlessly, standing abruptly from time to time to pace back and forth or to stand uneasily by her. The three moons bathed them in light, and a cool southern breeze washed the scent of campfires and pine trees over them. But Maewen knew that however tranquil the surroundings, before her was agony and struggle. Even at a distance, Maewen could sense the Chalaine's pain. Whatever the Chalaine felt exuded from her, the dark smoke of a smoldering soul.

"Chalaine, please," Dason, distressed, said at last. "I know you grieve for your mother, but you cannot go on like this! I can hardly bear it!"

"You are right. I cannot go on like this," the Chalaine agreed, voice distant. Before Dason could think to reply, the Chalaine uncovered her face. Even in the poor light, Dason winced and looked away. "So, how do you find me, Dason? A proper Queen? One you shall loathe and keep hidden away. Look at me!"

Dason turned his gaze toward her with effort. "Chalaine, you know . . . you know I would have you even if you, well, even if you. . ."

"Come closer, Dason. Look at my face. Closer!"

Dason reluctantly complied. Maewen knew what would

come next and rose as the Chalaine breathed on her Protector's face. Dason collapsed in a heap over the rock, landing with an uncomfortable thud. The Chalaine immediately stood and cast aside her cloak and veil. Maewen sneaked forward as the Queen turned toward the canyon. She wore the same dress she had worn to greet Mikkik at Echo Hold. While not close to its original splendor, the Chalaine had obviously cleaned and repaired it recently. The white fabric caught the moonlight, as did her eyes, but her skin was twisted and burned. Her hair, once a brilliant blonde, fell dull, tangled, and thin around her shoulders.

Maewen approached slowly, and as she feared, the Chalaine walked purposefully to the precipice of the deep divide. The young woman turned her face to the sky, a tear reflecting the moonlight as it ran down the black whorls and warps of the skin on her face. The Chalaine cried silently for some time before steeling herself. Maewen waited just behind the rock where Dason lay unconscious, arguing within herself about what she should do and whether or not it would work to deflect the Chalaine from her purpose. But as the Chalaine turned her gaze from the heavens to the canyon floor below, Maewen thought of Gen and spoke.

"I can give you a reason to live."

The Chalaine startled and fell backward before turning to peer into the darkness. "Who is there?" the Chalaine asked. "Just let me be!"

Maewen emerged from behind the rock and into moonlight, face sympathetic but stern. "You must come with me now, Chalaine. I have something to show you."

"Just go, Maewen," the Chalaine cried. "Let me be done with it. My time is over."

Maewen walked forward casually, trying not to alarm the fallen Queen. "Listen to me, Chalaine. After seeing what I have to show you, if you still want to take your life, then I will let you. Such a practice is common among the elves, although they do it to pass on from one joy to another rather than to escape the world out of despair. But I insist that you come with me. It is not far."

"What could you show me that could possibly make any difference? Will you do what my mother did and tell me to gaze upon the brave soldiers wounded to protect me because they believe in me? I doubt there is one man in this camp who would throw his life away for me now. If that is all you have, Maewen, then be gone."

Maewen stooped down and forced the Chalaine to look her in the eye. "I will show you a soldier, but one who has already thrown his life away for you. Come with me."

Maewen extended her hand, and after a moment the Chalaine, face questioning, grasped it and stood. The Chalaine's hand felt scarred and rough, and when the half-elf took it, ash-colored skin flaked off and fell to the ground. Maewen sorrowed at this evidence of the Chalaine's plight, wondering what it meant. She walked on the side of the trail closest to the cliff, forcing the Chalaine away from it, and held to her hand under the pretense of helping her along even though the ample moonlight along the naked edge of the cliff outlined the trail clearly, even to human vision.

"I must ask you to try to be quiet when we approach and not to speak. He is weary from the battle today, and we need to let him rest. There are other . . . complications . . . as well. This may be hard for you, but if it will help you seek life, then I am willing."

Maewen guided her off the main path, stepping softly among the old trees, careful to lead the Chalaine over the cushion of pine needles and avoid the twigs and branches that would announce their approach. The camp lay in a small hollow just over a low protrusion of white granite, well hidden from the trail and prying eyes. As they crested, Maewen stopped the Chalaine and pointed downward. Gen lay to their left, reclined against the lee side of the rock. The moonlight exposed the profile of his face, the shallow arrow cut running across his cheek. Maewen turned and watched the Chalaine's countenance. It was apathetic with a tinge of disappointment.

"This is the woodsman you travel with. Amos," the Chalaine whispered flatly, turning to go. "What does he have to do with me?"

"Look more closely, Chalaine," Maewen prompted, pulling her back around. "He has a beard and longer hair, but you know this man. Step closer if you can do it quietly. He is quite spent and should not wake if you are careful."

The Chalaine squinted and took two tentative steps forward. At that moment, a wind approached, rushing down the mountain from the east. As it blew through the clearing, Gen stirred and turned his face toward them in sleep. The bending trees let in a momentary shaft of moonlight that ran along the blade he embraced across his breast, handle by his head.

And that was enough. Maewen watched as the Chalaine's eyes widened and her hand slowly rose to her mouth. Maewen took her arm and led her away quickly, half carrying her as she stumbled about in a daze, shaking. Once back to the trail, Maewen helped her to sit, watching as tears ran down her face. Her emotion was difficult to read, her eyes alternating between surprise and fear. It took some time before the young woman could speak.

"It's impossible! I watched him die. I felt his cold skin and laid his sword in his lifeless arms! It cannot be him. How can you know this isn't some trick of the enemy?"

Maewen removed her own cloak and lifted her leather shirt, showing Chalaine the spiral scar across the top of her chest, a scar the Chalaine had seen burned into every one of her Protectors.

"I had Ethris do it when we were forced to leave him behind in Elde Luri Mora. I felt his death. I felt his return

112

to life. And I rejoiced when he joined our besieged camp. It is he. He has been with the army for days. Our escaping the beetles was his work. All the little miracles the men are talking about today were his doing. The strategy I presented to the council for our most recent battle came from him. And when the precipice collapsed this afternoon, it was no act of God or nature, it was Gen's. It completely exhausted him to do it."

"But he must hate me!" the Chalaine exclaimed. "How can he bear to look at me? What must he think of the nothing I am? Of his dying for a failed wretch?"

"What?" Maewen had not expected this. "How can you ask such a question? Why do think he came to this camp? For me? For your mother? For the armies of men? He came to watch over you! He blames you for nothing at Echo Hold. He feels you yet have a role to play, but I doubt he even cares for that. I know little of what the race of men thinks is love, but I have seen what I think it is. Gen has done and is determined to do anything in his power to see you safe. He is a god among men who has forsaken his own glory for the right to serve you."

"But. . ."

"But what?" Maewen interrupted, irritation rising. "I have never seen a man give as much for any woman as he has given for you. And with what reward? Does he have your tender embrace? Your sweet words? Does he get power, fame, or regard? Will it be his hand instead of Dason's that you take? No! He walks ignored and unknown, and he cares for nothing but to restore your happiness. How can you doubt his regard for you? What further proof do you need of his love, and what further proof could he possibly give?"

"There is a way I can know," the Chalaine said, now calm. "Lead me to him again."

"I cannot. He instructed me never to tell anyone who he was, especially you. I cannot chance his waking. I have

113

already gone against his wishes."

"Why would he not want me to know?" the Chalaine asked, sounding hurt.

"He feared discovery, which you know would be disastrous to him and what is left of this army. If Mikkik knew he lived, he would pull every creature and man at his command between Rhugoth and the ruins of Lal'Manar and send them south to hunt him, forcing Gen to flee from you to keep you safe. He also felt that you knowing would prevent you from fully seeking happiness in other matters."

"Marrying Dason."

"Yes. He knows you love Dason and doesn't want to complicate your relationship with him." The Chalaine turned away to hide her emotion, and Maewen waited until she composed herself, wondering what she was feeling.

"I have been truly cursed for that lie," the Chalaine finally said, and before Maewen could ask what she meant, the Chalaine continued. "You must take me to him. I swear I will not wake him. But I must know something, something I cannot afford to doubt."

Maewen considered the risk for several long moments before nodding her assent and leading the Chalaine back to where Gen slept.

"I must touch him, but only lightly," the Chalaine reassured. "It will only take a moment. If he is as exhausted as you say, he won't wake." Maewen feared ruin. Gen would never trust her again if he woke and discovered the Chalaine there.

The Chalaine approached him carefully. Maewen examined Gen's face, on guard for any sign he might wake, but from the rise and fall of his chest, she knew he still slept deeply. The Chalaine crouched at his side and stretched forth a trembling, scarred hand to touch his exposed arm lightly. Immediately, the wound on Gen's face healed, but Maewen saw something else—the skin on the Chalaine's hand turning pale and smooth.

114

Maewen again pulled her away and led her back toward the trail. The Chalaine wept for joy, hand over her heart as if it had just beat for the first time. Gradually, the skin on her face healed, her back and shoulders straightened, her eyes brightened, and her hair regained its color and thickness. Maewen was stunned at the Chalaine's restored majesty and beauty, and for a moment the Queen shone so brightly that she cast a perceptible light around her. Sinking to her knees, the Chalaine looked heavenward with gratitude, face humble and happy. The light around her gradually faded, though Maewen could still sense a brilliancy around her even after the transfiguration ended.

"Thank you, Maewen," the Chalaine said, standing to embrace her. Maewen returned it awkwardly, though with satisfaction at seeing life in the Chalaine's eyes. "I will not betray you. I will act as if I never knew him. But you must introduce him to me. I cannot live and ignore him."

"I do not think that would be wise," Maewen counseled. "He is perceptive."

"Do not worry," the Chalaine reassured her. "I have a good reason to wear the veil now, and I've had to act like I didn't love him before. You cannot deny me this, so do not try. Be assured, however, that I will not tell him what you have done. I owe you a great debt."

"Let us away from here," Maewen ordered, ignoring the Chalaine's request. "He can still sense you, and if he wakes he will know you are near, and I will have no lie to tell that will satisfy."

"Yes," the Chalaine agreed. "Let's go. We shouldn't leave Dason draped over a rock all night."

The next day, word gradually spread of the Chalaine's transformation, and for those who longed for a sign that the fortunes of their poor party had truly changed, the Chalaine was its revelation. Ethris and Lord Kildan stood amazed and pleased, all smiles, when they saw her the next morning. Just as strongly as darkness had exuded from her before, light and joy did so now.

"What happened, dear child?" Ethris asked, embracing her.

"Eldaloth revealed hope to me again. I know now that all is not lost, that another opportunity awaits me, awaits us all, to make things right."

And though they pressed her to be more forthcoming, she simply told them that she could not explain it. Everywhere she went that day, a beaming Dason behind her, bows and pleas for healing and blessing replaced the guarded whispering of the days before. With delight she shared her returned talent with the war-weary and wounded men, leaving in her wake soldiers with gratitude on their faces and hearts that would push forward when feet threatened to fail.

Lord Kildan let them take their rest and start late. Maewen took the lead at the head of the column, marking a path for them to follow.

"What happened last night?" a happy but puzzled Gen asked after seeing the Chalaine for himself.

"She and Dason left camp," Maewen said. "I followed them out onto the ridge. She cast the spell to make him sleep. I can only surmise that what she did was plead with God. She was alone for an hour, and then she changed. I can hardly describe it, but it was wonderful. I was a bit nervous, however, as she was not seventy-five yards from where you slept."

Gen smiled. "It was good to see her like her old self, like she was before her miserable wedding," he said. "Pity I could not have watched last night instead of you. I wish I could question her about it."

"Everyone who can has asked her. She merely says that

God gave her hope again, though most suspect a great deal is missing from her explanation. Whatever happened to her, the morale of the soldiers is the highest it has been since before Echo Hold. We need to use that to our advantage to cover some miles. I still reckon it will be three days before we get off the canyon ridge."

"I agree. Push hard. If we can make it to Rhugoth, we can see what we have left with which to mount a defense. The Chalaine and Dason can wed to unite Tolnor and Rhugoth, though it won't do much good if we can't convince everyone that the being they think is Eldaloth is Mikkik. "

"I doubt the Chalaine is in much humor to marry. She just lost her first husband, and her mother rides in the company of Athan on her way to Echo Hold and some unknown fate."

Gen raised his eyebrows in surprise. "An odd observation from you, though I think you are wrong. The Chalaine certainly needs no time to mourn Chertanne, and I would think wedding Dason would serve as comfort for her losses."

"In that case," Maewen said, "leave her in his care and turn your abilities toward greater things. I again tell you that it is you who needs to lead this people! No one has greater power, and because of Khairn's Training Stones, no one has more wisdom. Why do you continue this vigil of the Chalaine? Others can do it."

"Because," Gen replied with some heat, "Mikkik still wants her! Mirelle's little ruse will not last for long. Athan's Eldephaere may not know the difference, but others of his agents will. If Mikkik wants the Chalaine, then she is in danger, the kind that mere swordfighters cannot protect her from. The restoration of her beauty points to a part she may yet play."

"See reason, Gen. . ."

"No more, Maewen. My mind is fixed. Lead them out. I

am going back to my vigil, whether you think it necessary or not!"

For the next three days, they marched hard. The miles meant nothing to the Chalaine, who spent every moment scheming ways she could chance an encounter with Gen. But he was too clever in his avoidance, and Maewen was unwilling to offer any assistance in the matter, fearing discovery. The Chalaine knew the brand on Gen's chest let him know of her approach, so not even stealth could avail her. Every time she walked in his direction, no matter how she tried to appear as if she were headed somewhere else, he would turn and walk off at an odd angle.

But now that she knew who he was, she saw him everywhere. She wondered at how she hadn't noticed, even in her despair, his continual, watchful presence. He was skilled at masking his intentions and his movements, but she saw only his face in the crowd now, and it required discipline not to search for it at every opportunity.

Every day she longed to speak with him, remembering the comfort their conversations gave her as she traveled in the wagon and as they hiked alone toward Elde Luri Mora. She just needed a chance at his ear and some contrivance to give her an excuse to talk with him more frequently, something she hadn't quite worked out yet. She kept hoping that Maewen would invite him to the morning councils she took with Lord Kildan, General Harband, and Ethris, but the half-elf appeared firm in her resolve to be unhelpful. By the end of the third day, the Chalaine felt very cross and was quite short with everyone, including Dason, who had been jubilant and painfully affectionate since her transformation.

On the morning of the fourth day, however, Maewen

unwittingly provided just the opportunity the Chalaine had waited for. The company had descended steadily for two days, and Maewen announced the evening before that they should find the plain the next day and from there the Black River that would lead them to Rhugoth. As was her custom, the half-elf left before first light to scout ahead. At daybreak the Chalaine, Ethris, and Lord Kildan met as they always did, but for the first time since they started their journey, Maewen was late. Out of the corner of her eye, the Chalaine noticed Gen sitting casually against an oak tree eating bread not thirty feet from her. Maewen's tardiness provided the opening she needed.

Turning to Lord Kildan, she announced, "I will speak with the man she travels with—Amos, was it?—and see if he knows anything about her whereabouts."

With Gerand in tow, she strode quickly toward Gen. As she started walking in his direction, he pulled the brim of his hat down to hide his face. As it became apparent that she approached him specifically, he rose to go as naturally as he could.

The Chalaine's heart pounded as she approached. "Excuse me, Amos?" she called to him, subduing the excitement in her voice and trying to sound as if she were addressing a stranger. He turned to go. "Sir! Amos!" she called more loudly. He stopped, and she almost laughed at his obvious discomfort as he slowly turned to face her. When he did, he kept his face and eyes down, executing a bow and leaning on a quarterstaff.

"Yes, Holiness?" he asked. The Chalaine completely underestimated the effect that hearing his voice again would have on her. It was deep, calm, and wonderfully familiar. Wherever that voice spoke was her peace, her home. "Milady?" he said as she paused, and the fear that he thought she recognized him gave her the ability to tame her emotions and continue.

"I am sorry," she said, "but I didn't understand what

you had said, as you were talking at the ground. You are Amos, the one who travels with Maewen, correct?"

"Yes, Holiness," he answered.

"Well, look up, Amos, or shall I lie on the ground at your feet so I can see your face?"

He looked up reluctantly, though he did not meet her eye, focusing his gaze behind her. Now that she could get a good look at him, she marveled at his face, skin smooth and free of scars, but undeniably his. The long hair and close-cropped beard lent him a few more years, and despite his rustic attire, the intelligence of eye imbued him dignity and nobility, as she remembered.

"But I've interrupted your breakfast. Please sit and eat. I just have a few brief questions for you concerning Maewen."

"Thank you, Holiness," he said, returning his quarterstaff to the ground and sitting with his back against the tree. The Chalaine realized that this gave him the advantage of hiding his face again, so she surprised him and Gerand by taking a seat beside him.

"Please, do not be uncomfortable," she soothed. "Think of me as just another woman. I am quite tired of people treating me as if I were a spider who might bite or a bird who might fly away. Be at ease. I promise I mean you no harm."

"Forgive me. I am but a simple woodsman, Milady."

"You are forgiven. My questions are these. First," she said, "the council wonders if Maewen thinks we will make the river before dark, and if so, if we should camp close to it."

"We should arrive at the river before midday," he said evenly as he rummaged through his leather bag for some bread and nuts, keeping his face away from her as much as possible. "Our camping situation will be dictated by the disposition of the surrounding area."

"What?" she asked, amused.

"Did I say something amiss?" he inquired, taken aback.

"Well, not really. You said, 'our camping situation will be dictated by the disposition of the surrounding area.' Now, I've not had the pleasure of knowing many *simple* woodsmen, but that sounded like something Lord Kildan would say." She could almost see him chiding himself. "You don't happen to be a general in disguise? We could use another good one."

"No, Milady. The second question?"

"Maewen is late returning from her usual morning scout. We wondered if you knew if she intended to go farther ahead than usual and if she might be in some danger?"

He pulled his hat down. "She had intended to go forward far enough to see the plain, though she was unsure of the exact distance. I believe she wanted to see if we would find any danger there. She may be delayed for that reason."

"Should we worry?"

"I do not think so. Perhaps I should go see if the sentries have had any sign of her." He shifted his worn leather satchel to his lap and started to repack his food. The Chalaine thought hard for a way to stall his escape.

"Perhaps you should," she said before he could stand, "but may I ask if you would be capable of leading the column forward in her absence? I assume that since you are a woodsman with a staff and a bow rather than a wood ax and rope that you earned your title by something other than cutting and hauling lumber?"

"I am not as skilled as Maewen, but I could substitute in her absence."

"Excellent. Make your inquiries to the sentries and return and report to me what you find. If she is not seen inside a half hour, we will move without her, you in the lead."

He left quickly, and the Chalaine watched him go as she returned to Ethris and Kildan. While happy that she had

121

finally heard his voice, she felt thoroughly unsatisfied. She could already tell the pretended unfamiliarity would quickly wear thin and annoy her. She wanted a return to the way it had been, and she wanted it now. She could not dissemble forever, and she wondered when and how she could tell him that she knew and loved him. At the same time, there would be no way to visit and talk with him if he maintained his nondescript role as woodsman. But how could she elevate him without calling attention to who he was or revealing her regard for him?

Dason stood in the circle when she and his brother returned to the council. Her amorous Protector beamed at her, taking her hand enthusiastically and kissing it. The affection in his eyes pained her, and the expectation in his countenance filled her with dread. He saw no obstacle now to their wedding, and by the way his father smiled at him and her, he didn't either.

"Well, your Grace," Lord Kildan began before Dason could say anything, "what does—what is his name again—what does he say?"

"Amos is his name, Lord Kildan," the Chalaine answered. "He told me that Maewen intended to scout forward until she saw the plain, although she was unsure of the distance. He is capable of leading us forward if she does not return soon."

"Really?" Ethris said, jumping ahead of Lord Kildan. "I've been meaning to ask her the origin of her friend. I've never known Maewen to consort much with anyone, though she did seem fond of Gen."

"Doesn't seem the wholesome sort," Lord Kildan interjected. "I've seen him skulking about, hat low on his face. I don't remember him in any of the battles we've survived."

"I've noticed him lately as well," Dason added. "And if I notice him, that means he is nearly always close to the Chalaine, which gives me concern. However, I must trust that one as old and as wise as Maewen would be careful in her choice of associates."

"He seems quite harmless," the Chalaine commented offhandedly.

"Seeming and being are quite different, your Holiness," Ethris counseled.

"Yes," the Chalaine replied, "but I am not a complete failure as a judge of character. It may well be that Maewen set him to watch over me while she blazes the trail for us. Besides you and the Dark Guard, I believe Maewen feels the most responsible for my safety."

Lord Kildan and Dason objected fervently, and the Chalaine rolled her eyes up into her head while they proclaimed their utmost interest and concern for her welfare.

"Ethris," Lord Kildan ordered, "ask Maewen directly the next time you see her. I want to know if she did order this protection. If not, then some action may need to be taken."

"Ask me what?" Maewen inquired flatly, leaning on her bow just outside the circle. Sweat ran down her face, though she didn't appear to be laboring. The Chalaine searched for Gen, disappointed at not finding him nearby.

"Ah! Maewen," Lord Kildan exclaimed. "It is a small matter concerning the man Amos. But first, what report?"

"The way is clear to the plain, as near as I can tell. We should be to the Black River by dark and Blackshire castle by midday tomorrow."

"Excellent news! Gerand, prepare the troops to march." Gerand bowed and left. "Now to Amos. Dason says he's seen him near the Chalaine quite frequently and we wonder how well you know him and if you'd ordered him to watch the Chalaine."

If Maewen were surprised by the question, she didn't show it. "I know him better than I know any of you. I did ask him to watch over her because. . ."

"Do you not trust the Dark Guard and me," Dason

interrupted, obviously offended, "to provide an adequate defense? I must object!"

"I could hardly see how one charged to protect her could object to one more pair of eyes watching in her behalf," Maewen answered, annoyance plain. "Now if I may finish. I did ask him to watch over her because he is a skilled woodsman and can hear and see things you do not know to look or listen for."

"Seems a bit young to have enough skill or experience to lend much aid," Dason returned contemptuously.

"I'm sure," Maewen said, "that people said the same when you were raised to the Protectorship at such an early age." Dason turned red, and the Chalaine hoped he would hold his tongue before Maewen was forced to completely humiliate him. "At my age you all seem a bit too young for anything. But may I assure you all that Amos has the best of intentions toward the Chalaine and is a capable woodsman and an adequate fighter." The Chalaine smiled at her whopping understatement. Thankfully, Maewen's assertions put an end to all argument.

"I am satisfied," Lord Kildan said. "Lead us forward, Maewen. I would like to get somewhere more civilized and defensible soon."

CHAPTER 77 – BLACKSHIRE

A very different army from the one that had left Echo Hold descended from the alpine ridge to meet up with the county road that ran along the Black River at the southern edge of Rhugoth. While they had lost nearly half their number to the marauding Uyumaak, their thoughts now turned to home and family. The untamed wilds behind, they rejoiced to see the beginnings of the touch of human hands on the landscape. Squat stone farmhouses popped into view, set against green fields with corn and wheat nearly waist high. The lane widened and improved as orchard-draped hills and mighty oaks lined the way.

In the brilliant morning sunshine the Chalaine could almost believe that Eldaloth had returned, their danger having dissipated into the tree-choked mountains behind them. She glanced around, finding Gen nearer to her than he usually walked, speaking with Maewen in Elvish. The army no longer needed a guide to show them the way. Lord Kildan, General Harband, and Ethris were at the vanguard as they walked toward Blackshire, the estate her mother had promised to Gen and that Chertanne had given to Geoff and Fenna.

Perhaps now Gen would understand the love that her

mother had for him, for the Chalaine couldn't imagine a more beautiful, tranquil place to bestow upon a person. Everywhere the eye turned, something caught its interest, from the dark, flowing river, to the mountains rising on the east and south, to the rolling green hills and the pleasant breeze that rippled waves in the fields of grain. She knew Gen. She knew he would have loved this gorgeous country place. She loved it too, and just like the men around her she began that vain wishing that the war was indeed over. All she wanted was to drag Gen to the nearest Pureman and find a little home tucked away off down a distant lane and just live for him forever.

She peeked over her shoulder again but found that he and Maewen had turned, walking toward the rear of the column. For a moment, she feared that they would leave and strike out into the wilderness, but instead they stopped to speak with Cadaen, whose angry, sober face stood out in contrast to the rest of the smiling marchers.

While the Chalaine had spoken to Mirelle's Protector before to offer him comfort, she realized his thoughts had now turned to leaving the army behind and going to find her mother. The Chalaine surprised Dason by turning on her heel and walking back to join them. As she had come to expect, Gen yanked his hat down and leaned on his quarterstaff as she approached. She vowed to rip the hat off his head and burn it at the first opportunity.

"I cannot delay," Cadaen was saying. "Every minute I wait, she is in greater danger."

"You cannot leave me today," the Chalaine said. "I want my mother freed more than anything, but you must see me safely to Blackshire. Let us see what news has come. You must at least rest and re-provision tonight."

As the Chalaine said these words, she knew she would have to let Gen go again. Cadaen could not confront Athan and the Council of Padras alone, and Gen alone held the power to extract Mirelle from whatever prison she languished in. The Chalaine would suffer on with Dason and bid the one she loved farewell.

"But, Chalaine, I. . ." Cadaen protested.

"No more, Cadaen," she said, her voice breaking with emotion. "If you leave now and go alone, you will fail. You need rest, and you need help. Stay with me one more day, just one more, and you can go."

The Chalaine glanced at Gen before turning away, finding his eyes sad and affectionate. It was hard not to turn and run to him, but she steeled herself and continued forward with the rest of the column. He walked close behind her now, just behind Dason, watchful and caring as always.

As they crested the hill, the city of Blackshire sprung into view. The small castle at its center sat pleasantly atop a tree-covered hill, the town encircling it on all sides. A low wall, meant to fend off wild animals rather than warriors, surrounded the older part of the city, though many buildings had recently risen up around the outside. Most structures had a mortared stone foundation with a plastered wood slats at the top. Long, thin trees shot up all through the town, bending in the air with the motions of a breeze that was hazy with wood smoke. They stopped to regard it, the city Warden and a handful of men riding toward their position, no doubt alarmed at the large armed force closing on their homes.

The Chalaine found Gen regarding the scene serenely, a slight smile on his lips, and she wondered what memories the scene invoked for him. Good ones, by the look in his eyes. For her, it was all about the memories she wanted to make and the ones she wanted to forget. Her duties to others seemed over. Now she could serve her own purposes without the burden of guilt. Blackshire was the symbol of that new life. Mikmir and its underground chambers might be safe, but the memory of that place felt like a prison. Here, she was free to ride and roam and love as never before.

The Warden, a tall thin man with sun-darkened skin, approached warily. Lord Kildan and Ethris greeted him warmly to allay his fears. They had worked out the story in council the day before. The Chalaine listened as Lord Kildan explained that they had escaped a large army of Uyumaak, and that the Chalaine had come to Blackshire to hide from Mikkik's forces, who sought revenge.

"We just received word two days ago that Eldaloth had returned and the Ilch struck a blow," the Warden explained, "but that the Chalaine had been found and returned safely to Echo Hold! Lord Geoff of Blackshire ordered a week-long celebration. It is just underway this day. While I must consult with him, I can assure you we have nowhere to quarter such a large band of men."

"We can encamp in any place that is convenient," Ethris said. "We are weary, however, and in need of some provisions before we press on to Mikmir."

"I will ask the Lord how to proceed."

They waited for nearly an hour, resting on the side of the road, trying to ignore the smell of roasted meats that the breeze carried to their noses. At last, a procession of men wearing the device of the Black Tree rode forward, and the Chalaine could spot Geoff and Fenna riding at their head, smiles wide. A host of memories of her handmaiden flooded back to her, and the Chalaine had to grin at the thought of all their long conversations about men and love. Geoff still wore his green hat, but his clothes looked a little tight and his face a little full. The elevation to nobility had treated him well. Fenna rode sidesaddle, and her pregnant belly looked ready to pop, an uncomfortable but happy expression on her sweating face.

From the corner of her eye, the Chalaine saw Gen casually walk away. The couple dismounted, Geoff taking Fenna's hand and leading her forward in a regal style. The Chalaine stepped forward and her handmaiden embraced her warmly, belly interfering and reminding the Chalaine of her own pregnancy.

"It is dreadfully hot today," Fenna complained. "Lord Blackshire and I insist that you, the Dark Guard, and your officers come stay with us in the manor for as long as you need. Ethris and Maewen, too. We have such a celebration planned for tonight! You have come just in time. But let's get out of this cruel heat! We have heard so many stories! You must tell me everything!"

The trip into Blackshire proper only served to further endear the Chalaine to the place. Rustic and quaint, its rough cobble streets teeming with people seemed the happiest place in the world, though the lively festival all around her aided that perception. The girls twirled in brightly colored dresses meant to impress the young men, who had cleaned their boots and shirts to return the gesture. Performers and acrobats, food and song, all of it beckoned to the Chalaine who had tired of war and strife. If only her mother weren't imprisoned miles away, and if only Mikkik weren't making fools of them all.

One of the entourage had offered his horse to her, and she accepted it gladly. Gen brought up the rear, flicking coins to the children as he passed, gathering a cloud of youth until he feigned that he had no more to give. The smile on his face brought the Chalaine's heart to her throat. His hat was back and his face plain in the afternoon sunshine. Something about him was different, something she couldn't attribute to just his lack of scars or his beard. She couldn't place her finger on what it was, though his countenance was certainly more inviting and handsome than it had been when scars marred it into a testament of cruelty.

They crossed up the switchbacks to the castle proper, passing through the thick outer walls that—compared to the impregnable fortresses of Mikmir and Echo Hold— seemed paltry. But Blackshire had never seen anything of war, having been built and settled after the eclipsing of Trys and the end of the Second Mikkikian War. The interior of the courtyard was beautiful, decorative trees and bushes lining the modestly sized manor house and the keep, and the Chapel behind it. Summer flowers bloomed in colorful planters along the windows, and a mighty oak hung protectively over one side of the edifice.

"We must get you properly attired!" Fenna said as they dismounted. "You're all a-tatters! You will, of course, have a room all to yourself. We may have to double the others. I'll let Wilkes take care of it. Who is that bearded fellow that walks with Maewen?"

"That is Amos, a woodsman and fighter. He is a friend of Maewen's that helped us in our latest struggles."

After a brief tour of the cheery manor, Fenna led her upstairs, Dason following behind. They left the handsome Tolnorian prince outside the doors and entered, just like old times. In moments Fenna had dismissed her own handmaiden and removed the Chalaine's crude veil.

"There you are, just as pretty as ever," Fenna said. "We'll get a warm bath for everyone—you first, of course. So can you imagine such a strange ending to the prophecy? Who would have thought that Gen was the Ilch the whole time? I never really favored him much. There was always something not quite right about him. And those abominable scars! What a fright he was! You must have been shocked. And he tried to kill you just as you were about to be taken to Erelinda with your husband. How awful. He died, then?"

"Yes. He was killed by the Uyumaak."

"What? How strange! Why would they kill him?"

The Chalaine shook her head, realizing how torturous her encounter with Fenna would be. "There are many mysteries yet to solve, Fenna. I don't believe Gen intended to harm me at all."

"Well, we're all glad you're rid of him," Fenna said

firmly. "And do you think you will have Eldaloth send you to your husband in Erelinda, or will you, um, turn your affections elsewhere for a while? I couldn't help but notice that a certain eligible young man still follows you around. . ."

Inwardly the Chalaine groaned. "I will stay upon Ki'Hal. I must work to free my mother. I have no other object in view now." *Except Gen.*

"Your mother! What happened?"

The Chalaine invented a story about how Athan arrested her for treason for harboring and favoring Gen, a story the Chalaine fully expected to have come true.

Fenna gasped. "How awful! But Athan will set her free. Gen deceived all of us, the scoundrel!"

"Fenna," the Chalaine said, trying to sound friendly. "I am dreadfully tired. Would you mind if I bathed now and slept for a while? It was a long march through rough country, and if I am to enjoy this excellent celebration, it would be nice to be fresh."

"But of course!" Fenna agreed, giving the Chalaine's hair another stroke with the brush. "But there is so much news and gossip to tell you! I have been so happy. Chertanne was a bit rough, but I thank him for having the wisdom to pair me with Geoff. He must have seen what kindred spirits we were, after all."

With a little more prodding from the Chalaine, Fenna finally saw to the servants bringing in a large basin and warm water. After assuring the Lady of Blackshire that she needed no help bathing, she stripped her frayed and torn clothing away and soaked, the warmth lulling her eyes closed. When she did dream, Gen appeared in every scene, some of them as scandalous as the ones she had envisioned in her long days in Ironkeep. When she woke, the longing reflected in those dreams sparked a glow in her heart rather than the crushing guilt they had inspired before.

Fenna returned before dinner and brought her a

gorgeous plum-colored dress trimmed in gold. "It will be a bit tight on you," Fenna warned, "though you've thinned a bit from your wandering about the woods, I see. Anyway, I've had my maid stitch together a veil for you. It's not as fancy as those you once wore, but certainly better than the awful thing you were wearing when you arrived. You know, my maid is just a little tiresome. All she wants to talk about is this boy and that and how she can't do without them. Just one of the trials of nobility. I suppose it's my duty to sober her up."

After buttoning the dress and declaring her ravishing, Fenna left with a tease to Dason about how wonderful the Chalaine looked. The Chalaine admired herself in the mirror. The dusty, exhausted refugee was gone, and before her was a beautiful woman with long blonde hair, piercing blue eyes, and a dress to rival those her mother had worn in her attempts to drive Gen mad with passion. She smiled and hoped that Amos the woodsman was not above flirting with widows.

Affixing her veil, she opened the door and found an appreciative Dason who, despite all his propriety, couldn't help but glance over her, even if quickly.

"Tonight will be a night to remember, Chalaine," he said with a twinkle in his eye. She took his proffered arm, sick at the expectation in Dason's handsome, smiling face. He had found an opportunity to bathe as well, his uniform stitched and laundered back to something more presentable. He led her to the dining room, and everyone stood as she entered. Lord Kildan, the Dark Guard, and Ethris were there, but the Chalaine was disappointed to find Gen missing, Maewen sitting alone at a side table. Fenna and two other Lords and Ladies she didn't recognize were present as well.

Geoff thrust his glass into the air.

"To the Chalaine, who has courageously led us to this new era of peace and prosperity under the rule of Eldaloth!"

The agreement to keep their knowledge of Mikkik's fraud a secret kept the ebullience of the toast to a minimum, the Chalaine feeling sick at the deception. They drank anyway, but before the Chalaine sat, she called for attention.

"I thank you, Lord Blackshire, for your kind words, though I hardly feel I deserve them. But it is at this time that I wish to invoke a long-standing custom of the Chalaines. At the birth of their first child, every Chalaine has relinquished the title and taken upon her a new name for the remainder of her life. The name I have chosen comes from the ancient language. My name is Alumira'rei Se Ellenwei, or Alumira for short."

Maewen perked up. "Do you know what it means?"

The Chalaine remembered her conversation with Gen outside of her chamber so long ago. He had given her the name just after the demon attack when she had treated him crossly. "I think it means 'someone who picks fights.'"

The assemblage laughed, excepting Maewen, who shook her head. "No! That's not what it means at all."

"Then tell us," Dason prompted. "It certainly sounds as lovely as she is."

"The name means, 'My way out of darkness.'"

The Chalaine exhaled and gripped the table, trying to keep the tears out of her eyes. The name was Gen's tribute to her, his gratitude for saving him from Mikkik's poison. She remembered when she had told him never to call her that name again. There could be no more waiting. *I must find him tonight,* she thought. *He must know my heart.*

"Where did you get the name?" Dason prompted.

The Chalaine stifled the blooming of love in her heart, wanting to savor the private emotion away from the expectant faces. She swallowed hard, but her voice quavered as she said, "A dear friend."

Maewen nodded, the barest grin on her lips. The rest pressed her to be more forthcoming, but she refused, returning to her seat, mind drifting inward. Dinner was served. The conversation and blather in the room, whether meaningful or pointless, passed over and around her. Dason kept snaking his hand under the table to try to grasp hers, but she would snatch it away. He would grin, thinking she was playing coy. She fought the urge to stab him with a fork.

Thankfully, dinner ended, and they entered a modest assembly hall where they were joined by other members of Blackshire society and officers from the regiment stationed there. The people crowded suffocatingly around her, congratulating and thanking her for her grand part in the prophecy. They asked her when she would join her husband in Erelinda, and every time they did, Dason would wink meaningfully at her.

Once the dancing began, she reclaimed a little breathing room, save from her Protector, who stood uncomfortably close, rubbing against her arm or shoulder whenever he could get the chance. The Chalaine thought Gen might have decided to absent himself from the party entirely, but after a lively dance with Dason, she noticed him standing near a doorway with Maewen watching.

Like a bowshot she threaded her way to the door, Gen disappearing before she arrived. Dason, surprised by the sudden movement, was slow to catch up.

"Is Amos not to join us?" the Chalaine asked.

Maewen smiled that peculiar smile again. "He said he is need of some fresh air and went to one of the upstairs balconies. In truth, he may just need to rest. I have discovered that our young friend has a bad habit of not sleeping."

The Chalaine grinned. "I've heard that about him."

"I promised I would watch you for him," Maewen continued. "But it looks like a certain pair of eyes can hardly bear to be off you as it is."

"Milady!" Dason exclaimed as he arrived. "You departed

most hastily."

"I'm sorry, Dason," she said. "Please feel free to dance with other ladies. I wanted to speak with Maewen for a bit."

"How could any other woman satisfy me?" he said, taking her hand and kissing it.

She gritted her teeth. *I refuse to spend the evening with a man I wouldn't marry in a millennium while the man I would marry in a moment is upstairs!* The Chalaine bit her lip, her mind trying to grind out some way to be rid of her constant companion. Then the hard, reclusive Maewen unexpectedly intervened.

"Have you ever danced with an elf, Dason?"

"Of course not."

"Then come, and perhaps you shall learn how to do it properly."

Dason stammered as Maewen led him toward the floor, Maewen exciting a bit of comment, not just because of her race, but because she was a woman wearing pants in a room full of fashionable, expensive dresses. Dason glanced back at the Chalaine a couple of times, shrugging as Maewen led him away.

When he was fully occupied, the Chalaine dove out of the door and into the entryway where several people loitered. The hunt took a little longer than she liked, and she feared Dason would come traipsing after her at any moment. But after a frantic search around the second floor, she found Gen.

The second story balcony at the back of the house looked over the Chapel garden. Gen sat in a simple wooden chair, leaning it back against the side wall with his feet on the balustrade. His wide-brimmed hat he had yanked down over his face, and without a weapon had crossed his arms over his chest as if he were carrying one anyway. He was fast asleep.

The sounds and smells of the celebration and the fragrant garden below filled her with the same feelings of freedom and freshness as they had that morning, and her heart felt freed. She tiptoed to him and removed her veil. For several moments she just stared at him, unsure of how to proceed. His strong hands rose and fell slowly with his chest, and she wondered if he ever dreamed of her as she dreamed of him. She hoped so.

She wanted to see his face, to find what felt so different about it, but the obscuring hat covered everything but his bearded chin. That was it. That was where to start. With a grin and the flick of her hand, she yanked his hat off. He startled from sleep. With the speed of an adder he grabbed her hand before she could retract it and shot to standing, eyes roving over her in confusion. He finally let go. The Chalaine blushed as his gaze drank her in, eyes lingering just where she hoped they would before finding hers.

"Your Ladyship!" he stammered. "I. . ."

With all the energy of pent up desire and stifled affection finally let loose, she pressed into him and put her lips on his, kissing him deeply with every ounce of longing she had. It took him a moment to respond, but she didn't let up until his hands found her hips and then his arms enveloped her, pulling her against him.   Only then did she put her head on his shoulder, tears of joy falling like rain in the sunshine. He held her, the Chalaine relishing his tenderness and his touch.

At length she pulled back, kissing him again and grabbing his face in her hands. "I have missed you so badly! You could never understand. I have so many things to tell you that you must know," she said.

"It appears you already know more than is good for you," Gen replied. "It is dangerous for you to know who I am, Chalaine."

"I have taken the name Alumira'rei Se Ellenwei now," she said, and kissed him again. "And, as of tonight, I know what it really means. I have a heart full of things to say to you. Please listen."

"Let me find another chair," he offered.

"No, you sit down," she said. "I think pacing might help me get through it. But. . ." and she pulled his head in for another long pull at his lips, "you have no idea how long I've waited to do that!"

She shoved him down in the chair and stood in front of him. *Where to begin?!* He stared up at her patiently, and she rejoiced to see the tender affection there that she always hoped he felt for her. "Oh, Gen, how can I explain all this?"

Footsteps squeaking the boards inside the house startled her, and she cast about for the veil she had discarded.

"Your Ladyship?"

Dason! She dared not turn around without her veil. Gen said a strange word, and Dason collapsed, face impacting painfully with the balustrade on the way down.

"You have no idea how long I've wanted to do that," Gen said, and the Chalaine laughed. "But I find that it is a bit crowded here all of a sudden. Collect your veil, and we'll find somewhere with fewer unconscious people to bother us."

While he dragged Dason over to the chair and propped him up in it, she picked her veil off the floor.

Once he finished arranging Dason, Gen took her hand. "Hold on." He incanted again and she suddenly felt as light as air. With ease they drifted over the balustrade and down into the garden where their weight returned.

"You've learned a few more tricks," she said appreciatively.

"I use them to impress the ladies," he joked. "Come, the Chapel looks abandoned."

She took his hand and wrapped it around her waist as they walked through the garden and up the short stone stairs. The large wooden door swung open ponderously and they slipped inside, the building completely dark. Using his magic, Gen created a globe of light to guide them through the row of benches until they took a seat in the middle.

Gen sat and she sat on him, wrapping her arms around his neck. He let the light fade and drew her in, and they kissed, relishing one another's closeness.

"I believe you wanted to tell me something," Gen said. "But if you want to do this a while longer, I won't complain."

The Chalaine snuggled into him as deeply as she could and told him everything, her lies about not loving him, the guilt she felt for loving him, and her utter despair at seeing him killed at Butchers gap. She told him of her months of wedded loneliness serving Chertanne in his infirmity. She told him of the passion that had seared her soul with so much guilt before, a passion that now filled that same space with hope and joy. She told him how his touch had healed her that night on the ridge.

"I would ask if you still loved me, too, but I know," she said. "It's the only thing I know anymore."

"You are easy to love," he said. "I just never imagined I could have you."

"You have me, Gen," she assured him. "You've had me for longer than you know. Every part. And I will not have another."

"Dason's not going to be pleased," Gen said.

"Hang Dason! You have no idea what mortification I've been through with that man since I was healed on the ridge. How I ever became infatuated with him, I will never know."

Gen chuckled. "It's not even two years since we first met, and I feel like we were all silly children back then. I have felt so weighed down for so long. The kisses helped, so thank you."

She administered another dose to ensure he remained light of heart.

"You never seemed like a child to me, Gen. You were so severe and so intimidating when I first knew you! It took Fenna to soften you up a bit."

"No, Alumira. It was finding a purpose, finding you."

"And I'm glad you did. Fenna's lucky Chertanne forced her to wed Geoff. My mother probably would have assassinated her before she let you two get within a hundred yards of a Church."

Gen reached out and stroked her hair, and she closed her eyes to enjoy the soothing sensation. "Have you learned any way to stop the passing of time?" she said after a long while.

"I'm afraid not, or I would do it."

She exhaled and shifted off his lap, taking his hand and sitting next to him.

"Is something wrong?" he asked.

"Gen, I would never leave your side, but I'm afraid I must ask you leave mine one more time."

"Mirelle."

"I cannot leave her in Athan's hands. I'm terrified at what he will do when he discovers our ruse. In his eyes, she knowingly aided the Ilch and almost caused the second death of Eldaloth. When he knows he's been tricked, I fear he will be brutal. Cadaen wants to be gone already. Will you go with him for me?"

"I will," said Gen, "but please stay close to Ethris. The Dark Guard will do little good against the kind of magic that Athan and the Council of Padras wield."

"Do *whatever* it takes, Gen," she ordered, face sober, squeezing his hand to drive home the point.

"You know I will."

"If they have hurt her, let your wrath be poured out enough for the both of us."

"If they have hurt her, there will not be enough room for any wrath but my own."

A chill ran down her spine at the edge in his voice, and she pitied Athan if he had behaved in the way her imagination thought he might. She leaned against Gen's shoulder and they sat in silence for some time. How long would it take before someone realized that she was missing? Hours, if she were lucky.

"Now that my eyes have adjusted to the dark," Gen said, "I can see that you are an exceptionally beautiful woman."

She laughed quietly.

"Thank you for noticing. As for you, to be honest, I think I miss those scars of yours, and I'm not sure about this beard." She gave it a tug. "And that ridiculous hat should be burned."

"I don't know what to do about my identity. The world thinks me a villain, and—although I look different—it isn't different enough to fool anyone for long. Then there's Maewen, who wants me to rise up as a leader. All I want to do is keep you safe, but Mikkik must be dealt with. I just don't know how. What will you do when you get to Mikmir?"

"I think the truth has to start with me," she said. "Once I am safe within the castle there, I can publish my version of the events and at least help people start to doubt. What Mikkik intends to do with his usurped position, I cannot guess. What is his purpose?"

Gen thought for a moment. "He has always sought the eradication of all good creatures on Ki'Hal, but if he starts ordering people killed, then he would lose his control." He leaned back and ran his fingers through his long hair. "If he is patient, it may take time for him to reveal his scheme. We have to think and plan carefully."

"My mother would be better at that," the Chalaine said, feeling anxiety reasserting itself. "Can we go back to the kissing? I think I like that better, though just because I'm so willing to be affectionate, don't think that you can just take advantage of me."

"I wouldn't dream of taking advantage of you."

"Really? I've dreamed about it several times. You're quite a rake in my dreams. Now, don't be offended. Those dreams kept me alive. So let's see if I can't provide a little spark to inflame your imaginings a little."

She retook her perch on his lap pressed into him again, her passion now guiltless and rewarding as she shared her lips and her warmth until a polite "ahem" from the rear of the Chapel startled them both.

"Maewen?" Gen said, turning in surprise.

"Excuse my interruption," she said. "But the Chalaine must return to the house soon. She is missed."

"Just tell them I've retired to my room."

"I don't think that will do," Maewen replied. "Fenna's already checked your chambers. They may have found Dason by now. Did you hit him in the face?"

"The balustrade did," Gen replied. "They ought to fix that thing. Knocked him unconscious."

Maewen smirked. "We leave for Mikmir in the morning. Will you be coming with us, Gen?"

"No. I go with Cadaen to find Mirelle."

"Good. We need her wisdom. The whole world is careening to its doom and, dancing the entire way. I'll tell them I've found you, Alumira, and that you'll be in shortly. Don't be too long." She left, the door squeaking as she shut it.

"How did I not hear her come in?" Gen wondered aloud.

The Chalaine smiled. "You were preoccupied. But curse it all, I don't want to leave you now! Everyone else's company is burdensome to me. Promise me you won't leave tomorrow without seeing me."

"I promise. And I won't leave this Chapel until we have a dance together. I must atone for abandoning your birthday party."

"Yes, you must."

He stood and extended his hand, pulling her out into the aisle. There they danced to a rhythm only they could hear until caution bade them stop. They embraced one last time and kissed, the Chalaine reluctantly retrieving her veil and fastening it to her head.

"I love you, Chalaine," Gen said, hands cradling her face. "Remember that. Remember to love yourself. You are so much better and stronger than you think you are."

"Don't talk like that. It makes me think you aren't coming back. Bring my mother back to me, Gen. My love goes with you, and my love waits for your return. Be quick. Please."

"I will."

"And if my mother starts flirting with you again, tell her it's my turn. I'll see you tomorrow, early. Don't forget."

The Chalaine left reluctantly. As she opened the door, she turned to find Gen watching her intently and she nearly burst into tears. The best night of her life was ending, and she ached, fearing the greater bliss she longed for would never come.

CHAPTER 78 - PRISONER AND PILGRIMS

Mirelle gripped the bars of the prison wagon as it bounced along the uneven and newly repaired road up the canyon wall to the bridge at Echo Hold. So anxious was Athan to get the person who he thought was the Chalaine back to who he thought was Eldaloth that they had ridden through the night at great haste. Through the window on the left side of the cart, the rocky canyon wall slid by, and through the other window was a vertiginous and expansive view of the mountains in the late morning sunshine.

While Mirelle worried about what Athan and Mikkik would do to her once her true identity was revealed, she worried more for the Chalaine. They rode hard, not only to get back to Mikkik as expeditiously as possible, but to escape what Athan's soldiers considered a leaderless, marauding band of Uyumaak heading southwest toward their position. Mirelle overheard no reports about the size of the Uyumaak army, but Athan's soldiers numbered near six thousand, and they fled before it like a deer would from a wolf.

As she gazed upon the mountain scenery slipping by,

she concluded that the journey and her life quickly approached their ends. Only one event would bring her satisfaction, now—the moment that Athan found out that the woman in the cart was not the precious Chalaine he wished to present to Eldaloth to heal the wound Gen had inflicted upon him. Athan was dreadfully bad at enduring disappointment, and Mirelle couldn't think of a disappointment more stinging than being duped by the First Mother of Rhugoth on the most important mission of his life.

The road smoothed out as they crested the canyon and started across the enormous bridge. Mirelle smiled to see that the multinational force brought to fight at Echo Hold had all been marshaled to give the Chalaine a warm welcome back to the fort and to the embrace of her god. Trumpets blared and shouts were raised, and Mirelle played the part, waving out the barred windows as the soldiery applauded. Her real purpose, however, was to see if any of the Dark Guard she had placed within the Tolnorian ranks awaited her arrival. Captain Tolbrook had been among them, and if the Church hadn't ferreted him out, he would no doubt come to her defense, if he were able.

But the sea of faces was too vast and the window too small for her to search, so she settled back onto the pillows. Time was short. She would face death with dignity. To calm herself, she searched back through her memory for the pleasant times she always called upon to soothe her when life turned dark. Raising her daughter, ruling a kingdom, and her pathetic, desperate flirting with Gen all served to cheer her in her moment of need. *If only I could have convinced him to marry me!* she thought. Not winning Gen was her only real regret, besides not assassinating Chertanne when she had the chance.

The cart lurched to a halt, and the call to dismount and quarter the horses rang down the line. A large gate swung shut behind them, and Mirelle heard Athan's sharp voice outside the wagon.

"We must get her to him immediately!" he commanded. "Form a guard around me." The rear door of the wagon slid open, and a hurried but fawning Athan waited. "Lady Khairn, we must not delay. You may rest from your journey later, unless Eldaloth rewards you with the wonders of Erelinda first."

The voice-changing magic that Ethris had worked upon her had long since worn off, and Mirelle simply nodded and joined the Eldephaere guard that Athan had gathered to guard her. Their backs were to the keep of Echo Hold, rising square and high into the air. Before them the Hall of Echo Hold waited. It had been carved from the native rock, appearing as if two rectangular slabs of tan stone had leaned against one another and a recess had been chiseled away in the front. A short, fanning stairway led to a wide porch, three tall windows rising on the facade of the edifice. The doorway was shaped like a rectangle with a triangle on top, and new doors had recently been installed to replace those that had gone to rot.

The door swung open, and Mirelle frowned. The Church of the One had complete control of the structure, all the guards Eldephaere and all the attendants and administrators wearing the long robes and stoles of the Church. The interior of the keep bore rich appointments of maroon cloth and silver, no doubt brought to Echo Hold before the brief sham of a war they had fought.

One of the attendants approached. "We have prepared refreshment. . ."

"We have no time for refreshment," Athan said. "We must end Edaloth's pain immediately. Please inform him we are here with the Chalaine and await his pleasure."

The attendant slipped inside the interior double doors of the same size as the outer ones, returning a moment later and signaling them forward. Mirelle swallowed. She hadn't seen Mikkik before as her daughter had and was unsure of what to expect. As she entered, she nearly gasped. The Hall was empty save for a single, commanding figure sitting on a new throne of polished dark wood barely large enough to hold him. He wore a simple white robe and glowed with glory. Much taller than a man, he had upswept ears and deep, powerful eyes. All this majesty, however, was undermined by a slow trickle of golden blood dripping from the throne and onto the floor to pool before him, crusting around the edges. He was in pain, his face registering discomfort, anger, and an incontrovertible will. It scared her, and she could no longer blame Athan for his eagerness to please.

They bowed as they entered, the door swinging shut behind them. Only she, Athan, and two Eldephaere had entered and awaited Mikkik's pleasure. Torches added their light to narrow slits in the vertical walls. Above her, the two walls slanted upward to a point. Fresh wooden beams stretched across the top at regular intervals, three iron chandeliers hanging down. The candles were extinguished.

"Rise and approach," came the command, the rich voice echoing through the stony hall with power.

"Most Holy Eldaloth," Athan said, anxious and entreating, "I have brought to you the Chalaine. She will heal the wound and free you of pain."

They continued to approach, Mirelle trembling. Mikkik's searching gaze drilled through the veil, and he stood, wincing with the effort. A fresh stream of blood poured away from the throne. A sudden force ripped into her mind, and she staggered and fell, Mikkik rummaging through her memories with brutal ease before releasing her. She gasped, working to stand.

Athan stooped to help her up. "Are you. . ."

"You are deceived, Athan!" Mikkik boomed, returning to his throne and sitting heavily. "This is not the Chalaine. This is her mother."

"No!"

146

Still unsteady, Mirelle removed the heavy veil and threw it onto the floor. She drank in Athan's horrified reaction, his face draining to white before blooming to red again. He gritted his teeth and slapped her with every ounce of strength his diminutive frame possessed, bloodying her mouth and snapping her head back.

"You meddlesome woman! You will pay for your crimes!"

Mirelle wiped her mouth. "I don't think that is particularly fair, since we're all paying for yours."

"Where is she?" Athan asked. "Where is the Chalaine?"

"Let's see. I think you left her traveling south, being pursued by a large force of Mikkik's creatures. So nice of you to warn Lord Kildan they were coming. Oh, wait, you didn't because you wouldn't have cared if we all were slaughtered. What would Eldaloth say about your behavior?"

Athan's face reddened. "Eldaloth needs the Chalaine! Now! Where is she?"

Mikkik spoke. "She travels to Rhugoth and Mikmir. Mirelle hopes her daughter will pen a letter explaining that she believes I am not Eldaloth. The Ilch has deceived them most thoroughly. It is well that he is dead. The sorrow this woman holds for his death is so strong I almost pity her."

"She knew he was the Ilch and aided him anyway!" Athan reported. "She must be punished."

"Yes," Mikkik replied. "She has believed the Chalaine's Ilch-distorted version of the events on the bridge. It is the grossest deception. It could not be foreseen, Athan. You are to blame for nothing, but you are correct that this woman is guilty. She did not act blindly. She and the Mage Ethris knew who Gen was and ignored the warning of prophecy for their own ends. They have endangered the whole world, for while I bleed, I cannot protect my children as I have longed to do.

"Once this woman reigned in Rhugoth with much

power and skill, but she must be humbled, now. We must act quickly to make an example of her. Have her flogged and burned immediately, a notice sent to all nations that she is dead for her crimes against Ki'Hal. Ethris must suffer the same fate or he will work his poison upon the nations, and war will come again. But the Chalaine must be recovered so that I might undo the deceit that has been planted in her mind and speed her to her rest."

Mirelle stood tall, staring Athan down. "Is this the *merciful* Eldloth we have praised every day of our lives, Athan? If the Ilch has deceived me, shouldn't I be pitied rather than burned?"

Mikkik rose again. "What you did, you did with your eyes open in the daylight. What I do must be done, though I take no pleasure in it. You were a Queen. You know that examples must be made to maintain order in chaotic times. Mikkik's forces run rampant throughout the land, and I haven't enough strength to fight them while I languish here in a pool of my own blood! The traitors among your race must die, or the disease the Ilch has infected you with will spread."

"Will you kill my daughter, Mikkik? To keep the disease from spreading? It is she to whom Aldemar showed the vision of you slaying Eldaloth with a sword made from the blood of the Mikkik Dun who died at your command. It is she that will start the fire that will burn you, and by harming me, you will only make that fire hotter!"

Athan stepped forward. "She is right in her judgment of the Chalaine, Holy Eldaloth. I have seen the girl's heart. If we kill Mirelle—which I agree must be done—then the Chalaine will not aid us willingly. She was completely deceived by the Ilch almost to a greater degree than her mother. She will be angered beyond the power of reason to recover her if she knows her mother suffers."

"I can reclaim her, Athan," Mikkik said. "But she must come to me first. If we must delay this woman's death to secure the Chalaine, then let it be so."

"It is wisdom, for now. I will jail her. I will haste to Mikmir and bring the Holy Chalaine to you with as much speed as I can muster."

"I will not let you use me as bait, Athan," Mirelle hissed.

"You have no choice," Athan returned. "Guards! Bind her hand and foot and take her to the deepest cell. So she doesn't feel so alone, put with her a few of the friends she tried to sneak into Echo Hold before the war. I was ready for that one, Mirelle." To the guards he said, "Do not be over-generous with her food and water. Tell the outer guard to prepare the carriage. We depart for Mikmir immediately, and I will need the full help of the Council. Ethris travels with the Chalaine."

"I will smooth the road for you, my faithful servant," Mikkik said, and Mirelle wondered what he meant.

The two Eldephaere grabbed her roughly and pushed her forward, Athan striding out before them in as hurried a rush as he had when he entered. The guards led her back toward the keep, a fair number of Eldephaere sneering at her in disgust as they unlocked a door in a squat building nearby. They paused to bind her hands, and then forced her down a winding set of narrow stone steps into a haphazard catacomb with rough cells carved into the walls.

Dirty, wretched prisoners behind newly restored metal bars winced at the sudden light of the Eldephaere's torches. Mirelle scanned their hollow faces for anyone she knew, but only strangers stared back. Once they reached the last in the long line of cells, they unlocked the iron door and tossed her inside, the cramped cell not even as big as the closet in her luxurious room in Mikmir.

"You tie her legs, and I'll get her 'friends,'" one of the guards said.

As the other bound her ankles with rough cords, Mirelle tried to think why Athan would bestow the gift of company upon her when he clearly wished to strip everything else away. But when the other soldier returned, face grim and carrying an armful of severed heads, she finally knew the depth of Athan's cruel heart. With a sneer he threw them in and closed the door.

The light of the torch faded quickly. In its dwindling glow she saw the decaying face of Captain Tolbrook staring up at her in a rictus of pain, and she was thankful for the blessing of darkness and a place where weeping was a natural part of the chorus of despair all around her.

The sun had yet to rise as Gen walked softly down the hall toward the Chalaine's room. Maewen had relayed to Cadaen that Amos would accompany him on his journey, Cadaen informing her in return that he would leave at first light and brook no delays. Gen wouldn't be late and was itching to leave. The uncertainty of Mirelle's predicament tortured him all night, and, like Cadaen, his heart told him there wasn't a moment to lose. He quickened his steps, the old building creaking dreadfully with every footfall. When he rounded the corner to the hall where the Chalaine was quartered, Dason, groggy and a little bruised, was already looking in his direction.

"There you are!" her Protector said in an accusatory tone. "What were you doing with the Chalaine last night, and what did you do to me?"

Gen stopped. "Keep your voice down, man! People are sleeping. What the Chalaine and I discussed is none of your concern, and what I did to you was this."

And Gen did it again, incanting the same spell. Dason collapsed face first into the wall opposite him, skidding down until he was an uncomfortable lump on the floor. Gen stepped over him and opened the Chalaine's door quietly, entering the dark room where she still slept. The barest slivers of light from the predawn sky leaked through the shutters. The Chalaine was lying on her side, hair fanned out around her, face peaceful. As he sat on the bed, the wood squealed and she stirred.

"There you are," she said dreamily, taking his hand and pulling him in beside her and snuggling into him. "You are awfully forward."

"I must go," he said.

"Not yet."

He stroked her hair until her breathing slowed and deepened.

"I promise I'll come to you as quickly as I can," he whispered.

"I'll be waiting," she replied, still sounding as if she frolicked in a dream.

Gen leaned over and kissed her forehead and her cheek, her lips turning up in a smile.

As he stood to go, he used Trysmagic to create a thornless red rose and placed it on the bed next to her, drinking in her serene face before turning his own toward trouble. The trip, he hoped, would be short, as much because of his fear of leaving the Chalaine unprotected as for a desire to be near her again.

But he would not abandon Mirelle to torture and death. He stepped back out into the Hall and undid his spell on Dason, leaving before the man could recover. As Gen rounded the corner, Dason opened the Chalaine's door to check on her and the Chalaine told him to go away.

Cadaen waited in the kitchen. He had put aside his Dark Guard uniform in favor of a plain shirt and woolen pants and was hastily filling his bags with provisions from the larder. Gen tipped his hat to him and started stuffing his own bags.

"I ride fast," Cadaen said. "You get behind, I'm not slowing."

"I understand," Gen replied.

Their road would lead them northwest to the town of Embriss where a Portal to Tenswater would put them near the Portal that opened close to Echo Hold. Gen calculated a journey of three days to get to Echo Hold, worried they would not arrive soon enough. Gen knew enough of Athan's drive and temper to fear him, and with his own magic and the mandates of Mikkik, he was a force to be reckoned with.

At the worst, Athan would kill Mirelle outright, though Cadaen's brand only registered her physical discomfort for the moment. How long would Athan delay her death? Gen thought the man had enough theatricality to stage something public and brutal to act as a reminder to everyone not to cross the Church. That Athan thought Eldaloth would actually condone the actions he had taken to protect Chertanne and would likely take to punish Mirelle made Gen wonder if Athan thought of Eldaloth at all or only his own pride.

Gen and Cadaen galloped out of the manor on horses generously provided by Geoff. The morning skies were high and gray, but by midday they cleared. Gen feared that Cadaen would recognize him on closer acquaintance, but the old faithful soldier was completely absorbed in his own thoughts and the mission at hand. Gen rode behind him at a discrete distance anyway. As Cadaen promised, they rode hard, the animals laboring and frothing under the haste of their passing. This gave Gen the chance to use another trick of Mynmagic that the Millim Eri had bestowed upon him: speaking with animals. The animals expectedly had little to say, but he found he could implant simple ideas such as urgency and need. Combined with the restorative touch of Duammagic to revive the horses' flagging energy, they crossed through the beautiful, winding hills and valleys with such speed that they arrived in Embriss just before midday, hours before they had intended.

Their satisfaction at an early arrival was immediately

crushed. A column of people stretched out of the town, a mismatched array of the young and old, rich and poor. The poor carried bags, while others rode in simple farm carts laden with their equipage. The rich leaned out of carriages to see how far back they were from the city gates. The Eldephaere—not Rhugothian soldiers—patrolled the line, keeping order.

What are they doing in Rhugoth? he wondered.

"Excuse me," Cadaen asked a plump man with similarly sized wife and children, "is there a festival?"

"No, my good man!" he answered brightly. "We all make for the Portal and Tenswater! We travel to see Echo Hold and the place where the last battle was fought!"

Cadaen swore. "It will take hours to get to the Portal!"

"Here, yes," the merchant replied. "In Tenswater they say it can take a couple of days. Are you well, friend?"

Cadaen didn't answer, angry face staring at the line as if deciding whether or not to kill them all. "I cannot delay!"

"We've all got to wait our turn!" the merchant said, voice more subdued as Cadaen's emotion rose. "The Guild doesn't play favorites."

"We'll see about that!"

Cadaen rode off at a fair clip toward the town, mood souring as they entered within the gates and found Embriss a chaotic, packed mess of Rhugothians trying to reach the Portal or make money off of those who did. Gen thought the town had probably been pleasant once, but the reek of smoke and beer and sweat and garbage, combined with the constant roar of street hawkers and crying children, turned Embriss into something like the Damned Quarter, only with nicer buildings.

The long line of travelers disappeared into the wide, arched entry of a tall domed building in the middle of town, the blue glow of the Portal illuminating the faces of those relieved to at least be close. Those selling drink and food were doubly thick along the line, and Cadaen's face took on a determined expression that Gen figured meant that violence was about to ensue.

"Cadaen!" Gen yelled to pull him out of his dark scheming.

He turned toward Gen, face really considering him for the first time. Gen eased his horse closer so they could talk above the din.

"Before you start threatening people, let me see if I can pay someone to take their place at the front," he said.

"Do you have money?" he asked. "I have none."

"I think I've got enough. Wait here."

They dismounted, and Gen scanned the line for a likely prospect for his scheme. An impoverished farmer and his dirty brood seemed just the sort he needed. Gen approached and doffed his hat.

"Good day, sir," he said.

"Don't want nothin'," the farmer replied curtly.

"I'm not selling. I'm buying. I'll give you three gold pieces for your place in line."

Suspicious, disbelieving eyes regarded him, measuring him up. "You ain't got it."

Gen reached inside his jacket and formed the money in his hand using Trysmagic, extending it outward for the farmer to examine. "Think what you could do with it! Shoes, food, tools. A nice bonnet for the missus."

The farmer extended his hand and Gen pulled the money back.

"Gotta see if it's real!"

Gen took a piece and handed it to him. The farmer bit into the soft metal to test it and then examined it by closing one eye and squinting at it with the other.

"Deal."

Gen motioned Cadaen over, and, after relinquishing the money, they found themselves twelfth in line behind an old farm cart crawling with cats and children.

"You got enough to do the same in Tenswater?" asked a

considerably more relaxed Cadaen.

"It'll cost more, I'm sure," Gen answered. "But I'm pretty good at persuading people when I wish. Oh no."

Looking down the line, Gen caught the farmer and his family chatting with a brace of Eldephaere and pointing in their direction. Cadaen followed his gaze and shook his head at the Church soldiers.

"Creepy little emasculated buggers!"

"Be calm or they'll get nervous," Gen counseled. "Just let me do the talking."

The two Church soldiers regarded them warily, and Gen figured they couldn't miss Cadaen's impressive physique and the sword strapped to his horse. And, while Gen's outfit didn't scream *soldier*, a trained eye would no doubt pick out the posture and musculature of a man familiar with a fight. The soldiers, both of them tall and thin, wore the conical helmets and blue cloaks of their order, hands on the hilts of their swords.

"It is illegal to buy a place in line," one of the soldiers said. "You'll need to head to the rear of the line or depart the town entirely."

Gen decided to see just how much of a hassle the two were willing to go through to pursue justice for a petty crime.

"We didn't buy a place in line," Gen said, acting offended.

"The farmer says you did," the Eldephaere returned.

"I did no such thing," Gen lied.

"He showed me the gold you paid him," the Eldephaere retorted. "No farmer would have that much gold!"

"Do either of us look like someone who would have that much gold?"

The soldier opened his mouth and shut it. A point won.

He took another tack. "And I don't remember seeing you at this point of the line, either."

Gen shrugged. "I can hardly be responsible for what you

remember. But look, the farmer there can clear up this entire matter. Just go fetch him, and we'll have this resolved in no time."

The farmer was fifty yards away, and they were now seventh in line, nearly to the opening of the Portal building. The guard, a little flustered, finally managed to gather enough sense to do what Gen feared he would.

"Well, we'll just ask the people behind you, then!"

The person directly behind them was an old, bureaucratic-looking fellow who just wanted to be left alone. Gen caught his eye.

"Excuse me sir," the guard said, voice exuding confidence now that he had finally found the trump card. "Have these two men been in front of you the whole time?"

Gen created a gold piece and flashed it at the man surreptitiously. The fellow's eyebrows raised.

"Yes," he said. "The whole time."

"Are you sure?"

"Positively."

The guards looked back at Gen and he folded his arms. "There. What further evidence do you need? If you hurry, you might catch that farmer. . ."

The two guards scowled and left, grumbling under their breath. Gen waited until they disappeared into the crowd before flipping the gold piece to their benefactor. "Thank you, sir."

The Portal enclosure had no windows save for a circular opening in the very top. The brilliant blue of the shimmering Portal provided ample illumination, the Portal Mage sitting cross-legged on a decorative rug in meditative concentration to keep the Portal open for long periods of time. Another man in the robes of Portal Guild sat at a table, recording the names of everyone who passed through in a ledger, and two Eldephaere were at attention on the edges of the Portal. Gen and Cadaen both lied about their names and their purpose, but if there were any suspicions, the frantic, busy pace of the day kept anyone from acting on them.

They led the horses through the Portal, emerging into a dry, warm day in Tenswater.

"Unbelievable," Cadaen said, stunned by what he saw.

While Embriss teemed with people, Tenswater choked on them. The press of traffic along the streets almost prevented movement. Eldephaere walked among the throng in large numbers, trying to keep the irritated crowd from brawling and stampeding. As it was, shoves and curses abounded. As in Embriss, merchants took advantage of the influx of patrons by accosting passers-by and inflating their prices, and every inn or tavern seemed fit to burst. Some people encamped in alleys and parks, and from what Gen could overhear, the entire mass of humanity was bound for Echo Hold.

While they had expected a single column making for the Portal entry, instead the ebb and flow of the crowd went in every direction. After some inquiries they found that the Church had instituted a system to control the numbers making for the Portal. Every pilgrim had a mark stained on the back of his hand, a different mark for each day. The current mark was for four days out.

"Can we forge them?" Cadaen asked.

"I made some discreet inquiries," Gen answered. "They apparently have a way to separate the fakes when you get to the Portal. No one knows exactly how they do it."

"We've got to try. I am not waiting four days."

"Agreed. As you may have heard, I have some talent with Duammagic. I may be able to use it to aid us here, but first we need to get a look at what we need to mimic."

It took them a solid hour to work their way through the crowd to the other end of Tenswater where the line of people waiting for the Portal queued. The Portal to Echo Hold waited below ground. Workers had dug a vertical hole downward, a spiraling ramp descending into the pit. The line waiting to enter the hole stretched a quarter mile back and was moving slowly. The Eldephaere patrolled thickly, and Gen thought better of trying to buy his way to the front of the line again.

Thankfully, those in the line kept staring at the stained marks on the backs of their hands, done in a reddish ink. Gen used his magical gifts to discolor the skin and create the mark on his and Cadaen's hands just before the Eldephaere came to check them when they joined the end of the line.

While they waited, Gen availed himself of the exorbitantly priced services of a hay cart offering provision and drink for the horses.

"Any news from Echo Hold?" Gen asked as the thin farmer pulled hay out of the wagon.

"Those coming back say it's as packed as a barn on a wedding. Eldaloth's made an open invitation to the nobles and Warlords from any country to let them pass to Erelinda like Chertanne did. Biggest rumor, though, is that they got the First Mother on trial before Eldaloth himself. They say they'll probably execute her. Had lots of nobles show up today wanting to attend that, but I doubt any of them will make it through in time."

Gen glanced at Cadaen, whose smoldering, far off look portended trouble. Despite the ridiculous amount he had already paid, Gen tossed the farmer a silver piece before turning back to his distressed friend.

"Once we get through the Portal, it will still be two days' travel to Echo Hold," Cadaen lamented. "It will be too late."

"You don't know that," Gen consoled. "We'll ride quickly, just as before. I've been to Echo Hold, and I know a way we can bypass the crowd and get in without scrutiny. Keep faith, Cadaen. We haven't lost yet."

The words calmed him, but the irritating, slow grind of

the line only increased their anxiety. By the time they had descended the spiral ramp to the bottom, evening had fallen.

As in Embriss, the Portal Mage sat on a rug on the ground while another member of the Guild recorded names. A contingent of ten Eldephaere waited around the Portal, and the rumors on the street proved true. Every person passing before the Portal was forced to stick a stained hand into a bucket and have it examined by the Eldephaere. Due to the odd lighting, Gen couldn't figure out what was happening after they dipped it in. To read the mind of the soldier performing the check would take physical contact, and without knowing what the final result of the hand-dipping needed to be, he couldn't implant a suggestion, either.

"What do we do?" Cadaen asked.

"We ride," Gen answered. "If we're not fast enough, we might find ourselves riding half a horse."

As they neared the mark-checking station, they mounted their horses, Cadaen in the lead.

"Get down off there!" one of the guards growled.

"Yah!"

Like arrows sprung from the bow, they shot into the blue field before them. Curses erupted around them, and the guards drew steel. Half a moment later they emerged into a valley north of Echo Hold, a line of camp fires and lanterns stretching before them. Their pace prevented maneuvering, and they collided with a pack of riders that had gone through just before them. Horses reared and people fell, the dust churning in the firelight as the animals bumped and collided with one another. Gen and Cadaen pulled their horses around and bolted out into the night just as the Eldephaere from the other side of the Portal burst through, yelling at anyone who would listen to detain them.

Spurs to flanks, Gen and Cadaen fled into the night without a glance back.

CHAPTER 79 - A SMALL BEGINNING

By the time the Chalaine awoke, the sun streamed through the shutters of the single window in her room. The night's sleep felt luxurious and deep, her dreams vibrant and more inappropriate than ever. This morning, however, they didn't seem quite so inappropriate. They were the promise of a closeness to come, and she smiled, half wishing the rose Gen had left on the pillow next to her was instead the man who had left it.

One day, she thought. *One day soon.*

She and the army would leave for Mikmir after lunch, though she wanted to avoid the bustle evident in the creaking and rumbling throughout the house. While in her room, she could wrap herself in a cocoon that only consisted of her and Gen. The minute she stepped out the door, Mikkik, Dason, and duty would come calling, and the world would barrel forward in the frantic haste of purpose again. She had spent the whole of her young life worried about the expansive needs of the world, but since Gen's return her anxieties collapsed into a space that only admitted two.

But her mother's plight revived her to a sense of purpose, although she feared that the letter she intended to write and publish to the world would harm rather than help Mirelle. The gnawing worry pulled her from the sheets and back into life, and she put her feet on the floor. The door cracked as she rose, but Gerand's voice rather than Dason's greeted her.

"Shall I call for the maid?"

"Yes, please."

Fenna came instead of the maid, waddling into the room with a worn face. "This baby must come soon," she groaned. "Do the Chalaines have any magic that might convince a baby that it is time to make the journey?"

"I'm afraid not, Fenna."

"Does it hurt? Having the baby, I mean."

"It is . . . intense," the Chalaine answered, not really wishing to remember those hours of her life. "But you'll do fine. Just don't let Geoff be anywhere nearby in case you say something you might regret."

"So I saw Dason at breakfast this morning," Fenna said as she brushed the Chalaine's hair. "He seemed quite cross and appears as if he'd been in a fist fight with a Gagon. I hope you weren't cruel to him last night. Has he made his intentions known?"

The Chalaine sighed. "No. He is a gentleman and probably knows I would not think of courting while my mother . . . while my mother is away. We must return to Mikmir and home."

"I am sure Mirelle will not tarry to counsel with Athan long and will join you as soon as she can," Fenna consoled, "Although I have heard some strange rumors."

"Such as?"

"We had food brought in through Portal Gate, and the merchant told my cook that a whole host of Church soldiers had passed through there on their way to Mikmir. I suppose, though, that they would have been looking for you."

"Very likely," the Chalaine answered.

"Were you very lost?"

"We were in a trackless wilderness running for our very lives."

"Oh! But look! A rose!" Fenna said, abandoning the Chalaine's hair and retrieving it. "So! Dason perhaps expressed his affectionate intentions after all, even if he didn't use words! And look! It is thornless. It doesn't even look like it grew with thorns. There are no scars where they have been cut off. I wonder where he got such a variety? Not in my gardens. I shall have to ask him."

The Chalaine closed her eyes to settle her irritation. "He knows nothing of it. He didn't give it to me."

"Really!" Fenna plopped down beside her and started in on the hair again. "Then who?"

"A secret admirer. It was on my bed when I returned last night," she lied. It was toilsome to bottle up the love she wanted to shout from the tallest tower.

Not much longer.

"Then it was likely Dason," Fenna said. "I am so excited! I can't wait for the wedding! Will you have it in Mikmir or in Tolnor?"

"Fenna, enough!" the Chalaine said, trying to insert a friendly tone into a plea that proceeded from frustration.

Lady Blackshire finally did relent, though at breakfast, she cornered a grumpy Dason, and the two spoke at length. By the time they finished, Dason was beaming again and the Chalaine had lost her appetite. He resumed his duties as Gerand took the opportunity to get a few hours of sleep before they departed. Lord Kildan left with his Tolnorian soldiers first, the Duke bidding his sons farewell and promising to return to Mikmir as soon as he could to join in council.

The Chalaine pulled Maewen, Ethris, and General Harband aside after their departure and relayed Fenna's intelligence about the Church soldiers marching on Mikmir.

"I feared as much," Ethris said. "If Athan is looking for you, he knows you will make for Mikmir and will use every means to prevent you from getting inside. The Church is likely placing members of the Council of Padras in leadership positions, and Mikmir is key to controlling the nations. This may get very difficult, Chalaine. It may be up to you to rally your countrymen to take back Mikmir if the Church won't quit the city."

She said, "My mother would be better equipped. . ."

Ethris took her by the shoulders. "Your mother is a prisoner now, to save you. It falls to you now to fill her place."

"But the people rejoice! They won't believe me!"

"They will believe you. They worship you and will come to your aid if you can speak with conviction. You must wake them from this dream and bring them into the nightmare before Mikkik accomplishes his purpose."

"Where do I start?" she asked.

"You start here with Lord and Lady Blackshire. Their levy of soldiers is small, but with the Tolnorians marching for their own country, we need to reinforce. The Church armies were never very big alone, and if the armies of the nations are returning home or scouring the wilderness to fight the Uyumaak, then we may be able to muster a force big enough to put the Eldephaere to flight."

The Chalaine looked sideways at the jovial Geoff with his expectant wife, her longtime friend. Fenna placed a hand on the top of her protruding baby, waiting to feel a kick. Their happiness and celebration was a lie, or, as Ethris said, a dream. The Chalaine's stomach clenched. No one knew better than she that a warm, comfortable dream was often much preferable to the cold, hard truth.

"Will you stand with me?" she asked Ethris. "My word alone won't be sufficient."

"I will, child. You may find you have more iron in you

than you think."

Heart heavy and hands clammy, the Chalaine walked to the head of the table where Lord Geoff of Blackshire waited.

Be like mother, she told herself.

"Lord Blackshire," she said. "Ethris and I need to have a word with you and your wife."

"But are you sure, Lady Alumira?" Geoff said, face stunned. So far, he was the only one that had remembered to use her new name. They sat in his study, which was dusty from disuse. "I can scarce believe it! It is the most awful thing in the world!"

"It is true," she replied, finding that telling the tale out loud actually calmed her nerves. "What his purpose is now, I cannot say, but he has deceived the entire world. He played on the prophecy and turned it to his own ends. We are in grave danger, and I must get control of Mikmir to spread the word to a world that will not want to hear it."

"So Gen *was* the Ilch as the stories said," Fenna said, "but he turned away from his foreordained path out of love for you! And then to be killed! How he must have suffered."

"Yes," the Chalaine said. "But I do not tell you this merely for your information. I need provision for the men we have and what soldiers you can spare."

Geoff stood. "But of course you shall have what you need. I . . . I just can't fathom it. It did all sound a bit too easily done, and this kind of nefarious trickery does fit with all the tales told of Mikkik during the Wars. Thank you, Lady Alumira, for enlightening us. And I sorrow for your loss. Gen was every inch a man to be admired."

"Yes, he is," the Chalaine said before she realized her

mistake. "Was," she corrected hastily. "I thank you for your support. We will travel and try to gather men from the Regents as we go, though I fear that when the Church finds out we are coming, they may send soldiers for us directly."

"More likely they will stay fortified within Mikmir's walls," Ethris opined.

Maewen, who had insisted on coming, walked out of the corner. "I will go find Falael, who is no doubt enjoying the living trees near here. I will send him north to scout. I will remain with the Chalaine."

"Very good," Ethris said. "Let's get General Harband and get the men moving. We should stop in Embriss to speak with Regent Feldebrinne and then on to Kitmere to visit Regent Torunne. Having his nephew Volney with us should help."

They left the study, and the Chalaine breathed a sigh of relief.

Ethris beamed at her, eyes soft. "Well done, Lady Alumira. It will be hard for me to get used to calling you that."

"Call me whatever you like," she said. "You've earned it. Do you think the others will be as easy to convince?"

Ethris shook his head. "No. They have more at stake in angering the Church, but do not fear! You can actually be quite persuasive when you wish. And if we fail, we will move on to the next and the next until we have enough men behind us to make Athan think twice about facing us."

In order to allow Geoff time to muster his men and gather provisions, they delayed a day. During the night, Fenna at last had her baby. The Chalaine saw her through the difficult moments of labor and rejoiced with her when a baby girl howled her first cries into the night. Geoff already had a song at the ready—he had previously prepared one for a boy and one for a girl—and father and mother both laughed and wept at the wonder of it all. By the time the Chalaine sought her room and her bed, it was late.

"I will have a son as my first child," Dason said as they walked the hall.

"How do you know?" the Chalaine asked.

"I just know. Don't you feel the same?" he asked, words pregnant with meaning.

"Good night, Dason," she said as she opened the door to her room and shut it more loudly than she intended.

None of the candles in her room were lit, and the fire smoldered, extinguished in the hearth. Something about the room felt wrong, a smell or a change in the way she felt. She turned back to the door to open it, but her body would no longer move at her command. She opened her mouth to scream for help, but nothing would come. Something passed in front of the shuttered window, a dark shadow growing larger as it approached her, and then blackness enveloped her like a dark wing.

"Lady Alumira!"

The Chalaine opened her eyes and rolled over. It was still night, and she was surprised to find herself in her bed fully clothed and facedown as if she had been dropped there. She remembered coming into the room, but nothing after.

"What happened, Gerand?"

"You were gone! Taken somewhere, as far as we know. We all rode away to find you, but Ethris held us back, saying that what waited was too powerful for us to deal with. He wanted to go on alone, but Dason refused to stay behind. They disappeared over a hill, and we all sensed that you had returned here a short while later. I've just ridden in. What happened to you?"

"I . . . I can't remember. I came into the room and then I woke up here."

The Chalaine worked at her mind to try to unlock the memory, but she couldn't tease out what had happened in the missing interval. Long minutes passed, the night deepening as they waited for Dason and Ethris. She went to visit Fenna, who was feeding her baby. Her worn, sleepy face was troubled, and after she finished nursing, the Chalaine left to let her sleep. Pacing about the house— Gerand following behind her—was all the Chalaine could think to do.

A few hours before dawn, the front door swung open hard and everything turned to commotion. Men dressed in the livery of Blackshire hauled a body through the door. It was an unconscious Dason, his face pale and eyes closed. Charred holes were blasted in his uniform, the skin black and cracked underneath. A burned gash ran aslant down his face.

"He's barely alive, Lady Alumira," one of the soldiers said as Geoff burst into the room followed by Fenna. "We fished two bodies out of the water. Both of them were boiled alive by the looks of it. I think one of them is the Mage."

"Ethris?" Geoff exclaimed.

"We think so, Milord," the soldier replied as they placed Dason on the couch. "The clothes were his, anyway. Never seen the other one."

The Chalaine's heart sank. What had happened? She crossed to Dason as more people crowded into the room only to be dismissed by Geoff. Grabbing his hand, she crouched beside her injured Protector and concentrated. Charred wounds gaped all over his torso and arms. With her skill in healing, it took little to repair them, knitting the skin back together and restoring his handsome face so that nothing marred his visage. She broke contact and he stirred, sitting upright slowly as his mind cleared.

"Dason?" the Chalaine said, trying to focus his attention.

"Your Ladyship," he said reverently, standing and

pulling her into an awkward hug in front of everyone. "I had thought you lost. You were just lying there in the grass as if you were dead! Thank Eldaloth you are alive! I have proved myself to you now and atoned for my failure in Rhugoth. I can stand as a man before you. You are my love and my life, and I will never part from you!"

She pulled away gently but was unable to escape his adoring gaze or the amused smiles of those in the room. "What happened, Dason? I have no memory of what happened to me this night. Is Ethris dead?"

Dason reached for her hand. "I do not know. We all felt that you were moving away from Blackshire at great speed and gave chase. Ethris came with us, fearing that some sorcery was involved. We felt you stop your forward progress as we rode west into the hills. But Ethris felt something, something he said was powerful enough that swords would be of no use. He ordered us to stay behind, but *I* didn't. I could not be detained, though the *others* of the Dark Guard were more than happy to obey orders." He cast a meaningful glance at Gerand.

"So, abandoned by my brothers in arms, Ethris and I rode alone through the hills at great hazard to recover you. We crested a hill where a pond was nestled in a depression, and there we saw you lying in the grass next to an old woman. Ethris warned me that this was the Ash Witch and that I should return, but my heart wouldn't let me. That love which I have always had for you, Chalaine, prodded me onward. I could not let the hope of all my future prospects remain in the power of that evil woman.

"We rode forward to confront her. She simply waited, and Ethris was incanting, probably some protection. But my horse suddenly slowed and then fell over. Ethris rode on without me, but undeterred I drew my sword and charged forward, though the distance was great. Ethris stopped before the Ash Witch and they appeared to bandy words, but a tentacle of water rose from the pond, encircled him, and pulled him down into the depths. A great show of light and disruption flared in the water as if Ethris struggled against some unseen foe in its depths.

"The Ash Witch stood and watched until Ethris rose to the top of the water. From my position, I could not tell who it was, but when a bald head emerged, I knew Ethris had won the contest. My heart soared for joy, but the Ash Witch called down a mighty column of fire that set the pond to boiling. And . . . and I think Ethris succumbed.

"I understood, then, the Witch's terrible power, but my Chalaine waited, unconscious and unprotected on the grass, and I would not stop even if death were the price. Alone and friendless I charged forward, raising my sword to strike down the Witch, but a great blast of lightning lanced through me and I fell, not ten feet from where the Chalaine lay. I stretched my hand toward her at the last, but my deep wounds overcame my strength. But as I faded, I knew that the love in my heart would keep my body alive until my Lady could heal me, and it was as I knew it would be. All I ask now is a small locket of your hair as a token to mark my deeds, though I soon hope it will be within my power to ask much more."

"I shall fetch a knife!" Fenna said with a wink to the Chalaine.

"There is no need," Dason said, pulling one from his boot.

"Dason," the Chalaine said, "this is not the time! Ethris is dead, and we are in grave peril."

"It will just take a moment, Chalaine," he said, reaching out and grasping a strand of her hair that curled beneath the veil. The Chalaine gritted her teeth as he performed the act.

"I am Lady Alumira, now, Dason," she said firmly. "And I must see the bodies. I must know. You take your rest. I will have Gerand with me on this errand."

She didn't bother to turn around to see if her coldness

had stung him, asking the soldiers that had carried him in earlier to show her and Gerand where they had placed the bodies. The soldiers led them to the small Chapel where she and Gen had enjoyed their first open expressions of love for one another. Those memories seemed ages behind her, and she wanted their renewal. The lamps of the Chapel were lit, and a Pureman stood as they entered.

"I've been preparing the bodies, Milady," he said. "I am sorry for your loss. Ethris was a powerful man. I would advise you against seeing them. It is unpleasant."

"I will see them," she said, feeling numb.

The closer she came, the more her stomach turned. Both men were wrapped in white linen, their faces bloated and burned almost beyond recognition. While one corpse she could not identify, the other was unmistakable. Ethris had been killed in a trap set by his own mother, not that Ethris had ever hinted that he regarded her with any affection.

"I will leave you with him for a moment," the Pureman said.

"Wait outside," the Chalaine ordered Geoff's men. "Gerand, stay with me."

She stared at the grotesque body in disbelief. It was as if she was looking out a window, and a mountain that had always been there had crumbled. Of all the people she had known in her life, Ethris had always seemed the most indestructible. Even when he had been missing after the caravan had been destroyed, she never doubted that they would find him again. With Ethris dead, her mother missing, and Gen gone, she felt utterly alone. The foundations of her life were falling, and she struggled to balance. She could rely on no one but herself. While her feelings should have focused on the loss she had suffered, she instead felt a weight pressing down upon her.

"The passing of a legend," Gerand said reverently. "Dark times, indeed."

"What am I to do, Gerand?"

"Your duty, Lady Alumira," he said. "It is a very Tolnorian thing to say, I know, but he set you on a path before he died, and it seems wise to walk it."

"But now I walk it alone without his wisdom. I wish my mother were here."

Gerand nodded. "I wish Cadaen and his companion success. I pray for it daily."

"There is something I wish to share with you, Gerand. I hope you do not consider it a burden," she said. "But it is a secret, and a deep one at that. I have carried it nearly alone for some time, but I feel to tell you now. Will you hear it?"

"You have my word as your Protector and a Tolnorian," he said, "though if your secret is that you do not love my brother as he hopes you do, I believe that I know it."

"You can see that?" she said.

"Yes. My brother is a sword fighter to be feared, but he is also a romantic fool. I'm afraid he will likely persist in pursuing you even if you rebuff him," Gerand answered. "You may actually have to marry someone else before he gives up."

"That is not the secret, but it is related, in a way," She exhaled. Telling someone else was a horrible risk, but she needed support. "Gen is alive."

"Yes, he is," Gerand said.

"But . . . when did you know? How?"

Gerand smiled. "I had him treat a wound I had sustained. He might have thought the dark would aid him in concealing his identity, but it actually helped expose him. His voice, the way he moved, his profile, his mysterious appearance, all of it pointed to him. I was still hesitant to believe until I saw him and Maewen standing around chatting in Elvish like they always did. Unmistakable. You should take heart. If any man can get your mother free from Athan, it is Gen. It is him you love, is it not?"

"Yes," she answered, stunned by Gerand's

perceptiveness.

"You always did seem to have a bond beyond Chalaine and Protector. How he returned to life must be quite a tale," he added. "But why did you wish to tell me this?"

"First, so you would not think me unnecessarily cruel to your brother. Second, because—besides Maewen—I am the only one that knows. He is alone, and he needs the support of his former companions. He carries a great weight, as I do now. Can you support him? You don't believe he was secretly a traitor for Mikkik, do you?"

"Mikkik is crafty, but not stupid. If he were clever enough to move one of his agents into such an intimate position within the inner circle of prophecy, I'm sure he would have struck before the wedding even took place. While Athan may be confused, Gen acting under Mikkik's orders makes no sense. And of course, I will support Gen. I thought his return some plan or device of your mother's or Ethris's and didn't wish to interfere."

"No," she said. "He came of his own accord. You can't imagine my joy. Or perhaps you can. I'm sure your thoughts of Mena have given you a hope to cling to during these strange times."

"Of course," Gerand said, "although I am sorry to think that she is at home rejoicing in the false salvation of the world, deceived like everyone else. I dread having to break the news to her that the world is worse off than ever before."

The Chalaine regarded the corspes before her. "I know. I have to go tell all of Ki'Hal the same. It's going to be hard without Ethris. People feared and respected him. It will be easy for them to dismiss me as a silly girl who has been tricked by the Ilch."

"My father says that it is hard to respect a man without a sword or a woman without a will. If you really believe that Mikkik has stolen Eldaloth's name, and if you really have a fire in your heart to do something about it, the Regents will

173

respond."

"I hope so. We bury Ethris tomorrow, and then we march to speak with Regent Feldebrinne."

"There you are, *my* lady," Dason said from behind them.

The Chalaine closed her eyes for a moment to gather herself before turning around. "I thought I had ordered you to bed, Dason."

He had donned the green and black uniform of Blackshire and appeared to have bathed, his dark hair combed back and face scrubbed clean.

He stepped forward, face aglow. "I found that the excitement of this evening's events have quite overcome my need to sleep. I felt that I should be with you to console your heart during this most difficult of losses." He turned to Gerand. "I dismiss you, little brother."

"He will remain with us," the Chalaine said, a sudden idea striking her. "I wish to maintain a double guard about me. The dangers have multiplied, and without Ethris, I feel especially vulnerable."

Dason frowned, disappointed. "Well, I had hoped for a few moments to speak with you about something in particular concerning a future, desirable event."

"I have just lost one of my most trusted advisers, Dason. I find I am not in the mood for conversation at all. I must return to my quarters and get what rest I can. The night is nearly spent, and a journey awaits us tomorrow."

"Surely we must delay another day!" Dason importuned.

"I cannot wait anymore," the Chalaine said. "To honor Ethris, I must be bold. We ride tomorrow. I have no other object in view but the dethroning of Mikkik. Any events desirable or undesirable must be put aside until then."

Unless Gen wants to marry me, in which case I'll set Mikkik aside for a while, she thought, taking some cruel satisfaction at watching the light in Dason's eyes go out. She had clearly let his presumptions go too far. Out of respect she would try to spare his feelings as much as possible, but if Gerand was right, she would likely have to rip his heart out and feed it to a dog before he would believe her professions of disinterest and even disgust.

The brothers accompanied her back to her room, and when she entered and shut the door, she was surprised to find Fenna there nursing her baby. Lady Blackshire's eyes gleamed with anticipatory light.

"So, when is the wedding?" she said. "I've so wanted to go back to Mikmir! I can't wait. He is such a delicious man!"

"There will be no wedding, Fenna."

"But, he asked you, didn't he? How could you refuse him after his gallantry in your behalf this night?"

"You mean when he courageously ignored the instructions from a man more wise and powerful than he was and got himself nearly killed?"

"Chalaine! That is unkind!"

"My name is Lady Alumira now, Fenna," the Chalaine said evenly. "He did not ask, and I will not be drawn into romance and courtship during this time. The last weeks have been ones of toil and hardship. We are not at court during sunny, carefree days. There are dangers and horrors to fight and plans to be laid, and I must do it. I need no distractions from Dason or anyone else."

Fenna appeared on the verge of tears. "What has happened to you, Cha . . . Lady Alumira?"

"I've had to grow up, Fenna," she replied, softening her tone. "I am sorry if I was sharp just now. I know you mean well, but my heart is sealed. Get some rest, Fenna. Starting tomorrow, everything must change."

Chapter 80 - Sword of the Chalaine

The Chalaine found her brief sleep fleeting and uneven, but when she rose an hour after dawn, she didn't feel tired. Her mind buzzed with the arguments she must make in Embriss two days ride away, and she turned them over in her head, trying to hone them into something irresistibly persuasive. The only direct evidence of Mikkik's treachery would come from her experiences, but Ethris's arguments had helped show her that other circumstances would help in confirmation. The ease of the battle of Echo Hold, the unreasonable assumption that Gen had acted under Mikkik's orders, and even Ethris's own death suggested Mikkik's hand.

The smells of broiled pig and sweet porridge wafted up to her room, though the savory odors failed to induce hunger in her twisting stomach. She pried open the shutters. Outside, a gentle morning drizzle saturated the dazzling greens and reds and purples of the flowers and trees around the Blackshire Manor, though the light clouds and a brisk, fragrant breeze promised change.

The door cracked. "Shall I call for the maid?" Gerand

asked.

"No thank you, Gerand," she replied. "I will fend for myself this morning."

She brushed her hair and dressed, wondering if Gen had reached Echo Hold yet. If fortune had favored them, her mother might soon be free—or the both of them dead. The Chalaine tried to shove this gnawing worry away. Her mother had always tried to instruct her not to fret over things she could not control, but she had always found the notion a little strange. What one couldn't control was precisely what demanded worry.

Their party for the trip had shrunk to Maewen, Dason, Volney, Gerand, General Harband, and around five hundred soldiers. While not a formidable force, it couldn't easily be ignored, either. Maewen greeted her outside the dining room where she had packed her sparse provisions.

"Any word from Falael?" the Chalaine asked.

"Not yet," Maewen said. "It is hard to say when he will return. I offer my condolences for Ethris. His loss is a fell blow, indeed. I wish Amos were here now."

"So do I," the Chalaine agreed.

"It is my counsel that we stay off the road as much as possible," Maewen said. "We must move about unexpectedly to avoid a trap."

General Harband entered, his appearance as fierce and discomfiting as always.

"I will get the men up and ready to march," he said. "I hunger for an opportunity to bash in the heads of a few Church boys, creepy little geldings that they are."

The Chalaine smiled at the idea of someone as fearsome as General Harband possessing such a sentiment. She said, "I would like to leave within the hour. Two hours at the most."

He nodded and left, and the Chalaine went into the dining room to find Fenna and Dason talking in the corner again, and she groaned within herself. Volney and Geoff stood as she entered and she asked them to sit. Dason cast longing, hurtful looks in her direction and she ignored him pointedly. Gerand stood calmly behind her, and she wondered if his older brother's behavior shamed or amused him.

The anemic conversation did little to cheer the meal, but while they ate, a servant entered. "Lord Blackshire, there are three Puremen here who carry a message to you from the north and wish to dine with you."

"Let them in," Geoff said. "Illisa! We need three more plates," he shouted back to the kitchen.

Everyone turned as the three Puremen entered, and as soon as they crossed the threshold of the kitchen everyone jumped away from the table as swords were drawn. Padra Athan, Padra Nolan, and Padra Wolfram stood before them, Athan stretching out his hands in a placating gesture.

"We wish to talk and to eat," Athan said. "Nothing more. This does not need to end in bloodshed."

The Chalaine waved the weapons down, fighting to control her fear. Gradually the room relaxed, a nervous Illisa placing the three plates on an unused side of the table and retreating hastily back to the kitchen. The three Padras sat, and for several minutes they did nothing but eat their food while the rest of the company nibbled at theirs and watched them.

"How did you find me?" the Chalaine asked.

Athan threw her a disappointed look. "It was clear your army made for Rhugoth. It is really quite obvious that you would seek to rest and recover under the roof of old friends. Though even if you had thought to seek refuge somewhere more clever, I could find you anywhere in the world."

"So did you arrange a little bargain with the Ash Witch to kill Ethris last night to keep him from interfering?"

The trio of crinkled brows and surprised expressions answered the question, but Athan seemed incredulous.

"Ethris is dead?"

"His body lies in the Chapel."

"We had nothing to do with that," Athan professed. "The Ash Witch is his mother! This is indeed a strange turn of events, though I would be lying if I pretended to be sorry about the loss. But enough banter. Eldaloth has asked me to relay this message to you in good faith. If you do not accept this offer, then he will send an army to raze Blackshire until you relent."

"Your barbarity will only hurt your cause, Athan," the Chalaine said. "Every innocent you kill in the name of Eldaloth will only expose him for who he really is."

Athan wiped his mouth with the table cloth and retrieved his utensils. "Your deception is so ingrained and deep that it makes me pity you. Listen carefully. Your mother dies at dusk today. Eldaloth offers this: if you will consent to heal him, he will ensure that the death is dignified and will not have her run through the streets. If, after you heal him, you do not wish the passage to Erelinda, he will not force it upon you, but you must remain at Echo Hold under his protection. Do not answer now. Consider carefully what I have said. And eat. You will need your strength. His wound is grievous."

She asked, "And where is Mikkik? Must I go to Echo Hold to heal him?"

"Do not profane his Holiness!" Athan roared, pointing his fork tines at her. "Eldaloth has favored Blackshire with unusual condescension. He awaits your ministrations in the Chapel behind this building. Do make your decision quickly. Depending on what you choose, Lord Blackshire may have a lot on his mind. Such a beautiful country, here. It would be a shame to see the streets running with blood and its quaint buildings choked with fire."

Athan returned to his breakfast, eating heartily as if famished. The Chalaine sat back, defeated. She would not sacrifice an entire town on principle. Her mother might have the stomach for it, but the Chalaine's heart couldn't bear the thought. The entire company sat on edge save the Churchmen. Unbidden, tears came to the Chalaine's eyes. She would march to her doom and never see her mother or Gen again. Mikkik might make promises, but if he saw her as a threat, he would evaporate her into nothingness just as he had Chertanne. The Chalaine stared at the smug Athan, hand itching for a sword. He would ruin the world by his willful ignorance.

Athan cleared his plate and set his silverware down. "So what will it be, Chalaine?"

"Please call me Lady Alumira," she said. "I will go."

"No!" Maewen said. "You cannot fall into his hands!"

"There is no other way, Maewen," the Chalaine replied. "I will not have this place burned to the ground and its people slaughtered on my account. Give my love to my mother and . . . others . . . if I do not return. Let's get this over with."

"A wise choice," Athan congratulated her, smiling. "You will soon see that there never was anything to fear."

Dason, Volney, and Gerand fell in around her as they left the house and traversed the beautiful stonework path that led around to the Chapel. The Chalaine lifted her veiled face to the rain, offering a silent prayer to a God whose existence she had begun to doubt.

A slight glow emanated through the windows of the Chapel, the Puremen standing on the steps before the carved door. He bowed as they approached. "Welcome, brothers," he said, voice adoring. "Eldaloth has come to *my* humble Chapel. It is marvelous!"

"I will see him alone for a moment," Athan said. "Everyone else, remain here."

Athan entered and closed the door. The Chalaine's hands shook and felt clammy. She glanced about at her Protectors, each solemn and silent. They would die for her, but she would prevent that if she could. Athan returned a short while later.

"He will see you alone, Lady Alumira. He is quite pleased you have come, at last."

I am sure he is.

"We will go with her," Dason said, standing tall.

"Eldaloth says she comes alone," Athan said, voice regaining its edge. "And you will not disobey. Your swords will be useless against the magic of the Padras assembled here, and if you defy the wishes of Eldaloth, we will not hesitate to use it."

"Stay, Dason. Stay, Gerand and Volney," the Chalaine ordered. "No valiant notions or gallantry now. This is beyond the power of any of you. I will face this alone."

"But. . ." Dason protested.

"But nothing, Dason!" she said, raising her voice. "You will obey me! Do not follow. Athan is right. Your swords will avail you nothing, here."

She hiked up her dress and took the familiar stairs, Athan holding the door open for her as she entered. With an ominous, echoing boom he shut it, remaining outside. She walked forward resolutely, trying not to dwell on the pleasant memories of the place that would never bear fruit.

Mikkik, tall, regal, and shining, stood by the altar at the front of the Chapel, a wound in his side dripping golden blood onto the floor. As the Chalaine walked forward, a young woman came from a room at the rear of the Church wearing a simple white gown. Her face, while pretty, was severe.

"My child," Mikkik said, "you have come home at last!"

"You can drop the pretenses, Mikkik," the Chalaine said flatly as she approached. "I know who you are." As she neared the dark god, he seemed to flinch and pull in on himself. "You can hardly stand to be in the same room as me, can you?"

"Heal me," he said, stretching out a hand, unable to look at her.

"Why should I? You will only kill me."

"Because I hold in my hand the life of one you hold dear. It is in my power to make her death slow and painful, or quick and merciful."

The Chalaine could feel him push into her mind with alarming ease and power. There he implanted an image of her mother on the floor of her cell, weak, emaciated, and nearly unconscious. Three rotted heads lay on the floor about her, members of the Dark Guard she had sent into Echo Hold as spies. The image faded.

"Heal me," he said, "and I will be merciful."

With tear stained cheeks, she grasped the large hand, Mikkik convulsing at the touch as if burned by a white hot fire. The wound, a gaping hole in his back where Gen had stabbed him, seeped blood from a cut she could have put her fist through. She gripped the reluctant hand tightly and set her will to work knitting the wound. As she did, eyes closed, she felt a seal in her mind released, uncovering the memory of the night before.

The dark shadow in her room had approached and enveloped her. When she came to, she found herself on the edge of large pond surrounded by tall grass and a few large trees. The terrain appeared similar to Blackshire, but in the light of the moons she could see little more than the soft hills that enclosed the water near where she stood. An old woman hunched over next to the bank close by. A man sat with his feet in the water a little distance off, holding a fishing line. A soft breeze tickled the grass, but the pleasantness ended there. The ill-favored woman adjusted a dark cloak around her hunched frame and stepped forward.

"It is a pleasure to meet you at last, Highness," she said, voice scratchy. "Be at ease. I mean you no harm."

"Who are you?" the Chalaine asked, stepping backward.

"I am Joranne, Ethris's mother. That is his simpler brother, Dethris, just there."

182

The Chalaine shivered, trying to master her fear. The Ash Witch. She had heard the tales of this woman and her odd cycle of aging and rebirth, of her capricious actions that had both hurt and helped them.

"Do not fret, Chalaine. I've only come to relay a message, but first I must know how he died."

"Who?"

"Gen, the one known as the Ilch. I raised him until the Millim Eri took him from me."

"He died fighting the Uyumaak to buy me time to escape," she said.

The woman looked at her quizzically. "I don't want words. Give me your hand, and you can show me," she said. "And then I will show you why Mikkik wants you."

Joranne extended her hand, but the Chalaine pulled back. "You might just wish to steal information from my mind for your master."

"If I needed that, I could have just taken what I wanted in your room. I will only take what you give me."

Nervously, the Chalaine took the proffered hand, and Joranne concentrated. "Show me."

The fresh memory came easily, and when it was over Joranne broke contact, shaking her head. "An utter waste. But you don't seem as sad as I would have expected. The two of you shared a bond, no?"

"I have cried my tears, Joranne. Tell me what you want."

Joranne's eyes shifted to the pond. "I must share something with you, but I will be honest. I am here of my own accord and for my own purpose. In fact, what I am going to tell you is not by Mikkik's command but contrary to it. For that reason, when we are done I will hide what I have shown you, and it will only be triggered in the moment you need it to prevent prying eyes from seeing it.

"Athan has dispatched a great force to find you and bring you to Mikkik to heal him. He will succeed, sooner or later, whatever protections and schemes you may have. If he fails, then Mikkik will risk exposure of his true identity and send me to fetch you back. Once he has you, however, he will no longer need to keep up his little ruse, at least not for long. You hold the key to everything."

"How?" the Chalaine asked. "The holy babe is dead!"

"On the bridge of Echo Hold, Mikkik discovered something in you that he did not expect. You have Eldaloth's blood in your veins, Chalaine. I do not know how the Millim Eri did it, but with that blood, Mikkik can accomplish his purpose, to forge a weapon to still the spirit of Eldaloth that still abides in Elde Luri Mora. That presence tortures him without end. But that same weapon of blood can also be used to destroy him, so he must be cautious. And we must be cautious. You are familiar with blood magic?"

The memory of draining Gen's blood she would never forget. "It was used to revive Chertanne from death. It was horrible."

"Blood magic can only be used to annihilate or to heal. One can use the power of his *own* blood to heal another, but must use the willing blood of *another* to destroy. Blood ranges in power by race. The gods have the most powerful, while human blood holds so little power it is almost worthless. Almost.

"Within your veins, you carry the most powerful blood in Ki'Hal, and the power of blood is now the heart of the matter. I must show you why Mikkik is impersonating Eldaloth. It is an idea I gave him and that he amplified and twisted for his own ends. I must show you what happens to these pilgrims who have come to claim the offer of passing on to Erelinda. Take my hand again."

The Chalaine took her wrinkled appendage, and Joranne pressed a memory upon her. Before her a line stretched before the front gates to the keep at Echo Hold, the pilgrims chatting excitedly about their coming journey to a world without fear, sickness, or pain. Many of those who came were old and infirm looking for relief, but children and families came, too. The Eldephaere led them through the gates, taking twenty at a time through the door of the keep where a young Joranne waited in what looked like a small hall. She was dressed in ceremonial white robes, her benevolent smile and inviting face hushing them as she raised her hands. The Eldephaere left and shut the door.

Joranne stepped forward, clasping her hands in front of her. "You have all chosen a great gift, the greatest of all the blessings with which Eldaloth can bless you. I have seen the world into which you will enter, and it is glorious. Follow me. Leave all your worries and your possessions here. Eternal peace and a freedom from sorrow await. Come into the presence of Eldaloth and taste your reward."

She led the happy group through an archway and down a spiral staircase carved from the rock. Lanterns lit the way, and in that light the euphoria in the people's gazes faded ever so slightly as the descent took them unexpectedly deep into the earth. At last, the journey ended at a beautiful, gilded door encrusted with jewels. Joranne produced a key and unlocked it, signaling the group to enter.

She led them in, the lamp the only illumination. The room was cylindrical, a mighty wooden beam rising from the center of the floor and shooting upward to disappear into darkness of the upper area of the chamber. Grooves etched into the floor emanated out from the post, deepening as they reached the edge of the room where they terminated in holes drilled in the floor.

"You may wonder why such things must be done in the deep of the earth," Joranne said to the eager faces. "It is from the earth that life sprang, and Eldaloth's power courses through these underground passages like the blood in your veins. I will leave, and the room will be dark. Kneel and pray these words which I give you:

Freely I give my body.

Freely I give my blood.
Freely take my life
To rest in Erelinda.

When Eldaloth hears you, a great light and a rushing like a mighty wind will carry you to Erelinda and a life of rest."

With joy the pilgrims embraced one another and then knelt, smiles and tears gracing their faces. As one their chant to Eldaloth rose, and Joranne stepped out and shut the door. On the wall an iron lever waited, and she reached out and pulled it down. The rushing sound she so reverently promised came, not of wind but of something heavy falling. It terminated in an awful clang that shook the chamber. She opened the door, revealing a heavy metal platform that had descended and crushed the supplicants, their blood draining down the grooves and through the holes.

The Chalaine pulled away in horror, ending the vision. "You monster! Whose side are you on?"

"It's not about sides, Chalaine," Joranne scowled. "It's about survival! Listen to me carefully. In order to get the power that he needs to destroy Elde Luri Mora, he will need the blood of countless thousands of the race of men. It may take months. Eldaloth needs your blood drained only seven times, which will save him time and more lives than you can count. But he fears you because that same blood is what is needed to destroy him, as the blade the Ilch used against him almost did.

"This is what matters. When you are before Mikkik, the only way his scheme will work is if you are willing to give the blood. You have the power to bargain. He may try to bargain for the life of your mother, who now stands condemned to die."

"When?!" the Chalaine asked, mortified.

"Nothing is fixed. Athan will use her to try to persuade you to come, but even if you disagree he will take you. But

186

when the time comes that you stand before Eldaloth, you must remember this: whatever the cost, the only bargain you should make is for your own life. If you do not, he will unmake you just as he did Chertanne and your baby. Once he has your blood, he will make the weapon. He cannot abide your presence for long. You may need to use that to your advantage. Remember, give your blood only in exchange for your life. You must remain alive if there is to be any hope of ending Mikkik."

"Mother!" Dethris said, pulling in his pole and laying it in the grass.

"He comes?"

"Yes, he does."

Joranne sighed. "It is time, then. Chalaine, I will make you forget this until it is the proper time. Mikkik may search your mind, and he cannot know what I have done. When you remember again, remember that what I do, I do so we can survive."

Joranne reached out and took her hand, and the Chalaine collapsed.

The Chalaine released Mikkik's hand and stepped back, gasping at the horrible memory. The woman who came with Mikkik regarded her intently from behind her master was the Ash Witch, Mikkik's crony with some agenda she could not understand. Mikkik, now healed, probed his healed back and stood upright.

"I have one more need of you, Chalaine," he said. "I need your blood. I need you to give it willingly. If you do not, I will ensure that your mother is killed in the most brutal manner. She will scream loud enough for you to hear it."

The Chalaine looked at Mikkik and at Joranne. She couldn't bear the thought of her mother's torture and death, but if Joranne was right, then Mikkik would unmake her, and the virtue of her blood would be lost. Her thoughts turned to Gen and Cadaen and if they were too late. The chances had never been good, but *Gen* and *failure* never seemed to enter her mind together at the same time.

She said, "I will only give my blood to you willingly on the condition that I am left alive, unchanged, and free when you are finished. I will accept no other terms, and if you go against them, then the contract is void. That is my only offer."

Mikkik regarded her coldly. "I cannot let you live."

"Then kill me now. I will not willingly give you any blood of mine."

He stepped forward, towering over her. "Perhaps I did not make it plain what I can do to your mother! Perhaps I did not make it plain what I can do to this town!"

Again he pushed into her mind, showing her scenes of depravity and destruction that chilled her heart and weakened her knees. Her mother yelled in agony under blades and flames of torture unending. The buildings of Blackshire burned with the families inside, the bodies of the soldiers ripped apart by the wild animals drawn to the carnage. Men, women, children, her mother, all stared at her with pleading eyes, begging her to give them release.

The vision faded and she nearly fell under the emotional weight. Joranne, standing just behind her master, regarded her intently.

Breathing in deeply to collect herself, the Chalaine stood tall. "I stand by my conditions—take them or leave them."

Mikkik stared death at her for several moments and then turned on his heel. "So be it." With a thought he turned the altar into a wide stone basin. "Joranne, seal the doors and bleed her seven times. When finished, erase the memory of this encounter. I will need the support of the Padras a little while longer. I will return shortly."

Mikkik disappeared into the rooms behind the altar, leaving the Chalaine with Joranne, who glanced at her meaningfully. The Chalaine ascended the steps, Joranne signaling for her to lean over the basin.

"You have done well," Joranne whispered, pulling a thin knife. "I am sorry for this necessity."

For what felt like the entire morning, the Chalaine found herself reliving the nightmare of Gen's bleeding. Watching the blood drain from her arm and the accompanying weakness sickened her. She vomited twice, unable to bear glancing at the gathering pool of blood. After the seventh bleeding and healing, Joranne appeared spent. Feeling unsteady, the Chalaine descended to the first bench and threw herself onto it.

"What is he going to do?" the Chalaine asked.

Joranne opened her mouth to answer, but Mikkik striding forward from the back of the Chapel closed it. He carried a simple sword in his hand, one that might be found in the scabbard of a common soldier. Face twisted in discomfort, he stopped well short of the bloody basin.

"Take the sword, Joranne," he instructed. "Lay it in the blood."

Joranne complied and stepped back. Mikkik did not approach any closer, but the dark speech flowed smoothly from his lips in subdued tones. The Chalaine remembered the familiar words from the vision Aldemar had shown her. His incantation lasted but moments, but when he was finished the blood was gone and the sword shone with power. Mikkik produced a dark cloth from nothing and handed it to Joranne.

"Conceal it and give it to me."

Again Joranne obeyed, and once the sword was obscured, Mikkik's eyes closed in relief and he took the sword from her.

"At last it is finished. At last I shall have an end of agony and Eldaloth be silenced forever. Cleanse her memory while I go instruct the helpful Padras about their next task. Meet me in Echo Hold. We have work to do."

"Give me your hand," Joranne said as Mikkik strode to

the doors.

When the Chalaine placed her hand in Joranne's, she could feel Joranne come into her mind again, but instead of covering the memory of the sword's creation, she spoke.

"I will not erase what you know, but understand that Mikkik now holds the power of your blood in a weapon like the first he used to strike Eldaloth down. He will use the Churchmen to take it where he and I cannot go, to the heart of Elde Luri Mora. He will trick them into destroying Ki'Hal. More of his plans I do not know, but now you know the doom that awaits the world. It falls to you to stop it, if you can. Remember, the weapon he has created can be used to destroy him!"

Joranne released her and left hurriedly through the back, leaving the Chalaine stunned and confused. Her body wanted to stay inert, her sluggish mind still trying to churn out what she was to do. Could a sword really destroy Elde Luri Mora, and Ki'Hal with it? Was her blood that powerful? She needed Gen's knowledge and her mother's wisdom, and again she prayed for their deliverance from Echo Hold.

The Dark Guard ran into the Chapel, Dason charging down the aisle. He knelt before her. "We have failed you. We felt the blood being drained from you, but Athan kept us from coming to your aid! Are you well."

"Help me up, Dason. I am well enough," she said. "Get Maewen and General Harband. We can't delay."

She stumbled, and Dason grabbed her arm to steady her. "You must rest!"

"There is no time. Is Athan gone?"

"Yes. Eldaloth or Mikkik or whoever ordered them to leave immediately for Echo Hold."

"Then time is short. We will ride, even if you must tie me to the horse."

CHAPTER 81 – RAGE

The vulgar, jeering crowd clogged every avenue of Echo Hold, the Eldephaere overwhelmed by the sheer number of spectators hoping for a glimpse of the First Mother of Rhugoth being dragged to her death. Gen and Cadaen muscled their way forward. The late afternoon sunshine beat down like a hammer on the uplifted, rocky forge of Echo Hold. The sweat and humid stench of the mob was nauseating, but no inconvenience could slow or deter the two from their purpose. They shoved and elbowed citizens and soldiers alike without reservation.

"Once we get to the next intersection, we must bear left!" Cadaen shouted over the crowd, his stern, determined face more than enough to convince most people to clear out of his way. "She is moving."

During their two day journey toward the mountain stronghold, Cadaen had felt Mirelle weakening from lack of nourishment. After he and Gen had entered the city that afternoon, Cadaen gritted his teeth and reported that she had endured a whipping, and that her bonds had rubbed her wrists and ankles into festering wounds. Gen felt his ire rising, and only the Shadan's training kept him under control. In the back of his mind he knew that as soon as he saw Mirelle bruised and beaten, there would be no damming up the fiery indignation he could feel beginning to burn in his heart. Cadaen's steadily reddening face let Gen know that the same fire consumed him, as well.

Cadaen stopped short. "They are dragging her!"

A shout erupted at the intersection in their view, and the people surged forward. A cavalry unit of Eldephaere trotted by escorting a Padra, the blue pendants adorning their lances streaming behind them. A mighty black warhorse ridden by the executioner slashed through their view, rope tied to its pommel, a rope Gen knew was tied to Mirelle's wrists. Another cavalry unit followed, the people surging into the street after it. Cadaen froze for a moment in horror, and Gen used Trysmagic to create a simple sword in Cadaen's hand.

"Here!" Gen said. "Follow me!"

Cadaen expressed no surprise at Gen's sudden production of a weapon, and they turned right into an alleyway running parallel to the street along which the cruel procession traveled. Some spectators ran with them, hoping to catch up with the spectacle. Others plodded along, but the time for shoves and polite elbows had ended. Gen and Cadaen simply blasted anyone in their way onto the ground or into the wall. Cadaen let out a ferocious yell, brandishing his sword, and people dove out of their way.

The alley ended its parallel track and forced them back toward the main street, the mob thick as it pulsed forward at a jog. Cadaen yelled for people to move as he sprinted behind Gen, and at the corner of the street they met their first resistance in the form of three Eldephaere who had been alerted to the inexorable sprint of two madmen, one armed. The soldiers pulled their weapons and hefted their circular shields as Cadaen and Gen approached. They didn't slow.

Using Trysmagic, Gen undid cracks of metal along the swords where the blades met the hilts, and as the

Eldephaere pulled them back to strike, the blades simply fell to the ground useless. Gen unleashed a hard shove to one as he pushed by, Cadaen decapitating another as the two of them tried to work their way into the main flow that was chasing the suffering First Mother.

The Eldephaere raised a shout and tried to chase them, putting their shields to good use to push the intervening onlookers out of the way. Gen scanned ahead. The horse units and the executioner had reached farther than he had hoped, disappearing around a corner as the procession pushed toward the town square. The sheer number of people would make it impossible for even a tenth of them to witness the burning personally.

Behind them the Eldephaere pressed toward them. Ahead the dense crowd compressed into an impenetrable shield to bar their way. The more they pushed toward the square, the more trapped they became. Cadaen roared, using his sword to encourage people to move, slicing anyone who thought to impede them.

The pursuing Eldephaere continued to scream and yell, and along the edges of the crowd, their fellow soldiers left their posts along the route and pressed into the crowd in an attempt to reach them. Gen formed a sword in his hand, creating an edge so sharp that when he turned and hacked at the Eldephaere behind him, the blade passed through the shield as if it were nothing more than paper. The soldier fell in a splash of blood, the sudden violence pulling the people behind to a halt, only to be bowled over by the Eldephaere coming up from behind. Cadaen ran another soldier through, and he collapsed in a heap to be trodden on by those trying to escape the bloodshed.

Gen turned to try to keep moving forward, but the soldiers thickened as the hopeful spectators thinned, realizing that a fight was in the offing. As Gen and Cadaen reached the rear boundary of the crowd wall outside the square, they found themselves surrounded by nearly twenty soldiers. The spectators forming a ring around them, bets changing hands.

Shield at the ready, one of the Eldephaere stepped forward. "Drop your weapons and. . ."

Gen hacked him down, his blade thrusting through the shield with ease and puncturing the soldier's heart.

We don't have time for this! Gen thought as shout erupted from the square behind them. But the Eldephaere rushed and forced his concentration back to his own survival. The initial five soldiers came at them cautiously, but after Cadaen and Gen hacked them down with speed and skill they had never seen, the rest backed off a space to reconsider. The bets began in earnest.

Cadaen came to Gen's side. "I only have seen three men fight like you do."

Mirelle's agonized scream from the square and Cadaen's petrified countenance made his next words unnecessary. "She burns!"

The Eldephaere appeared ready to rush again, and the crowd near the square began to chant, "Burn, burn, burn!"

"Go, my brother," Cadaen said, a tear running down his cheek. "If you have the power to stop this, then do it."

Gen nodded and turned, and within his heart an agony and a rage built to a crescendo that all his control and all his training could not stop. Between him and the square was a wall of people thirty feet thick, and pulling in the power of Duam he yelled the ancient words of the incantation with all the anger he possessed.

"Shui' Shei!"

A mighty gale of wind blasted into the crowd like an unseen battering ram and threw bodies up and away to slam into buildings and to fall into and crush the crowd. Gen sped down the newly cleared avenue as screams tore the air. He could see her now. Mirelle was tied to a pole above a burning pile of wood, the flames reddening and peeling her legs and setting her dress on fire. She screamed and wept in pain, red face soaked with tears.

The executioner and the Padra stood nearby, and Gen killed them both with a thought, undoing veins in their heads. They slumped lifeless from the platform, the executioner falling into his own fire and throwing up sparks.

The Eldephaere crowded into the gap that he had created, but with a Duam-powered leap, he sailed over them, landing twenty feet from Mirelle. Gen's fury burned white hot and without remorse he unleashed his next assault.

"Forua Kael!"

The fiery pile of wood underneath Mirelle exploded outward from the center, the wood whistling through the air with deadly, burning velocity. The heavy logs plowed avenues of death through the terrified Eldephaere. They continued on to level the forward ranks of the bloodthirsty crowd. The burning branches and sticks punctured unprotected bodies and knocked even more revelers to the ground. In terror the crowd reversed course and ran in the opposite direction.

Not a single twig remained beneath the charred First Mother, who hung unconscious from the abandoned pole. Gen rushed to her, using Trysmagic to free her hands and feet of her bonds. Limp, she fell into his arms, face blackened and legs charred. He had little of Duammagic left to avail him, and he spent the last of its strength to heal her lungs and to alleviate the damage of her legs. Even so, he could not tell if she would live, so bad was the damage. Tears welled up in his eyes as he carried her beaten, burned body away from the square. He needed to see if Cadaen yet lived.

A group of Eldephaere approached from the other side of the square, crossbowmen coming to the front. Gen killed them with Trysmagic before they could even raise their weapons. The determination of the rest failed them and they backed away. All before him fled as he ran back down the avenue. He found Cadaen lying in the street amid a pile of dead Eldephaere, blood running freely from many wounds. Gen had nothing left with which to heal him. Cadaen reached up and stroked Mirelle's hair, his eyes heavy with approaching death.

"She is yours now, Gen," he said. "Help her live. I am done."

The old Protector closed his eyes and his breath left him. With difficulty, Gen fought down his emotions. They had to survive, and to survive they had to evade a city teeming with enemies. He ducked down an alley and made a series of confusing turns before finding an old, crumbling building carved from the stone. He darted up a flight of treacherous stairs. The edifice was abandoned, and he ducked through a doorless entryway and used Trysmagic to create a slab of stone that would make it appear to the passerby that there was just a wall.

A single window on the opposite wall he covered with shutters, and with the rest of the Trysmagic he possessed, he created the herbs and water he would need to treat Mirelle's damaged body until his Duammagic recovered enough to heal her completely. Only Mynmagic was available to him now, and as he began his mundane ministrations he hoped for several hours of peace. Getting out of the city would be impossible until Mirelle was healed—and it would prove difficult even then.

Shutting away the commotion outside the window, he bathed her charred legs, hoping to keep them from festering to save her body's strength from the task of fighting infection. With the water, he cleaned her face and arms the best he could, whispering to her unconscious mind to hang on a few hours more. The brutal pace of the last few days and the heavy expenditure of magic exhausted him. After forcing some water down her throat, he lay back on the floor and drifted off to sleep as the heat of the day cooled to evening.

The sound of Mirelle groaning in pain wrenched him out of slumber a couple of hours later. It was dark, but he sought her hand and used Mynmagic to trick her mind into feeling no pain at all. She relaxed and fell back into a peaceful slumber. Standing, he opened a shutter for a view of the dark street below. They hadn't gone far from the square, and the marching of feet and clamor of shouted orders echoed everywhere. Closing the shutter, he lay back down.

Throughout the night, the sounds of soldiers passing beneath the windows woke him, though not until morning did he hear them searching the building where they hid. He waited quietly as they poked around the ruin, but no one was observant enough to realize there was a window on the outside that opened to a hidden room, and they left.

By midday, his reserves felt strong enough to attempt to heal her, but before he did, he used Trysmagic to dissolve her ruined dress and create a modest dress for her in its place. He chose one that a simple country girl might wear, to help her blend in when they attempted escape.

Delving deep into his reserves, he took her hand and poured the healing energy of Duammagic into Mirelle's flagging body, restoring the flesh, undoing the swelling, and killing the infections already starting to take root. To heal her completely took all the Duammagic he possessed, but her legs were still scarred from the fire. Her eyes fluttered and then popped open, and Gen helped her to sit up, bringing her water.

"Where am I?" she asked, a little frightened.

"In Echo Hold," Gen said. "You are safe for the moment."

She drank, her eyes regarding him skeptically in the dim light admitted from the shutters.

"And who are you?"

"I am called Amos these days, but under a different

name I was one of the few men who enjoyed the favor of the First Mother of Rhugoth. And, I might add, one of the few—if not the only—to ever kiss her."

The water fell out of Mirelle's hand and onto the floor, and her mouth gaped. She leaned in for a closer look. "Gen? It can't be! The voice is yours, but, the face. . . Sweet Eldaloth, it is you!"

She dove at him and knocked him to the ground, lying on top of him and kissing him, her tears running down her face and onto his. She finally sat up, straddling him and inspecting his face.

"How are you not dead? How dare you not be dead! I held you in my arms and made this horrible blubbering scene crying over you! And where did all your scars go? And a beard?"

Gen laughed. "It's a long tale, but. . ."

She leaned down and smothered him in kisses until some thought struck her. "But if you're alive . . . does my daughter know?"

"Yes," Gen said.

Mirelle rolled off of him and onto the floor, staring up at the ceiling. "Curse it all. No, I don't mean that. But you must marry her, Gen. You must love her and make love to her and make her smile. She wants it so desperately. Oh, why couldn't I have conned you into marrying me before all this happened? I worked so hard at being persuasive and seductive and charming. Tell me I was good at it."

"You were unnaturally good at it."

"Not good enough, apparently. Damn it all! You must marry her—and quickly. We need to the put the world under your leadership as soon as possible."

Gen reached over and took her hand. "Ki'Hal needs to be under your rule, Mirelle. You are gifted in ways I don't think I ever will be. Remember that I'm a villain to the whole world. I can't marry anyone, much less lead anything. I look different, but not different enough to fool anyone for long."

"Maybe," she said. "But I need all the details of what happened to you and between you and the Chalaine. Just leave out the romantic bits—if there are any—so I don't get jealous. Are there any? Romantic bits, I mean?"

"Mirelle. . ."

"But who is a better kisser? Be honest."

Gen chuckled. "Do you have any idea how bizarre this conversation is? You look very young, but to think I've kissed a mother and her daughter in a romantic way is a little . . . uncomfortable."

"So you have kissed her!" Mirelle exclaimed, and then frowned and changed her tone. "So you have kissed her. You are right; this is tending toward the bizarre. Being in love with your future son-in-law is terribly low class. On with the story, then."

Gen related the tale of his awakening and their flight through the Black Forest, the Chalaine's illness and sudden recovery, and his brief stay in Blackshire. When he related leaving Blackshire in company with Cadaen, her hand went to her mouth as she predicted the truth behind his absence. Gen held her as she cried softly, telling her of Cadaen's concern for her and his fight to keep the Eldephaere at bay.

"He bought me the time I needed to get to you," Gen said. "He died bravely and was an excellent soldier and a dedicated man."

Mirelle wiped her eyes. "Well, he got what he wanted in the end. Ever since he lost control and tried to take me for his own, he has been searching for a way to die for me. I guess he found it. I will miss him. It will be like turning around and finding your shadow gone. Oh, Gen, this last week has been so dark and comfortless in that cell. I had lost you. I thought I might lose my daughter to an Uyumaak horde. I bandied words with Mikkik and saw his dark heart. By the time they dragged me out of that cell this morning, I was almost glad to die." She reached out and touched his face. "But now that you are here, and here with power, there is light again in the world."

Gen took her hand, "I still can't see what I can do, although I will fight for any good cause."

"I have some ideas," she returned, "but how long must we hide, do you think?"

"We'll just need to wait for the patrols to die down," Gen said. "At some point they'll think we've already escaped. I know a few tricks to get us away safely, even if they don't, so if it takes longer than a day or two, we'll risk it."

"Then would you mind conjuring up a mattress or a pillow? I assume you can do that with Trysmagic," she said.

"Yes. The plainer, the less power is required, so forgive something simple."

"Well it doesn't need to be big," she said. "You and I can be cozy for as long as it takes."

He grinned at her. "You're doing it again."

"What?"

"Flirting."

"Well, I can't help it," she said. "The Chalaine doesn't have to know *everything* that happens here. Thank you for the dress, by the way. Not quite my style, but it will do."

Gen created a thin mattress big enough for them to sit comfortably on. As she sat cross-legged, she noticed the burn scars on her legs and sighed. "It is a shame," she said, rubbing her hand over the uneven skin. "They were quite lovely, I would have you know."

"I can restore the skin with Trysmagic," he said. "You will have your legs back. I will . . . I will need to see them to do the work required."

She smiled teasingly. "Who is being forward now?"

200

After a day of resting and hiding, Gen decided they should risk leaving, as much as for the frustration they both felt over their confinement as the need to keep his relationship with Mirelle from barreling headlong into the inappropriate. She clearly found it difficult to bridle her affections. Mirelle was ever intoxicating, and she sorely tested his control with her copious affection.

Thankfully, the patrols had died down and the city had returned to its natural hum and flow, and he judged it was time to move. By way of disguise, Gen conjured up some drab, dirty peasant attire, and he used Duammagic to lengthen his beard and his hair until he appeared almost wild. Gen stared over at Mirelle, who had just finished laughing at his disguise.

"The clothes might say peasant woman," Gen said, stroking his beard, "but you still look like a beautiful noblewoman wearing a costume. Isn't there something you can do to look more ignorant and unattractive?"

"Now that is a rare request," she said. "I'll let you give me a bad haircut, and we can smear some filth on my face. Maybe you can expand the dress, and we can stuff something in it to make me look pregnant. Then we can pretend you're some wild beast of a man who just travels into town to father children. Like Chertanne."

"Sounds awful, but it might work," he said.

"Just promise me that you can use your magic to put me back to normal before we see anyone I know. Do you need to check my body anywhere else for burn scars before we go?"

"You've got to stop. . ."

"I'm serious!"

"No. If you find any more, then you can let me know."

"I'm sorry, Gen," she said, eyes that had been playful for the last day finally turning melancholy. "I am such a wretched contradiction of emotions that I think I might just tear myself in half. When we leave, it will be time to get to work, and that will help."

"I understand, and I want you to know. . ."

"But," she interrupted, stepping close, "a man who saves an aristocrat's life must be rewarded."

"There is no need," he replied, smiling at the memory of their conversation after the attempt on her life on the streets of Mikmir.

"Yes there is," she replied. And then she kissed him deeply with tender emotion and sincere love. Gen could feel his knees buckling.

"There," she said, putting her hand on his cheek. "Something to remember me by."

Gen swallowed. "Mirelle. . ."

"Come on, Gen," she ordered. "You've cooped me up long enough. I want to see my daughter as soon as I can. We need to have you sitting on the throne of Mikmir with my daughter by your side as soon as we can arrange it."

"The people won't accept me!"

"No, but they will accept the return of Aldradan Mikmir."

"You can't be serious!"

She smiled one of the devious, plotting smiles that he loved. "I am. Mikkik likes a good ruse, and so do I. We've a long way to go. Hear me out. You might like this little plot of mine."

CHAPTER 82 - THE PROCESSION OF GLORY

"She isn't in town," Gen informed Mirelle once they arrived in Embriss on horses Gen had paid for with conjured money. "She's just north of here a couple of miles. We're almost there."

Dusk had fallen on the dirty, noisy town packed with pilgrims. Gen thought the chaos was worse than when he and Cadaen had traveled through just days before. He figured that every merchant from any town within reasonable distance had come to take advantage of the mob, and the overworked Eldephaere had lost the war against the drunken rowdy.

Gen and Mirelle's path led out of the city and toward the manor house of Regent Feldebrinne, who lived down a country lane walled by trees. Even here, many of the pilgrims waiting for their chance to pass through the Portal had set up crude camps among the tree boles, small fires weaving their smoke through the forest and across the lane.

"This is a mess," Mirelle commented. "I wonder that Feldebrinne has let it spiral so far out of control."

"The Church appears to be in control—or not in

control," Gen observed. "Since this is the closest Portal to Echo Hold, I'm guessing Athan wanted a stranglehold on it. I haven't seen any soldiers dressed in the colors of the Regent."

"We'll need to change that," Mirelle said. "I've been wondering who has been in charge since Eldaloth's supposed return. I hunger for news. My mind needs something to work on besides you. Can you put me back to normal now, please? I miss my hair."

"I thought the Chalaine might enjoy seeing how well I cut hair with a knife," he said.

"And I might enjoy giving you another kiss you can't forget," she returned.

"You win."

"I really haven't."

The pilgrims lining the road thinned as they proceeded farther along the curved, forested road. The lighted windows of the manor house perched on a low hill winked in and out between the trees as they dismounted and walked the horses to rest them. A cool breeze in the twilight brought relief from a hot day of hard travel that had exhausted both them and the animals. Once they were sure that there were no prying eyes, Gen restored Mirelle's long hair and used Trysmagic to create a more regal riding dress that befitted her station. He changed himself back to Amos, complete with his wide brimmed hat.

"I hate that hat," Mirelle commented.

"So does the Chalaine," Gen replied, "but it is necessary."

"Not for long."

The call of the Silver Loon greeted them, and Gen stopped. "Maewen is here. Let's tie the horses and find her."

"How do you know that?" Mirelle asked.

"The bird trill we just heard. That bird does not frequent this area of Ki'Hal. It's a signal we've used before."

They secured the horses to a tree branch and walked into the dimming woods. Unlike the Black Forest, the woods around Embriss were cleared of fallen branches and brush, and instead of densely packed pines, majestic oaks and maples rose into the air. Maewen stood on the stump of a recently sawed tree, leaning on her longbow and regarding them both with pleasure.

"Well met," she said. "I feared to tell the Chalaine that Gen neared until I was sure he had you with him, Mirelle. But I see it was not without trouble. Cadaen has fallen, then?"

"Yes," Mirelle confirmed.

"I feel for you," Maewen said, placing her hand on Mirelle's arm. "But I rejoice that you have come. You and Gen are needed, and the time is short. Gen, I do not think you can maintain your disguise. Events of a serious nature have occurred in your absence, and your knowledge and power are needed now."

"Gen and I have a scheme ready," Mirelle said, "but tell us what has happened."

The more Maewen talked, the more alarmed Gen became. Ethris was dead. Mikkik had bled the Chalaine and created a weapon of immense power, and the dark god only needed to dupe someone not of his creation to walk into Elde Luri Mora and use it. Time was, indeed, short.

"To add to our difficulties," Maewen continued, "the Church has spies and soldiers all over. They are well aware that the Chalaine is visiting with Regent Feldebrinne and are probably aware of why. I've killed two spies who came onto the Regent's land, which I doubt will foster good will. Falael returned yesterday from scouting to Mikmir. Mikkik has set a Padra on each of the thrones of the three nations, and each stronghold is held by a sizable force. Mikmir is no exception."

Mirelle shook her head. "Mikkik has run this little ploy of his expertly. This is dire news."

"It gets worse," Maewen continued. "Lord Kildan returned to his homeland and was immediately arrested by the Eldephaere and killed as a traitor."

"No!" Gen and Mirelle said in unison.

"His sons found out about three hours ago and are eager for some kind of revenge. But the most intriguing news to come this evening was of your escape and an invitation from Eldaloth, well, Mikkik. He has invited anyone who formerly claimed right of leadership or nobility in any of the nations to join him on a Procession of Glory led by the new Pontiff, Athan."

"Procession of Glory?" Mirelle asked. "Sounds overly dramatic and pretentious. What is it?"

She reached into her pouch and pulled out a piece of parchment. "Read it for yourself."

To the Esteemed Lord Feldebrinne,

To celebrate the healing of Eldaloth from the wound cruelly inflicted upon him by the Ilch, you, in view of your past service to the prophecy, are invited to join a Procession of Glory. Eldaloth and Pontiff Athan will lead to Elde Luri Mora those whose leadership during the hard months before the rebirth proved critical in defeating Mikkik and his allies.

With his power fully restored, Eldaloth will march to Elde Luri Mora and restore Ki'Hal to a wholeness that has not been since Mikkik struck him down. You are privileged to be called up to join the company to witness these events firsthand and join in a celebration the likes of which you will never forget.

All those wishing to join this Procession of Glory to see Ki'Hal restored should report to Echo Hold on the Seventh Day following the next. Food and provisions will be provided for you, but you should provide your own horses and raiment. May Eldaloth continue to bless us with his glorious return.

"This is outrageous!" Mirelle said. "The Regents and nobles and Warlords cannot be stupid enough to fall for this! He'll kill them all, and the world will be leaderless!" Mirelle exclaimed.

"Mirelle," Gen said gently, "remember that you have seen nothing but hardship since the fraudulent return. You have spoken with Mikkik himself and nearly been killed. Most of the people have been rejoicing and feasting for days. This is just more good news to fuel their celebration. We need a way to awaken them. I'm not sure our little plan will be enough."

"What is it that you propose?" Maewen asked.

"The return of Aldradan Mikmir," Mirelle said.

"He's dead, Mirelle," Maewen replied, face skeptical. "I buried him."

"That is true, but if Mikkik can assume someone else's identity to lead people around like sheep, then we can do the same. The legend of Aldradan Mikmir runs through all the peoples of Ki'Hal. He was a warrior, he was a Magician, and he came at a time of dire need." Mirelle pointed a finger at Gen. "Sound familiar?"

Maewen's eyebrows raised, and a smile slowly formed on her lips. "That is the most ridiculous and wonderful thing I have heard in a long while. But there isn't a lot of time. Even with Gen's power, he just can't cleanse Mikmir of Eldephaere and Church soldiers by himself. Even the company of soldiers we have brought out of Blackshire would be insufficient. We have six days before this Procession of Glory moves out of Echo Hold. In four days' march they can be on the shores of Elde Luri Mora."

"It begins here," Gen said. "Tomorrow, Aldradan Mikmir will come to Embriss and speak of Mikkik's treachery to all the pilgrims lining up for Echo Hold. They will carry the story to Tenswater. Using the Portals we can get fast riders to send the word to all of Rhugoth and most of Ki'Hal within two days and tell them to bring soldiers to Mikmir. It will be war from the start. The Church will block the use of the Portals as soon as they find out, but we hope to make it difficult for them."

"How?" Maewen asked.

Mirelle grinned. "By announcing an irresistible wedding and inviting everyone in Ki'Hal to attend."

"And whose wedding will that be?"

"Aldradan Mikmir and my daughter. She has taken the name Alumira, then?"

"Yes," Maewen answered.

"We have to get her consent, of course," Gen said. "I won't have her marry against her will again."

"I think gaining the Chalaine's consent will be the easiest part of this plan of yours," Maewen said. "Dason's been quite forward with his intentions concerning her. This will be a cruel blow to him."

"He'll recover," Mirelle said. "But we do need to talk to my daughter about all of this before tomorrow."

"Come within the outer walls of the manor," Maewen said. "There are too many threats that lurk out here in the dark. There is one complication; Mirelle, you are a fugitive. Few know it as yet, but Regent Feldebrinne is still divided about what Lady Alumira has told him. If he sways in another direction, he could try to detain her."

"Try would be all he would do before Gen leveled his manor," Mirelle answered confidently. "Part of our ruse is that Aldradan Mikmir rescued me from Echo Hold. I think my presence will only sway the Regent to our side."

Maewen nodded. "The manor is surrounded by pleasant little wilderness. On the northern side there is a low hill with a pavilion. I will bring her there. Gerand is on duty, but don't be surprised if Dason comes looking for her when she wanders away. He is more like her pet than a Protector."

Together they walked back to the road, and Gen offered

Mirelle his arm as they traveled the short distance to the manor gate. A wall of mortared stones two times as high as a man surrounded the entire estate, encompassing several outbuildings and the forest for a mile in every direction. The soldiers of the Regent still held power on the Regent's property, and the swelling numbers of strangers in the town had required a similar increase of soldiers to patrol the Regent's lands.

Two lanterns hung from the walls by the arched entry, four soldiers standing at the ready by the closed gate. Maewen approached first.

"These are two more members of Lady Alumira's party," Maewen explained. "I have been waiting for them. We are ready to enter."

"Who are they?" one of the guards asked.

"This is Amos and the Lady Alumira's mother, the former First Mother of Rhugoth."

Mirelle flashed them a smile, and the soldiers looked on in astonishment.

"We heard you were burned as a traitor and then that you escaped!"

"I was rescued," she replied, "by someone greater than us all. You will know more soon. Thank you for your watchful diligence. May we enter, please?"

The power of her pleasant, feminine beauty unlocked the gate and they passed through, the road inside the wall paved in cobble. They passed low barracks ensconced in trees where soldiers were quartered. Other buildings waited down wide forest tracks, lanterns casting lights among the trees. The road led steadily upward, night birds favoring them with their song. As they cleared a bend, they could make out the steeply sloped gables of the manor above the trees. Gen could sense the Chalaine there, and his heart rejoiced to see her again.

"Take the side path here northward," Maewen instructed them. "Follow it until you reach the pavilion. I will come with the Chalaine as soon as I can."

Maewen continued on toward the house while Gen led Mirelle down the dark path between the trees. She leaned into him, and an odd sorrow rose within him. He stopped and faced her, and she regarded him questioningly. He took her hands.

"Mirelle," he said, "I need you to know something before we rush headlong into the whirlwind of trouble you and I have concocted together. You have been so kind and generous and loving to me that I could never repay you everything I owe you. You have cared for me, defended me, and rewarded me with every good thing you could. How you knew me well enough to know that I would love to spend my days in Blackshire, I can only guess. That you are willing to give me your best gift, your beloved daughter, stirs me with feelings I cannot give words to.

"You are the best and brightest of all women I have ever known, and please understand that if circumstances would have been different, you are just as beautiful to me as your daughter and I would be just as happy and fortunate to wed the First Mother of Rhugoth. I would have loved you no less, Mirelle. Do not think that just because I love the Chalaine, that I do not love you. Earning the love of one beautiful woman is good fortune; earning the love of two is a peculiar kind of torture."

Mirelle wiped her eyes. "I am sorry if I made this harder on you than it should have been."

"Don't apologize," Gen said. "I only grieve to see you alone. I owe you everything, and I want to see you happy."

"Then marry my daughter. I am a mother, Gen, and I am no longer the first concern of my heart. I will take great joy in seeing her happy, especially knowing all the trouble and sorrow she has passed through with Chertanne. That said, do know that when you see me crying at your wedding, most of the tears will be for my daughter, but some few will be for me."

"One last kiss, then, before you become my intimidating mother-in-law?"

"I hoped you would ask."

To spare them both, Gen kept it short. He pressed his forehead against hers for several long moments, breathing in her scent, before pulling away and leading her forward. They walked in silence, winding around a low, tree-covered hill until they found the pavilion that Maewen had spoken of. It provided a good view of the surrounding area, the moons' hazy light playing evenly over the trees. The lights of the packed town and the manor house were bright pockets in the darkness. They sat together, Mirelle leaning on his shoulder while they waited.

"Any advice you want to give me about your daughter before I marry her?"

"She has matured a great deal this last year," Mirelle said. "I think you are wise enough and know her well enough that any advice I give you would be redundant. I really have no charge to give you other than to make her as happy as you can, and I don't believe you need to do much more than be yourself to do it. She trusts and loves you completely and will be overjoyed to take your hand. She will at last get to do what was promised to her at her birth—marry the best of men."

"She is coming," Gen said, rising as he felt her near.

Mirelle stood as well, straightening her dress and peering into the darkness. The Chalaine, Maewen, and Gerand crested the hill, mother and daughter racing to each other and embracing, crying for joy. To Gen's surprise, Gerand approached him and extended his hand.

"Well met, brother," he said, smiling. "It is good to know that the best swordsman on Ki'Hal has returned in these difficult times."

Gen took the hand, surprised. "How did you know?"

"Your disguise isn't that good, though without the scars you aren't nearly as frightening as you were back then. The

Chalaine also told me of your return, but I knew before then."

"Do Volney and Dason know?"

"No," he said. "Should we inform them?"

"Not yet. My condolences for your father. He will be missed."

"I don't have words, Gen. They burned him, just like they tried to do to the First Mother. If I didn't have responsibilities here, I would ride for vengeance now."

"We will make this right, Gerand, I. . ."

Gen turned just in time to catch the Chalaine as she leapt his arms and clamped onto him. Gen wrapped her up.

"I knew you would save her," she said, "I just knew it. Thank you."

"You are welcome," he returned. "It's good to see you again. I missed you."

She moved in close to his ear. "We need to be alone so I can take this veil off and give you a proper welcome."

Gerand cleared his throat and they turned to find everyone smiling at them sloppily.

"Why Gerand," Mirelle said, "there was no need to interrupt them! I think it was just about to get more interesting. But we do have a lot to talk about and to do. Let's sit for a moment. Gerand, I understand that you know who Gen is. I will let you stay to hear this if you will swear that if you cannot support what we are about to do, that you will at least keep silent on the matter."

"I swear it."

"What do you intend to do, mother?" the Chalaine asked. Gen intertwined his fingers with hers.

"We intend to take back Mikmir in a rather unorthodox way," Mirelle explained. "I'm afraid it involves you getting married to someone famous and a lot older than you."

The Chalaine's fingers dug into Gen's hand. "I will not marry anyone except for love, mother! How could you even think I would consider. . . Why are you all smiling?"

Mirelle asked, "What if that person was Gen, dear?"

"I accept."

"And would you still accept it if Gen was impersonating Aldradan Mikmir?"

"What?!" Gerand and the Chalaine said at once.

"You heard me."

"I would marry Gen if he were a gong scourer, but why Aldradan Mikmir?"

As the First Mother explained her reasons, Gen watched the Chalaine carefully, trying to gauge her reaction to the plan he and Mirelle had carefully put together over the last two days. She had lived her entire life with the weight of expectations upon her, and probably wanted nothing more than to fade into a life of safety and solitude with those that she loved. As her mother talked, the Chalaine leaned into him, her grip tight and her posture tense. She was frightened.

Mirelle continued. "Once Gen is on the throne as Aldradan Mikmir, and with you at his side, we should have enough support to put a good force into the field to see if we can stop this travesty. I can see Mikkik sending an honored and delighted Athan into Elde Luri Mora flanked by the nobles from three kingdoms. What a great laugh Mikkik will have when Athan destroys us all."

Maewen broke in. "Gen, do we know what will happen if he uses the sword there? Lady Alumira heard Mikkik say it was the destruction of Ki'Hal, but how, exactly?"

Gen thought for a moment. "In lore, Elde Luri Mora is the heart of Ki'Hal, the place from which Eldaloth's life-giving force flowed. When we were there, did you note the eternal blossoms on the trees? Once they bore fruit. When Mikkik struck Eldaloth down, Elde Luri Mora and the world still lived, but the holy place was wounded in the same way I wounded Mikkik. It is an injury that has no power to kill, but no power to heal, either."

"I saw the difference between the world before Eldaloth

was struck down and after," the Chalaine added. "Aldemar showed it to me. Before Eldaloth died, the world was marvelous and vibrant, and it was a feeling more than anything, a vibrancy that filled Ki'Hal. If Elde Luri Mora is what is left of Eldaloth, then destroying it will be dire in scope, I am sure. Its existence has tormented Mikkik for centuries, but he needed my blood to finish it, and I gave it to him. Perhaps it would have been better that I died than let him take my blood as he did."

Gen pulled her in close. "He would have had his blood one way or another. He was willing to bleed every living creature on Ki'Hal dry until he had enough essence to do it. This is our chance, now. That sword can destroy Elde Luri Mora. It can also destroy him. It will be out in the open during their journey, so it's time to turn the tables on Mikkik and do to his caravan what he did to ours. They wanted the Chalaine. We want the sword. I will lead what army we can muster in the next few days and take them east to do it. Mirelle and the future Lady Mikmir will remain safely in Rhugoth while I get this done."

"Lady Mikmir," Mirelle smiled. "I like how that sounds. It is settled, then. Tomorrow Gen will become Aldradan Mikmir. Maewen will work with him to get the details of his clothing and armament right. The rest will be up to Gen. Remember, Gen, that you were to be a bard. It's time to review your lessons on theatricality and performance. You're about to put on an act like the world has never seen, and we need a virtuoso performance on the opening night."

"It is bold, and it is cunning," Gerand opined, "but time is your biggest enemy. There is only one Portal close to Echo Hold, and as soon as the Church gets wind that there is a rebellion in the offing, they will guard that Portal with everything they've got. Even if the word gets out that Aldradan Mikmir wants to muster men, a week will hardly be sufficient to organize everything, especially with most of the armies scattering and going home celebrating. Getting

Mikmir under our control in that amount of time would be difficult. And why the need for the wedding? Though I can see it is a desired event."

"The wedding serves a number of purposes, besides the obvious one of bringing two people together who love each other together," Mirelle answered. "At the very least, I hope it will draw some of the leaders away from the Procession of Glory, sparing them whatever horrific end Mikkik has in mind. Given the choice of a four or five day journey through the wilderness or a wedding celebration of a legend returned from the dead, we are hoping more than a few will choose the wedding. This will give us an opportunity to persuade them and get their support.

"Besides that, the massive influx of people through the Portal will make it nearly impossible for the Church to control it without causing a rebellion. If we can get the leadership to bring soldiers with them, then we will have the force ready to march.

"But your point about time is well taken, Gerand. The fighting for the Portal to Echo Hold we cannot avoid, and I fear it will be bloody, but I hope to take Mikmir without shedding any blood whatsoever."

"How?"

"Aldradan Mikmir will simply walk in and ask for it back. When he rides through the streets of Mikmir with the Chalaine at his side, a mob will follow, and I am betting that the Church will not want to dampen these festive times by engaging in a bloodbath of innocent people. Gen assures me he is powerful enough to make them miserable for trying.

"If all goes well, the wedding will take place in five days, and Gen will march the sixth day. There will be blood on the streets of Tenswater, but that cannot be helped. Once through the Portal, they ride hard to catch the Caravan. This all begins tomorrow, and we will be working through the night to prepare. Now, how stand matters with Regent

Feldebrinne?"

"He is still wavering, I'm afraid," the Chalaine answered. "We've worked at him all afternoon, but he fears repercussions to his estate since a Portal to Tenswater is nearby, and I can't blame him."

Mirelle sighed. "I'll see what I can do. If I fail, then a personal visit from Aldradan Mikmir may be in order. Now, let's leave Gen and the Lady Alumira together, since I don't believe the marriage proposal has been properly made yet. I have given Gen my consent to marry my daughter earlier."

The party broke up, the Chalaine hanging onto Gen until they left. Gen tried to calm his mind. Impersonating a legend would prove taxing, and he hardly knew where to start. But he tried to push his concerns aside as a beaming Chalaine lifted her veil and greeted him properly as she promised. During all the planning with Mirelle, he had failed to even consider that he would need to ask the Chalaine to marry him in some proper manner. Since her first marriage was forced upon her, it would be doubly important to impress her.

"Well?" she asked, face expectant. "Don't you have something to ask me?"

"Lady Alumira. . ."

"You know," she interrupted, "the *Lady* on the front of the name makes it much too stuffy. Just call me Alumira like you did back in our canyon days together."

"Very well. Alumira, when I look back over the past two years of our acquaintance. . ."

"And I don't want some long, sloppy speech, either. Your actions toward me have said a thousand times more than words ever could about your feelings."

He knelt before her. "Alumira. . ."

"Stand up for pity's sake!" she said, this time without mirth. "You will never kneel before me. Ever."

A little flummoxed, he stood and took her hands. "Will you marry. . ."

"Yes, of course I will. What took you so long?" she joked, greeting him properly several more times. "I've waited so long! This will be the best night of my life."

"Just a few more days, Alumira, and you'll be back home and be a proper Queen, just as it should be."

"Not exactly correct," she said, lowering her veil and guiding him away from the pavilion. "I will be home in a few days and a proper Queen in a few days, but I will be a married woman tonight."

"What?"

"You heard me," she said. "That wedding will be a big show for the world. The wedding tonight will be just for us. Regent Feldebrinne's Pureman lives just behind the manor, and I'm sure we can persuade him."

"Are you sure?" Gen asked.

"Aren't you?"

"I just thought that since things turned out so miserably for your first marriage that you would want something glorious this time, with a procession of knights and trumpets and screaming celebrants and a cake and good food and everyone telling you how beautiful your dress is."

She laughed. "No. I just want you. You ride off to war in a week, and I will not spend another night alone dreaming of how I want it to be. If I dream of you, I want to wake up and make the dreams real. I have sacrificed, and I have been patient, and I have stifled my feelings, and I am done with it all. I have longed for you for what seems like an age, and I will have my way tonight."

"You're going to have to tell Dason," he warned her.

"Nothing says, 'I don't love you' like marrying someone else."

"I just hope he takes it honorably."

"I really don't care," the Chalaine said. "I have suffered a great deal these last few days with all his fawning and bald-faced hints. The best mercy I can afford him is not to let him know how small he has become in my heart."

"This will be a poor wedding night," Gen said. "I have a lot of work to do before morning."

"I know. Let's fetch the Pureman quickly and be wed. I will retire to my chambers. You do what work you need to with Maewen. When you are finished, come to me. I will wait for you. I promise tonight will be memorable, even if there is no cake."

Gen smiled to himself as he and the Chalaine descended the hill into the woods and worked their way around the manor house toward the small Chapel at the rear. Few people frequented the estate, though Embriss's soldiers still patrolled the grounds thickly. The ancient Pureman was still at work cleaning the inside of the small stonework Chapel. Lanterns bathed the ancient interior with a cheery light, revealing the marks of age on the old edifice and its furnishings. The Pureman eyed them both with a friendly smile and straightened himself with some effort.

"Good evening, Chalaine," he said. "I received word that you were with us. I am honored that you have come to see me. And who is this that you bring with you?"

"His identity is a great secret for now, but you may call him Amos," she answered. "And what is your name?"

"Pureman Talis," he answered.

"We have a favor to ask you," she continued. "We wish to be wed immediately."

He blinked, the unexpected request requiring some time to grind through his brain. "To be married?"

"That is correct," the Chalaine continued. "This instant, if you would."

"But aren't you just widowed?" he asked.

"It is true, but I assure you that what I ask of you now is the sincerest wish of my heart."

"And mine," Gen added.

Talis appeared stuck, his aged visage registering confusion. After sorting through his mind for an objection, he shrugged his shoulders. "I am a poor country Pureman for such an honor as this."

"We seek no other gift than your power to bind us," Gen added. "Will you do this?"

"If you wish it," he answered. "Though it seems a hasty thing to me. Let me fetch the ribbon to bind you."

He shuffled off through a door, and they walked forward to the altar. There they waited for some time, the sounds of rummaging and muttering echoing through the empty Chapel. At last he returned, a frustrated look on his face.

"I'm afraid I can't find it. I think that Haddis boy took it after his wedding two days ago."

Gen created one in his hand. "Will this do?"

Talis regarded it with surprise. "Yes, it will. Put your hands on the altar and I'll bind them together."

The old, shaking hands took some time to get it right, and Gen smiled at the Chalaine who was unconsciously tapping her foot in impatience. At length, Talis finished and stood behind the altar.

"This is most unusual," he said. "No one's even here to witness it."

"The two most important ones are here. Please proceed," the Chalaine instructed. "And my name now is Lady Alumira Se' Ellenwei."

"Alumira what?"

It took a few tries to get it right, but at last Talis seemed to get the hang of the unusual moniker.

"Since you are determined to proceed, let us do so promptly."

"Yes, please," the Chalaine said, Gen stifling a chuckle.

"I, Talis, Pureman of the Church of the One stand before you duly authorized to bind you together as husband and wife. The tie which binds your hands represents the binding between your hearts that can only be broken when love is betrayed by a heart unfaithful or starved by a heart neglectful. It is a bond that should be so soft as to afford

219

peace and comfort, but of such strength to resist every hammer blow of life's afflictions. Are you prepared now to enjoy every pleasure, to endure every hardship, and to resist every evil as husband and wife?"

"Yes," the Chalaine answered.

"Yes," Gen added.

"Then I, Talis, pronounce you, Amos, and you Alumira Se' Ellenwei, man and wife."

The Chalaine leaped into Gens arms. "I am married! And there were no demons, and no one died or anything."

"The night is still young," Gen quipped.

The door creaking behind them turned their gaze, where they found it slightly ajar. No one was there.

"The wind does that from time to time," Talis said. "Now, let me go get my book and record this. Amos and Alumira, correct?"

"Yes."

Talis wandered off, and Gen lifted the veil and kissed the Chalaine, who returned it passionately.

"Now," she said, voice teasing as she played her fingers over his chest, "do not be overly long with the half-elven hussy. I will retire, and when you are ready, use one of your little tricks to come up to my window. I'll show you the correct one. If you're very polite, I'll let you in."

"I will be sure to say please," he said.

He led her back to the manor house where Maewen loitered outside. She fetched Gerand to take over her protection.

"Remember," the Chalaine said, "don't stay out too late. And be polite."

"Yes, Alumira. I will remember and obey all your instructions."

She left, and Maewen gave him a quizzical look before speaking with him in Elvish.

"It is good to see her happy again," Maewen commented. "She is an interesting girl. She is so young and simple, but has been thrust into such complex circumstances. Her protected life kept her naive, but hardships have tested and hardened her. I am glad that you will marry. It will be good for you both."

"It will."

"I do sorrow for Mirelle, though. She loves you just as much, as I think you are well aware."

Gen felt his hear sink. "I'm trying not to think of it just now. I hope she can find love."

Maewen nodded. "As do I. Many men would marry her, but I think she will go to her grave alone."

"Let's get to work," Gen suggested, not wanting to revisit his feelings for Mirelle.

Maewen led him into the trees, and they found a small clearing away from the stone wall. The moonlight was strong in the hazy light, the night birds singing softly in the still air. Maewen sat on a stump.

"I assume you will use Trysmagic to create the armor and sword you need?"

"Yes."

"The detail of the sword you have seen. The armor of Aldradan's later years was extremely ornate with a filigreed eagle on the breastplate and greaves. The shield had one too. You may find this exhausting."

"It must be done."

"Before we begin, do you know what errand Dason is about?"

"I've been with the Chalaine. Perhaps the First Mother sent him somewhere. Why do you ask?"

"He rode away from the manor not long before you came. He appeared angry, and I wondered if he'd been dismissed or sent on an unwanted quest. I just found it peculiar that one so pegged to the Chalaine's side would leave her. I'll ask Mirelle about it tomorrow. Let's begin. I'll try to be as descriptive as possible so you don't need to do many alterations. We need to get you to bed. You've had a long journey and will need your rest tonight."

"Yes, I would like to retire as soon as possible."

Chapter 83 - Aldradan Mikmir

Pontiff Athan sat upon the throne of Echo Hold in Eldaloth's absence. He rubbed the rough, stony edges of the arm rests with his hands and grinned with satisfaction. While not a king, he fancied that at this moment he held more power than Chertanne ever had, and he certainly used it with more skill than the dimwitted, cowardly, and tragically short-lived monarch.

The Ha'Ulrich had played his part badly, but in the end Eldaloth's purposes had been served. Athan took comfort in Eldaloth's mercy. If one such as Chertanne with all his fumbling and stumbling could earn Eldaloth's rest, then surely the man who had succeeded in facilitating his healing by bringing him the deluded Chalaine would earn splendorous rewards untold. That Eldaloth had chosen him to use the Sword of the Chalaine to restore Ki'Hal to its former glory was an unexpected and humbling assignment that thrilled him.

Today he sat in audience in the ascetic Great Hall, a place that suited his notion of propriety. The lack of frippery and fashion pleased him, the hard, earthy nature suiting the simplicity and strength he had always wished to project. The entire edifice had been carved directly from the stone, a building born from nature itself. Its heavy ceiling exuded a sense of dangerous weight that had been properly subdued for the use of man.

Today Athan hoped to hear the first reports of those accepting the invitation to join the Procession of Glory. Busy days awaited to prepare for such a momentous journey, but all the pieces were in place. His Padras ruled the nations, the people danced in the streets in adulation, and whatever Eldaloth needed was freely given. Their God had left to prepare the way east to Elde Luri Mora.

Athan scoffed at the fools that had arranged the first, disastrous caravan. So many mistakes. So little discipline and control. Only Eldaloth's merciful care had spared them from utter ruin. *I will do better*, he promised himself. He would honor Eldaloth with a caravan that would praise his name and protect his subjects with orderliness and efficiency. He had prepared for every contingency, from weather, to the still-troublesome Uyumaak, to some desperate attempt by Mirelle and her allies to stop them.

The door to the hall swung open, admitting the first visitor of the morning. Athan corrected his posture, gripping the Pontiff's staff and sitting erect even though the guest was his longtime friend and confidant, Padra Nolan. Pontiff Athan regarded him with a friendly expression until Nolan's quick gait and anxious face prompted concern. The man, long used to difficult news and hard decisions, appeared genuinely alarmed. He didn't even bother to properly genuflect as he should have done.

"It is most extraordinary," Padra Nolan began.

"Be easy, Padra Nolan," Pontiff Athan said as his friend stopped before him. The poor man was out of breath.

"I don't think we can be easy about this, Padra Athan. We are in danger of losing control of Rhugoth."

Athan stood. "What? Mirelle?"

"Not exactly."

"Who would do this? The Regents?"

Padra Nolan took a moment to collect himself, and Athan slid back on the throne, bracing his back and bracing for news. *We cannot lose control of Rhugoth so easily,* he reassured himself. *I placed enough soldiers there to crush any rebellion!*

"It is not Mirelle or the Regents, though they surely lend their support and their men. Rhugoth has its king again. Aldradan Mikmir has returned."

Athan reeled. "Impossible! Church scholars have confirmed his death. This is some trick!"

"It may be, Pontiff," Padra Nolan agreed, "but he comes with mighty power! We've wondered who it was that rescued Mirelle with that display of magic, especially with Ethris dead. Aldradan claims that responsibility, saying that Mirelle's need pulled him away from his rest and into the world again. He wields a sword that can cleave anything, as he amply demonstrated in Embriss, dismantling the Eldephaere with the telltale blade. It was his first appearance as Aldradan, apparently.

"If the stories are to be believed, he rode into the city practically glowing, sword drawn and calling for the pilgrims to hear his words. Our Eldephaere went to stop him, but just as he did on the streets of Echo Hold, he destroyed them with little effort. By the time he left, even the Eldephaere who remained believed he was the King of Mikmir returned, and the word is spreading quickly through Tenswater—and hence the world."

Pontiff Athan calmed himself. "We have an army in Rhugoth, and there is no way they could. . ."

The door to the Great Hall opened again and an acolyte jogged forward. Athan called for silence from Padra Nolan. There was no need to start rumors and create panic. The acolyte handed Nolan a letter and withdrew quickly. Nolan read it and turned as white as a sheet.

"It is confirmed. Mikmir is out of our hands."

"No! So quickly?"

"Padra Madred is dead. It says that Aldradan came into the city, accompanied by the Chalaine, after having gathered a mighty mob of people along the way. The gates were shut, but he opened them with a word of command. Our soldiers simply fled. Apparently Madred tried to confront Aldradan but fell dead without so much as a whimper. From all reports, King Mikmir looks and acts the part. Mirelle is with them, and Aldradan is preaching her belief that Eldaloth is indeed Mikkik."

"This is some scheme of hers," Athan said, face livid. "I should have killed that woman a hundred times by now! Where she conjured up an Aldradan Mikmir, I cannot guess. But this is the true fraud. I must inform Eldaloth at once. He will know how to act to stop this treachery."

"There's more," Padra Nolan continued. "Aldradan Mikmir will wed the Chalaine in Mikmir in three days and has invited everyone of importance to attend—the same list we sent to join the Procession of Glory, I assume."

Athan tried to keep his boiling anger under control for the sake of Padra Nolan. "She is just spitting in my face, now," he ranted. "They must all be punished. We must expose this fake King for whoever he really is and quell these doubts. I can't believe this. Please keep me informed of any further developments. I will call a council this afternoon. Please get all the Padras here who can attend. We have some holes in our ranks to fill, and quickly."

"I will, Pontiff," Nolan said, bowing. "But there is more. We have a very unexpected visitor. Do you remember Dason, Lord Kildan's son?"

"Yes. His father was just executed."

"He wishes an audience with you."

Athan's eyes widened. "He left the Chalaine? Is this some further device of Mirelle's?"

"I do not think so," Padra Athan said. "I have him under guard outside. Will you see him?"

"This is indeed strange. Yes, see him in and stay with me

226

to ward against any treachery."

Athan resumed a formal posture on his throne as Padra Nolan returned with their unlooked for guest. Dason had sided with the Ha'Ulrich, Athan remembered, when Gen had turned everyone against him. He was Tolnorian, a skilled fighter, and every inch a courtier. When he entered, his handsome face was twisted in an unhappy scowl, though Athan thought the cause might be the binds and escort, both an affront to his honor.

"Dason, Protector of the Holy Chalaine," Athan said. "You choose an odd time to see me. Do you come of your own accord or as Mirelle's little puppet? Perhaps you wanted to join the Procession of Glory? You are invited, but I thought your devotion to the Chalaine would preclude you from the trip."

Dason said, "I come of my own accord, and I come because I believe the Chalaine has been ill-used and is in danger."

"Really? How so?"

"When we were driven into the woods, fleeing the Uyumaak horde, a man came among us using the name of Amos. He claimed to be a friend of Maewen the half-elf and a worker of some small magic. He was always lurking in the shadows and the edges of the company, his eyes always on the Chalaine.

"During the battles we fought, he was rarely seen, but stories of his magic and his prowess spread throughout the soldiers. But more troubling, while we were in Blackshire, I caught him with the Chalaine on a couple occasions, and it seemed as if he had won her ear."

"I do not see the danger," Athan said skeptically.

"Two nights ago he and the Chalaine were married in Embriss, a secret affair."

Athan's brows furrowed. "Is this the same man that was sent to retrieve Mirelle from Echo Hold?"

"Yes."

"Are you aware that he is claiming to be Aldradan Mikmir returned?"

Dason's bulging eyes and slack jaw revealed the answer. "Aldradan Mikmir?"

"Yes. You say they were wed, but we received news today that the wedding is set for three days from now. Perhaps you saw the betrothal?"

"I . . . I don't think so. But it must be a lie. He is no Aldradan Mikmir, surely. Even so, the Chalaine wouldn't consent to marry him so quickly!"

Athan saw what was really troubling the handsome Dason, but he needed to draw it to the surface. "And why shouldn't she? She and Chertanne certainly did not share a deep love. In fact, I was quite sure she was enamored of someone else."

"Precisely!" Dason said, rising to the bait. "She and I have always had a high regard for each other, and since Chertanne's death there was an unspoken understanding between us that we would wed to unite Tolnor and Rhugoth. But the more time she spent with this Amos, the more distant and unusually cold she became toward me. It was unbearable."

"It is hard to see someone change so quickly," Athan said. "You suspect that some magical influence was used?"

"When I saw them hand in hand at the altar, no one but him present, I knew something was amiss. Twice Amos used his magic to incapacitate me, so I dared not approach, but is it possible to use magic to sway one's affections so quickly?"

"Quite possible, yes," Athan confirmed. "But what would you have me do? She has turned her back on Eldaloth and on me. I don't see how I can help you."

"You must help me remove her from the clutches of that man!" Dason pled earnestly. "I do not have magic to counter his, and I fear the Chalaine is under some influence too strong for one of my meager talents to break. I came to you because I am beginning to see what you have always believed, that Mirelle and the Chalaine are under some dark influence from the Ilch or someone else. I must rescue her. I know you cared for her once, watched out for her those long months in Ironkeep. You know she has been protected and shut away. She is naive and innocent and might fall under the influence of a Magician easily."

Athan nodded, seeing an opportunity. "I feel for you, but I worry that we can do little. With the Chalaine inside of the fortress of Mikmir, she is no doubt under wards that not even I can pass. We simply cannot get to her to rescue her."

"I have the brand!" Dason said. "I can get to her, but if Amos is there, he will defeat me."

"I hadn't considered that you had the brand," Athan lied. "I believe I may be able to help you." To the soldiers he said, "Unbind him and get him a good meal. I will come to you shortly with instructions. Do you think that Mirelle and the Chalaine will accept you back if you return?"

"I believe they will," Dason said as soldiers cut through his bonds. "There is a secret Portal inside the Chalaine's chambers. If I can see her there, I can get her out to Renberry Cathedral."

"Good. The only hope the Chalaine has is in you, her truest Protector. You will need to leave soon if you are to keep her from being pulled into this farce of a wedding to an impostor. Once she is free of his influence, she will no doubt return that love she once felt for you, only doubly so. Take your rest now, and I will send you instructions soon."

Dason smiled, a gleam returning to his eyes, and Athan knew he had him. *Just the tool I need,* Athan thought. He waved the swordsman away, trying to keep the grin off of his face. A fool in love was easily manipulated. If only Chertanne had been so pliant and willing.

"Is that all, Padra Nolan," Athan asked, "or do you yet have more surprises for me this morning?"

"That is all, and I'm sure more than enough."

"Yes. Keep me informed. Now leave me. I must call to Eldaloth and inform him of what has happened."

Athan stared at his staff of office, admiring the beautiful quartzite crystal formed from Eldaloth's drying blood on the earth when he was struck down. *Who would have thought that his return would bring such chaos and disbelief!* Even dead, Mikkik spread his poison, dividing and tearing asunder when unity should have come. *The sword will set things right and help people have tangible proof,* Athan thought. When Ki'Hal was restored to its full glory, none would dispute the identity of the one called Eldaloth, and all of Mirelle's careful plots would crumble in shame.

Once the doors to the Great Hall swung shut, Athan stepped down from the throne and prayed, invoking the name of Eldaloth and imploring his aid. He could sense the bright light descending and opened his eyes. Eldaloth smiled upon him, as beautiful a being as any living had ever seen. How could Mirelle and the Chalaine doubt when such power and glory were before them?

"Eldaloth," Athan said reverently. "I have dire news."

"Rise and speak, my chosen servant."

In a rush, Athan repeated what Padra Nolan had told him, taking strength from Eldaloth's calm presence. Only Eldaloth's eyes were troubled, and when Athan finished, he reached out and placed his holy hand on Athan's shoulder.

Eldaloth's penetrating eyes held his. "This is indeed the work of Mikkik," he intoned. "We cannot wait any longer. We will proceed with the Procession of Glory as planned to keep them unaware, but you and Padra Nolan must leave in secrecy immediately for Elde Luri Mora and perform the ritual there as I explained it. On fast horses with a small party, you will reach it in three days. Do nothing more. I will put an end to this pretended Aldradan Mikmir."

"We have an unexpected ally, Holiness. It is one of the Chalaine's Protectors who has come to his senses and realized that she is being manipulated and tricked by those around her. He may be able to get to the Chalaine and pull her away from those that deceive her. He claims he can get her to Renberry Cathedral in Mikmir, one of our Church strongholds there. Do I have your permission to attempt to reclaim her?"

"Of course. I will take care of the predator if you can arrange to rescue the prey. This will show the people my power and put an end to this upstart rebellion."

Athan was pleased. "I will see it done. In three days, the world will at last be set right. Your glory will shine through the world, and the traitors will be put down."

Eldaloth smiled at him, Athan's heart leaping at having brought pleasure to his glorious master.

"Is there more that you require, most Holy Eldaloth?"

"Leave me and let me meditate upon my throne for a moment," he said. "You have done well."

Athan bowed and left.

The pile of rocks crushed him without end. He lay mangled and smashed, left alone and buried by Ghama Dhron which had been acting under Gen's command. Sir Torus hungered for food, the souls of sentient creatures that he so craved. Starvation had weakened him, and he could hardly think for the continual weight that could not kill him even though every part of him was pulverized. His only freedom from despair was the unconquerable need to feed that pushed aside all other ruminations that might have driven him mad.

But in the darkness, a voice came to his mind, the voice of the one who had changed him into a creature of appetite, a creature that he loathed.

The time for your freedom has come, Mikkik said. *I have come to my power but have one enemy left. When she is dead, I will free you from your curse, and you will be free to seek death.*

Anything to be free, Sir Tornus begged. *Anything to feed!*

My servant comes to your aid. Be ready. The silencing of the world is at hand.

Gen lay on his back staring at the canopy of the Chalaine's bed, wondering if Gerand and Volney were getting suspicious that he insisted on guarding the Chalaine personally during the night, since his duties as the returned King of Rhugoth would certainly require him to get a good night's rest. The royal chambers built into the Great Hall to await the return of Aldradan Mikmir had lain dormant and unused, a museum piece, until Gen had shocked the world by taking upon himself the title of King. While Mirelle had informed Volney of Gen's true identity—which shocked and delighted him—no one, not even Mirelle, knew that he and the Chalaine had already wed.

He stroked the Chalaine's hair as she slept peacefully. She rested as she had every night with her head on his shoulder, an arm across his chest, and one leg stretched across his. While he relished her unconscious embrace, he couldn't help but think she draped herself over him to prevent him from leaving without her knowing.

Her sweet, trusting love always pushed away the intense hardships of the day, most of which were spent in court with the Chalaine receiving visitors and issuing instructions, or with Mirelle trying to firm up plans for the wedding on ridiculously short notice. Once the wedding was complete, only about half of the force they had hoped for would be ready to march on Tenswater to get to the Echo Hold Portal, and reports had already trickled in that the Church was planning to contest their entry by force of arms.

In spite of his worries and the myriad of items demanding his attention, returning to Rhugoth brought him great pleasure. While he still preferred the country lanes of Blackshire over packed city avenues, Mikmir felt like the place of his second birth. Here he had found purpose. Here he had risen in power and importance. Here he had found the woman he called wife and who loved him without reservation. Following the Chalaine through the maze their first night back came as naturally as if he had never been away, though retiring with her for the night in her chambers felt strangely inappropriate until she made it feel otherwise.

More than anything, seeing her happy every single day— bright and carefree and smiling—felt like a victory over every darkness and evil he had struggled against for two years. The most important battle had been fought and won. The Chalaine practically danced around the castle of Mikmir, shining like a second sun everywhere she went. With the Chalaine happy, Mirelle was happy, too, in spite of the immense stress of the logistics and planning that absorbed her. It was a dream. And as the Chalaine had expressed to him nearly every night as they lay together, she wished with all her heart the Mikkik would simply go away and let them live in peace and joy.

But it wasn't to be. This morning he would be a King and hold a council with his generals. This evening he would be a King again and wed the Chalaine. Then tonight, one last time, he could be Gen and she could be the Alumira, alone together and in love. Then it was time for war and death and a desperate ride to Elde Luri Mora. He couldn't guess what would happen if Mikkik succeeded in plunging the sword into the heart of the ancient city, but he also couldn't fathom what would happen if the dark god failed and they won the day. Would he still go on pretending to be Aldradan Mikmir, living out his life as a lie?

He stirred and tried to gently pry the Chalaine off him,

but as he did she woke enough to clamp on to him even more tightly.

"No, you don't," she said sleepily.

"Alumira, I have to get outside the door before Gerand arrives, or he may begin to suspect that I have behaved in an improper way toward you. Reputation is very important to Tolnorians."

"Just go back to sleep. You need your rest for our wedding night."

He smiled and disentangled himself from his clinging wife of nearly a week. She pouted in protest but quickly fell asleep. Gen smiled at her as he donned the regal uniform he had fashioned for himself for playing the part of Aldradan Mikmir. Both Mirelle and the Chalaine had praised the black pants and deep blue shirt with gold trim, saying it accented his features and colors nicely. They sized him up like a bull at the fair, fussing about the length of his hair and the shape of his beard, but both had separately told him that he looked every inch a king.

Belting the replica sword of Aldradan Mikmir to his waist, he opened the door quietly and stepped out, and just in time. Footsteps in the maze signaled Gerand's approach, and Gen stood at attention, trying to look like someone who had just spent a night in solitude and boredom rather than the reverse.

"Good morning, my Lord Mikmir," Gerand said, executing a bow. "I've come to relieve you."

"Gerand, I know we need to keep up pretenses, but bow to me as little as possible. It's hard enough to accept from complete strangers, but we are sword brothers and equals."

"Sword brothers, yes," Gerand said, "but equals? I think not. Aldradan Mikmir was not born a king, and neither were you, but you are both gifted leaders. The people are ecstatic and praise you highly."

"Thank you for your kind words," Gen replied. "But it will be a long time before I am used to this. And thank you for arriving promptly. I've got a council to prepare for this morning."

Gen left and wound his way out to the antechamber of the Chalaines where Mirelle waited for him as she had every morning since their arrival. She had clearly slept little, red eyes ringed with dark circles.

"Good morning, Lord Mikmir," she said with a teasing smile.

Gen offered her his arm. "And to you the same, First Mother. It appears you need to follow the example of your daughter and sleep a little later. You seem to be at the point of exhaustion."

"I am tired, though I might comment that you seem a little too well rested for someone who has been performing guard duty at night and hardly has a moment to himself during the day. I would compliment you on the idea of personally guarding the Chalaine, however. The story that Aldradan Mikmir protects the Chalaine has played well with the people. I am happy that she is so *closely* protected every night."

"And how is Volney working out?" Gen asked, changing the subject.

"It is odd to have someone so young and impressionable walking in my shadow," she said. "I gave him the day off to visit with his wife, since you will be with me almost all day."

The unification of the shards had not so neatly joined the tunnels between the shards where the bridge once spanned the gap. Workers had cleared a rough tunnel to the spiral walkway that led up to the Great Hall of the castle. Gen took breakfast with Mirelle on the balcony, and they talked strategy for the council meeting and final plans for the wedding.

"I only lament that it will be a simple affair," Mirelle said. "I had wished to throw the most luxurious and expensive wedding for my daughter, especially since this is a wedding we can both wholeheartedly look forward to."

"It is enough for us," Gen said. "I'm surprised you've arranged as much as you have on such short notice. You are very efficient."

"It is one of my better qualities."

A weak voice below the balcony tried to rise above the din of the workers decorating the Great Hall for the wedding. "Lord Mikmir?"

Hurney Fedrick waited on the floor, his once commanding voice having crumbled during Mirelle's absence. "My Lord, you have a visitor who wishes an audience."

"Who is it, Chamberlain?"

"Dason Kildan."

Gen's eyebrows raised. "I will come down in a moment. I wish to make him wait for a while."

"Very good, Milord."

"So the prodigal Protector has come home," Mirelle said, face troubled. "I confess his departure has worried me a great deal, as it was so unexpected. Do you mind if I tag along and sit on my throne one last time?"

"Not at all. Let's finish and go down together."

They took their time with the food and then descended, Gen dismissing the decorators and the court scribe so that they could talk with privacy. Gen took his seat on the massive throne of Aldradan Mikmir, Mirelle sitting on the smaller one just below. Gen signaled to Hurney, who went to retrieve the visitor.

"Dason Kildan," he croaked a few moments later in a barely audible voice. The last few days of constant visits had nearly incapacitated the old man.

Dason, now dressed in the black uniform of the Dark Guard, strode in. Gen sized him up, remembering Shadan Khairn's training on reading the details of stride and posture and expression. The Tolnorian's steps lacked confidence and his entire demeanor was tentative, but his face was resolute, eyes full of purpose. Whatever he felt, he

236

had a hard time meeting their eyes, and Gen couldn't tell if he felt shame or harbored some secret anger toward them. Dason knelt and bowed his head.

"Rise," Gen commanded, tone forceful. "You are brave to come to this hall after your desertion of the Chalaine, Dason Kildan of Tolnor. If you have come to beg for a return to your position of honor after such an act, then you are wasting your breath."

"Lord Mikmir," Dason said, face earnest. "I realize my error in leaving unannounced as I did that evening, but I was a man disappointed in a love I thought mine alone. Since the passing of the Ha'Ulrich, it was my deepest wish and understanding that the Chalaine and I would be wed to unite Tolnor and Rhugoth for strength against the schemes of Mikkik. It was my understanding that my feelings of love and affection were reciprocated by the Chalaine. We have shared a closeness since my former appointment as her Protector. When her love and person seemed at last within my grasp, I cannot tell you what joy filled my heart.

"Imagine my despair when I found out that this dream was not to be! That she had given her heart to some obscure woodsman, that I only later came to know was Aldradan Mikmir. I was crushed and hurt, the very joy of life ripped from me cruelly. It was as if death had found me. I felt she had betrayed me, and my world had gone as black as the grave! I fled from her glorious presence and my pain, and in my despair I wandered, my duty to her lost beneath my sadness.

"I return now knowing my position is lost, but begging only one favor. I wish to be in her honor guard at her wedding. I can only hope that my years of service as a Dark Guard and a Protector can earn me some leniency for the disappointment she must feel at my dereliction of duty. This one favor I ask, and no more."

Gen regarded Dason closely. It wasn't difficult to hear the shattered heart in his voice, and Gen remembered the

Chalaine's tale of their stolen kiss of regard while he was her Protector. The Chalaine had grown out of her infatuation while his infatuation had grown into love or at least some expectation of it.

"I cannot blame you for your feelings, Dason," Gen said. "Nor will I render judgment on your request immediately. I will consult the feelings of the Chalaine, who, I believe, has always considered you an excellent man and a good friend. From those close the the Chalaine, I know you have rendered good service in the past, and I do not wish to be punitive at this time of celebration. Take a room at the Quickblade. I will send our decision to you before midday."

"I thank you, your Majesty," Dason said, appearing relieved. "I will await your word."

Dason strode away and Gen glanced at Mirelle, who leaned in close. She said, "It is a cruel thing, poor man. It was the wish of his father that they wed. The Chalaine should have spurned his advances more forcefully."

Gen shook his head. "She had a great deal of affection for him once."

"Once," Mirelle agreed, "but she hasn't thought of him that way for a long time. You taught her what love really was, and she never looked back."

Gen nodded and sat back, pondering as Dason disappeared behind the double doors. He could pity the man. To lose the love of the Chalaine would crush anyone, though it appeared that Dason's surety of the Chalaine's reciprocation of his love proceeded from a healthy imagination fed by vanity.

"Should we make a wager on whether the Chalaine will allow him in the honor guard?" Mirelle asked. "I'll wager fifty gold she says yes just to spare his feelings."

"I accept your wager and say she won't," Gen replied. "She was powerfully annoyed with him before he left. When she found out he had ridden off, she said, 'Good riddance.'"

Mirelle grinned. "We shall see, Lord Mikmir. A mother knows her daughter."

CHAPTER 84 - SHATTERED SKY

The Chalaine stood in front of the Walls, staring at the people gathering on the square in preparation for the wedding. As was custom, they formed two lines, holding lanterns and candles to create an avenue of light for her and Gen to traverse. The evening deepened on a perfect summer day, and she couldn't help but draw comparisons to the betrothal ceremony she had so dreaded with Chertanne. Tonight, the right man would be on the horse, and dutiful Churchmen had scoured the Chapel to ensure that no uninvited demonic visitors would interrupt the ceremony. More than anything, she wished she could tear the veil from her face and toss it into the crowd so they could see the life and happiness in her face.

Her mother worked her hair to perfection, smiling as she twisted and looped and tied. The Chalaine felt profound relief at the warmth and serenity of Mirelle's countenance. She had feared for so long that her wedding to Gen would break Mirelle's heart, but she appeared perfectly content and happy to give her daughter to the man she also loved. The love of a mother was still a mystery to her, but in time the Chalaine hoped she would have the chance to understand the depth of dedication that a woman could have for a child.

"How are you feeling, dear?" Mirelle asked. "You don't seem as nervous as you should be."

"I am at peace," the Chalaine answered truthfully. "This is the kind of man I wanted to marry in the first place, and I know and love Gen so well that there is simply no room for fear in my heart."

"You need to call him Lord Mikmir from now on, Alumira," Mirelle chided. "One slip in the right company could prove disastrous."

"I know, I know," the Chalaine said. "It just seems so awkward and formal. I'll be careful. There's just some part of me that wishes that everyone knew that I was marrying Gen and not some legend I've barely known a week. I want the whole world to see that I loved the man who fought and bled and even died for me. He deserves that recognition and that reward."

Mirelle adjusted her daughter's dress, shifting the veil to precisely center. "*You* are the reward, and since I know Gen, I know he wishes for nothing more than you. And speaking of reward," her mother said, voice teasing, "are you ready for the honeymoon, such as it is?"

The Chalaine blushed. She didn't have the heart to tell her mother that she had been thoroughly enjoying her honeymoon for days. Since Gen had to leave Mikmir the morning after the wedding, they could not travel to some exotic place to be alone. The honeymoon would consist of a stay in the Chalaine's Tower, a place where her decoys had lived and to which she had never been.

"I will hardly speak of such matters with you, mother," the Chalaine replied. "Gen—I mean, Lord Mikmir—will do quite well, I'm sure, and we will keep such matters private, as is proper."

Mirelle chuckled. "I love it when you blush. Just don't keep him up too late. He's going to need his wits about him tomorrow. But don't cheat him, either. He deserves the love of his wife before he rides into danger."

"That's quite enough advice on the topic," the Chalaine said, pulling at a strand of hair. "I'm sure we will be sensible."

"But not too sensible, for pity's sake!" Mirelle admonished, picking up her daughter's veil from the bed where it was carefully folded. "It's supposed to be memorable, after all."

A knock at the door hurried Mirelle's efforts to secure the veil to her daughter's head.

"Come in!" the Chalaine said.

Gerand poked his head in. "Dason has arrived and wishes an audience with you, Lady Alumira."

"Let him enter," the Chalaine said, suddenly feeling sick to her stomach. She had agreed to let him serve as honor guard out of respect, but since Gen had brought the news of Dason's return to her, she had chastised herself for not making her feelings—or rather the lack thereof—plain to Dason. She never wished to cause him pain, but as he entered, it wasn't pain but purpose that she found in his eyes. He bowed.

"Thank you for this honor, Lady Alumira," he said.

"You have earned it, Dason," she said. "I am sorry if I have hurt you. I did not wish to make you think I felt more than I did for you."

This stung him, but he seemed resolute, straightening and stepping near her. "I beg you to reconsider this marriage," he said, voice intense. "I love you and only want the best for you. You are being deceived!"

"Dason!" Mirelle said, stepping between him and the Chalaine. "Leave at once!"

His face screwed up into a scowl of righteous anger. "I'll leave, Mirelle!"

Dason stepped forward, and with a powerful shove pushed Mirelle backward with such force that she tumbled over the bed. Entangling bed veils clung to Mirelle, and she grunted when she landed hard on the floor. Before the Chalaine could think, Dason grabbed her arm in a vice-like grip and placed his other hand on the Walls.

"Renberry Cathedral!"

The Chalaine screamed for help as the interior of the old Church resolved into view. The door exploded open, Gerand entering with sword drawn.

"Let her go, brother!" he yelled.

But to the Chalaine's surprise, Dason walked forward and then into the Walls. He pulled her in after, her room disappearing in an instant.

She and Dason stood in the deserted Cathedral, a stone wall behind them where they had crossed through. A single lantern hanging askance from the wall created a small pool on the deserted benches halfway back. The Cathedral, built on the edge of Kingsblood Lake, stood at the center of an Eldephaere stronghold. Its dark, thick stone and ascetic interior was meant to reflect sobriety and service rather than to stun a parishioner into reverence. Unlike other Church buildings with ornate windows and glass, only thin vertical slits in the walls allowed the dying evening light to slice into the room. The Chalaine stared at the boxy interior with disbelief. Her Walls were a Portal! No one had never told her!

"What have you done!" the Chalaine yelled, yanking her arm from Dason's grip.

"What I had to do to save you, Chalaine. You have been gravely deceived and are, I fear, under the influence of magic," he explained, voice placating. "I love you and only wish to see your mind and heart put right again."

"You are the one who has been tricked!" the Chalaine spat. "How dare you do this to me against my will! Gen will come for me, and you will pay for this treachery with your life!"

"Gen is dead, Chalaine!" Dason said, trying to place his hands on her shoulders. She moved away. "You are clearly not in your right mind!"

"You are fool, Dason," she said, cursing her slip of the tongue. "There will be no mercy for you this time."

Dason shook his head. "We'll be gone before anyone can find us. Athan will provide protection and undo whatever lies have been foisted upon you."

"Athan!?" she yelled. "You really have lost your mind! Athan is a deluded fiend!"

She waited for Dason to respond, but as his eyes searched the Chapel around them, his countenance lost its confidence. The Chalaine followed his gaze. Around the edges of the floor Eldephaere soldiers lay dead, and a Churchman was draped over the altar behind them.

"Dason?"

A man rose in the darkness near the back benches and walked toward them calmly. He had a soldierly stride and stance, but he wore no weapon. A glint of anticipation shone in his dark eyes as he approached.

"Good evening," he said. "Welcome to Renberry Cathedral, Chalaine. It is an honor to know you at last."

The Chalaine backed instinctively away, and Dason pulled his sword.

"Who are you?" Dason asked.

The man smiled. "Sir Tornus of Echo Hold. Forgive the mess. I have been very hungry lately."

Gen examined himself in the mirror and almost couldn't recognize himself. Even more disturbing, the man who returned the gaze looked like an actual King. A week of having every servant and aristocrat call him Lord Mikmir hadn't helped the lie sound like the truth to him or lessened the feeling that he was a fraud and an impostor. But now, staring at himself bedecked in rich blue and gold, a simple crown atop his head, an uncanny invitation to believe in his own abilities and destiny called to him. Mirelle beaming at him with unabashed pride as they sat in council or in court almost convinced him that Kingship was a calling he could fulfill. But something of the peasant boy of Tell still remained within him and refused to let the conversion fully take place.

The chambers of Aldradan Mikmir had received a hasty cleaning and restoration after he arrived, though the scent of dust still clung to the side chambers in particular. A cadre a servants swirled about, some to ensure his clothing was in proper order, and others asking about this detail or that. The drama of his arrival and his display of power had nearly convinced everyone that Aldradan Mikmir had indeed returned, although skepticism still bred in some corners of Rhugoth, especially among those dedicated to the Church of the One.

"I believe you are ready, Milord," his servant said after inspecting the golden cape. "Your itinerary states that you are to retrieve your stallion from the stables and proceed to the front of the Great Hall to await Lady Alumira's approach. Shall I review the rest, or are you confident of the procedure?"

"I know it well enough, thank you," he said. "You and your fellows may retire and enjoy yourselves."

"You are most gracious, Lord Mikmir," the servant said. "A thousand blessings to you."

Gen nodded. He promised himself not get used to the fawning and scraping. As yet, there had hardly been enough time for the Regents and Generals to curry favor with him, but he knew it would begin in earnest if he sat on the throne much longer.

A servant opened the door for him and an honor guard of six Rhugothian knights fell in around him as he strode down the hall to the side door near the kitchens. The Great Hall was a blur of servants placing tables and food, and amid the chaos he spotted Marna firmly in command, rolling pin in hand. It was her scepter, and she prodded and smacked as much as she rolled dough.

"Marna," Gen said, "I have heard your sweetbread is second to none. Please have some taken to the Chalaine's Tower tonight."

The poor cook nearly fainted, but she composed herself and bowed, blushing furiously.

"I'll bake it myself!" she said. "Don't fear! It'll water your mouth right good."

Gen winked at her and she giggled girlishly, returning to her work with redoubled fervor. The grounds outside were thick with children playing in the cool evening breeze. All activity stopped as the impressive guard and a King exited the kitchens and into the night, tiny faces agape with awe. Gen smiled and lifted his arm in a friendly wave, though only two of the group had the courage to return the greeting.

The din of the crowd waiting outside the front entrance to the Great Hall filled the air with a lively rumble as they approached the stables. A thick, dark stallion awaited him, arrayed in armor, and Gen mounted the beast carefully, sensitive to the massive power the warhorse possessed. With a gentle incantation and a push from Mynmagic, the horse settled itself and walked forward without prodding spurs or commands. The knights walked three to a side as they approached the side gate that would lead them to the square beyond. Hard pressed soldiers kept the immediate environs of the gate free of revelers, but once the trumpet sounded to announce the approach of Aldradan Mikmir, a surge nearly overtook them.

To a chorus of shouting he rode forward, two lines of soldiers forming a lane toward the Great Hall where nearly two hundred soldiers stood at attention, all sporting the device of the rose, the Chalaine's symbol. Gen sat up tall and willed the horse forward. He set forth at a walk, projecting an exultant, friendly air as the horse sauntered down the temporary avenue and then up the stairs toward the porch of the Great Hall. He turned toward the crowd, raising his hand for silence. To his surprise, it actually fell, and quickly.

"Good people of Rhugoth," he said, using Duammagic to enhance and project his voice. "It is with a feeling of great honor that I share this night with you. As in days long past, the people of Rhugoth are indeed the best and most loyal of people. I thank you for your trust and support in these difficult times as we once again must be the tip of the spear that will pierce the heart of Mikkik and lead the world out of deception and destruction.

"I am most humbled and gratified that I have the great privilege of marrying the most glorious daughter of this nation, and I swear to you that I will dedicate my life to filling hers with peace and joy. Now return to your revels while we await the favor of the Lady Alumira. Let there be feasting, let there be song, and let our joy be unrivaled in Ki'Hal!"

A wave of applause and cheering shook the air and Gen dismounted, keeping an eye on the double doors in anticipation of seeing his bride. The Chalaine had expressly forbidden him from seeing her arrayed in her chosen dress, wanting to surprise him. More than anything, he wanted to see her and have the whole procession and ceremony done. The people needed the pomp, but he wanted only the private moments before riding off to battle the Church soldiers in Tenswater and then on the plain around Echo Hold.

He could feel her presence somewhere below, still in her chamber. But as he turned to watch the crowd, she moved in an instant to somewhere on the other side of the city. He waited for a moment, alarmed, disbelieving his own senses. But her position did not return to the hall behind.

Dason! he thought. *He came to stage a rescue of his own!*

Gen placed his foot in the stirrup of his horse, but gasps and expressions of surprise filled the air before turning to silence. The music died, and even the rowdiest of revelers held his peace. Gen turned and gazed upward to see a figure burning like a white hot sun descending from the sky as if plucked from the stars. This same trick of glory Gen knew from the battle at Echo Hold. Mikkik had come for him.

The crowd shied back as Mikkik settled on the stones of the courtyard with a graceful step, striding forward toward the stairs. Gen drew his sword and swallowed. How would Mikkik approach him? As an enemy? A wayward child? After dying and being revivified by the Millim Eri, Gen had used Trysmagic to reapply the protection against transmutation, but would his will be strong enough to counter the force of a dark god bent on destroying the world?

"Remain here," Gen commanded his knights.

Working up his courage, Gen marched down the stairs with a regal step, keeping calm. A burning sword of fire ignited in Mikkik's hand as they closed upon each other. The god knew when to apply a little theatricality. Mikkik towered over him, his simple white robe and golden belt so bright that it illuminated the faces of the stunned crowd around them.

"I have come to end this treachery," Mikkik's voice boomed. "I am Eldaloth, the only King of Ki'Hal. There may be no other, especially not one who unworthily takes upon himself the name of one of my great and noble servants of times past." Mikkik raised his sword. "I will cleanse this place of you and redeem Rhugoth from this farce!"

Gen raised his sword to defend, but suddenly Mikkik pressed upon his mind with brutal force, sending his thoughts scattering in a hundred directions. Gen's vision blurred as Mikkik threw images and emotions from his life at him as if pelting him with rocks. His concentration wavered, unable to push aside the memories and feelings enough to gather his thoughts to defend himself. Mikkik would crush him with the first blow.

Gen retreated inside himself, trying to find the will to dispel the confounding swirl of his mind and center his thoughts on the shining blade arcing unopposed toward the space between his neck and shoulder with enough force to drive the sword deep into his chest. He fought Mikkik's spell, but the Mynmagic was too strong. He would not escape.

Run Chalaine! Gen willed. *Run!*

Pontiff Athan rubbed the unfamiliar growth on his face and let his fingers wander up to the tired eyes that had scarcely rested since departing Echo Hold over three days before. Padra Nolan and ten of the elite Eldephaere had accompanied him on their crucial mission to restore Ki'Hal before Mirelle and her schemes could endanger it. Eldaloth would deal with her, Athan was sure, though he need not fear her interference any longer. The goal was in easy reach.

They rode at a casual pace across the bridge over Mora Lake toward the still and quiet city of Elde Luri Mora. The journey eastward had passed in blessed ease. No storms or Uyumaak had menaced them as they pushed the horses to their limits. Athan would not let any idleness or overconfidence or neglect put his sacred task in jeopardy. He had regimented their travel with uncompromising efficiency and with some cost to their health and the welfare of the horses.

But they had come fast and they had come far, and when Ki'Hal was restored, then so would they be. An end to sickness and famine and even death awaited a weary world, and the sacred sword bundled in oil-slicked leather would return a joy and brightness to the world that had been lost since Mikkik's treachery. That Eldaloth would entrust him with this final task was a supernal reward that would immortalize the name of Athan forever.

Elde Luri Mora sat as it once had when he and the doomed caravan had entered it. As then, it was a place of refuge and safety, sleeping in an eternal spring, unable to mature to the sweet fruit of summer. Very few of Athan's memories of that time brought him cheer, though the old Pontiff Beliarmus tossing an insolent Gen across the sacred hall would always bring a smile to his face. How they had all survived those tumultuous days eluded him, but *miraculous* was an apt description for their deliverance.

Of course, no great act of history was accomplished without losses and setbacks, but tonight would see the end of evil, the end of nefarious schemes and demented Queens. He would be the instrument in Eldaloth's hands. Pontiff Athan would bring peace. He would bring health. He would bring joy. The thought nearly overwhelmed him with anticipation, and he fought back the urge to push his exhausted horse into one last gallop.

Evening had passed, only a dim veil of light rising up from the horizon before him as they finished their traverse and the hooves of the animals trod upon the cobbled roadways of Elde Luri Mora. All three moons shone brightly in summer sky, highlighting the edges of thin clouds riding just above the forested hills that encompassed the lake and the island. The scent of blossoms caressed their worries and weariness away, and Athan smiled in anticipation. Fireflies swarmed and blinked aimlessly in the gathering darkness, pushed about by a gentle evening breeze.

"Is that the great hall of Elde Luri Mora?" Padra Nolan asked as the edifice slid into view as they crested a rise. The tall domed structure waited just as they had left it.

"The Hall of Three Moons, yes," Athan answered. "Unless the Ilch made some other provision, the bones of my predecessor await somewhere in the darkness there. You will see where Chertanne and the Chalaine were wed. The babe was conceived in that dwelling just across the way. When Eldaloth reigns here, I imagine all will be welcome to come see the places where such momentous events took place. I hope that I will dwell here with him. It is the most beautiful of places.

"Let us make haste. This task should not be delayed. I truly pity all the unfortunate nobles in the caravan. How disappointed they will be when they realize they will not be a part of this great moment. I hope they will understand the need for our haste. At the very least, they will be among the first to visit the great city after its glory is restored."

"It will be a disappointment," Padra Nolan agreed. "But Eldaloth will reward them some other way, I am sure."

"Exactly, brother. Thank you for accompanying me. Now, let's be about our task quickly. I am anxious to discharge this duty."

They dismounted their horses and ascended the familiar stairs toward the arched entry, Athan clutching the Sword of the Chalaine to his breast. As they approached, the fireflies gathered and swarmed in an enormous cloud and streamed inside the Hall of Three Moons, illuminating it in a yellowish light.

"Marvelous!" Padra Nathan exclaimed.

"Yes. More wonders will come," Athan said. "Guard the way," he commanded his soldiers. "This should take but a moment."

Before them stretched the map of Ki'Hal etched upon the floor, and on the far side of the room, Pontiff Beliarmus's dark robe and desiccated skeleton moldered on the ground.

Athan shook his head in disgust. "I suppose it is no surprise that the Ilch and his companions could not show even the least bit of decency to provide a great man a proper burial. We will attend to it when we are finished."

They reached the center of the map, following Eldaloth's instructions. Reverently Athan knelt, unwrapping the sword entrusted to him. It was a simple blade, but he could feel the power of the Chalaine's blood—Eldaloth's blood—coursing through it. Once inserted into the holy ground of Elde Luri Mora, Eldaloth's power would flow from the sacred blade and enliven the world.

He exhaled. "The time has come." He remembered the words, thick upon the tongue, given him by his master: "Kekkat. Gundrued Ki. Gundrued Tekkix. Gundrued Zhas. Kekkat!"

The blade began to glow, the air vibrating with power. Grasping the hilt with both hands, he raised the sword above his head and jammed it downward, the point sliding into the stone floor like a sharp dagger into soft flesh. It slid all the way to the hilt and Athan released it, raising his head to the sky. "It is done!"

The ground beneath his feet buzzed like the air. "It is happening, Nolan! It is happening!"

As if blown by a gale, the fireflies streamed out the door, leaving them in darkness. The buzzing beneath their feet progressed to a tremor, a horrible low moaning of grinding rock pummeling their ears. A mighty shake of the ground threw them to the floor, a wrenching, cracking noise bringing their hands to their ears to muffle the penetrating thunder that shook their bodies to the core. The great glass dome of the ceiling crashed down, cracks in the masonry of the dome loosening in chunks and throwing down sections of the ceiling and walls all around them.

Athan struggled to his feet as the shaking subsided, casting about to find Padra Nolan crushed beneath a heavy stone, his blood pooling outward. A great fissure stretching the length of the floor had swallowed the sword, but Athan knew he was in grave danger and could not linger.

Swaying as he tried to keep his bearings, he went to cast a spell to steady himself and calm his nerves, but his incantations issued from his mouth in vain. Stumbling over fallen rock and debris, he reached the broken entrance finding that his soldiers had fled to the base of the stairs to escape the crumbling building. As one they looked to the sky, mouths agape, unaware of his presence.

Athan's eyes followed theirs to the sky. The moons had gone, or rather they had been obliterated. Nothing but expanding clouds of what seemed to be fine dust remained, as if each had exploded from the very center. The power of magic was gone. The blessed feeling of life in Elda Luri Mora was gone.

What have I done? Athan thought, stumbling and falling down the stairs in shock. Battered and bruised, he regained his feet, eyes ever upon the sky as the clouds of shattered moons swelled the sky, streaming in every direction.

"The trees!" one of the soldiers exclaimed.

The blossoms that had clothed every tree in splendorous pinks, purples, and yellows had wilted as one, their leaves falling like a rain to carpet the ground beneath them. In seconds, the branches were barren and colorless, the soothing breeze that once blew gently kicking up into a gale that swirled the detritus around them in a whirlwind.

Athan was numb. He had to make it back to Echo Hold. There had to have been some mistake! Had he said the wrong words? Misplaced the sword? But as he reached his horse and clung to its bridle, the horrifying possibility that he had dismissed as folly started to reassert itself. Had Mirelle been right? Had they all been duped? *Impossible!* All the signs were there! Every event detailed by the prophecy had happened. Eldaloth had come!

"We should go, Pontiff," one of his soldiers said, breaking through his confusion. "Something is not right, here."

"What is it?"

"Look."

Athan lifted his gaze to the city around them. In the last of the evening light, every tree, every blade of grass, every creeping vine and flower was turning black and shriveling into a gray powder as if burned by some invisible fire. Terror and despair gripped his heart as his own flesh and that of the horses began to dry and peel.

In haste they mounted their skittish horses and fled, the affliction of flesh lessening as they rode away from the ruined Hall of Three Moons. Their skin gradually smoothed and regained its elasticity as they galloped across the cracked bridge above the dark, still water. The gate, bent and hanging from one hinge, squealed in the wind.

Elde Luri Mora was dying.

I killed it. Athan lamented. *I am a fool!* His righteous anger, his arguments, his adoration for the being who claimed Eldaloth's name faded and disintegrated with all the suffering life behind him. A poisonous dread seeped as deep into his soul as the exultant honor and pride he had felt just minutes before, the vast gap between the two emotions a crater into which his very soul plummeted in freefall.

Nearly insensible to all around him, he let the horse follow its companions through the gate to find that the road that had so invitingly welcomed them into the city had completely disappeared, leaving nothing but wilderness ahead of them. Their pace slowed as they tried to pick their way through the uneven ground in the deepening dark.

"Shall we encamp here?" one of the soldiers asked. "The horses cannot go on again! They've barely rested!"

Athan hardly heard him.

"Pontiff! Shall we encamp here?"

Athan snapped out of his reverie, regarding the soldier with sober, bleary eyes. There was only one way to remedy this error, only one way to restore the world. If the blood of the Chalaine could destroy, then it could also heal. She must be bled again, only this time in a world without moons, a world where no magic could heal her. If all had gone well with Dason's plan, then the Chalaine would be safely on her way to Echo Hold, though if she reached it, he feared what Mikkik would do. Surely he knew that only she held the key to the restoration of Ki'Hal.

"No. We don't camp. We ride for Echo Hold."

CHAPTER 85 - NIGHT FIRE

The Chalaine shrank from Sir Tornus, trying to pull Dason away from him. Her former Protector stood firm.

"What house do you come from?" Dason asked Sir Tornus, who looked at him like a savory meal ready to be devoured. "I've never heard of any Sir Tornus from anywhere."

"He's a Craver, Dason," the Chalaine explained. "He betrayed the nations at Echo Hold in the Second Mikkikian War."

"The Lady knows her history!" Sir Tornus said, smiling. "Pray, who did you learn it from?"

"Gen," she said.

Sir Tornus nodded. "Ah, yes, the man with no soul. You know, I tried to devour him and his companions. I felt dreadful about it, but essence of Uyumaak simply grew too tiresome. It's not like you can season an essence with herbs. It was, therefore, simply impossible for me to pass up an opportunity for something a little sweeter. But you, Chalaine, are the sweetest soul I've come across in ages."

Dason's brow crinkled. "Cravers are a myth!"

Sir Tornus regarded him with a wicked grin. "Oh, how I wish I were a myth! I've tried to disbelieve in myself for some time, but I keep turning out to be real. But you, my friend, you will learn differently soon."

Dason stepped back. "Pontiff Athan said he would send a force to protect us. You'd best flee while you are able."

"I think I devoured your protection," Sir Tornus explained. "Strange people, these Eldephaere, castrating themselves so they wouldn't be attracted to a woman they haven't been allowed to guard for nearly a century. I know traditions tend to linger, but let's face it—castration is a really poor choice of tradition. It seems a simple vote to end the practice could hardly fail. Quite a deterrent to recruiting, I would imagine."

During Sir Tornus's musings, Dason grabbed the Chalaine's arm and led her sideways, away from the center aisle. The Eldephaere soldiers lay in heaps in the shadows, forcing the Chalaine to step over them and on them in order to reach the side aisle and make for the rear door. Sir Tornus simply strode back to where he had come from to block their way.

"You can't leave yet!" he said. "The sign hasn't been given! I've one last duty to discharge and I'll at last be free to die. You young people can hardly understand how the years grind on in boredom, but they do. Death isn't a punishment or a disease—it's a relief!"

"Let us pass, or I will cut you down!" Dason threatened.

"Haven't you been listening? You can't cut me down! It is my dearest wish that you could! Give me a good whack, young man. Give it all you got. In fact, I wrote a little song for these occasions. I even have a little dance to go with it."

Hit me hard and cut me deep.
Cleave me in two,
From my head to my feet.

Stab my heart, hack off my head,
Slice off a limb,
Or run me through instead.

Break my bones and spill my guts.
Burn me with fire,
Pound my chest to a mush.

You will stare, and I will sigh.
Oh, how I wish
You could make me die.

While he sang he danced an awkward jig that ended in a
bow as if performing for an audience. Dason pulled the
Chalaine forward.

Tornus straightened and cut off their retreat in a
heartbeat. "I said not yet!"

Dason yelled, "You are mad! Move aside!"

"Mad? I am hungry!"

Sir Tornus's arm shot out, Dason slapping it aside with
his blade and then plunging the sword into Sir Tornus's
heart. Dason twisted the blade while Sir Tornus looked on
in boredom. Neither man moved for several moments until
Sir Tornus threw up his arms.

"See what I mean? Trust me, the fact that I am not dead
is more disappointing to me than it is to you."

Sir Tornus's hand shot out again and grabbed Dason's
arm at the wrist. The madman's eyes flared and Dason's
face went slack, an energy pouring from his eyes and into
those of Sir Tornus. The Chalaine screamed and shoved
Dason away from Sir Tornus's grasp, her Protector falling
to the ground, alive but face wan and devoid of intelligence.
The old knight's malevolent gaze turned on her and he
backhanded her to the floor.

"Never take away the meal of a starving man when he is
but half done!"

The Chalaine, ears ringing, tried to get back up, but Sir
Tornus had already lowered his face above Dason's,
consuming what remained of her Protector's essence before

she could recover. Once finished, he stood and shook his head, an odd expression of regret flashing over his features, before turning his attention to her.

"Who sent you?" the Chalaine asked.

"Mikkik, of course," Sir Tornus said, voice suddenly melancholy. "You know, I . . . I never wanted to do this. The hunger. It is too strong. I can't stop it. I can't!"

"Are you going to kill me, too?"

He regarded her, face sad. "Yes. But not until he knows that he doesn't need you anymore. It shouldn't be long. I am sorry. And on your wedding night and everything. You look quite stunning, I must confess. Such a nice dress. Tell me, is that really Aldradan Mikmir on that throne?"

"He is the King."

"Not quite what I asked." He rubbed his chin thoughtfully. "Your evasion answers the question. No matter. Mikkik should be busy killing him right now. Aldradan Mikmir—or some good impostor—against Mikkik. Quite a contest to amuse the populace. It's a shame that we aren't there to see it. . ."

The Chalaine gasped. Mikkik? In Mikmir? She sprinted for the door, but Sir Tornus knocked her to the floor with his forearm.

"I am so sorry. I was a gentleman once. I can still remember it sometimes. Opening doors for the ladies, throwing out compliments they didn't deserve. . ."

The Chalaine slid to a sitting position, leaning against the wall and regarding her captor. He seemed so distracted and lost, but clearly he burned with a purpose that rose up whenever anything threatened it. He offered his hand to help her stand up and she refused, shaking her head. He sighed and retracted it, staring at her with the same hungry expression with which he had sized up Dason. The Chalaine stared back at him, trying to choke down her fear.

Then the world changed.

She could feel it, like a subtle shift in the wind or the

weaker quality of light when autumn has at last conquered summer. A wrongness pervaded everything at once, a feeling of stillness and death. She shot to her feet, noticing Sir Tornus with his eyes closed and face troubled. She darted toward the door, her wedding dress streaming behind her. *If I can just get outside!* The closer she got to the door, the louder became the shouts of exclamation and dismay rising from the streets. Had Gen been killed? Was the news spreading that Eldaloth had come and slain the pretended Aldradan Mikmir?

With a frantic shove, she pushed the heavy oaken door aside and stepped out onto the wide, square porch of Renberry Cathedral. Revelers in the streets beyond the Church complex had all stopped to turn their gaze to the deep blue evening sky. To the Chalaine's amazement, the moons had gone, their solid, beaming faces replaced with mighty clouds of dust expanding steadily outward and thinning. Trys, Myn, and Duam had been destroyed, and with them something else, a vibrancy to everything—living and inanimate—around her. It was palpable to her, and, by the expressions on the faces of those nearby, she could tell that they felt it, too.

An iron grip closed around her arm. "Come back inside, Chalaine," said Sir Tornus. "The sign has been given, and the bargain must be completed. This is, I admit, most unexpected. The moons have shattered like little clods of dirt tossed against a stone. Is this the end of magic, then? No matter. I am nearly free. Come. We wouldn't want to frighten these people more than they already are! It would be bad manners, don't you think? You see, I am not as heartless as you think me."

She wouldn't go willingly. With all her strength, she struck out with a sharp kick to Sir Tornus's knee, but whatever damage or pain she hoped to inflict did nothing to the Craver who held her bound. Roughly he dragged her back toward the Chapel, and the Chalaine screamed for help. No one seemed to hear her cry, and Sir Tornus shoved her back inside and closed the door.

"Now, Chalaine," he began, standing erect and taking on a formal air. "It is time for me to apologize for what I must do. I cannot help it, nor would I." The hunger crept back into his eyes. "It is nothing personal, I assure you. In fact, in other circumstances, you and I might have been good friends. But a bargain is a bargain, and I must fulfill!"

His hand shot out and caught her by the neck, his eyes alight with anticipation.

A voice behind him pulled him up short. "Stop, Sir Tornus! Or you'll doom us all!"

He released the Chalaine's neck, keeping an iron grip on her wrist, and turned. Joranne, now in middle age, approached them down the center aisle. She appeared troubled and did not approach Sir Tornus closely.

"Doom?" Sir Tornus said. "This is my freedom! He will release me if I do this! Or do you wish to kill her yourself? Did he promise to end your curse, too?"

"Yes," Joranne confirmed. "Two of his pawns sent for the same purpose and promised the same reward. But he cannot make good on his promises now, Sir Tornus," Joranne explained.

"Why not? Is he dead?"

"No," Joranne replied. "He is powerless. He did not expect this. The only magic left powerful enough to heal either one of us is in her blood. If you kill her then neither of us can escape our fate!"

"No!" he thundered. "No! No! No! He promised me!"

"Quit acting like a child, Tornus!" Joranne scolded. "We must work together or he will not free us!"

Sir Tornus let go of the Chalaine, who stumbled backward, caressing her neck. *No magic!* Mikkik was powerless, but Ki'Hal felt wrong. Joranne and Sir Tornus eyed each other, two predators trying to decide how to deal with a shared prey.

"See reason, Sir Tornus," Joranne argued. "Mikkik is the only one who knows how to undo what was done to us." The Craver's eyes still burned, but, his brow crinkled in thought. "Think," Joranne continued, coming closer. "Her blood was the only power that could destroy Elde Luri Mora, but it is also the only power that can restore it to life, which he does not want. As long as we have her, we have a way to manipulate and control him."

A thought struck the Chalaine and she approached the middle ground between the two. "There is someone else that may know how to heal you, someone who will listen to me."

"No one knows all the secrets of blood magic except Mikkik," Joranne said. "He would not give them all, even to me."

"Gen knows them," the Chalaine said, trying to sound confident. She wasn't sure what Gen knew of blood magic, but she had to conjure a way to get herself out of the power of the two people seeking to use her as leverage.

"Gen is dead," Joranne said, face skeptical.

"He isn't. Who do you think is parading around as Aldradan Mikmir? Mikkik isn't the only one who can play tricks."

"How can this be?" Joranne asked. "He was killed! I am sure of it."

"He did die at Butchers gap, but the Millim Eri returned him to life using the blood magic of which you speak, though they were loathe to do it."

"Loathe?" Joranne exclaimed. "They were expressly forbidden by Eldaloth from its practice, as were all of the elder races who had the power of magic."

The Chalaine said, "If you take me to him, I may be able to persuade him to help you. I dare say, you have a better chance of convincing him than trying to persuade Mikkik to use the power of my blood to help you rather than himself."

Sir Tornus rubbed his chin and something unspoken passed between him and Joranne.

"I agree that it is worth a chance," Sir Toruns said, "but there is a problem."

"What is that?" the Chalaine asked.

"Mikkik went to kill Aldradan Mikmir."

Mikkik's spell released, and Gen found himself in possession of his own mind again, but not soon enough to avoid the bite of Mikkik's blade. Gen dropped to his right just enough that the sword—its magical flame now extinguished—hacked deeply into the meaty part of his shoulder instead of his neck. He ignored the pain and rolled to the right, happy to sacrifice an arm to keep his head on his shoulders.

When he came to his feet, he took stock of his enemy, now stripped of all his pretended brilliancy. On Mikkik's upturned face played an expression of ecstasy, a release from hundreds of years of torture inflicted upon him by the very existence of Elde Luri Mora. His bloodied sword hung limply in his hand. Gen raised his own to strike, but the horrified expressions of the crowd and the odd feeling of loss within him stopped his hand.

He turned his eyes upward and joined the throng in dismay as Trys, Myn, and Duam disintegrated before their eyes in a deep purple evening sky. The exploded moons had robbed Gen of his magic, but the entire world felt palsied and weak, as if inflicted with a withering disease from which it would never recover. Mikkik opened his eyes and began to laugh and cry at the same time, as if witnessing a sublime beauty only he could comprehend.

"It is done," Mikkik said in the ancient tongue. "At last the world will be free, and I will be left eternally and blessedly alone."

263

He dropped the sword, the metal clanging against the stones as he turned and walked toward the gates of the castle without a look back. Infuriated, Gen grabbed his sword and charged at the retreating Mikkik. As he sprinted to close the distance, a sound from behind him pulled him up short. A dark cloud of sleek, black birds descended from the sky, the beating of their wings and the shriek of their call rolling toward the square like a storm. Gen backed away and uselessly hacked with his sword as the flock of birds rushed by, surrounding him in the haunted cacophony of their horrible cry. They were the size of ravens but clothed with feathers that glinted like metal armor. Slender, sharp beaks the length of a finger gave the suggestion of a poniard. Three slammed beak-first into Gen's body, puncturing his chest, abdomen, and right leg, only to extract a portion of blood and then fall dead to the ground, just as the beetles had.

Gen fell and rolled into a ball, receiving two more wounds before the flock passed him completely. Blood seeped from five wounds, and he rolled over. The birds swirled around Mikkik in a globe, attacking anything or anyone near the dark god as he walked away unchallenged. The people fled. Gen pushed himself up, leaning heavily on his sword. His knights rushed forward and surrounded him.

"I need a horse!" Gen yelled. He knew he needed to staunch the deep wounds dripping blood around him, but he couldn't wait, wondering what treachery Athan and Dason had set against the Chalaine. The knights complied without question.

Gerand, Volney, and Maewen found him moments later, aghast at the portents in the sky.

"Lord Mikmir!" Gerand exclaimed.

"Don't mind me. Get a horse and get to the Chalaine."

"Get him inside!" Maewen yelled at the knights.

"No Maewen," Gen said. "I've got to find her."

"Not like that, you won't!" she said firmly. "You can

hardly stand. Send Gerand and Volney and the knights. You can follow when we get you well. There is no magic to help you, now."

Gen signaled his men on, and Maewen threw his arm over her shoulder as they thundered away.

"This brings back memories of our little excursion against the Uyumaak," Maewen said in Elvish as his concentration wavered. "I had to help you walk then, too. Perhaps you should try not getting hurt so badly."

Once they passed through the doors of the Great Hall, a handful of servants helped carry him to his bed chamber. A trail of his blood ran through the hall.

"Shall we fetch the chirugeon?" one asked.

"Only if you wish him to die," Maewen said. "Leave him to me. Bring Mirelle here."

Maewen pulled a knife from her boot and cut away his robe and tunic, sucking air through her teeth. "They bleed more badly than they should. One of Mikkik's nasty tricks."

"There are two on my back, as well," he groaned, feeling weak.

Hastily, Maewen sliced away the rest of his clothes, leaving him in nothing but breeches. As she began slicing chunks of the bed sheets away for bandages, Mirelle burst in through the doors, face concerned.

"What happened!?" she exclaimed.

"No time to explain," Maewen said. "Take these bandages, Mirelle, and press them wherever he is bleeding. Tie one around his leg, and he's got two more wounds on his back. The ones on his chest and belly are the worst. I need to fetch my bag from my room."

Mirelle nodded, and Maewen sprinted away. Hastily Mirelle complied with the half-elf's instructions, Gen's blood slicking her hands and staining the beautiful white gown she had worn for her daughter's wedding.

"I sent Gerand and Volney after the Chalaine," Gen said weakly. "I will go after her, too, as soon as I can."

"Hush, now, my Lord," Mirelle said, face pale and sad. "Save your strength."

"You know, trying to marry the Chalaine really seems to be a deadly business."

Tears ran down Mirelle's face as she worked. "You should really shut up now, my love. You have to fight it, Gen. Look at me. Fight."

Gen stared up at Mirelle's beautiful face. He reached up to stroke her hair, but she pushed his hand down. By her cursing, he could tell her attempts to staunch the bleeding were failing. His vision swam, and he felt drowsy and disconnected from the world around him, a heavy dullness pulling him comfortably down into a warm embrace. The pain of the wounds didn't concern him. He was tired. He needed sleep. Just a few moments wouldn't hurt, and he deserved it, anyway. He slipped away into blackness, feeling numb.

"Gen!"

His eyes snapped open. The Chalaine, her dress dirty and torn, sat on the bed next to him. Her touch had healed his wounds. He sat up in his blood-soaked bed, a tableau of relieved faces surrounding him. Mirelle, face tear-streaked, was covered in his blood, crying quietly as she sat next to her daughter. Gerand, Volney, and Maewen looked on with satisfaction as color and health returned to Gen's face.

"I wondered if your gift would still work," Gen said, taking her hand.

"It will work as long as you love me," she said.

Gen regarded himself, noticing his nearly nude, bloody state. "I am a mess."

"I will send the servants with a bath to clean you up," Mirelle said, wiping her face. "I wish you could rest, but you have some unusual visitors."

"Who?" Gen asked.

"It is Joranne and Sir Tornus," the Chalaine explained.

"Athan plotted with Dason to take me to Renberry Cathedral. Mikkik plotted with Sir Tornus to kill me once Elde Luri Mora was destroyed. Joranne convinced Sir Tornus that now that the moons are gone, Mikkik has no power to make good on his bargain to remove the curse they each suffer from. My blood is, apparently, the most powerful source of magic left in the world, and I convinced them that you had the power and knowledge to help them."

Gen frowned. "It won't work. Blood magic can heal, even from death, and destroy to the point of annihilation, but it cannot do the work of Trys and remake them to what they were before they made a bargain with Mikkik. And without Duammagic to heal, bleeding anyone for the purpose of using their blood will likely result in death."

"I didn't know if what I said was true, but it convinced them to bring me to you rather than to Mikkik," the Chalaine explained.

"Well done, Alumira." Gen thought for a moment. "Joranne is powerless, now, so there is little she can do to us, but Sir Tornus is a Craver and is nearly impossible to kill."

"All he wants is death," the Chalaine reported. "My blood could provide him that."

"Yes, but I won't risk bleeding you or me for *his* sake. He can be locked away and restrained, if need be."

"There's more," the Chalaine said. "Joranne said my blood had the power to undo what Mikkik has done to Elde Luri Mora, that my blood held the power to heal it. That's why Mikkik sent Tornus to kill me, to make sure what he did could not be undone. He couldn't kill me until he was sure he didn't need me anymore."

Gen's mind spun with the knowledge, and he realized immediately that it was true. If the power of her blood could destroy Elde Luri Mora, it could restore it as well. The Chalaine still bore the burden of the world's salvation on her shoulders. With tenderness he regarded her. If only she could be free. If only she could escape her fate and be the beautiful bride and wife and mother she longed to be. But peace, it seemed, was ever to be denied her.

"I need time to think," Gen said. "I will speak with the people to calm them first, then I will see what Joranne and Sir Tornus have to say."

"What about the marriage?" Mirelle asked.

Gen glanced at the Chalaine, who shook her head. "We can wait," he said. "This is not the time for celebration and feasting. It is a time to mourn and to plan. Maewen, I need you to go see if the portals still work."

The room cleared as the servants worked to wash Gen and clean the room of his blood. His mind churned, trying to find a way to keep the Chalaine from another horror-ridden trip to Elde Luri Mora to be bled in an attempt to heal what Mikkik had destroyed. To bring the dead back to life required the beneficiary to be bathed in blood. How could they bathe the entirety of Elde Luri Mora in the Chalaine's life essence? How could they bathe the city even in a small part without killing her?

Pushing aside the impossible quandary, Gen donned another set of royal robes and descended to the Great Hall. Again his knights formed around him, relieved to see him well again. Outside, the populace awaited news, and a great hail rose as he emerged from the doors. With a practiced air of calm that he did not feel he reassured them. There was no time for flowery speeches. He promised that he would lead the march against Mikkik in the morning and returned to the Great Hall where Mirelle and the Chalaine waited by the throne.

"I would that the two of you not be here," Gen said. "Cravers are unpredictable and dangerous."

"We will not leave your side, Lord Mikmir," Mirelle stated firmly. "It seems most everything is dangerous, anyway."

Gen nodded and sat on his throne, Mirelle signaling for

the Chalaine to sit in hers while she came to stand by Gen. Volney and Gerand flanked the dais.

"Are we sure that Joranne can do no magic?" Mirelle whispered.

"She can do blood magic if she knows it," Gen answered, "but no more than that. We are equals now, save that her curse puts her in a precarious position. With Mikkik and her magic no longer sheltering her, she needs our protection, which means we can use her. She knows Mikkik's plans and schemes and strongholds. Unfortunately, I have nothing I can offer her in return without bluffing, and I fear she knows enough about blood magic to know I cannot help her. Let's see what she has to say. Bring them in!"

Chamberlain Fedrick, sill dressed for the wedding, signaled for the guard to open the door. Joranne, now looking nearly as aged as the good Chamberlain, shuffled into the room, Sir Tornus coming slowly behind her as he took in the glory of the hall.

Gen dismissed his scribe, the Chamberlain, and the guard. The strange pair came cautiously, Gen trying to weigh the attitude of the two cursed creatures approaching the throne. Joranne, always haughty and in control, appeared humbled, but Sir Tornus still maintained his air of aloof lunacy that he had demonstrated from the first time that Gen, Gerand, and Volney had met him at Echo Hold.

"You will bow before Lord Mikmir!" Gerand commanded when it became apparent they wouldn't do it.

"There's no need for ceremony here!" Joranne returned. "I know the man who sits on the throne. As an infant he drank of my milk and grew strong. I would recognize him anywhere, even if the Chalaine hadn't told me who he was. You are bold, indeed, Gen, to assume such an honor as the throne of Mikmir. The need for power was something the Millim Eri somehow bred out of you, but you seem to have come to your senses now."

"We don't need a history lesson, Joranne," Gen said. "We need answers."

"I would just like to die, if you don't mind," Sir Tornus said, eying the Chalaine. "It would be good for everyone if you could kill me before I get really hungry again. I'm stuffed full of Eldephaere right now, but I am not very disciplined about denying myself a little snack now and again. Joranne tells me that just one bleeding of the Chalaine ought to do it." Suddenly, the Craver's eyes shot wide. "But you have a soul now, Gen!"

"What?"

"Yes! Yes, indeed!" Sir Tornus exclaimed, excitedly. "When we first met, you were as empty as a drunkard's bottle, but there is something in you to feast on now, something not quite human!"

Gen blinked in surprise, finding everyone looking at him with awe.

"Mikkik created him," Joranne said. "Gen has no natural father and mother. As the Ilch he never had a soul, but the Millim Eri have gifted him one, somehow. Do you know how it was done?"

Gen said, "The subject of my soul can wait! First I need to know what Mikkik plans."

"He has no more plans," Joranne answered, "or at least he won't until he finds out that the Chalaine is alive. Once he knows that, he will have but one plan: to kill the one woman whose blood has the power to undo all of this. He will throw every dark creature, Uyumaak, and all the Dhrons at her to do get it done."

"How many Dhrons are there?" Gen asked. "I have met Ghama and Hekka. Were the birds another?"

"Yes. That was Sethra Dhron. There is another, the unspeakable horror Khrona Dhron, an abominable amalgamation of men. But these are not your immediate concern. Mikkik commissioned Sir Tornus and I separately to kill the Chalaine and report her death to him. Only then can his victory be total and irreversible."

"Report where?"

"Elde Luri Mora," Joranne said. "It is no longer denied him. He will go to enjoy the spoils of his work. It is there he promised that he would undo the curse he put upon me, but I no longer believe he has the power to do so. I have sought so long to be free of him, to be rid of all the elder races. I helped the Millim Eri find you, Gen, to blunt his influence over you. I swear it. I only ask now that you help me be free of this curse."

Gen doubted her information and her sincerity. "In exchange for what?"

"My help! I can aid you! If we work together, we can conquer. But first you must protect the Chalaine. She must be dead to all and hidden away. Sir Tornus or I must report it to Mikkik, and soon. Since he is without Mynmagic, he will no longer be able to pull the information from our minds as he once did, so we can lie to him."

Gen nodded. "Even so, I cannot see how to restore Elde Luri Mora, even if we can get the Chalaine there. I can raise a person from the dead with the power of blood, but a city? With Chertanne, I had to reach into the Abyss and pull his spirit back into his body. Where is the spirit of the city?"

Joranne tapped her lip thoughtfully. "The city was suffused with some essence of Eldaloth that tortured Mikkik for ages. There must have been a place, a center from which it emanated. It is Athan who carried out the deed and to him that Mikkik gave instruction on how to destroy it. He must know."

Gen rubbed his bearded chin and sat back to consider, rifling through all of the lore packed away in his mind, finding that the knowledge of his three trainers availed him little in such a unique circumstance. Deep inside he knew the attempt had to be made, but was loathe to do it. But as he allowed himself to accept the necessity, possibilities started to unlock in his mind that he had not considered.

"If the Chalaine is bled, and must be bled multiple times, we have to have a way to heal her," Gen said. "If I teach you, Joranne, you could use the power of my blood to heal her. She can heal me with a touch."

The Ash Witch's clouded eyes brightened. "Yes! That should do nicely."

"But we must act quickly, and I must put everyone in danger. I will do what I can to grant you of your wishes, Joranne and Tornus, but you must help me in this."

"What are you suggesting?" Mirelle asked, face concerned.

"Sir Tornus will travel to Elde Luri Mora immediately, but he will tell Mikkik that the Chalaine lives and is hidden away in Mikmir."

"What?!" Joranne exclaimed.

"The Chalaine, Joranne, and I will travel behind him a couple of days. When Mikkik sends his might against Mikmir to kill the Chalaine, we will enter Elde Luri Mora and perform the bleeding. Mirelle, I will need you to impersonate the Chalaine here while we are gone. Will you do that?"

She nodded. "I will."

"Volney, I will need you to continue on as Mirelle's personal guard. Gerand, I am promoting you to ambassador to Tolnor. You will leave immediately to gather support from your nation and bring it here. You will coordinate with General Torunne and General Harband on how best to protect Mikmir upon your return."

"I will," Gerand said, bowing.

"There is one thing you aren't considering," Mirelle warned. "The Church."

"True," Gen admitted. "It will be difficult to gauge their reaction to what has happened. If Athan is convinced of his error, then we may have an ally, but the man was so blinded by Mikkik he may still attempt to thwart us."

"And what of Aughmere?" Gerand asked.

"Ulean Mail was the Shadan there before the rule of the Padras," said Gen. "I will send a letter asking for his support and strength, but we have no strong ties there. If there were time, I would challenge him for his throne. A host of Aughmerian soldiers would aid us a great deal, and I never thought I would find myself saying that.

"As for my absence, tell the people I have gone to gather strength to Mikmir, to raise army to defend it or some such nonsense. I will take some of my knights with me, but the defense of Mikmir will fall to the regents and Generals. Even if we succeed in Elde Luri Mora, Mikkik's creatures may still press the attack until they are utterly destroyed."

Plan set, Gen leaned back in his throne and regarded his somber friends and the two fiends. One more night of peace was all he could offer any of them.

"Volney and Gerand, go and take an evening and a day with your wives. I will watch over the Chalaine tonight. Sir Tornus, I'm afraid I will need to lock you up."

The Craver grinned, "You are wise."

"We prepare tomorrow and leave early the day after."

A sudden orange glow in the dark windows flared, lighting the Great Hall in a fiery light. It subsided and flared again, like a flame blown down by a gale only to burn brighter. Maewen entered the hall at a jog.

"Lord Mikmir," she said. "Portal magic still works, but you should see the sky. It is on fire! I have never seen the like."

As one they left the Great Hall, striding out into the dark to find a sky filled with smoke and long tongues of flame as the small fragments of the moons cut streaks of fire across the blackness. The celestial conflagration crescendoed, the orange and black sky filling their vision with a roiling, churning storm of flames.

Gen pulled the Chalaine close.

"Is this the end, Gen?" she asked, voice subdued.

"The sky weeps fire for the loss of the moons," he replied. "The sun will rise in an angry sky tomorrow, and we will rise with it into a new day. You are still our hope, Chalaine, and while you are alive, the end is not yet."

CHAPTER 86 - THE APPROACH

Mirelle ascended the Tower of the Chalaines for the first time in her life. Volney had tried to convince her that such an ascent was a poor idea, but the young man's complying nature could never hold a resolution long enough to cross her for too long. Cadaen had been four times the stubborn mule that Volney was, and she had managed that old soldier for most of her life. The tower, used to house a decoy for the Chalaines, was also the best vantage point for a clear view of the Kingsblood Lake and the city of Mikmir that surrounded it.

A clear view, however, was hard to come by anymore. The burning sky had persisted for two days before finally subsiding, and the smoke and haze had turned the days into twilight. Some of the flaming chunks of the moons had driven craters into the ground and set fields ablaze, though as for that, since Elde Luri Mora had been destroyed, the crops and trees had withered steadily, whether from the darkening of the sky or some loss of the essence of Ki'Hal, no one could say.

Unused to the veil she had worn since her daughter left, Mirelle had to pick her way carefully up the dark, narrow staircase that led to the circular upper room and its advantageous prospect. Since the events of Echo Hold, the decoys had retired from their post, so when Mirelle and Volney opened the gilded door, they found the richly appointed room dusty and smelling stale. Mirelle thought the furnishings and decorations had probably not changed since the first decoy for the Chalaines had roomed there. The tapestries were faded, and the blocky, bold furniture was out of style with the more modern, delicate pieces that tended to curve and sport clever filigrees. The reds of the carpets and dark woods of the rooms' appointments almost gave it an Aughmerian feel.

Not bothering with the closed shutters, they crossed to another door that opened onto a balcony that encircled the entire tower, allowing a view in every direction. It was stuck fast, and only a vigorous yank from Volney freed it.

"We shouldn't spend too much time out of doors," he said firmly, and Mirelle smiled. She could almost feel like the Chalaine again back when she had been overprotected and shut away.

"We won't be long," Mirelle promised as they stepped out.

The sense of vertigo took a moment to beat down. A chest high balustrade protected them from a fall, but regularly spaced arched cutouts left enough of the precipitous view in sight to send her heart into her throat.

Volney paled. "I grew up on a plain," he lamented by way of explanation.

From the tower, the smoke and the haze actually seemed worse. An enthusiastic breeze did little to alleviate the gritty dust and ash grays soiling the air. The sharp smell of smoke pervaded everywhere, some columns of fire still rising from burning fields without the city walls. Feeling more comfortable with their elevated perch, Mirelle leaned against it while Volney stood at obedient attention with his back flat to the tower wall as if stuck to it.

Four days ago, Falael and Maewen had encountered the vanguard of Mikkik's awful host as they reached the eastern edge of Rhugoth. The people there had long since fled, but Mikkik's servants had not lost an opportunity to raze and burn everything in their path. If Maewen was correct, the army would reach the fortified lower wall of Mikmir by nightfall with one purpose—to root through every building until they found the Chalaine and deprived her of her life.

Mirelle peered to the east. There was nothing save some procrastinating stragglers who had taken their time before heeding the warning that had followed on Gen's and the Chalaine's heels after they secretly left the city.

The thought of the two of them stung Mirelle's eyes. She missed them both terribly and had been so distraught when they said farewell that she hugged her daughter for so long that she and Gen had started much later than they intended. Mirelle had even kissed Gen on the lips in front of his intended bride, though she hoped it was a short enough peck to avoid suspicion of her true feelings.

The two of them were all she truly loved in the world, and to send them off to an uncertain and dangerous fate, far from where she could help or counsel either one, aggravated her emotions and made her restless. Even worse, she felt useless. She was bait. The Generals knew far better than she how to handle the impending war, but she desperately wanted to grab a sword and *do* something.

The inner courtyard of the castle below her stirred with relentless activity, the once-beautiful grounds now littered with temporary accommodations and the refuse of the soldiers who lived there. The bulk of the combined armies of Tolnor and Mikmir occupied the streets of the city. The mass of fleeing citizenry they had sent north and west out of the path of Mikkik's creatures, but many people had refused to leave and found themselves host to soldiers quartered with them. As yet, no word had come from Aughmere, though Mirelle still held out hope that they would come to Rhugoth's relief. While Maewen had been unsure of the exact numbers of the enemy they faced, she assured them that to her eyes it appeared Mikkik had scraped every nook and cranny of Ki'Hal and sent what he found to Rhugoth.

"We should descend, Milady," Volney suggested after a stiff wind kicked up.

Mirelle turned toward him. "Where did you send your wife, Lena, and her boy?"

"To family in the north. I have a grand uncle there who has a fortified estate that is a bit out of the way. It's the best I could have hoped for."

Mirelle nodded. "She'll be much safer than any of us, you most of all. I must thank you again for volunteering for this duty. I am sure you would prefer to be in the streets with Gerand."

"I am honored that Lord Mikmir—well, Gen or whatever—chose me for this post, though I certainly could not fill Cadaen's shoes. I wish I would have been with him and Gen in Echo Hold when they came for you."

Her days imprisoned in Echo Hold and being dragged along the streets to the burning pole seemed a blurry haze in her mind, and she wondered if Gen had done some trick of Mynmagic to soften the memory of those awful events. All she could remember was the rapturous joy of finding Gen alive and making sure he felt her delight. Her sorrow for Cadaen's death, while poignant, had lost its weight in the revelation of Gen's return from the same fate.

"Look there, Milady," Volney said urgently, finally taking a step away from the tower. "In the eastern sky."

"I see nothing but a cloud . . . but no."

"That's a flock of birds," Volney said. "I wasn't there, but didn't some flock of birds attack Lord Gen?"

"Yes. Joranne called it Sethra Dhron, which apparently means *the horror of birds*. Hekka Dhron was the beetles. Gen thinks he destroyed it."

"This just gets worse and worse. Snakes. Beetles. Now birds."

As the lustrous, deadly birds neared the city through the murky sky, their awful, shrieking call pierced Mirelle's and Volney's ears. Trumpets and commotion responded in the streets below, and a cloud of arrows rose to meet the avian threat. Some few birds plummeted from the sky, but the entire flock swarmed downward into the ranks of soldiers in the city, diving and then rising again. A small pocket of birds broke away from the main group and pushed against the wind toward the tower where they watched.

Volney grabbed her arm. "It's begun. You're underground from now on."

She didn't resist as he pulled her away and slammed the door shut. No one was sure how many of the magical protections about the Chalaine's complex still worked. As they closed the gilded door and started down the stairs, the sound of broken glass and snapping shutters preceded the raucous din of Mikkik's birds streaming into the deserted room. They had come for her, and it was time to hide.

------◆------

Gerand fussed with his helmet, unused to wearing one. In his younger days training with his father, he would hardly be caught without one, but now a helmet was proving a nuisance. He sat astride his horse in the streets of the inner city of Mikmir. The outer city was abandoned, save for the most stubborn of the citizenry, and the main eastern gate was shut. General Harband and his hardened army took the honor of defending the main approach, and Gerand was glad; when he had arrived in Tolnor as ambassador, he found that with the death of his brother he had become the Duke of his estate. He felt ill prepared to lead the men he had mustered to come with him.

His portion of the Tolnorian army, consisting of three hundred foot soldiers and fifty knights, occupied a road two streets north of where General Harband's men waited for the impending attack. Between them was General Torunne, Volney's father. General Harband placed most of the Tolnorian regiments in support positions since they were, as a whole, unfamiliar with the city and exhausted from frantic preparations and travel. They came ready to fight, however, and Gerand was proud of them for taking up a cause not immediately their own. Of course, most hoped to catch a glimpse of the famous Aldradan Mikmir, and the legend's absence fueled some disgruntled talk. Why would the King abandon his city in its time of need?

Gerand kept to the standard explanation: the King was traveling to drum up more support and had no doubt been hindered by the dangerous paths he was forced to tread. It held up for the most part, but if the leaders ever put their heads together and discussed it, they might find that Aldradan Mikmir had bidden no one come; messengers had spread the word, and the Regents and soldiers of Mikmir had answered the call of their missing monarch.

To Gerand's left, Baron Rikken sat staring into the dirty sky, the skin around his blue eyes lined from his many hours out in the sun. His bronze and silver breastplate held the device of a bear. The man was built straight and tall and had the look of old leather. Gerand was glad to have him. He was an experienced soldier who had won much honor during the war with Aughmere when King Filingrail withdrew from the Fildelium.

But even more soothing to Gerand was Maewen, who stood at his right, also peering into the sky but with her head slightly cocked. Why she had chosen to fight alongside him instead of General Harband or anyone else was a mystery to Gerand, but he wouldn't complain. On her back, her quiver brimmed with long arrows crafted after the elven fashion, and her hands were on the hilts of her curved long knives.

"What is it?" Gerand asked.

She waited, silent for a few moments. Baron Rikken

leaned over, listening.

"It will begin soon," she said. "I hear their voices on the wind."

"Whose?" Gerand asked.

"The fell shrieks of Sethra Dhron. Get them up and ready. The vanguard will be upon us soon."

Gerand gave the signal to the herald, and he blew the call to arms, his men scrambling from alleys and houses to gather to the street. A single knight bearing the white hammer device of the Torunnes rode up from the next street over and approached.

"General Torunne asks why you have sounded the call to arms?"

"Sethra Dhron is nearly here," Gerand explained. "Get your men ready."

"We have seen no threat."

"You will hear it first," Maewen said. "Your poor ears could hear it now if you would quiet yourselves. The cry of the birds is heavy on the air."

Gerand signaled for silence, and the rider waited. For several moments, only the sound of the wind whipping along the street rewarded their attention, but just as everyone started to relax, the horrifying shriek of the fell birds carried over the wall and into their ears. It sounded like the cries of a hundred girls screaming in pain. No more explanation was needed, and the rider galloped away while the men and horses formed their lines.

"It would be best to preserve the horses," Maewen counseled. "They will give you no advantage against the birds. Hide them in houses and alleys. Do it quickly."

"My Lord Kildan," the Baron objected. "I see no need to. . ."

"Just do it," Gerand said, dismounting his horse. "I've long since learned not to argue with someone who is over two hundred years old."

Maewen nodded appreciatively as Gerand gave the order

to the rest of his reluctant knights, finding himself needing to put a little angry fire in his commands to get the soldiers to respond with the proper celerity.

"Now listen!" Gerand yelled, raising his voice over the swelling shriek of the birds. "Lord Mikmir encountered these birds when he stood against Mikkik. Do not think of attack first. Use your shields to keep them away from exposed flesh. Their beaks wound like long daggers, and if you are stabbed, you must treat the wound immediately. There is something foul in their beaks that makes a wound bleed long and hard. A puncture cannot be neglected.

"Now, gather your courage! These are but birds that can be defeated if you are disciplined and careful. You will face worse in the coming days. Most importantly, do not flail wildly at them. If you have a clear chance to kill one, take a sure stroke, but it is most important to weather this assault without injury!"

No sooner had he given the advice than the dark cloud of the flock rose over the outer wall to their right and dove downward toward Harband's men. A volley of arrows took a small toll on the birds, but the mighty swarm pelted downward below the roof line. The yells of men and the terrified screaming of horses echoed down the streets, and the birds burst again into the sky, flying low and driving down again in a different spot, spreading themselves farther apart from each other.

An armored horse, riderless and eyes wild, galloped in a frenzy toward Gerand. Blood ran in streams down its flanks and belly from several puncture wounds leaving a red trail on the road. A single bird clung to the horse's head with sharp talons, and with a thrust of its own head drove its beak through the horse's skull and into its brain. The animal collapsed, the bird taking flight until an arrow speeding from Maewen's bow brought it down.

Gerand regarded his soldiers, sweating and nervous to a man. Give them a line of Aughmerian soldiers, and they would all lick their lips at the chance for battle; throw a flock of Mikkik's birds at them and they were shaking. Every eye scanned upward for the dark fowl peppering the sky and then disappearing just as quickly. Gerand hoped to escape their notice altogether, but such luck did not attend them.

"Prepare!" Maewen yelled, the men pulling their shields close. Gerand stepped close to Maewen, who had nothing with which to protect herself. She didn't refuse his aid, and then the birds were upon them. The pounding wings hammered them as the demonic birds descended upon them in a cloud of fury. Beaks and sharp talons whined against protective shields and armor, and curses and gasps of pain from the wounded mingled with the horrible cries of the birds.

"Damnable things!" Baron Rikken yelled, swiping the air with his broadsword, cleaving a bird in two, but one of its companions streaked down and avenged it, beak sinking into the Baron's eye. Dropping his shield, the Baron fell hard to the ground and rolled over onto his stomach, two more birds taking advantage of the exposed backs of his legs. Gerand batted them away with his sword, a bird slashing down and grinding against his arm greave before leaping away.

The birds rose as one and departed to terrorize some other part of the city, and while only seconds had passed, Gerand felt weary. How could he lead men against such a foe? The safest move seemed to be to abandon their posts and get inside the dwellings and buildings around them, but he feared that was what Mikkik wanted so he could sneak some other horror inside the walls with no defense prepared. They bound the wounded quickly. A pool of blood gathered around Baron Rikken's stricken eye. Despite Maewen's quick ministrations, he died in minutes.

"How can such a thing be fought?" Gerand muttered under his breath.

Maewen heard him anyway. "Gen said that one of the creatures hosts the spirit that controls the rest. He told me he used Mynmagic to locate it when he fought Hekka Dhron, but we have no such aid now. We must endure it and exact what vengeance we can upon it."

"It will sap the morale of the men."

"Morale is your responsibility," Maewen said, patting him on the shoulder.

Gerand ground his teeth. His morale wasn't particularly firm at the moment, and he didn't have much to offer other than to be with his men. In the respite from the attack, he wandered among them, trying to sound confident and in command, but he felt like a child when he looked into the weathered and battle-scarred faces of the more seasoned warriors around him. *Any one of them would be better at this than I am,* he thought. In a moment of idle reflection he wondered if the Chukkas even bothered to check on their Uyumaak charges after a battle, and that's when the thought struck him.

"Maewen!" he yelled, running back toward the front. "Come with me!"

Gerand gave command of the men to one of his knight lieutenants, and he and Maewen ran forward toward the walls, wary of the erratic rise and fall of the birds.

"What are we doing?" Maewen asked.

"There are two kinds of Kings when it comes to war," Gerand began. "One is the kind who loves his men and rides with them into battle. The other dwells on his own importance and sits back and commands others into battle while he sits back and surveys and executes strategy."

"How does that help us now?"

"I'm not sure it will, but it's worth a chance," Gerand said. "I'm guessing the Dhrons are led by the latter kind of King that wouldn't risk himself in the thick of a fight. We need the vantage point of the walls."

They jogged to the left, where chiseled stone stairs led to

the top of the outer wall that looked eastward over the city. Nearly all the men had hunkered down behind its fortifications to wait out the attack of Sethra Dhron. The dust from Mikkik's approaching army rose in the afternoon sun, his army coming ever closer to the abandoned lower city. A Captain Eagen joined Gerand and Maewen as they crested the wall.

"What do you need?" the Captain asked, looking frightened.

"Just a look about," Gerand answered. "Maewen, use those elven eyes and look to the sky. Can you see any bird not with its fellows?"

The three of them scanned the skies, Gerand keeping half an eye on the flock still rising and falling from place to place, leaving screams and curses in its wake. From the height of the walls, Gerand spotted horses running rampant through the streets and men diving indoors to get away from the assault. Blood ran in the grooves of the cobbled roads, the men's hemorrhaging wounds resisting all attempts to staunch them.

"There!" Maewen said, unlimbering her bow.

Gerand followed her gaze. To his eyes, it was just a speck of black against the smoke and dust, but there, hovering on the wind, was a single bird. "Can you hit it?"

"It is a tricky shot with the distance and the wind. . ." she said, bow creaking as she pulled it back. Gerand held his breath as she sized up the shot and then loosed the arrow, bowstring singing. They followed the arrow into the sky. Upward it went into the dust and wind, almost impossible to see. To Gerand, the faint spot jerked ever so imperceptibly, but then it tumbled downward, wounded.

"I hit its wing," Maewen said, disappointed. She lined up another shot as is spiraled down, but the jerky movements of its descent helped it avoid the killing shot, and it fell behind a nearby house. The flock of birds behind them continued its bloody work, but a group broke off from the main swarm.

"I've got to get down there!" Gerand yelled. He peered over the twenty foot drop. A house rose from the street, its roof ten feet below. Without taking time to think it through, he stepped up onto a crenellation.

"What are you doing?!" Maewen exclaimed.

"Cover me!"

Bending his legs, he leapt outward with all of his strength, aiming for the shake-shingled roof below. While he intended to land in the middle of the sloped side, the weight of his armor and shield rendered his leap much shorter than he had envisioned. He impacted with the lower eave of the roof shield-first, sending a numbing shock up his arm. Grunting, he slid down and landed on a decorative wooden planter not intended to take the weight of an armored man. It gave way in a splintering crack, soil and flowers and wood accompanying him to slam into a small gable over a window. He hit the ground with enough force to take the wind out of his lungs. Bruised and battered he scrambled to his feet and ran for the spot where he had seen the bird fall.

"They're coming!" Maewen shouted.

The birds screeched and flapped close behind him. Churning his legs with everything he had, Gerand sprinted around a corner, birds wheeling behind him. There on the ground he saw it, a single bird hobbled and hopping away from him. Gritting his teeth he bowled after it. The small flock of birds engulfed him, their beating wings and shrieks deafening. To his surprise, they did not attack, but passed him to land about their wounded comrade in an attempt to confuse him as to which one held Sethra Dhron's mind. But Gerand knew his target, and with a leap he came down shield-first among the small gathering of birds, a satisfying crunch rewarding his efforts while his arm took another painful shock.

The birds that could still fly exploded away like crows

scared out of a cornfield by the barking of a dog. Gerand rolled over and found the sky filled with a disorderly scattering of birds fleeing masterless in every direction. Coming to a crouch, he looked down at the pulverized remains of Sethra Dhron. *One horror down,* he thought.

Taking a couple of moments just to breathe, he stood and walked back to the walls, trying to rub and roll his left arm back into shape. As he cleared the building a great shout and applause rose from the men on the wall, Maewen staring down with a barely perceptible grin on her face.

"Your wife would not approve!" she yelled. "You are a crazy fool of a man!"

"That's *Duke* Crazy Fool of a Man, if you please!"

<hr />

The Chalaine's hand went to her mouth as she stared through the gates of Elde Luri Mora. Everything inviting about the city had gone, the entire island a ruined waste. The plants had not just withered and died, they appeared rotten, like spoiled fruit, black and covered in thick clumps of mold. The lake, once clear and blue, now looked sterile and black, corrupted and befouled. The white buildings, while having lost their splendor to a dusty dinginess that clung to them, still stuck out against the decay all about them.

Worse, however, the lands all around Elde Luri Mora struggled to live, trees and grass wilted despite the mildness of the summer, and what wildlife they saw moved listlessly, if it moved at all. The entire world was falling under a withering lethargy that all in their party could feel wrapping its weight about them every mile closer they came to the stricken city.

The Chalaine latched onto Gen, finding his face wrenched in sadness. They had speculated that the destruction of Elde Luri Mora would ruin the world, and every step toward the dead city bore witness to it. The effect was spreading. The city had to be restored to its glory and beauty, and they could not delay. But knowing what had to be done had not helped them conjure up a way to do it, and Gen appeared more concerned every day. That she had to bleed, they knew. Where and how much remained a mystery.

The journey had favored them with good fortune for the most part. The Church had not impeded their progress through the Portals, and Sir Tornus's ruse to draw away Mikkik's forces had left their trail empty of foes. Having Gen with her helped her stay calm enough to sleep, though she was pretty sure that all her stealth had failed to conceal from the five knights that accompanied them that she sneaked into Gen's tent every night—and didn't come out. What they might think of her, she could hardly care. She knew she was Gen's wife and resolved never to pass through the night without him.

"We should be about it," Joranne said. "It is late afternoon . . . I think. The haze is just as thick here."

Gen nodded, wearing his worry openly, and pushed the tall gate open. They led their horses forward toward the cracked bridge at a slow pace, the deadness of the place calling forth an instinctual wariness. But they had hardly stepped inside when the skin on their bodies started to desiccate and turn gray. The horses whined and became restless. Only Joranne seemed unaffected.

"Go back!" Gen ordered. The Chalaine grabbed his hand, and all at once the effect dissipated on both of them, their skin returning to its natural color and suppleness. The knights retreated behind the gate, and Gen and the Chalaine led their horses back to safety.

Just as Elde Luri Mora rejected Mikkik's creatures before, it invited them now. All good creatures would suffer under the gross corruption of the city. Gen shook his head. The Millim Eri had changed him and he was no longer Mikkik's creation. The city rejected him now just as it had when he had entered for the Chalaine's wedding.

"Stay here," he ordered his men. "I do not know how long this will take, but it will be some hours."

"How can you endure it, Lord Mikmir?"

"Lady Alumira's healing power keeps me safe. Joranne is a creature shaped by Mikkik, so this place does not harm her. Be wary. Mikkik may have left a guard about."

The Chalaine knew Gen's true fear. What if Mikkik himself remained? They had no means or magic to destroy him, though the Chalaine, who wore a blade for the first time in her life, hoped for some opportunity to stick him. If the bleeding succeeded and Elde Luri Mora was healed, they had agreed to attempt the creation of another weapon to end Mikkik for good.

Hand in hand they turned toward the city, Joranne already halfway across the bridge as if anxious to explore a place once forcefully denied her. The Chalaine looked up at Gen's sober face and rubbed the beard on his cheek.

"If the world is put right, I will make you shave that awful thing," she said. "It was cute at first, but I miss your naked face. Sometimes I even miss the scars."

He smiled weakly, still distracted, eyes absorbing the wasted landscape. "Joranne!" he yelled. "You shouldn't wander too far ahead. There may be dangers."

"Gen," the Chalaine whispered. "What's wrong?"

"I just don't know how this will work, Alumira. I want to be sure that what we're about to do is worth the risk. Then I imagine Mikmir in flames, everyone wondering why the legendary King skipped town just before battle. At least I would know what I was doing there. Here, I'm just afraid we're putting your life at risk for a plan we don't know will work."

"Have faith, Gen," she said, squeezing his hand. "When I first came here, I was a lost little girl, afraid of what I had to do. Now the city lays before us blighted and forbidding, and while I feel sadness, I am not afraid. I can't explain it, but I feel that this is where I should be. It may not be as beautiful as it once was, but both times I have come to this place, I have had the love of the best of men. And this time, I don't have to hide from it."

She stopped, lifted her veil, and kissed him deeply. "No more sour faces, Lord Mikmir. We will succeed and take our rest from horror and pain."

He kissed her forehead and embraced her. "Your will, my love."

"Are you two done yet?" Joranne hissed from the end of the bridge. "Remember that I am getting older every moment!"

"As are we all," Gen replied.

They pressed forward, the eerie silence of the city unnerving. No wind stirred the stale air, and the once-blossomed branches now stretched across the road like the gnarled legs of dark spiders. Their footsteps and their voices echoed through the empty streets, and even the jaded Joranne pulled back to walk more closely to her companions.

The Chalaine reached up and touched one of the twigs hanging down, and, to their delight, it turned green and healthy again under her touch. But once released, it settled into its previous putrefaction.

"Now you see," the Chalaine said. "It is my blood that will heal this place."

Gen smiled uncertainly, but the Chalaine thought she could catch a glimpse of hope in his eye as they walked up the stairs toward the half collapsed Hall of Three Moons. Joining Joranne, they stood at the threshold and regarded the wrack of the once-proud building, now a jumble of broken stones.

"I wonder if Athan survived this?" the Chalaine said.

"He must have," Gen speculated, "or we wouldn't have had so easy a time at the Portals, I think. But I can see a hand sticking out beneath some rubble. Be careful where you step."

They entered tentatively, their feet crunching small rocks as they pressed forward. A large crack transected the center of the room, spanning it from side to side. The four thrones on the opposite side of the room were all charred, as Mikkik's throne was when the first visited.

"You can see where the crack began," Joranne said, "just there in the center of the room. It is there the weapon pierced the floor. It is there she must be bled."

The Chalaine swallowed and they approached the yawning crack. Even with the light streaming through the dusty particles in the air, the chasm appeared to have no bottom, a great yawning hole into nothingness. The Chalaine stepped back, feeling vertigo. How could a weapon formed of her blood have split the very ground in two?

"We will lay the Chalaine on this stone," Joranne began, "and let her blood cover the floor and drip down the crack. It should. . ."

A scrape behind them spun them around, hands on weapons, but Sir Tornus's familiar shape in the archway put them at ease.

"So you have come at last," he said. "Mikkik told me to remain here, and there simply isn't a thing to eat, so you can imagine how hungry I've become. You see that I did my job well. Mikkik left for Mikmir immediately and left me all alone. Did I mention how hungry I am? It may be best to destroy me first thing."

"You have fulfilled your end of the bargain," Gen said. "Once we are finished here, I can use my blood to destroy you. I have the essence of the Millim Eri flowing through my veins, and only one bleeding should be sufficient to end your life."

Sir Tornus's eyes bulged. "Did I mention that controlling my appetite isn't one of my strong suits? When

I see a delicious soul, I really just stick my fork right in it, so to speak."

"Do be quiet, Tornus," Joranne said acidly. "Why don't you run off and keep watch? Mikkik may have left a surprise or two for anyone who might enter here."

"I do believe I was to be the surprise," Sir Tornus answered. "Very well. Do hurry."

He wandered off toward the door muttering to himself. The Chalaine let Gen help her recline close to the great crack in the center of the floor. She squeezed his hand and felt a little lightheaded. From her previous experience, she knew the cuts would hurt, but even worse was watching her blood spill from her and feeling the warm, comfortable slipping away that brought her close to death. With Gen to watch over her, she felt more sure, but Joranne she could not trust despite her assertions of common purpose.

"Teach me the words of healing for blood magic," Joranne said.

Gen complied and then reclined next the Chalaine, keeping a tight grip on her hand. He said, "She and I will bleed together. When we begin to get faint, use my blood to heal her, and then she will heal me. We cannot touch while we bleed, so the curse of this place will be upon us for a short while. You must watch closely, Joranne. Lose either one of us, and all is lost. Do you understand?"

"Of course," Joranne said. "We must begin before I become too old for my eyes to be of any use."

Gen reached down and removed the dagger from his boot. "I am sorry, Chalaine. I hoped there would be another way."

"It must be done. Let's get it over with."

Gen cut her wrist and then his own. She flinched at the pain, sucking air through her teeth. Gen had long since accustomed himself to cuts and wounds and didn't seem the least perturbed as he bled out onto the floor with her. The darkening and drying skin overtook them almost immediately when they no longer touched, the familiar ashen curse covering her as it once had when she fled in despair from Echo Hold.

Her blood spilled away from her onto the floor to drip down the sides of the chasm, Gen's flowing the other way toward the watchful Joranne. Just as the woozy sleepiness took her into her own mind, she was healed, and she reached out to Gen immediately, their strength and skin returning to health.

They rested for a few moments before Joranne prodded them onward. "Six more times."

Time after time they bled, each time the summer sun sinking lower and the room dimming. Joranne aged with every passing minute, her hair grayer every time the Chalaine woke from being healed. Blood slicked the floor in both directions, fanning away from both of them as they endured the awful cutting for the last time.

The last time!

The Chalaine's heart leapt with hope. The task was nearly done, and the pain and weakness would end forever. As her life force slipped from her after the seventh cut, she fell into one of her favorite daydreams of living with Gen in Blackshire. They walked among the woods and rivers hand in hand, evening sunlight streaming down as they swam naked in forest pools and laughed around a campfire in the moonlight.

And then she awoke, healed and staring through the broken ceiling into the sky. The smoke and dust in the air from the night of fire cast the sunset into a vibrant orange and blue, ragged clouds taking up the rich colors as they sped past above her. She smiled and turned, reaching out to heal Gen. His blood still flowed away from him, and she was alarmed at how pale he seemed. A foot smashed her hand to the ground and she yelped.

"Not so quickly, dear," Joranne said.

CHAPTER 87 – PUSH

Evening had fallen, but the cool breeze and soft shadows brought no relief from the toil of war. Gerand and ten of his knights waited astride their horses in an alley close the the Quickblade Inn. After the fight with Sethra Dhron, his contingent of men had the only intact cavalry left, owing to Maewen's advice to hide the horses until the birds were vanquished. His heroics in slaying the Dhron had earned him respect and renown from the men under his command, although it had also left him with a shield arm that ached terribly. With magic healing an impossibility, he had to rely on Maewen's ministrations. Herbs and poultices, while welcome, took time, and time was not on their side.

Once Sethra Dhron had been defeated, the surge of hope and enthusiasm among the armies defending Mikmir lasted a short two hours until Mikkik's host poured into the city. Heavy arrows fell from deadly Archers, and the armored Gagons pounded down the gates like they were made of rotten wood instead of reinforced oak. Uyumaak sprinted and leaped and marched into the city in droves, and brutal fighting spilled from street to street.

Despite the heavy bloodshed, pride and purpose remained firm until Ghama Dhron made an unwelcome appearance. The memory still chilled Gerand's spine. It came in the shape of a giant man, snakes coalescing to form a chest, legs, arms, and even a wicked head, all of it constantly slithering and slipping about, its constant angry hiss a poison to the ears.

What archers dared stick their heads above the walls shot arrows into the roiling mass, only rewarded by single snakes dropping away from the main body. But as Ghama Dhron approached the walls, the man shape simply fell apart, the vipers scattering in every direction among the ranks of soldiers, biting horses and legs, the venom of such potency that death claimed its victims with alarming speed. Bodies blackened everywhere, dark lumps in the dimming street.

While Gerand wished he could repeat the same trick he had pulled with Sethra Dhron, the slithering chaos of serpents made it impossible to find the body that hosted the spirit. His men had nothing but the force of arms to butcher the snakes one at a time as they darted about with uncanny speed, sinking fangs into their prey and then fleeing to hide in nooks and crannies to await another victim. Gerand had lost nearly twenty men and six horses to the serpents, but as the day wore on, they encountered them less frequently, and he hoped they had at last killed enough to consider Ghama Dhron vanquished.

Fires burned throughout the city, the thick smoke adding to the already hazy sky. Every intake of breath tasted acrid, and the entire company reeked of fire and sweat. Their enemies had pushed them back to the castle wall of Mikmir in one day, and Gerand feared the city would fall before the sun rose the next morning. General Harband had ordered one last assault before nightfall to try to push their enemies back to the outer wall, but Gerand thought the real reason was to buy them time to get inside the castle to prepare for a night of anguish and hard fighting.

Nothing they had done all day seemed to dent the ferocity or capability of their foe. However many they killed, more simply poured through the ruined gates, and the enemy never retreated or rested, exerting a constant pressure that Rhugoth's forces could hardly match, despite the advantages afforded them by the city.

A trill whistle rang through the air. Maewen's signal. Gerand raised his hand and his knights readied themselves. Out on the street, his foot soldiers were drawing a contingent of Uyumaak toward a killing field of their choosing. It was the first offensive strategy they had attempted since the battle began, and Gerand was determined to make it count. Archers poised at the ready on nearby roofs and his cavalry were secreted with him in the alleys at the top of the hill. His footmen served as unfortunate but necessary bait. They would draw the Uyumaak to the street, the archers would let loose, and then the cavalry would charge down the hill and decimate them from the rear. The half-elf's whistle meant the footmen were within a quarter mile, and—if they obeyed orders—were in a fighting retreat.

A second whistle, but too soon. A fighting retreat should have taken longer. In a few moments, he could hear his men yelling and the thumping of Uyumaak drums, but the expected clash of weapons and yelled orders from his captains were conspicuously missing. This was not a fighting retreat or an orderly one; his men were running for their lives. After a few moments more he knew why. The very stones beneath their feet shook with its coming.

A Gagon.

"Gagon," Gerand said, though he felt his announcement was unnecessary. "Switch to spears."

The third signal. His men had rounded the corner. The Uyumaak would be charging up behind. His men readied their weapons as the first of the bowmen began to loose their barrage, the pounding of the Gagon's feet close.

296

When the fourth whistle came, Gerand hefted his heavy spear and tore out of the alley with a mighty yell. The other line of cavalry galloped out of an alley on the opposite side, and in two columns they descended the hill.

So few! Gerand thought as he surveyed the scene. Not even half of his footmen had survived the ruse. As they ran to escape their pursuers, the footmen darted to the side to allow room for the horses to do their work. As Gerand had intended, the Uyumaak had pooled at the bottom of the hill. Only the Uyumaak Warriors continued their pursuit of the fliers. The Bashers had stopped, hastily forming a line in preparation to cut down the horses with their wicked battle axes. The Gagon bringing up the rear had turned about, arrows from the archers protruding from its back while it used its massive club to beat at the buildings from which the archers shot. The Uyumaak Archers returned in kind, their deadly aim thinning Gerand's men at an alarming rate.

An Uyumaak Warrior raised its club and Gerand took it on the shield as he flew past. The shock and pain of his injured arm watered his eyes in agony. The Basher ahead of him raised its ax to strike his horse's legs, but one of Maewen's arrows punched into its face through the tiny visor in its helmet and it fell. Gerand shot through the gap and knocked down an Uyumaak Archer before unleashing his heavy spear toward the raging Gagon which was stomping about twenty feet ahead. The spear flew true, sticking the Gagon at the base of the neck between its helmet and back armor. It collapsed without a twitch to the street, limbs flaccid and body crushing the unfortunate Uyumaak nearby. The rest of the knights unleashed their spears at the Uyumaak Archers and Bashers, felling enough to allow Gerand's archers to resume their work. Sword drawn, Gerand rallied his foot soldiers and knights to him, and in minutes they had butchered every Uyumaak in the street.

Wincing, Gerand dismounted as Maewen left her perch at the top of the hill and ran to him.

"Well done, Lord Kildan," she complimented. "You are earning a name for yourself today."

"It cost too many men," he lamented. "We won this battle, but paid a heavy price. Would you mind helping me unbuckle this shield? I'm afraid I haven't had time to find a squire yet."

"How is your arm?" she asked as she carefully lifted his shield and undid the inner buckle.

He sucked air through his teeth at the painful movement. "It's worthless. I can't lift the shield anymore. I'll be better without it, though if another Sethra Dhron shows up, I may ask for it back. Knight Captain Gremaine! Get everyone together and let's see what we have left for the push."

Maewen handed the shield to one of the nearby foot soldiers and probed Gerand's arm, shaking her head. "You've broken it. Try not to move it too much."

"I think an Uyumaak Warrior broke it for me when I came down the hill."

"I think you broke it yourself when you jumped off the wall like a madman."

Gerand smirked. "This from the person who took Gen along for a little suicide run on an Uyumaak unit."

Maewen leaned on her bow. "I didn't say I disapprove of what you did. After all, the brave are merely the stupid who live through their poor decisions. I just hope we can live long enough to tell Lord Mikmir about your exploits."

"I wish Lord Mikmir would arrive," Gerand said. "I have every confidence in General Harband, but somehow I think our mutual friend would have done better at the defense of the city."

"I agree."

At last his men had gathered, and Gerand had to stifle a frown and put on a proud face instead. He had lost nearly half his men in less than a day of fighting, and the ones that remained were bloody, beaten, and exhausted. They had one more battle to fight before night completely fell, and Gerand sought the words to tease a flame from what embers remained of their enthusiasm.

He raised his good arm for silence. "Well done!" he yelled. "Well done! I am fortunate to have the bravest and the best of men under my command. We have sacrificed dearly this day for a good cause, but we have made the enemy pay for every inch forward. I could ask for no finer men in this dark hour than the ones that stand bruised and bleeding before me. I am honored to call you countrymen, and no man can fault our valor and skill at arms this day.

"Now, our half-elf friend tells me that I have broken my shield arm and can no longer protect myself. My arm may be broken, but my spirit is not. When the trumpet sounds, I will ride this horse and I will take my sword and cut the enemy back to the gates of this city. . ."

As he said the words, the trumpet sounded, but not for attack. It sounded for retreat.

Things are worse than even I thought.

"We are being called within the gates!" he announced. "Let's go with all speed and see what deeds of valor await us this night. Cavalry, to the back! Form on me! Foot soldiers, walk at the head!"

They traversed the wrack of the streets with the best speed they could, bodies of monsters and men littering every thoroughfare and alley in all directions. They met up with the main column of men streaming uphill toward the main gates, a ragged collection of the weary, wounded, and fearful shuffling eagerly toward the greater protection of the main wall.

Rhughoth has enjoyed uncontested peace for so long they have forgotten the rigors of war, Gerand mused. While his soldiers fared little better, the war with Aughmere at least had ensured him veteran fighters in his ranks. They merged in with the stream, several looking on the mounted knights with jealousy. Mikkik's minions had taken a heavy toll on the horses in the city, and the loss of that advantage was felt keenly.

They rode in silence through the deep archway of the massive stone walls, their sturdy construction and imposing height inspiring some comfort. Even the most colorful imagination would find difficulty conjuring up an enemy that could breach such a fortification, but Mikkik, so far, had proven his genius at finding ways to overcome every device they had to defeat him. Only now could the soldiers who had served at Echo Hold appreciate the deceptive joke Mikkik had played on them during their carefree days of archery practice against the hapless Uyumaak streaming up the road to be slaughtered.

In the waning stages of twilight they emerged into the courtyard, the thick press of men rendering the immense space cramped and noisy. A Captain of Rhugoth unhelpfully ordered them to "find a spot" to encamp and to have the healthiest half of his men to report to the base of the walls. This duty done, Gerand found Maewen and made their way toward a pavilion set up in front of the Great Hall where the Generals consulted together, all looking as ragged their men. Even the steely-eyed, half mad General Harband appeared spent. Three of Tolnor's Dukes were among the party, and they perked up a little as Gerand and Maewen joined them.

"How are you, lad?" General Harband inquired as they approached the table.

"Lad?" Duke Greenwall protested. "This is Duke Kildan, and you should render him the respect he is due!"

"Be at ease, Milord," Gerand said. "He and I need not stand on ceremony. What is our situation?"

"Dire!" General Harband reported. "We have had no answer for this kind of a war! No one's fought an army of this magnitude and composition in two hundred years! We paid for our naiveté today."

"We should have abandoned the city and fought them from here, behind the walls," General Torunne opined. "We thought we would have the advantage in the streets—but birds with dagger sharp beaks? Poisonous vipers? Gagons at every turn?"

"How many men have we lost?" Gerand asked, fearing the answer.

"It's hard to say," General Harband replied, rubbing his thin goatee. "At least a third are dead. Only about half of what remain are in fighting condition. Let's just hope the walls are enough to buy us some time to heal and wait for Aughmere or Lord Mikmir to show up with reinforcements. I thought we would hold the city for days, not hours."

"We'll hold this wall forever," General Torunne stated confidently. We've got ballistae for the damned Gagon, and they would grind their battering ram to powder on the gates. We'll hold."

"Where do you want me?" Gerand asked.

"He should rest," Maewen piped in. "He has a broken arm."

Gerand shook his head. "I can still lead and swing a sword. Put me on the wall somewhere."

"Go there now and take the southern side," Harband commanded, "but when the fighting starts, I'll pull you down to rest and bring you in reserve if needed. I know your mettle, boy, but trying to mount a wall defense with a broken arm will get you killed. Don't worry, I'll be there to beat them back. Besides, defeating that cursed flock of birds has earned you a pass."

Gerand bowed and left, striding through the makeshift camps with Maewen in tow. He didn't want a pass!

"I'm sorry if I put you in a bad light in front of your peers," she apologized, "but they are right. You cannot lead a defense along the wall as wounded as you are."

301

Gerand gritted his teeth. He could not afford an injury! "Do you have any of that pain draught that you gave to the Chalaine when she broke her wrist?"

"No, but if I could borrow a fire and a pot, I could brew it."

"It would help."

Maewen left, and Gerand ascended the steps to the south wall, relieving a General Forswright of Rhugoth. The men on the walls were Rhugothian and fresh, having been stationed inside the protective fort for the duration of the battle. They wore the blue capes and silver breastplates of the Castle Guard, and although clean and rested, their faces registered the same sober worry as the men who had passed through the now-sealed gates.

While Gerand diligently inspected and enforced discipline, in the end there was little to do but wait while Mikkik hatched some further plot or threw some new horror at them. Without the moons in the sky, sundown brought a darkness compounded by the choking smoke that hung over the city in a cloud. Pockets of orange beneath the haze created pools of flickering, diffuse light that brightened and dimmed as the fires breathed and then starved when the fuel ran out. The constant chatter and commotion behind the wall made the abandoned city seem all the more dead by comparison, a giant graveyard for the brave men hewn down during the day.

Maewen coming up the stairs holding a waterskin brightened Gerand's prospects. His arm ached horribly, and the constant pain robbed him of vigor and clouded his mind.

"Take only a sip every hour or so," she warned. "It will make you sleep if you drink too much."

He nodded and eagerly took the dosage prescribed while she watched to ensure he didn't overdo it.

"Any developments up here?" she asked.

"No. Nothing has approached the walls as yet, and it is

simply too dark to see anything. They must know not to let us rest. They have us on the edge of exhaustion and fear. A bold push now could end this battle tonight."

"We can hope the wall is as strong as they say," Maewen said, coming to a crenellation on the edge and peering into the abyssal darkness. "There is movement in the streets, though to what end it is hard to say."

They remained on the wall for nearly an hour while Maewen surveyed the city, using her superior eyes to try to give some advanced warning. Gerand made one last inspection of the men, and when he returned, he could tell by Maewen's posture that something was amiss, her face registering an uncharacteristic shock.

"What do you see?"

"Look down at the base of the hill," Maewen said, pointing. "I can hardly make sense of what it might be."

Gerand peered. There was something there, something big, but in the poor light, it was impossible to make out, even as it started to move.

"Holy Eldaloth!" Maewen said, stepping back. "I've got to warn them!"

She darted away without explaining, and Gerand turned his gaze back to the winding cobble road that led up to the castle. It took a while for what Maewen saw to become plain to his human sight, but when it did he joined the rest of the soldiers along the wall in muttering an oath. Mikkik had unleashed his last horror upon them. Khrona Dhron: the Abomination of the East.

———◆———

Before the Chalaine could react, Sir Tornus roughly dragged her off the ground in a bruising grip that pinned her arms to her sides. Gen continued to bleed, clearly weakening with each pulse of the blood from the cut on his wrist. Without her touch, the curse covered both her and him in charred, ashen skin. Joranne stood next to him, watching as Sir Tornus dragged her backward toward a greenish light now casting ghoulish shadows across the rubble and reflecting off the slick blood.

As he pulled her back, they jostled against scaly Uyumaak who were staring at the lantern, just as she had seen on that final night on the shores of Shroud Lake. By the sounds of scraping and crunching, more were filing in through the archway behind her.

"What are you doing?!" the Chalaine yelled, struggling in vain against the embrace of her captor. "He'll die!"

"I don't want to kill him," Joranne said, stooping and gray with age as she joined Sir Tornus in the midst of the Uyumaak. "He has information I need, and he won't give it up without a little incentive. The way you two have been getting on, I think you'll be just what I need to persuade him!"

Joranne concentrated and muttered the healing words of blood magic. Hidden among the Uyumaak, the Chalaine had to crane around the transfixed creatures to see Gen slowly rise, drawing his sword as he noticed the enemies filling the chamber around them.

"Joranne!" he yelled. "What's the meaning of this? Let her go right now, or you will not leave here alive!"

"I will not let her go. If you incant one word of blood magic, I will kill her and Sir Tornus will let loose the Uyumaak. Listen to me very carefully. . ."

"If you want my help," Gen said, "you will let her go!"

Joranne scowled. "Sir Tornus you can aid, but you can't help me, and you know it!" Joranne returned angrily. "And did you think I would let you restore Elde Luri Mora while we were still in it? You know what would happen to us. You will uphold your end of the bargain to Sir Tornus, but I want something else. I want all the incantations of blood magic. Mikkik taught me once so I could teach you, but then he took the knowledge from me. I know how to heal, but I want the rest of it. Teach me the words to bind power to a weapon. Teach me how to bring someone back to life."

"To what end, Joranne?" Gen said. "It's over! There are no more cards to be played for your personal gain! Help me restore Ki'Hal before it dies, or there is no point to any of this!"

Joranne pulled a long thin dagger from her boot. "The words, Gen! How do you bind the power of blood to a weapon? Now!"

"How do I know you won't just kill the Chalaine and set the Uyumaak loose anyway?"

Joranne put the point of the blade to the Chalaine's neck, dimpling the skin. "The words!"

"Stop! I'll tell you."

With the painful point at her throat, the Chalaine kept as still as she could, listening as Gen repeated the words she had heard Mikkik speak in Aldemar's vision of Eldaloth's death, the invocation of the dark speech seeming to darken the room further. Joranne absorbed the knowledge greedily, eyes shining.

"Good!" she crowed once Gen finished. "Tell me, Chalaine, would you give the power of your blood to release Sir Tornus from his long, tormented life?"

"Yes, of course," the Chalaine answered.

Joranne removed the blade point from her neck, and the Chalaine took a deep breath of relief. With a quick jab, the Ash Witch plunged the blade into her side. The searing pain emptied the Chalaine's mind of thought, a soundless scream issuing from her open mouth until her lungs caught up enough to issue it out loud. If it wasn't for Sir Tornus's inescapable grip, she would have collapsed in agony, Joranne keeping the blade inside her body while she groaned. Gen started to incant.

"Stop or she dies!" Joranne yelled. "I want all the incantations, Gen. Do it now, or this will get messy."

"Sir Tornus, let her go," Gen begged. "You were a knight once! Let her go, and I will destroy you now!"

Joranne twisted the blade in the Chalaine's side, her blood dripping down her hip and leg, staining her riding dress. Her screams brought Gen up short.

"The words!" Joranne demanded while the Chalaine cried. "And if I sense for one second that you are using them to heal this place, she will die."

"Take the knife out of her side, and I will tell you!"

"Tell me and then I'll take the knife out of her side! Quit bargaining and do what I say!"

"But the incantations are long!"

"Then you had best begin."

As Gen recited the spells to Joranne, the Chalaine felt life draining from her, the pain of the knife dissolving slowly under her weakness as the room around her seemed to dim and spin. She rallied herself, prodding her eyes open with sheer will.

"Now let her go!"

"One last thing," Joranne said, smiling wickedly. "Throw yourself into the chasm, and I will let her live. Take a step forward or attempt to use magic, and this blade goes to her heart."

"Let me heal Ki'Hal!"

"I will heal it after I am far enough away!" Joranne said. "You are no longer needed. In you go." She punctuated the command with another painful twist of the blade that brought the Chalaine out of her haze to writhe in agony.

Face ashen and eyes wet, Gen turned toward the edge.

"No, Gen, don't," the Chalaine cried, tears sliding down her face. "Please. I cannot live without you. I won't!"

"Goodbye, Chalaine," Gen said, sheathing his sword and peering down into the darkness. "Whatever you do, live. Live and love!"

"Wait!" In her weakness, a blind fury awakened, a primal need to keep Gen alive, to repay every goodness he had blessed her life with. He had saved her enough; it was her turn to repay. A surge of energy—her last—rose within her, and with all her might she pushed her body into Joranne's blade, twisting to drive it deep within her. Blood flowed freely, streaming down in a cascade of red. Gen howled in rage, and the Chalaine knew no more.

Chapter 88 - Abomination and Absolution

Gerand fought to keep his nerve. Horrors he had faced. Horrors he had beaten. Horrors he had endured. But with every step of Khrona Dhron's approach, his senses and courage reeled, duty and honor serving as the last anchors against turning away from the battlements and running as some of the men on the wall now did. Mikkik's evil truly knew no bounds. Gerand had to fight off the amazement seizing his tongue. He had to find the words to stiffen the shaking knees and feet now standing in puddles of urine.

It was half again as high as the walls, a single mass of hundreds if not thousands of human bodies clinging together to form a single mass in the rough shape of a man. Some were naked, others clothed in rotting rags falling away with every heavy footfall. The desiccated, rotting forms of men, women, and children with gray, tattered skin compacted together in one form, but each twitched and moved individually as the creature lumbered forward with dark purpose. The rotted hands and arms and legs of each individual member clung to their neighbors to form the creature's shape and musculature, and, like a gigantic brute of the Abyss, it came steadily forward, pounding toward them in the wavering light of the fires and torches on the walls.

But while its appearance shocked, its smell sickened, the rank odor of decay, stale sweat, and feces wafted before it in an invisible, poisonous cloud that challenged the fortitude of every stomach in its path. As it neared, the wails and moans of Khrona Dhron's corpses unnerved even the sturdiest soldier, every man on the walls stupefied and waiting to wake from a nightmare that dwarfed their darkest imaginings.

Maewen grabbed Gerand's hand. "You must raise your voice. Get them moving!"

Gerand shook his head to clear it. "Stand your ground!" he yelled sprinting along the wall. "Arrows and ballistae, fire now! Fire now! Get the spearmen ready!"

His calls echoed along the wall, and the other commanders picked it up as the Generals and Dukes sprinted up the stairs from below. Awakened from their torpidity, the arrows and heavy bolts of the ballistae poured from the walls and into the creature. To Gerand's dismay, the arrows did little, the bodies convulsing and wrapping around each other to snap the protruding arrows off and present fresh flesh for targets. The ballistae ripped holes in the great mass, only to have them filled again.

"Archers down, spearmen forward!" Gerand yelled as Khrona Dhron loomed above them. "We must push them off the walls. They're coming!"

The switch of soldiers had only begun when the creature lurched forward with renewed speed and crashed into the walls above the gate. The bodies of the top disconnected from one another and crashed onto and over the wall, spilling into the main courtyard while the rest clambered up the backs and appendages of their fellows to stream over the massive barrier with inhuman celerity. They ran fully twice as fast as any human Gerand had ever seen, and the long fall from the walls seemed to do little to slow them.

With bony fists, ragged teeth, and clawed hands they beat and scraped and wrestled down everything in their path with a ferocious purpose. Once they felled a foe, they took his weapons and continued on their deadly rampage.

"They're headed to the gatehouse!" General Harband screamed. "Keep them away! Fight to the last!"

The men in the courtyard streamed forward, but it was too late, the steady stream of Khrona Dhron's quick and deadly minions too fast to prevent the slaughter of the gate guard and the slow opening of the mighty doors and portcullis. The remnants of Khrona Dhron crammed through the slowly opening gap and joined their companions. Once again they gathered, climbing up and over each other, forming into a solid mass. With monstrous feet and fists, Khrona Dhron pounded and crushed the soldiers in the courtyard while making its way toward the doors of the Great Hall.

Gerand swore and tore down the stairs, Maewen following. "We have to chop them down one at a time!" he yelled to any soldier that would listen. The courtyard was an unruly mess, the creature outpacing and outmaneuvering every attempt to form an assault against it, all the while smashing down with heavy feet to crush anything that approached near it. Some of the corpses in the lower legs still held weapons and would reach out from their clinging positions to swipe at anyone who got too near.

In frustration Gerand realized that nothing could stop it in time. It would reach the Great Hall and slaughter its way to the chambers where Mirelle waited as decoy. She would be trapped and defenseless. Her only hope would be to escape out a side entrance and try to win free of the city.

"The Uyumaak are coming!" someone yelled from the wall.

Gerand swallowed his panic and bolted to where his horse waited with the wounded of his company. His injured arm reminded him of its existence as he pulled himself up onto the horse.

"I'm going to get Mirelle," Gerand yelled to Maewen. "See if they can get the gates closed before the Uyumaak get here!"

She nodded and sprinted away. Gerand dug his heels into his mount and crashed into the square, heedless of bowling away friend or foe as he tore ahead of the abomination that was dismantling everything in its path. The men had clumped thickly before it, slowing but not stopping its progress, and Gerand rode around them and up the stairs to the Great Hall. The creature would be there in minutes, and Mirelle would die.

Through his brand, Gen felt the Chalaine's life fade and then flee. He watched Sir Tornus release her, her body collapsing in the midst of the Uyumaak mob still mesmerized by the green lantern light. Gen drew his sword. The blood on the floor could still save her. He need only bathe her body in it. He could bring her back. Shoving away the doubts in his mind, he let the anger and sadness loose, yanking his sword from its sheath.

Joranne slunk back, face panicked. With a quick glance at Gen, she muttered the words of blood magic under her breath, the bloodstained dagger in her hand flaring with power. Sir Tornus eyed it.

"Stay away," she said, retreating back toward the fallen archway, "or Sir Tornus will set them loose."

"That dagger is the only thing that can end your life, Sir Tornus," Gen said. "I won't help you after what you've done, so it is your last chance."

Sir Tornus needed no further prodding. Like a savage animal he bolted after Joranne, who dropped the dagger and darted away into the gathering darkness of the Hall of Three Moons. With reverence Sir Tornus lifted the weapon

311

from the floor, regarding it with a smile of gleeful anticipation.

"At last. At last!" he said, kissing the blade. "Oh, sweet oblivion, my only forgiveness!" With a decisive downward thrust, he plunged the knife into his breast, closing his eyes with pleasure. A glow gathered around Sir Tornus for a brief moment, and in an instant the white hot radiance consumed him, the hilt of the now bladeless dagger falling to the ground.

"That was quite a show," Joranne cackled, voice emanating from somewhere in the motionless horde of Mikkik's creatures.

Gen walked among the Uyumaak and found the witch with her hand on the lantern. Amid the scaly, color-shifting legs of the Uyumaak, the Chalaine's body lay still, though the raspy, burned skin of her arms and the brittle hair had changed back to their natural color and luster. He struck out toward her body, but Joranne shuttered the lantern, and in the near total darkness, the Uyumaak awoke and smelled an enemy near.

Gen backed out of their reach as they came to their senses. Wary of the slick blood and the chasm's edge, he angled away deeper into the chamber. Debris littered the room, making movement treacherous. As one, the Uyumaak slapped their chests and darted after him. Gen turned and dove behind a rubble pile to keep them all from falling on him at once. Flinching away from a dark arrow loosed upon him, he laid into an Uyumaak Warrior that had followed him over the stone. Gen gutted it with a single stroke of his sharp blade, kicking the body away. With a back stroke he decapitated a Basher rounding upon him. *I've got to get to a wall!* he thought, seeing that they could surround him at any moment. With two powerful strokes he hacked two Hunters in half and bolted for a section of the wall that would keep the creatures off his back.

Negotiating the room tested every sense he had, his

enemies at his heels stumbling along behind him. Another arrow sped by him, nicking his shoulder as he at last reached the protective wall and spun with a wide stroke, killing one Warrior and amputating the arm of a Hunter, who tripped and fell. With all the speed and skill of his training he fought, Joranne's echoing laughter mocking him.

In the end, there were too many, the desiccating curse upon his skin slowing his movements. A claw dug away a furrow of flesh from his chest. A sword carved a bloody gash in his leg. A Basher's hammer pulverized his arm. Still he fought on until an arrow he could not avoid dug into his belly, slamming him into the wall and knocking him to his knees. Almost all was dark now, and he felt as he had at Butchers gap—spent and waiting for the last blow to send him to Erelinda. Send him to the Chalaine. A Basher raised its hammer above its head, and Gen closed his eyes, welcoming death.

But it never came.

He opened his eyes to find the ruins again bathed in green light. The Uyumaak retreated back toward the other side of the hall where the Chalaine lay. Gen couldn't move, and he awaited Joranne's jeering face to come mock him before finishing him off. But instead of the old and bent witch, a robed figure strode purposefully toward him, staff in hand. He pulled his hood down around his shoulders as he bent down. Even in the weak light, and despite the burned skin, Gen recognized Athan, Pontiff of the Church of the One.

"Lord Mikmir?" Athan asked.

"Yes," Gen answered.

"I can heal you with some of the power of the blood on the floor, but if I know your purpose, I fear it may spend the virtue needed to do your task."

"Help me to the Chalaine. I will do it. Where is Joranne?"

313

"I hit her rather hard in the head."

"Throw her in the chasm."

"It is not my nature to do such things, not anymore" Athan objected, extending his arm. Gen took the proferred arm and used it to rise, his ravaged body screaming with pain. With a yell he snapped the Uyumaak arrow in his gut in half and tossed the shaft away.

"Set me by the blood. Bring the Chalaine's body to me."

Athan helped him over and placed him carefully against the stone where they had lain to bleed. "What do you need her body for?"

"To bring her back."

"But you need to heal Elde Luri Mora with that blood!"

"If she lives, I can do both with your help."

Athan nodded and wove between the entranced Uyumaak to drag the Chalaine over by the armpits and into the blood on the floor.

"Soak her in it," Gen ordered. "You've done this before."

He nodded, the drying blood making his task difficult. Anywhere the Chalaine's blood touched Athan's skin, the flesh healed, and he glanced at it amazed.

"Now step away from her," Gen commanded.

Weak and dizzy, Gen recited the words of power, opening a Portal to Erelinda to find his beloved bride. Athan gasped in awe at the beautiful splendor of green trees, tall waterfalls, and blooming verdure that filled their vision. In a deep blue sky overspread with full, white clouds flew every kind and color of birds. The animals of the forest wandered wild and free among the spirits of men and women who walked among the flawless beauty. But more than sight, the feeling of rapturous joy and peace emanated through the Portal, the light narrowing their eyes with its warm brilliance.

Gen smiled as he found her, walking in wonder with her arms widespread to flit along the hazy petals of flowers, her blonde hair streaming behind her in a caressing breeze. She wore a loose white dress hemmed in purple with no other device adorning her body. In her perfect face rested a peace Gen had never seen play upon her features, a contentment that could only come from an absence of worry or toil. She was at home. Gen called to her across the distance, and she turned and smiled, her unparalleled beauty an object of worship.

She stared back, unclouded eyes full of love. "It is time I healed Ki'Hal," she said. "I know what to do now. Again I thank you, Gen. I knew Erelinda before I came to it. I felt it with you. Now the whole world must know. Do not be sad. One day you will know this joy as I know it."

Gen creased his brow as the Chalaine neared the Portal, her form dissolving into a bright shining presence the closer she came. On the floor, her body caught up the brilliance, losing its shape and burning like a sun to light the entire room. Gen closed his eyes as the Chalaine's spirit passed through the Portal, the Hall of Three Moons reverberating with power. The power of her blood was gone, and the spell died, Portal winking out. The room shook and swayed. Athan fell.

"Look!" Athan said.

Gen opened his eyes. The Uyumaak, the lantern, and Joranne's body had all been blasted to dust to be carried away on a wind that swirled about the hall and then dove into bowels of the shrinking chasm. In amazement they watched as the Hall knit itself together, stone rising to meet stone, cracks closing as if never sundered, and the glass of the arched dome rising to fit perfectly into place. The mighty chasm pushed together and the trembling stopped.

Athan helped Gen to his feet, draping his arm over his shoulder. Their skin had healed of its affliction, and they stumbled outside to watch the restoration of Elde Luri Mora. The fireflies streamed toward them from every direction, hovering around them to create a warm evening light wherever they walked. The rotting, blackened trees and bushes greened, swelled, and flowered as if spring had blown an entire season of warming winds in an instant. The befouled water of the lake turned clear and smooth, reflecting the starlight on its mirror surface.

Tears fell from both their eyes as they witnessed the return of the city's spirit, a familiar spirit to Gen, youthful, pure, and one that he would always miss. He lifted his hand to a nearby blossom, and at his touch a plum grew and ripened, falling into his palm. In his heart he instinctively knew what it was for, and he took a bite of its sweet flesh, the wounds of his body closing and healing as new.

Athan, haunted and humbled, turned his face to a sky filled with fireflies and stars. "I am sorry!" he said. "I was a fool. Forgive me, Chalaine. Forgive a stupid, prideful man."

Gen sat on the street and put his head between his knees. He cried as the price of Ki'Hal's salvation was collected and carried away from him. In the earth, in the air, and in the water he could sense her, but her touch and her smile and her words were gone. How long he mourned on the street, he couldn't say. Athan wept nearby, head bowed.

A bird call trilled in the air. Gen stirred, lifting his head to the sky. He wanted to sit and rest, to mourn the loss of his wife and let the returning vigor of Elde Luri Mora work to soothe the ache within. But Mikkik and his armies were gone to Mikmir, and there Gen knew he must go.

As his thoughts turned to Rhugoth, a group of fireflies broke from the swarm to dance in a loose globe in front of him. Slowly they moved away, and Gen followed. Athan trailed meekly a few steps behind, Gen still not ready to forgive or forget what the man had done in the pursuit of his zealotry. Gen could pity him, for he was Mikkik's biggest fool, but until he could get the image of Mirelle hanging from a pole while fire charred her legs, he could feel nothing but loathing for the man.

The globe of fireflies passed down the main avenue of

Elde Luri Mora before turning into the thick green grass and toward the lake. They reached the shore, and the globe hovered out over the shallow water near the edge. Gen squinted. Something glimmered beneath the calm surface of the translucent water. He removed his boots and stepped in, reaching down. Feeling about in the sandy silt, he closed his fist around a rough, porous rock the size of an apple. As soon as he gripped it, the power of the moon Duam exploded within him, a reserve of energy flowing from the stone into his body. He pulled it out of the water, examining its blackened, rough surface. A chunk of the moon fallen to Ki'Hal.

"What is it?" Athan asked.

"Power," Gen replied. "I need to get back to Mikmir."

"That will take nearly a week."

As soon as Athan said the words, a flash of blue spilled a brilliant light across the lake. Just behind them in the grass a Portal waited.

"Amazing," Athan said, awed.

"Are you coming?" Gen asked as he pulled on his boots.

"No," he answered. "Tell them I was killed. I have penance to do in this place, and I will stay. The Church must go on, but it will go on without me. But I must know, are you really Aldradan Mikmir? There is something familiar about you I cannot place."

"Believe what you will. I have a kingdom to see to."

Gen took a deep breath and plunged through the Portal.

CHAPTER 89 – DUAMSTONE

Gerand practically threw himself from the horse. The animated corpses of Khrona Dhron had taken notice of his race for the door, and a pocket of corpses had broken away from the main body and charged forward using weapons confiscated from their victims to cut through the resistance. Gerand glanced over his shoulder. *They are so fast!* There was no time to lose. The guards at the door cracked it for him.

"You can bar it from the inside," one of them told him.

Gerand slipped in, noticing a beam lying on the floor that had been brought up for that purpose. A contingent of guards waited at the ready in the antechamber.

"Bar this door and any side doors. It is upon us!"

Gerand sprinted down the well-known halls, pausing just for a moment to take a swig of Maewen's numbing draught. Guards lined the entire path to the antechamber of the Chalaines, and Mirelle and Volney waited at the entrance to the maze that led to the Chalaine's old chambers. Mirelle wore the veil and dress to complete the disguise, but there was no more need.

"We've got to try to get out of the city," Gerand said. "The castle is nearly lost, and there is nothing we have that can stop what's out there. Quick, Mirelle, get something on that you can run and fight in. I need to rest for a moment."

Mirelle nodded. "Don't forget the pool, Duke Kildan," she said before leaving.

He had forgotten. The clear water had been enchanted to heal wounds. Eagerly he thrust in his hand and drank, the water restoring movement and strength to his arm.

"What's happening out there?" Volney asked, face worried. "Is the castle really lost?"

"I'm afraid so, my friend," Gerand confirmed. "You remember those beetles and snakes?"

"Yes. Are they back?"

"The snakes and birds we have killed. But what came tonight was the most awful thing I have ever seen." Gerand tried to explain Khrona Dhron, but he doubted he conveyed the full horror to Volney, who opined that he thought the snakes the worst.

Mirelle emerged wearing a black divided riding dress, hair pulled behind her. She had removed the veil. "What is your plan, Gerand?"

"The courtyard is filled. We need to leave through the kitchens and see if we can get horses. Horses or not, we leave through the postern gate and work our way through the city. We ride for Tolnor."

They turned to go, but a sudden feeling of rightness flooded over them like a fresh wind pushing away the heavy haze they had become accustomed to. The clarity and rightness of feeling stopped them where they stood, inviting a moment to pause and savor what had been lost when Elde Luri Mora was destroyed.

"They've done it," Mirelle smiled.

"It is incredible!" Volney exclaimed.

"Yes," Gerand said. "But this isn't over yet. With Elde Luri Mora restored, Mikkik will be after the Chalaine twice as hard so he can bleed her again and destroy it. We still need to get far from him and his horde. Let's go quickly."

They had resumed their march toward the upper levels when Mirelle suddenly stopped, Volney nearly crashing into her.

"What's wrong?" Gerand asked, seeing wonder dawn on her face.

"We're not supposed to go that way," she said.

"Why do you think that?" Gerand asked.

"We're supposed to go to the tower. I can't explain it. He'll be there."

"Who?"

"Gen."

Altering course, they took the ramp up and then proceeded through the hallways and locked doors that led to the tower complex. Upward they climbed, around and around until they reached the door that led to the quarters of the decoy Chalaine. Volney inserted a key and they entered, finding the room dark. Shattered shutters were strewn about the floor, evidence of Sethra Dhron's attack.

"No one's here, Mirelle," Gerand said, squinting in the darkness. "We can't stay here. We'll be trapped with no way to. . ."

A Portal bloomed to life in the middle of the room.

"Whoa!" Volney said. "Was there a Portal here?"

"No," Mirelle answered. "There were no Portals in the entire complex save, the Walls in the Chalaine's quarters."

Gerand drew his sword. "We don't know what's on the other side."

Volney stepped in front of Mirelle and drew his blade as well, but a single figure passed through the blazing field of blue and it winked out. Mirelle darted around Volney and embraced Gen.

"You did it!"

"Elde Luri Mora is restored," Gen said. "What of Mikmir?"

"The situation is dire," Gerand reported. "Khrona Dhron is destroying us, and the Uyumaak are at the gates. We were about to flee with Mirelle."

"Has Mikkik appeared?"

"No."

Gen turned and jogged to the door that opened out onto the balcony. His companions joined him. Together they stared down at the battle below, all save Volney, who kept his back to the tower and muttered that the height was worse in the dark. Below in the courtyard a group of Uyumaak had formed a solid wedge, Khrona Dhron at the head, and they were driving through what was left of every soldier that could still fight.

"Gerand," Gen said. "Get back with the men. Tell them that Aldradan Mikmir is coming. Sound the trumpets. Go now. Volney, stay here, but I need a private word with Mirelle, please."

Gerand turned and ran back down the stairs, heart pounding in his chest. Knowing the Aldradan Mikmir was near would inspire the men, but would inspiration be enough? Gen was shrewd and a powerful fighter, but nothing they had done seemed able to stop Mikkik's forces. The addition of one man—even if a King—didn't seem enough.

He charged back to the antechamber of the Great Hall, startling the guards by commanding them to unbar the doors for him.

"Bar them again when I am through. Take courage. The King has come!"

The heavy doors opened and Gerand passed through, finding himself at the rear of the throng of soldiers waiting their turn to die as Khrona Dhron and the Uyumaak wedge sliced through them like and ax passing through rotten wood.

"The King is coming!" Gerand yelled, trying to find where any of the Generals or Dukes were. Their strategy was clear: clump everyone at the doors for a last stand. Spears and arrows sped into the Uyumaak wedge and the frightening creature before them. Axes and swords chopped and hewed with ferocity born of terror, the corpses of Khrona Dhron leering and howling in mockery at the futility of the resistance.

Gerand tried working his way to the front, yelling at the top of his lungs that Aldradan Mikmir had returned, but no one listened—or those that heard didn't care. He turned back to the doors, hoping Gen would make his appearance and rally the defenders, but a collective gasp from the soldiers turned him around and pulled his gaze upward.

As Mikkik had done on the night of the failed wedding, Gen descended from the sky. But rather than white, holy light, he came in a fiery burning, the glow of the flames casting a wide halo about him in the haze. A low rumble reverberated through the air, and the ground quivered beneath their feet as he descended like a meteor from the sky. Gen hit the ground hard, and the resulting quake knocked half of the fighters—foe and friend—to the ground.

No sooner had he landed than he incanted, and a great wave of fire burst away from him as if driven by an angry gale, setting aflame the entire center column of the Uyumaak horde. Silently the creatures burned, their mute mouths affixed in expressions of agony as they flailed and staggered and died. The flames licked the legs of the massive Khrona Dhron, who turned from his deadly work at the flank of the column and pounded forward toward the new foe, the heads of the many bodies craning around to regard the King of Mikmir with malice.

Closer it came, and Gen waited a moment more and then incanted again. A torrential swirl of wind and fire descended from the sky and ripped into Khrona Dhron. The mighty whirlwind tore the conglomerated bodies apart, flaming corpses ejected into the air and flung in every direction to slam into walls and to drop into the midst of the Uyumaak and men.

But when the flames and wind lifted, Gerand's eyes widened in disbelief. At the center of Khrona Dhron was

Mikkik, his majesty gone and his face twisted in the weary pain brought on by the restoration of Elde Luri Mora. Burns covered his body, but as Gen strode toward him, they healed.

Mikkik turned to run into the midst of the wrack in the courtyard. With a complex series of words, Gen gestured, and Duammagic called thin columns of pale stone from the ground, surrounding Mikkik in a prison from which he had no power to escape. The dark god yelled in rage and humiliation, cutting his hands on the sharp, glassy rock as he pushed and pulled against his prison bars.

What was left of the enemy milled about in shock and disarray. Gen turned toward the soldiers of Rhugoth and Tolnor and pulled his sword. "Drive them out of this courtyard! Drive them out of the gates. Drive them out of the city! Drive them back to the abyss!"

The men raised their swords in a shout and charged, Gen at the forefront of the wave of reinvigorated soldiers. Everywhere Gen went, there were bursts of fire, flashes of lightning, and blasts of wind that sent the enemy to the ground or running for the gates. Gerand took charge of the Tolnorians, a thrill building in his breast as he joined the unstoppable drive toward the gates, a day of defeat and retreat turning to the sweetest victory that he had ever known.

———◆———

"Shut the gates," Gen commanded hours later as the first signs of dawn broke into the sky. "Get the Generals and the Dukes here immediately. We need to rest and get organized. We will rest for a time and then drive them out of the city. If they leave, we will follow them out and slaughter them to the last creature."

In moments the portcullis and the gates whined shut, and Gen turned to survey the courtyard littered with bodies. The stench and smoke of burning hung over everything while the soldiers finished their work, killing anything that still twitched or moved. Mikkik waited in his prison, having sunk to the earth in despair.

Maewen ran up from the direction of the Great Hall. To Gen she said in Elvish, "It is good to see you."

Gen turned, finding the half-elf a bloody mass of cuts and bruises, an Uyumaak arrow broken off in her shoulder. Using the Duamstone, he healed her, her face registering relief.

"How is it done?" she asked.

Gen opened his hand to reveal the stone, which had shrunk to the size of an egg. "It is a fragment from Duam that fell. There will be others. No doubt many have been collected without their owners knowing what they are capable of."

"It is a secret best kept between us for now," Maewen said. "If Mikkik found out. . ."

"I know."

"And what of the Chalaine? Is she safe?"

The battle had helped him put aside the hurt, a sadness compounded by the necessity of telling Mirelle. The First Mother's sobs of agony and anguished cries broke his heart. He glanced up at the tower where she no doubt still wept curled up against the balustrade, head in her hands while tears streamed down her cheeks. He couldn't leave her alone. He would put his army in order and then go mourn with her.

Maewen noticed the sadness in his face and closed her eyes. "I am sorry, Gen. You turned a timid girl into a courageous young woman. I am and will always be proud of you both."

"There is more to her death than you know," he said. "It was an ending, but a beginning as well. I will tell you more by and by. I have a war that needs a King for a short while more. But do you remember your offer to me, to show me the wild places and wonders of Ki'Hal? I will need it. I will need it, to forget for a time."

She put her hand on his shoulder. "My offer still stands. You only need ask. But you are right. Let us finish this. Then we will rest. I'll get atop the walls and see what the Uyumaak are up to."

General Harband, beaten and bloody, arrived and leaned on his heavy war club. "We could have used you sooner, Milord," he said with a slight tone of accusation. "We lost a lot of men tonight."

"We lost more than that, General," Gen returned with emotion. "I have restored Elde Luri Mora, but at a great cost. Where are the other Dukes and Generals?"

"I believe I'm the only one who can stand. Two were killed, and the rest are gravely wounded."

"Take me to them, and I will heal them. I have a story they must hear so they can know that this sacrifice was not a vain one."

"Lord Mikmir!" Maewen shouted from the battlements. "What is it?"

"They've come!"

"Who?"

"The Aughmerians!"

General Harband rolled his eyes up into his head and he straightened, hefting his club. "Oh, no they don't! They'll fight off what's left and then take credit for saving the city! Heal me, Lord Mikmir, and let me gather what men are. . ."

"General Harband!" Gen barked loud enough to break the man from his frenzy. "General. Let the Aughmerians have their turn to bleed."

The meeting with the army's leadership was short, and Gen was gratified to see that General Torunne was not among those who had died, even though he had led the charge against Khrona Dhron to buy Gerand time to get Mirelle to safety. When Gen revealed that the person they thought was Lady Alumira was instead her mother, the

Dukes and Generals were shocked and angry that Mirelle and the city had been used as bait, but when Gen related the events of Elde Luri Mora, they nodded soberly and seemed to accept the necessity of the ruse.

"You have all won the freedom of this world," Gen said, "and much honor and glory besides. It has been an honor to serve and fight with you. I will see the Uyumaak dead, but I must leave you again soon. There is a task that I must complete before I can rest again and before the world can be at peace."

"What about Mikkik?" Gerand asked. "You just can't leave him imprisoned in the middle of the courtyard."

"I have to for now. When I return I will bring a weapon that will end him forever. Look for me before the summer ends. Do not let anyone approach him or give him anything, but let the people see him and know that he is, at last, beaten."

Emotionally spent, Gen left the pavilion, not wanting to field questions or make decisions. He walked into the courtyard as the light of dawn tried to scratch through the haze to lighten the sky. Mikkik glared at him from his cage, and Gen approached, pushing through a circle of gawking soldiers edging in for a look at the dark god of legend. While extraordinary to them, Mikkik no longer held any fascination for Gen.

Gen regarded him coldly and spoke to him in the ancient tongue. "I will come to release you from your suffering soon. You will suffer the same fate you designed for Eldaloth. I do not know if this brings you comfort, but to the world it will bring release."

"You will have to bleed many to have enough power to end me!" Mikkik sneered. "I have servants still. One will free me, and I will begin again and bleed thousands of the weak-blooded until my purpose is done!"

"The blood of the Millim Eri runs in my veins," Gen returned. "I will bleed forty-nine times with a smile on my face and *my* servant will come for you and rid the world of your treachery."

"Who are you?" Mikkik asked. "Where do you get your power from when there are no moons in the sky?"

Gen stepped closer and whispered, "You mean you do not recognize your creation?"

Mikkik's eyes went wide. "No! I stripped you of your power, and the Uyumaak destroyed you! Only Millim Eri could have restored you with blood magic, and they would never use it! Who are you?"

"I am Aldradan Mikmir!" Gen said loudly for the soldiers' sake before turning away. "And I have defeated you."

"Where does your power come from?!" Mikkik raged.

The soldiers parted and bowed as Gen passed through, searching the courtyard until he found Maewen standing on the wall watching the sun rise over the wounded city. Gen leaned on the battlements next to her, wondering what her eyes could see that his could not. The dawn cast an angry red glow where it prepared to rise into the haze of dust and smoke.

"Can you see to the plain?" Gen asked.

"The Aughmerians are bleeding now, I believe," she answered, "at least from the sound of it."

They watched in silence for several moments before Gen turned toward her. "I want to thank you for everything you have done," he said. "You have proved yourself invaluable, risked your life, done your duty, and helped me so many times I could never say thank you enough. For one such as you, I'm not sure what I could do to reward you or make plain my gratitude."

"Killing Uyumaak is pleasure enough for me. What do you intend to do?"

"I need to enlist your aid one last time, if you are willing."

"Are you ready to see the secret places the world?"

"Not just yet. My blood must be used to end Mikkik for good, and I'll need Athan's help to do it. I must return to Elde Luri Mora to find him. When that is done and Mikkik is finished, then we will walk the world until my heart is at peace. I must mourn with Mirelle and bid her farewell, but after that I have a task to put you to while I see to the creation of the weapon."

"I am ready."

CHAPTER 90 – ETERNAL

Mirelle had never watched the sky with such earnestness in her entire life. Over one year had passed since she had been visited by Athan, cowled and bearded in disguise. She hated him and would have cast him from her sight, but he had come with an extraordinary mission—to hand her a sword that would kill Mikkik in his cage.

It was the sword that would avenge the blood of her daughter, a sword of power formed by the virtue of Gen's blood. Along with it came the Training Stones Gen had gifted to her daughter with instructions to wear them so that Samian might give her the basic skill with the blade that she would need to make the killing stroke.

"Gen will come for you next year," Athan had told her, "when the first snow falls."

She wore the Training Stones for two weeks until she could manage a solid thrust and then announced to the world the date of Mikkik's execution. On a golden fall day over a year before, all who could fit in the courtyard watched her stride from the Chapel at dawn, face solemn. Mikkik flinched when he saw the blade, his cruel features twisted in the agony of his torment.

"For the Chalaine," was all Mirelle had heart to say. Extending her arm as she had been taught, she plunged the

329

blade into Mikkik's gut. The dark god had closed his eyes and sneered before disintegrating in an explosion of light. The crowd had cheered and would have pressed her into some speech, but she had no more words to speak that day. She had returned to her chambers to mourn afresh while the rest of the world feasted for a week.

And so began the longest year of her life, and the most agonizing autumn. While she waited for Gen's return, she had acquiesced to the aristocracy and agreed to stay on as Regent to be an anchor in Aldradan Mikmir's absence. There were funerals to attend, a city to rebuild, and alliances to renew. She knew her familiar face and familiar ways were needed, and to dull her own pain she used work to bury her grief.

The spring took her to Tolnor for the coronation of Gerand Kildan. He and his lovely Mena were striking in their royal garb of deep red and gold. While it was a joyous affair—free of demons and dark gods—Mirelle felt empty and alone without the people she loved best in the world, and she left a few days early under the pretense of needing to address Rhugoth's pressing concerns.

After she returned home, the Regency of Rhugoth tried to press her into service as the First Mother of Rhugoth, but without Gen and without her daughter, she simply had no taste for it. Only one desire burned in her heart—to fulfill her lifelong ambition to be a proper wife and to relive the joy of motherhood again. And there was only one man she would accept to walk with her in those desires, a man she pined for on some days and was furious with on others. How dare he leave her for a year! How dare he leave Rhugoth without his steadying presence! How dare he not come to see the end of Mikkik!

While she understood Gen's reasons for staying away and more than understood his grief, she had desperately needed him. She still did. She had cried her tears for her daughter, she had done her duty for her nation, and she had waited long enough without any word.

The loss of the Chalaine had carved a hole in her heart to add to the loneliness that already gaped open wide there. It needed filling, and while Gen had promised to come for her, he hadn't promised to love her or to wed her. The mystery and uncertainty nearly drove her mad as she willed Ki'Hal to hurtle forward, for the warm summer winds to cool and leech the green out of the leaves. Now she watched the leaves jostling in the wind and begged them to dry and fall, pulling one from every branch she passed to hasten the process.

Now with the branches mostly bare, she leaned on the balcony of the Great Hall in the late afternoon, shawl wrapped around her shoulders as a thick mass of dark clouds crawled toward the sun, bringing a biting chill that kicked up and rustled her hair and cooled her face. Sweet coldness it was to her. She dressed her best every day since the breezes began to cool, ready for that familiar voice and that familiar step. How he would come, she didn't know or care. Where they would go, she could guess, for she longed to see the place where her daughter had died, or perhaps still lived but in a way she couldn't now understand.

"Shall I fetch your cloak, Milady?" Volney asked.

"No," she said, turning to regard him. He had been faithful to Gen's charge to protect her, even though Mirelle no longer saw the necessity of his protection. Her only enemies now lived inside her, the doubt and fear she had to beat away with every sunrise and sunset.

The dark hours in her bed were the worst, and she nearly despised her bed chambers for the hopeful longings and dreadful imaginings they provoked within her, tearing her apart. The worst was the feeling of age that she had never felt. While the virtue of the breeding of the Chalaines blessed her with a youthful appearance, she knew it would not last. Gen would never age, eternally a man in his youth. One day she would wake up and look like his mother, and she wondered how he or she would deal with the disparity.

Another blast of chill wind squinted her eyes, this one truly numbing. The clouds spilled over the sun, ending whatever warmth was left in the air. *It is here,* she thought. *He had best keep his promise, or I will hunt him down and make him regret it.*

Volney let out an audible gasp as the frigid air washed over him. Mirelle smiled. He was such a contrast to Gen. With no wars to fight and with home and hearth putting good food in his mouth, Volney's uniform had tightened and his face had filled out. Family life suited him, and Mirelle hoped he would take what rewards and treasure were his and be with his wife and son. They couldn't ask for a kinder father.

Something cold touched her face and she looked up, finding the swirling flakes descending upon them, driven by the wind. She lifted a hand before her, and a flake fell upon it and melted under her heat. It had come. Winter with its first snow was upon them. He would come now. He had promised he would, and she would not let him break this promise.

Reasserting her more confident nature she turned away from the balustrade just as a brilliant shimmering field of blue appeared behind Volney, who jumped back and drew his sword. Mirelle crossed her arms in front of her and waited, a thrill building inside her. Quickly she loosened her hair the way Gen liked it and smoothed red her dress over her curves.

"Were you expecting this?" Volney asked, noting her distinct lack of anxiety.

"Yes. Be at ease."

He didn't sheathe his sword, but his body relaxed.

And finally he came. He dressed not as a King or a soldier, but as someone who wandered the wild. Mirelle hardly cared, taking in his clean shaven face and intelligent, sober eyes. But his smile was all she needed, and she fell into his extended arms, forgetting all the bouts of ill will she had suffered over his neglect. He kissed her hair and then took her hand, turning toward Volney.

"Your work is done, my friend," Gen said. "Put your sword away, go home, and never take it up again. Thank you for all you have done."

"It has been an honor, Gen, Lady Mirelle. I will always think of you." He bowed and left.

Gen turned her toward the Portal. "Are you ready?"

"I've been ready for a long time, Gen," she said, choking on the words and stifling tears. "I am ready."

He led her forward through the shimmering Portal, and in an instant they stepped out on into warmer air and clearer skies upon the bridge across the lake of Elde Luri Mora. The Portal shut behind them, and Mirelle gazed in wonder at the splendor of the city, now even more vibrant and alive than when the bedraggled survivors of the caravan had set foot upon it. The light of the afternoon sun painted warmth and health on every building and hillside, the blossoms of the city open wide to its light. It felt vibrant and whole, and, while she could not explain it, it felt intimately familiar.

"She is here, isn't she?" Mirelle asked reverently.

"She is," Gen said. "I hope this can bring you some comfort. If you want to feel close to your daughter, she is always here, and always will be."

Mirelle nodded, unsure of how to feel. The whole notion was so odd, but beautiful in its way. She grabbed Gen's arm and pulled in close. "Thank you for coming for me. I have missed you terribly."

"And I you. I am sorry to have been gone during such a hard time. It was hard for me, too. I regret it if I caused you pain, but I haven't been idle, and I haven't been avoiding you. I just needed to think. I needed to sort out what good I could do with the rest of a long life ahead of me. Maewen tells me I need to return as a King, but that isn't what is in my heart."

Mirelle nodded in understanding, not wanting to pry or force him to explain everything. Being near him and being in Elde Luri Mora were enough for now. As they neared the opposite shore, the rich scent of the blossoms greeted her, invigorating and refreshing her spirit. The chirp of a bird or the soft stirring of the trees were the only noises besides theirs, the blessed silence of the place washing away her cares. Whatever would come would come, and she would be content.

"I have some explaining to do," Gen said. "I need to show you something."

Gen guided her toward the Hall of Three Moons, and Mirelle tried to push away her unpleasant memories of the place. Watching the Chalaine wed Chertanne had hurt, and leaving Gen behind, bound to the floor by magic, had filled her with fury. But even as these thoughts sought to overwhelm her, something soothed her. It was as if no dark thought could prevail in Elde Luri Mora, the city casting out every care. Something was stronger about the city than it had been the first time she came, and Mirelle wondered why.

But what she saw at the center of the floor turned her attention outward. Three piles of blackened rocks sat in the beautiful chamber illuminated by the sunlight from the circular dome in the ceiling.

"Have you been collecting rocks?" Mirelle asked.

"Yes. Maewen and I have brought as many as we could find to this place."

"Why?"

"They are rocks from Duam, Myn, and Trys, chunks that fell to the ground at the death of Elde Luri Mora. They possess great magic."

Mirelle understood. "So this is what you used to fight Mikkik in Mikmir."

"Yes. I only had a Duamstone then, but the results were

powerful."

"Why horde them?"

Gen shook his head. "Not horde them. Hide them. If anyone figures out what they can do with these stones, there will be wars fought to get them. Elde Luri Mora is hidden to most, so they will be safe here."

"And if I looked in that bag of yours, I don't suppose I would find a few stashed away?"

He smiled. "Well, I thought it would be prudent to have a few around—for emergencies."

"I see."

Mirelle walked farther inside, standing on the map of unified Ki'Hal. "Is this where she died?"

"It is," Gen replied, turning to stand in front of Mirelle and placing his hands on her arms. "She did it to save me. I wish it would have been me instead, Mirelle. You must believe me. I hope you can forgive me for failing her in the end. I was stupid and naive to think that Joranne and Sir Tornus could serve any other need besides their own. Not a day goes by that I don't regret my part in her death, even if the world was saved. I was terrified to tell you what happened. I wouldn't blame you if you hated me."

Mirelle wrapped her arms around him and laid her head on his shoulder. "I never blamed you. I know you loved her, and in a way it seems she was led to this end. She was forced by expectations and prophecy to marry Chertanne. The sacrifice here she chose, and in this place she chose her path out of love for you. Perhaps it was only that kind of sacrifice that could save Ki'Hal. And you should know that I could never hate you, although I will admit to some unkind thoughts over your absence for the last year."

Gen led her out of the Hall of Three Moons and they meandered through the scented streets of Elde Luri Mora in silence. Mirelle glanced at his face, finding it sober and thoughtful. She leaned into him, wondering how badly his heart hurt and what questions troubled his mind.

"So, is Athan still here?" she asked as they approached a small pavilion by the lake.

"He left on an errand. He wanted to return his staff of office before coming back. I thought it best he not be here when you arrived. For all his penance and piety, I still cannot look on him without anger."

"You are wise," Mirelle agreed. "I am not ready to confront him without killing him, nor do I think I will ever be."

Gen nodded. "He wishes to make amends to you, but having suffered from your wrath a time or two, I knew that he would best serve your feelings by simply never showing his face again."

They ascended the pavilion, the structure delicately carved entirely from a white stone that gleamed in the sun. The sunlight played long the ripples on the lake, and they took a bench that afforded them a view of the dazzling water.

"What is weighing on you, Gen?" Mirelle asked.

He took her hand in his. "How to do right by you."

She swallowed hard, suddenly fearful. He was trying to find a way out, a way to politely part ways without harming her feelings. She fought down the urge to let her tears flow as they had so often for the last year. She wouldn't beg. She wouldn't throw herself at him. She wouldn't tease and flirt and seduce. She would let him go if that's what he wanted.

"You need not worry for me," she answered once she had control of herself. "I am quite well provided for and can care for myself."

"I know you don't need me, Mirelle. You never have," Gen said, taking her hand. "Your independence is something I have always loved about you. I believe that when you choose to love a man, you do it freely because you want to be with him, not because you need a protector or a provider. I know you loved me that way once. After all that has happened, after I failed the one person you considered the most precious in the world, can I still be that man? My respect and love for you only grows every minute I am with you. I would never part from you from this day onward if you could love me like that again, if when you looked at me, you didn't see the man who led your daughter to her death."

The tears refused to be shut away. She smiled at him, her heart beating with such strength she could feel it pounding. "Oh, Gen, you think too much! Nothing could separate you from my love! I am already yours in every way."

Leaning forward, he kissed her. It was loving, and it was sweet, and Mirelle simply closed her eyes and enjoyed it until he broke it and held her eyes.

"Thank you. You are, I would have you know, the most amazing, intimidating woman I have ever met, and I hope you never change."

A tickle on her hand turned Mirelle's gaze downward. A flowering vine had crept up the side of the pavilion and slithered at them, entwining about both their wrists before blooming in deep red flowers, rich and luxurious to the touch.

"More of your magic?" Mirelle asked.

"No," Gen said. "Not my magic."

Mirelle knew what it meant and whose approval of their union it was, tears coming again to her eyes. She would have the gift she had always meant for her daughter—when she wasn't busy wanting it for herself. They stared at the verdant ribbon of flowers about their wrists in wonder for many minutes, leaning together in quiet peace.

"It is my opinion that we are officially wedded now," Mirelle finally announced. "Thus we can avoid any marriage ceremonies—which mostly end in disaster anyway—and the honeymoon can begin."

"No, Mirelle," Gen laughed. "We will be proper and do this the right way. We just won't set a date. The first

Pureman we stumble across we will press into service and be done. Though I really had hoped to see you all dressed up in a beautiful gown."

"You'll just have to settle for seeing me all undressed," she quipped. "But where will we go?"

"I had a little country place in mind. It's not Blackshire, but it has the wonderful rolling hills and trees and flowers."

"Sounds nice," she said dreamily. She kissed him, and while it was loving and sweet, she put a little fire in it to encourage him to perhaps seek out a Pureman rather than simply wait to stumble upon one.

"So, it's settled then?" Maewen said, startling them both.

They laughed while the half-elf and Falael looked on with some amusement.

"Yes," Gen answered. "It is settled."

"Then she will accept our gift?"

"What gift?" Mirelle asked.

"Falael and I are ready to pass on, now," Maewen explained. "We would give your our blood. With blood magic and a Trysstone, Gen can give you your youth. You can be as immortal as he his. Will you accept this gift from us?"

Mirelle said, "Maewen! I . . . I don't know what to say!"

Maewen's face scrunched. "*Yes* would be the word, I believe. Don't annoy me with any human sentimentality, if you don't mind."

"Yes, then," she answered, almost too stunned to speak.

"Very well," Maewen replied. "Then let's begin. I believe there is a Pureman to be hunted for."

Falael said something in Elvish, and Gen and Maewen smiled.

"What?" Mirelle asked.

"Well," Gen explained, "Falael says he has only one regret about passing on."

"And what is that?"

"That he won't be able to see what our children are

338

like."

EPILOGUE - AN ORDINARY LIFE

Pureman Whatman of Chesborough shut and locked the door of his white stone Church as his acolyte led his white gelding horse around from the stable. The Pureman had few dark hairs left upon his head, but those he had he let grow so he could flop them over the territory abandoned by their brothers. In his wisdom, he had dressed in his best white robe of office and even shaved so that he would inspire the reverence that was due him and the respect that was needed to accomplish a delicate task.

Young people, he disparaged as he mounted and set off at a steady pace. Why Eldaloth had designed the race of man to have the most passion, vitality, and power when least able to use them wisely was a mystery of creation he had yet to settle in his own mind. While not old himself, his back hurt after performing tasks as mundane as fetching water from the well, and his eyes no longer permitted him to study by candlelight for more than half a watch. More subtly, when the young women of the Church interacted with him, they treated him with the notice they would give a father rather than an eligible man, though he castigated himself for even noticing.

But age held some advantages besides wisdom. It brought an ability to convey gravity and solemnity, and these abilities he needed today to deal with the young Mr. and Mrs. De'Bellamaine. When the two first took Greenwood cottage on Bristlebridge Lane during the winter (an odd enough time to move in, as it was), they did not seem disposed to much troublemaking and kept to themselves save for their steady attendance at Church each Seventh Day (for which Pureman Whatman was initially satisfied with regards to their moral characters). Soon after their settling in, several parishioners complained that the two had slighted them by refusing invitations to dinners, dances, and other social occasions, besides the apparently unforgivable crime of not hosting any themselves. Pureman Whatman agreed that Greenwood cottage had long been abandoned and needed visitors, and the master and mistress of Greenwood, being so young, would profit from good society.

But as winter wore on and eventually thawed, their reclusiveness melted with the snow. They visited and were visited in turn. They attended every event for which they received invitation and a few for which they had not, much to the consternation of the hosts. For the last year, the alarming reports of their behavior had trickled in, and for a year the Pureman ignored them. Nothing Mr. and Mrs. De'Bellamaine did, technically, violated any principle that it was his calling or the Magistrate's to address, but the fastidious Mrs. Foresythe, a widow and close neighbor of the De'Bellamaines, had at last worn him down with her nagging.

As she explained it, the parents or family of the offenders were the ones normally applied to in order to deliver censure and effect restraint in these cases. Since the De'Bellamaines hailed from a distant country and had no near relations, Mrs. Foresythe felt the burden of corrective intervention naturally fell to their religious authority. The Pureman doubted this logic, but the stalwart widow's droning would only be silenced upon the performance of this task, and as the city proper faded behind him, he felt at peace with what he would do. Perhaps he could inspire some good sense in the De'Bellamaines after all. Besides, he had never called on them personally as he should have done when they first arrived in town, and a closer association with a Pureman would also aid them in acquiring a bit more sobriety.

Bristlebridge Lane rolled over low hills lightly peppered with white spruce and a few yellow maples. A wide, shallow stream banked in thorned locust bushes divided two of the taller hills, and the gray stone bridge that bore the lane's namesake carried him over water ponderous in its movement south. Ducks paddled about with webbed, orange feet, as complacent in movement and purpose as the stream that carried them.

After the bridge and a turn in the road, a blooming cherry orchard exploded into view, branches cheerful with snowy spring blossoms. A Mr. Fotsman owned the orchard and the title to the cottage the De'Bellamaines rented. His sleek hunting hounds bolted out of the orchard, yapped at the horse, and bit at its heels until the Pureman cleared the last of the trees and headed out into open country again.

The lane was well kept; the inhabitants of the pleasant country were nearly all well-to-do and traveled frequently enough to keep encroaching plants from obscuring the road. Mrs. Foresythe was forward enough to complain to the Magistrate in the event that the road ever did become too overgrown, too rutted, or in any other way unsatisfactory.

He crested another hill and descended the steep slope on the other side. There was the abode of Mrs. Foresythe—Farrow cottage—and the De'Bellamaine's residence, Greenwood cottage. The lane separated them, though their front doors were no more than a fifty yards from one another. *Part of the problem,* he concluded. The theme of Farrow cottage was grass and field, while

Greenwood's was tree and garden. The structures, however, were of similar design, two-story affairs of a light gray stone with two high arched windows on either side of the door in the front. While the walls of Farrow cottage were scoured and clean, vines had spidered over the front of the other, water dripping from the slate roof, discoloring the stone.

He pulled the reins and guided the horse down the short cobblestone drive that circled a garden wild with untamed flowers and fecund plants. Towering spruce lined the lane and sheltered the house beneath their thick boughs as if protecting and warming a treasured egg. Woodland debris littered the modest lawn that surrounded the cottage, which brought to mind one of Mrs. Forsythe's complaints. Peculiarly, the De'Bellamaines employed no servants or gardeners, and, as a result, the upkeep of the grounds wanted attention. No doubt the interior suffered in a similar fashion.

Tying his horse to a post near the circular flower bed, he started toward the door when sounds from within the house caught his attention, stopping his foot on the first stair. An irregular clacking sound was punctuated by the vigorous voices of a man and a woman. The Pureman ascended, thinking, perhaps, the young couple engaged in some altercation. But as he neared the door, face lined with worry, he could hear their conversation more clearly and relaxed.

"I think I've taught you better than that, *Merta*. Maybe I'll need to tie *both* arms behind my back next time."

"Oh *really*, Lord De'Bellamaine?" The clacking resumed, along with the sound of furniture being violently pushed aside. A dull thwack.

"Ow!" Merta cried out.

"And maybe I'll tie a sack full of potatoes to my legs, as well."

"Impertinent dog!"

It occurred to Whatman that they were engaged in

swordplay with one another; Mrs. Foresythe had not invented that little detail. *What decent man would teach his wife the blade, and what decent woman would submit to the instruction?* he wondered, realizing now his task was more mountain than molehill. A vase crashed to the ground, shards tinkling about the floor.

"That vase was expensive!" Merta complained.

"Oh really? Was this one?" Another crash.

"I actually *liked* that one!"

"I apologize, dear. You really should avoid coming toe to toe with someone stronger than you. In this position, he could have his way with you."

"Hmmmm," Merta cooed. "And do what?"

The Pureman remembered to knock at this point. Another whack.

"Ow!" yelped Mr. De'Bellamaine. "That was uncalled for. Most dishonorable, not to mention cowardly."

"Don't be a baby. We have a visitor!" Merta said cheerfully. "Put the furniture in order, and I'll see who it is."

The door opened and the Pureman laid eyes on Merta De'Bellemaine. He had seen her before, a lovely blonde woman, buxom, thin-waisted, and with eyes blue enough to sink in, but he had never seen her attired in such a fashion. She was barefoot, wearing tight leather breeches and a light, sleeveless shirt that emphasized every pleasing curve. She held an air of confidence and command that unnerved him. The Pureman colored a little as she leaned the wooden practice sword against the door frame and smiled at him.

"Oh Frederick, dear, it is the Pureman come at last to pay us a visit! Do come in, Pureman Whatman. We are most happy to receive you."

"I am much obliged, Mrs. De'Bellamaine."

The Pureman walked into the sitting room, scanning the floor to avoid pieces of the vase he might step on. Mr. De'Bellamaine put the couches and chairs back in their proper order on top of a series of muted gray and blue rugs patterned to resemble a clouded sky. The room filled with light from the high windows, and the Pureman thought it very cheerful. Mr. De'Bellamaine had his shirt off, his lean, shockingly muscular torso sliding the chairs, couches, and tables about with little exertion. The furniture itself was plain but comfortable, and Mrs. De'Bellamaine motioned for the Pureman to sit in a padded chair near the fireplace where banked embers glowed. She sat opposite him, but as Mr. De'Bellamaine crossed to join her on the couch, she held him up.

"Dear, I believe you should put a shirt on for the Pureman," she suggested.

And you *should put on a dress,* the Pureman added mentally. *Shameless.* Mr. De'Bellamaine disappeared into the rear of the house while the Pureman collected his thoughts in spite of the distracting scrutiny of Merta De'Bellamaine.

She smiled at him. "We had quite despaired of receiving a visit from you, Pureman Whatman. I do hope we are not such troublesome parishioners as to cause you discomfort. I know how unpleasant tasks are often delayed as long as possible. I would hate for us to be one of those."

"I do apologize, Mrs. De'Bellamaine," the Pureman said. "I am tardy in my attentions to you and your husband. I can offer no excuse. I am typically very preoccupied during the winter months with caring for the sick and afflicted, but this year Chesborough has been blessed with uncommon good health. I've hardly had occasion to leave the Church at all. Have you and Mr. De'Bellamaine enjoyed good health the past months?"

"Indeed, we have."

Mr. De'Bellamaine entered the room, still working at the top buttons of a high collared white shirt. The Pureman was gratified to see he had the decorum to wear a coat as well. The Pureman stood as the master of the house crossed to him and shook hands with him, noticing a bruised lump sprouting on the top of the young man's hand, no doubt received from their earlier swordplay. They both returned to their seats. Mrs. De'Bellamaine smiled affectionately at her husband, snuggling up next to him as he sat and placing her hand on his thigh. The Pureman fought to keep his countenance, but in that instant, the whole of their life history unfolded before him.

Frederick De'Bellamaine, he speculated, *is probably the second or third son of some minor lord in the south, for surely the family would not let the oldest son mingle with such a woman! He was probably destined for the Church when he met up with this coquettish tart of a lady. Since he was a lesser son, the parents likely thought nothing of their being together until he forsook his family obligations and eloped. She probably had already fled some prior indiscretion before throwing herself at Mr. De'Bellamaine.*

But as they exchanged more pleasantries about the country and the weather, he noted that whatever their ill judgments in the past, these two genuinely cared for each other. The complete ease and playfulness with which they engaged one another, the pleasure radiating from their eyes and faces, and the way each one's words would complement, amplify, and weave in with the other's—even in interruption or amendment—struck the Pureman. Here was no stiffness or awkwardness, no conversation where the spouses' words and thoughts knocked together like strangers in the dark, no unnatural concealment of affection or regard. What they felt, they demonstrated plainly and without device.

Pureman Whatman recalculated. These two had known each other for some time, most likely since childhood. Long familiarity eroded those barriers and mores that normally accompanied an engagement and persisted into the marriage state afterward. *They are definitely from the country,* he concluded. *They have not had much experience in society to witness proper examples or to endure the kind of scrutiny that would mold their behavior appropriately. It will be difficult to change them.*

One should straighten the tree while it is a sapling.

"So, Pureman," Mrs. De'Bellamaine began after a lull, "you mentioned that good health has blessed us. Are there no cases of sickness, even now?"

"There is, unfortunately, one situation that is outside the normal run of headaches, nerves, and coughs common in all seasons. The Barnes, a poor family that live on the Downs, have a young girl, Alna, afflicted with the pig fever. She is a dear girl of only six years, her voice as pleasant an instrument as ever tuned by Eldaloth's hand. I've just received word and will attend to her this evening. She is a bit young to overcome the sickness, I fear, not to mention that her family's situation isn't such that encourages health or recovery. I have little hope of her improvement." He noted the concern in Mrs. De'Bellamaine's eyes.

"That is unfortunate," she said.

"We should visit them this afternoon," her husband commented, face grave.

"Yes," she continued, "and see what we can do to support them."

"Do you think they could use a blanket for the child?"

"I believe so," Mr. De'Bellamaine answered thoughtfully. "Wholesome food would certainly be in order."

"They do scrape by down there," Merta said. "I wonder if they are cleaning as they should?"

The Pureman jumped in before they could continue. "I think it best if you leave it to the ministrations to the Church. We will know how to succor them. It would be dangerous and . . . inappropriate . . . for you to go there. It is a filthy place."

"Why, Pureman," she remonstrated, "we shall hardly be deterred by a little dirt. As for the danger, surely you noted that we have some skill with weaponry. We have metal swords to go with the wooden ones. Would you like to see them?"

347

"Ah, no," he declined. "But may I ask, do you fence with each other often?"

"When we get the chance of it," Mr. De'Bellamaine answered. "I like to keep my skills sharp, so I have asked her to ambush me about the house unexpectedly."

Pureman Whatman frowned. "I'm sure we could find other young men in the country who would be happy to spar with you."

"No doubt they would be happy until they sparred with me," he stated matter-of-factly.

His wife laughed. "Oh, Frederick, you mustn't be so cocky! I'm sure the Pureman could arrange for some eligible opponents, though they may object to being smacked on the bottom as you do to me. I would love to watch a match. It's been so long since I've seen you humiliate someone."

The Pureman couldn't believe the forwardness of the woman. "Yes, yes. The young Darby Mills is quite handy with the blade, as is the Sheriff. Either one could provide you ample sport without you needing to put upon your wife for such an office."

"I am not put upon, dear Pureman," she objected. "I quite enjoy the instruction. I was actually thinking of asking the other ladies about town if they should wish to learn."

The Pureman snapped his jaw up. *Where* did *these people come from?* "I assure you, Mrs. De'Bellamaine, that such invitations would be universally despised and rejected. But the disclosure of your plan allows me to address, now, the object of my visit. I do not know your history or the land of your upbringing, but several of my parishioners have commented on how your manners are quite different from what is typical of the people in this area of the country."

"Oh, really?" Mr. De'Bellamaine said, though the Pureman failed to detect much gravity in his face. Hers was a mask of saucy amusement. "I do hope we have not caused overmuch offense. We have enjoyed the neighborhood, though Mrs. Foresythe does seem a bit rigorous in her vigil of our house."

"Do be clear, dearest," Mrs. De'Bellamaine put in. "This is a Pureman, and we shan't beat about the bush. What you meant to say was that Mrs. Foresythe is an insufferable spy."

The Pureman coughed. "I assure you that she is an honorable, though observant, woman."

Mrs. De'Bellamaine laughed again. "Observant! Very good, Pureman. Very good. It's like saying Aughmere and Tolnor were merely uncomfortable with one another and that Mikkik suffered from a bit of distemper."

Mr. De'Bellamaine grinned widely at his wife's quip. *I am losing control of this conversation!* the Pureman fretted. He cleared his throat loudly. He really had no idea how he would divulge the long list of complaints leveled against them, so he just plowed into them—in the kindest way he could imagine.

"Mr. and Mrs. De'Bellamaine, I urge you to hear me with all seriousness. In this part of the country there are some matters of decorum that must be heeded if you are to endear yourself to the community here. We believe women are too delicate for the coarse nature of handling weaponry. While it behooves every man of substance to learn the art of war for the defense of his honor, his home, and his country, the female sex should pursue those occupations for which kind hearts and gentle hands are best suited.

"Then there is the matter of staying out of doors until all hours of the night. Genteel people should keep respectable hours save for the direst of emergencies. What good could come of wandering the dark, or what good could those who witness such wandering think of those who wander? The dark hours are for the idle and those of disrepute. It would be a danger to the person and the honor of anyone to be about during the late watches."

Gen perked up. "But Pureman, isn't this a bit like

children accusing their siblings of opening their eyes during the oblation when they themselves would have had to open their own eyes to witness the infraction? Or did the idle and disreputable tell you this of us?"

"It is Mrs. Foresythe," Mrs. De'Bellamaine conjectured. "Watching us is her chief form of entertainment. Since she stays indoors to do it, she can stay up late without tarnishing her reputation. I guess that makes her idle, but not disreputable."

"Please, I do not mean to offend," the Pureman soothed. "Mrs. Foresythe. . ."

"But, Pureman Whatman," Mrs. De'Bellamaine interjected, "haven't you seen the stars at that time of a clear winter night when the glow in the west has dissolved into utter blackness and every lamp in the city is extinguished? They shine and twinkle like a room full of the eyes of the happiest children ever to breathe a blessing on the world. If those who view this habit as amiss would just sit up late, walk into a midnight field, and look up, then their censure for us would turn into a sympathetic joy! Have you seen them, Pureman?"

The Pureman was taken aback by her sincere passion. "Of course. I am about late on many errands to the sick," he answered, though he admitted to himself that he never had quite taken notice of the sky. He changed the subject quickly. "But in addition to this, you win too much at cards, often arrive at functions to which you were not invited, and insist on keeping no servants, which places you in the position of doing low work when you should instead be about the improvement of your minds and attending to some social obligations that are your duty to perform.

"But lastly, and perhaps most seriously, it has been noted by several of the people in this demesne that you two are frequently, and in public places, guilty of that sort of . . . affectionate contact . . . which discomfits those who may, perchance, view it. Such activities are for the discreet confines of your own walls, here, in private. Wouldn't you agree?"

Mrs. De'Bellamaine smiled oddly. "Frederick, I do believe the Pureman is desperately trying to convince us to stay indoors a great deal more, despite the warming weather. I don't think we ever been *that* demonstrative, have we Frederick?"

"Dearest," Mr. Bellamaine said, "remember that time at Mrs. Chisolm's, on All Peace Day? The wine cellar?"

"Oh! I had forgotten about that! Why would Mrs. Foresythe ever come down to a wine cellar? Seems it would be beneath her dignity. And now that the subject is broached, I do recall the balcony at Mr. Lourde's ball, though I would hardly think Mr. Havelton could be *that* shocked that two newlyweds would be kissing in the moonlight. Surely he isn't that stodgy at his age."

"You are mistaken, Merta," Mr. De'Bellamaine corrected. "Miss Greene found us at the ball—remember her shriek? Mr. Havelton stumbled upon us in the thicket at Winter Park."

"Yes, that's right. Was that ever cold, especially when the snow shook off the branches and . . . well, what business did Mr. Havelton have in that particular thicket at that time of day, anyway? I'm sure I don't want to know and thus spoil the memory."

Mr. De'Bellamaine turned back to the Pureman. "You have a point, though in our defense, I would argue that the problem isn't that we aren't discreet. We just aren't very good at it. Please continue."

The Pureman, however, was done, vaguely mumbling that he was finished and hoped they hadn't taken offense, though he doubted they were capable of taking any in the first place. There was some hope for Mr. De'Bellamaine, though the wife was clearly beyond amendment. The Pureman decided he would need to talk to Frederick alone. Perhaps by inspiring him to more judicious behavior, he might exercise some control over his spouse. Of course, Eldaloth was patient, and a few years might invest them both with a bit more sobriety. A devastating trial might do them good, as well. The sound of a horse and cart entering the drive cut short the Pureman's announcement that he was leaving.

"Is it Davis?" Mr. De'Bellamaine asked of his wife who had crossed to the window.

"Yes."

"Good. We'll have him ready the horses."

"My thought exactly. I'll find a blanket for Alna"

The Pureman furrowed his eyebrows. "Davis Korbett?"

"The very one," Mr. De'Bellamaine confirmed.

"What have you to do with the lad?" the Pureman asked, intrigued. "Have you hired him for some purpose?" He could think of few things worse than exposing impressionable children to people such as these. Davis was but ten years of age. His mother was a widow seamstress, quite poor, her son a bandy-legged, sickly wretch whose disability prevented him of being much service to his mother or anyone else besides. The Pureman reminded himself to pay Mrs. Korbett a visit, as he hadn't seen her since Harvest Festival.

"He performs some work for us around the house," Mr. De'Bellamaine explained. "In exchange, Merta teaches him letters, and I am teaching him the care of horses and how to shoot a bow."

Is everyone to learn weaponry? The Pureman grumped to himself. *Next he'll be teaching me to swing a club and Mrs. Foresythe to knife fight.*

Mrs. De'Bellamaine crossed to the door and opened it before Davis could knock. "Good morning!" she greeted him brightly, embracing her freckled, sandy blond student, who received it gratefully and familiarly.

The Pureman turned and his mouth dropped open. When last he saw the lad, he was a walking horseshoe, legs so severely bent he couldn't manage steps or walk at more than a turtle's pace. His face had been ashen, his eyes dim, and his manner so languid that he scarce could be placed in the category of the living. While there could be no doubt this was the same boy, the alteration in him was severe. Legs as straight as broomsticks supported a frame full of vitality. The Pureman stood and greeted the boy, amazed at the clarity in the brown eyes and the energy that beamed from a perfectly sanguine face.

"But Davis!" the Pureman exclaimed. "You are so much improved since I last saw you I can scarce believe it! What blessing is yours? How have you come into such health?"

As with most youth his age, he shrugged his shoulders and looked at the floor. "I dunno. Just got better, I suppose."

"Eldaloth has indeed favored you! I am very gratified."

Mr. and Mrs. De'Bellemaine looked at the boy with a great deal of pride and satisfaction, Mr. De'Bellemaine wrapping his arm affectionately around his wife's slender waist.

The Pureman shook his head and took his leave, resolving to visit the Widow Korbett immediately to inquire further into the matter of her young Davis. Surely there was some miracle there he could use to inspire his congregation.

He untied his horse and mounted, noticing Mrs. Foresythe watching him expectantly from her front porch across the way as he rode out to the lane. No doubt she wished to speak to him, but he would defer that conversation until later. If the De'Bellamaines were to notice him with her directly after visiting them, it would seem as if he were reporting to her and thus confirm that she was indeed the instigator of his visit.

The warming air and steady canter of the horse relaxed him after what he could only label an ordeal of a visit, but while at first his recollection of his visit to the De'Bellamaines only brought worry and irritation, as he rode by the spring fields and orchards burgeoning with life, his mind drifted on another tack.

Satisfaction with his calling and his life had always accompanied him through the years, but amid the buzzing of insects, the blossom of the trees, and flood of sunshine, his heart felt sensible of some loss he couldn't quite grasp. He tried to dispel these thoughts and feelings, but they persisted through his arrival in town and his half-hearted greetings to the men and women crowding the streets as he rode.

As he turned toward the widow's house, the passionate words of Mrs. De'Bellemaine sank into his heart. He sighed and smiled, making a quick resolution: *Tonight, I will study late, walk into Farmer Justin's pasture, and look up.*

Thank you for reading the Trysmoon Saga!

Find out about upcoming releases and projects on
briankfullerbooks.com and
facebook.com/briankfullerbooks

Made in the USA
Lexington, KY
31 May 2015